THE
EVER
CRUEL KINGDOM

RIN CHUPECO

THE
EVER
CRUEL
KINGDOM

HARPER TEEN
An Imprint of HarperCollinsPublishers

HarperTeen is an imprint of HarperCollins Publishers.

The Ever Cruel Kingdom
Copyright © 2020 by HarperCollins Publishers

Library of Congress Control Number: 2020942279
ISBN 978-0-06-282190-4

Typography by Molly Fehr
Map illustration by Virginia Allyn
20 21 22 23 24   CPIG   10 9 8 7 6 5 4 3 2 1

First Edition

To all the abandoned cattos who keep claiming sanctuary in my house with neither advance warning nor permission: you are all freeloading, garden-destroying, chaos-inducing little buggers, and you will always have a home here.

AE

THE FIREPITS

BRIGHTHENGE

THE DEAD FOREST

THE
SALT
SEA

THE SAND SEA

THE GOLDEN CITY

THE SKELETON
COAST

THE GREAT ABYSS

ON
Unknown Territories
The Spirit lands
Aranth
The Lunar lakes
Riverwinds
Acidfall

Chapter One

ARJUN AT THE SKELETON COAST

─────────── ☼ ───────────

I WAS GETTING REAL DAMN *tired* of sand in my mouth again.

I lifted myself up on bruised elbows and spat out a gob of grit, the familiar scrape of dust and wind swirling around me. The sun beat down relentlessly on us, the heat familiar and unforgiving. I'd grown too accustomed to clouds and the temperate weather in the weeks we'd traveled west, and now the light reflecting off the dunes was blinding even to me, a stark reminder that I'd been gone far longer than I expected to be. I staggered to my feet, looked around.

The first thing I noticed was that we were back on the Skeleton Coast. *Great.*

The second thing I noticed was that the portal we'd scrambled out of was still hovering in the air behind us, dark and angry against the otherwise bright sky. The creatures that made their homes in the depths of the Great Abyss were crawling toward us; still snarling, still roaring, still clamoring for blood. Behind them loomed the black, horrifying mass that was the corrupted form of the goddess Inanna. There was a sharpness to the shadow's edges, like the darkness was fabricated from the same things fangs and blades were made of.

I drew out my Howler and fired a shot straight into the portal, taking out a few writhing shadows that had drawn uncomfortably close, but that only emboldened the rest. More monsters skittered toward the opening on what passed for feet among that horrific lot. A fresh round from my gun obliterated the front row.

Haidee pointed, and winds formed into Air-whetted knives that sliced through the hole, bisecting a good swath of the demons. The Catseye, Lan, was already swinging her sword, decapitating all the goddessdamned horrors that had drawn close enough to the portal to stick their heads through. Her companion Noelle jabbed at the monsters with a long spear.

But Haidee's twin, Odessa, was frozen to the spot, her eyes locked on the shadows as they slithered closer, many reaching for her and failing only when Lan's blade lopped off their limbs. Odessa was almost the spitting image of Haidee, down to her pale eyes and colorshifting hair. But the other sister wore her hair longer than Haidee's shoulder-length cut, down almost to her waist, and had fairer skin—from a lifetime, I gathered, spent in a storm-swept city that hadn't seen the sun in almost eighteen years.

"Close it!" I hollered at the others. "Someone close the damn thing!"

"I don't know how!" The sweeps of cutting Air from Haidee had transformed into a full-blown gale. She gritted her teeth, brows furrowed. But shadows kept streaming out of the Great Abyss, their sheer numbers pushing them forward against the heavy gusts. "It's not like there's a lever to pull!"

"Well, it's gotta have *some* kind of switch!" I redoubled the patterns rattling in my gun, the cylinder smoking as I willed more blue fire in. With my next volley, the whole landscape within the portal gate burst into flames, but the creatures were undeterred, climbing over the bodies of their scorched brethren.

"I can see them," Odessa whispered.

"Obviously." I was tiring fast; conjuring incanta took a hell of a lot out of Firesmokers in particular, made us ripe for both fatigue and injuries. I reloaded my gun, but the next bursts were weaker. In ten minutes I'd be tapped out.

"No. I can see *them*. The galla with the blue jewels."

I followed her gaze, and saw a group of galla standing to one side, not participating in the attack. I could almost swear that parts of them were glowing blue.

We hadn't known each other long; Haidee and I had met Odessa and her guardians only a few hours before, discovered that Haidee's twin sister, the girl Haidee had believed was killed at the Breaking years ago, had been alive all this time. It had been a tearful reunion.

It could wind up being a short-lived reunion, too.

"What are you doing?" Haidee shrieked, but I paid her no attention, planting myself in front of the portal and unloading on any galla that came too close, while also trying not to panic, blast at everything, and exhaust myself in the process. Lan moved to stand beside me; her broadsword didn't have my range, but she was an army all on her own, cutting down shadows. I only had time to nod my thanks before shooting again, and she returned one of her own as she stabbed through a creature's head. Noelle had retreated to a defensive position by the girls, singling out any galla that drew too near.

We knew what would happen if they succeeded in fighting past us. I had family out here. If these bastards got through . . .

Another wave of patterns seared the air. It slammed against the edges of the glittering portal. With a loud screeching sound, like the harsh scrape of metal against metal, the gateway began to shrink, so quickly we could only watch. Within seconds it was gone, and the Great Abyss and its rabid minions along with it. All that was left was familiar territory: the wide expanse of sand hills I'd seen almost every waking moment of my life, and the shining air-domes of the Golden City a few miles away.

"I did it!" Though short of breath, Haidee sounded pleased with herself, the incanta fading from her eyes. "I remembered! The goddess Nyx wrote about this in her journal. She talked about channeling all the gates at once to open the Gate of Life. She brought a bird back from the dead that way, but she also believed it could be used for other kinds of creation spells. I didn't know what she meant, but I realized that a portal *was in itself* a creation spell, technically speaking, so it should also wor—"

"Haidee."

"Don't you *Haidee* me! And you! What possessed you—the *both* of you—to place yourselves in harm's way like that? You're good, but two people could not have lasted long against that horde! If I hadn't figured out a way to—"

"Haidee." I was breathing hard, still on a terrifying high from—I don't know, *avoiding getting eaten by moving shadows*, to start—and eager to ease my agitation the best way I knew how. "Just shut up and come here."

Haidee all but flew to my side, and I kissed her hard. Her eyes were still glittering when we finally broke apart. "I would have been happy with a simple 'thank you,'" she said.

"Thank you." Satisfied that she wasn't hurt, I gave myself the once-over, checking to see if I was intact. Feet and legs, torso, head, both ears and eyes, nose and mouth, left arm and right stump, Howler. Yup, all there.

"It's too hot out here," Odessa muttered, her eyes screwed nearly shut. Gently, Lan tugged her lover's hood up over her head, to keep the sun's glare out of her eyes.

Too hot, and too bright. The Golden City was shining, and I realized that we were closer to it than I would have liked. Haidee had speculated that her mother, Latona, had emerged from the Great Abyss through a similar portal after the Breaking, that it had dumped her here in much the same way it had us. Given our proximity now, she was probably right.

Noelle flinched, shielding her eyes with a hand. "I can barely see," the redhead announced, like she hadn't been expertly stabbing monsters only minutes before. "What is this place?" She bent down and scooped up a handful of sand, letting it trickle down her fingers, amazement crossing her features.

"Never seen sand before?" I asked.

"Nothing as small and fine as this. And not everywhere." Her eyes narrowed as her gaze drifted downward before she, to my surprise, fell to her hands and knees and began to dig.

"What are you doing?" Lan asked.

"This isn't sand I'm standing on. There's something buried here." The hole grew as she dug deeper, then made a startled sound. "Parts of what appear to be a statue."

I shrugged. "That's not unusual around here. The desert's reclaimed a lot of ruins over the years."

"But this one's different. And very familiar." Noelle pushed more sand away, revealing the eroded remains of a head made of dark granite. Its features had been worn down by the elements, but there was no mistaking its similarities to the statue that had marked the entrance to Brighthenge. The same statue the portals had originated from.

"Shit," I said, staring.

"I agree. It's smaller in size, so I would surmise this guarded a smaller temple. But it could explain why the portal leads out to here. Perhaps several such shrines were consecrated to Inanna in the past?"

"I presume this place would be Haidee and Arjun's home? It's . . . drier than I'm used to." Lan was already on her feet, dark eyes searching the sandscape and assessing all possible dangers. She pointed. "You both live in this city?"

I guffawed. "Haidee does, but it sure as hell ain't my home. It's also why we gotta hightail it out of here. My clan's located several miles out; the faster we start walking, the earlier we'll reach the cave. Mother Salla will want to question you—"

"I want to go back to the city," Haidee said immediately.

I stared at her. "Look, your mother *might* forgive you because you're her daughter, but the first thing she's gonna do is hang *me* by my ankles until I bleed dry."

"I want some answers from her, Arjun." The anger in her voice was palpable. "The world's turning again, but monsters are still climbing out of the Abyss. Something's wrong. If we'd healed Aeon like we should have, then this wouldn't be happening. Inanna's spirit would have been appeased."

I stared up at the sky. Then I stared back down at the ground. I had no idea what a turning world looked like, but it didn't look all that different from a world that hadn't moved its ass in decades, like the one we'd always known. "How do you even know that the world's started moving again?"

"I just do." Haidee turned to Odessa. "You felt it too, right?"

The other goddess nodded, still pale and shaken. Lan crouched down beside her and wrapped an arm around her shoulders. "Something else is coming," Haidee's twin said weakly. "Something bad. I can feel it."

"Unless you found something at Brighthenge that says otherwise, your mother was responsible for destroying the world to begin with," I reminded Haidee. "She's done nothing about it for the past seventeen years. If you're looking to her for a solution, you're wasting your time."

7

"Is she?" Haidee asked softly. "Is she my mother?"

I'd almost forgotten. Latona had never given Haidee a reason to believe that she wasn't her daughter. But Latona's twin sister, Asteria, hadn't just survived the Breaking; she'd also been raising Odessa on the other side of the world. Haidee and Odessa had both grown up convinced the other was dead, that they were the only surviving twin. The older goddesses had each claimed to be their mother, further complicating matters. Personally, I thought Latona and Asteria were equally deceitful and I didn't trust them as far as I could kick sand, but then again, I'd never been raised to have a good opinion of the goddesses who'd broken the world.

"I have to know, Arjun. I deserve to know why she's been lying to me this whole time." Haidee turned to her sister. Something unspoken passed between them, an understanding that needed no words; they both nodded at the same time, wearing similar expressions of determination.

"It's not over, is it?" Odessa asked. "I thought that with Aeon turning the way it once did, we would be done. I thought destroying that demon meant it was finally over. But we were wrong, weren't we? We didn't kill it. That was only the beginning."

"All the more reason for me to talk to Mother." Haidee turned to me. "I won't ask you to go back with me to the city. But she has to stop pretending that there isn't a world outside the dome, or that what happens outside of it will never affect her."

"How are you going to convince *her* that Aeon's started turning?"

Lan raised her sword. "You might not have to travel to the city to let her know."

The cloud of dust rising from the east was the first clue. I caught sight of the familiar green and bronze colors of the Golden City army among dozens of jeeps headed our way. Many of the rigs carried cannons, sparking as their fuses were lighted. The armored wheels overtook the marching army, guns trained in our direction as they quickly closed the distance.

"Please tell me this is a welcoming party," Noelle murmured.

It was most definitely *not* a mother-daughter talk.

"Fat chance." I tugged at Haidee's hand. "I don't think your mother's happy to see you. I highly doubt that she'll be over-joyed to see the rest of us."

Haidee didn't answer. Instead, she stepped forward and raised her hands over her head.

I didn't know what she was planning until I saw a stream of patterns weaving around her wrists, spiking the air with sharp hues—I could only clearly identify the patterns of Fire, mix-ing in with others that I couldn't. She stood there, unmoving, until the first of the rigs drew close enough for me to make out the faces of the men behind the wheel. She brought her hands down, and the patterns whipped themselves into a frenzy around her, churning up dust and pebbles.

"Haidee!" I yelled, just as a sandspout erupted from under-neath the nearest vehicle, sending it hurtling into the air.

Another abrupt gesture from Haidee dissipated the wind, and the jeep landed with a loud crash, throwing its passengers out several yards to bounce along the sand. She was mad, albeit not enough to actually kill them.

She repeated it with the next two rigs; by the time the third unsalvageable wreck came crashing back down, the rest had reversed their engines and retreated, stopping only long enough to haul away their injured. Haidee regarded the smoldering rigs with satisfaction. "You're right. The time for talking is over. We're shouting now."

Damn, if that wasn't a turn-on.

"Is this wise?" Lan asked her warily.

"I know my mother. The instant she regains control of the situation she'll dig in her heels and go back to ignoring me and restricting my movements. I'm not giving in this time."

The ranger eyed Latona's men. "That's very admirable, but there's only five of us and a lot more than five of them."

"We can try running," Noelle suggested. "Though I fear they would catch us soon enough. There doesn't seem to be anywhere to hide out here."

"Haidee!" The voice was loud, amplified by tendrils of Air. A woman strode toward the front of the army, in a gold flowing dress that glittered against the light and was an absurd choice of clothing given the circumstances. I shifted my Howler out of reflex. I'd never seen the Sun Goddess in person before, and it was disconcerting how much she resembled an older Haidee.

Anger seized me without warning, and I set the Howler's sights against my eye in an instant, training my gun on the approaching goddess. The first time I met Haidee my instinct had been to hesitate, my gut telling me she didn't mean any harm. With Latona, it was the exact opposite.

Haidee shot me a warning look, but I refused to lower the Howler. Latona might be her mother, but she was the reason there was nothing here but sand.

"What foolishness is this, Haidee?" the older woman snapped. "Stop your silly tantrums and come home this instant!"

"Not until you hear me out!" Haidee yelled back. "I—we— did it! We went to the Great Abyss! Aeon is turning again, the way it's supposed to be!"

"Oh, did you?" Latona's eyes flared red; smoke curled around her as flames licked at the tips of her outstretched fingers. "Did you think the world had simply stopped on nothing more than a whim? Do you ever think about the consequences of your actions? You disobey me, flee into the desert with traitors, and now you think you hold all the answers to the universe? It will take months, years, to undo what you've unraveled in your arrogance. Save the world? You've just fashioned its coffin, hammered the final nail into place!"

I saw the words hit home, saw Haidee jerk back, visibly stung. "I wasn't the one who destroyed Aeon! I was trying to save it!"

"And there will be consequences! Repercussions that extend beyond what you can even begin to imagine!"

"Maybe if you hadn't lied to me about everything, I would have believed you! You lied about my father, about my sister! Why should I trust what you say now?"

Latona's voice softened. "Whether you wish it or not, I am still your mother. I only want what's best for you, even if you don't understand."

"And what about me?" Odessa stepped forward, and her hood fell to her shoulders.

Audible gasps of amazement from the soldiers. Latona's eyes threatened to start out of her head; she grew pale, her hair leaching color. "Impossible," she whispered. "A mirage. You're nothing but a mirage. Odessa died years ago."

"You're wrong." Odessa's voice trembled, but she took her place beside Haidee, taking her sister's hand. "I lived. I grew up on the other side of the world. I survived the Breaking. Haidee found me. My—I always believed you were dead."

"Impossible!" Latona shouted. "What are these illusions you use against me, Haidee? Do you truly hate me, to hurt me this way?"

"No!" Haidee looked alarmed. "Mother, this is neither a mirage nor an illusion. This is Odessa, my twin. She was separated from us. She came from the city of Aranth, was raised among other survivors! They live in constant night just as we do in perpetual day, and she—"

"Aranth? How dare you." Latona's rage was frightening to behold. The sands before her churned, erupted into fire. Balls of flames leaped from her hands. "Aranth? How dare you say his name. *How dare you say his name.*"

I'd been in enough incanta fights to know what was coming. So did Lan. We grabbed Haidee and Odessa and dragged them away. Latona's fireballs were aimed at Odessa, so Lan all but tucked the girl underneath her arm, dodging the flames thrown their way until they skidded to safety behind a large sand dune, Noelle following close behind.

The rest of the Golden army, fortunately, had horrible aim. I slid us down behind a second knoll, Haidee still protesting, as more shots flew past us. I let go of her and lifted my Howler, trying to will Fire patterns in faster. Despite their imprecision, the soldiers had more firepower and better weapons, and it was only a matter of time before one of them got lucky. Even as that thought crossed my mind, they were already pushing one of the large cannons forward, stacked to overflowing with glowfires.

"I wasn't in danger!" Haidee yelped at me. "She won't hurt me, no matter how angry she gets!"

"Might be, but can you really trust her flunkies not to hit you, even by accident? Your mother is on a rampage." I glanced up at the sky, where bright sizzles of light gathered around the army, crackling with the promise of more violence. One of those bright balls of energy struck the sand nearby, and it felt like every hair on my skin stood on end from the impact.

"Lightning," Lan called out to us. "We've seen more than our share of that where we come from."

Haidee lashed out with an arm, and a giant wall of hardened sand rose up, a shield from the army's volleys and the older goddess's wrath. "She's never done this before," she said, sounding uncertain for the first time since returning. "She's always kept her composure. I've only seen her lose her temper once."

"Seeing Odessa unhinged her brain." I shifted my Howler, opening the fire-gate in my eyes again.

"Don't you dare, Arjun."

"Of course not. But you better figure out how to calm her down before this whole place goes to hell in a kettle."

"Your mirages hold no water!" Latona was gone. In her place was a madwoman. Her hair flew around her, sticking straight out of her head as she wove more and more incanta, the air steeped in their potency. "Odessa died at the Breaking!"

"Mother!" Haidee shouted. "Stop it!"

Lightning raked the ground before us, but Haidee's sand walls took the brunt. Several more bolts struck a couple of the army's rigs, setting them alight. The older goddess didn't seem to care; it was as if she were fighting an invisible monster the rest of us couldn't see, and we were all targets for her fury.

A cannon fired. A giant fireball hurtled toward the hill where Odessa, Lan, and Noelle had taken shelter. Haidee gestured, and a fresh wall shot out of the sand, breaking apart when the glowfire hit it, but stopping the attack.

"Odessa!" I heard Lan cry out, and saw the other twin rising to her feet, mimicking the combination of patterns that swirled around Latona. She clapped her hands together just as another arc of lightning crackled toward us, and her own lightning met it halfway. Both fizzled out in midair; the energy from the collision made my teeth hurt. There was too much of it everywhere.

Latona lowered her arms, rationality returning as she stared at her other daughter, as if finally seeing her for the first time. "It can't be you." The words came out slowly, fearful.

Odessa stared back, looking like she'd seen a mirage of her own. "You look exactly like Mother."

The Sun Goddess drew back. "Don't ever say that. She's not your mother!"

"Mother, listen!" The sand wall crumbled, and Haidee rose. "Everything we knew was a lie. Odessa's alive, and so is Asteria!"

A sudden rumbling noise made us all look up. I thought it was a fresh assault from the older Sun Goddess, but Latona's expression was also one of genuine shock.

Dark clouds were spreading rapidly overhead; the rumblings grew louder.

A figure blurred into view in between us and the army; a human-shaped form bound in a cloak of gray, features obscured by a hood. I drew in a sharp breath. It was a mirage. More than that, it was a mirage of a Devoted, one of the many dead servants of the goddesses that wandered the Skeleton Coast. I swore I could feel its gaze on us.

One of the soldiers fired a desperate shot at it. The cloak fluttered, and the flames stopped in mid-flight, settled instead against its gloved hand. The fire changed color, glowed a deep and unearthly blue before disappearing in a quick puff of blue smoke.

A *Firesmoker*. The undead Devoted was a damn Firesmoker.

A Firesmoker who could channel blue flames.

Just like me.

My mother had once led the Devoted, Mother Salla had told me. And Firesmokers with blue fire were rare as hell.

I didn't want to think about it.

I aimed my Howler.

The ground to the right of the figure exploded, kicking up grit and dust, but the mirage didn't move. I shot at the sand to its left next, with the same results. It said nothing, didn't retaliate. I couldn't see its face, but I know when I'm being stared at.

"Who the hell are you?" I didn't want to know what was behind that hood, whether or not whatever face was behind that cowl might resemble mine, or if death and rot had stripped that away. I didn't want to admit that those blue flames had shaken me, thrown me off guard. I didn't want to have anything in common with this creature.

The mirage didn't bother with a response. Its shoulders arched and its head tilted back, as if seeking some strange benediction from above.

There was a hissing noise that sounded like it came from everywhere at once.

There were three seconds of hushed, fearful silence.

And then water swept down from the sky; it fell like fine mist, and then like a raging river. I cupped my hand and stared, astonished, at the clear liquid collecting in my palm.

"Rain," Noelle said. "It's raining."

Nothing could have prepared the Golden army for this. However rigid their training had been, it was clearly not enough. Many fell to their knees, staring up with mouths agape, while others scrambled away, back toward the safety of the dome.

I couldn't blame them. I'd never seen the sky weep before.

A peculiar howling echoed across the desert, and I didn't think it had come from the rain or from any of us present.

"Let's get out of here," I growled at Haidee. On the heels of the rain and that mournful howl was a familiar, welcome sight: heading straight at us, a rig painted with the colors of the Oryx clan.

Haidee hesitated. "Mother—"

"Won't listen. You're dumping a lot of painful realities onto her lap all at once, and she's in no shape to deal with any of them."

The rains finally snapped Latona out of her rage. Her hair was now wet and plastered to the sides of her face, the water soaking through her robes. She looked down at her hands, the patterns around her fading, then up at the dark clouds overhead. "What have you done, Haidee?" she cried out, but the rest of her words were lost amid the howling winds.

The rig screeched to a halt beside us, Faraji's ugly mug grinning from behind the wheel. "Let's go!" Mother Salla roared from the backseat, her own Howler already trained on the few soldiers who still held their ground. Some of them were working frantically at the cannons, trying to set off a second round of glowfire.

Odessa's eyes glowed, an almost sickly green. Thick brown vines emerged from the ground around the cannons, wrapping themselves tightly around the weapons until every surface was covered in a seething mass of leaves and thorns. The glowfires faded, and the men scrambled away from the heavy artillery like the metal had come alive.

"How'd you know we were here?" I panted as I helped the girls in.

"A conversation for later!" Mother Salla's tone was all I

needed to know I was in trouble. "Get your butt in here, young man! You've got some explaining to do yourself!" Her eyes widened as she took in both Haidee and Odessa, but she pursed her lips with obvious effort and said nothing other than, "Faraji, floor it!"

He stomped down on the gas, and the rig spun, tore out at high speed. I could see the soldiers attempting to shoot at us again, but if they were close enough to hit us that meant I was close enough to hit them. I aimed my Howler. I fired.

The nearest cannon blew up, and abruptly water wasn't the only thing raining down on them, as men and women tried to scamper out of the unexpected hail of machinery bits. I saw Latona with her fists clenched, a look of utter despair on her face.

"What are we going to do now?" Odessa asked.

Haidee looked at her twin, and I saw in their faces mirror images of despair.

They thought they'd saved the world. Hell, we all did. The rains were the clearest signs that something had changed. That was something to be happy about, right?

So why wasn't the uneasy feeling in my gut going away?

I remembered the galla trying to claw their way out of the portal, reaching for us.

Odessa was right. This was only the beginning.

"I don't know," Haidee whispered. "I really don't."

The rain fell harder.

Chapter Two

'LAN AT THE ORYX LAIR

———————— ☾ ————————

"WE TRAVELED HALFWAY AROUND THE world only to find more rain," I groused, and Odessa, despite the gravity of our situation, couldn't completely rein in a giggle.

This storm wasn't as bad as the ones we often weathered in Aranth—I doubt anything else would be, excepting the acid rainfalls a few hundred miles northeast of the city—but most of the Oryx clan was transfixed by the sight. A couple actually wept openly. It was a sobering thought, that something I had always taken for granted was a rare, precious commodity to them, one that made all the difference between life and death.

It seemed even more inconceivable to me that anyone could have survived living in the dry, arid climate on this side of the world until now. The rain did little to stave off the heat, and the moisture clung to the air, my hair sticking to my skin in the most uncomfortable ways. I had already shrugged off my heavy woolen cloak and armor and stripped down to a sleeveless tunic, but I was still drenched in sweat. Odessa had done the same, and it was hard not to notice the softness of her curves, revealed by the absence of multiple layers of clothing. Arjun and Haidee, both apparently used to the insufferable heat, barely looked discomfited despite wearing more. Much to my irritation, Noelle was similarly unruffled, like she was incapable of perspiration altogether.

While the goddess Latona and her army had lacked hospitality, the clan mistress of the Oryx had, at least, opened her home to us. One of her charges, a pretty girl named Millie with goggles pushed up over her forehead, offered us small bowls of soothing tea as we sat on rocks sanded down for makeshift seating. The place was surprisingly spacious, with small rooms carved out within for privacy, and rudimentary utensils for cooking and cleaning.

I didn't sit for long. And then I couldn't stop pacing. I couldn't stop thinking. It was roughly sixty strides from the cave entrance to its deepest end, marking it approximately 120 feet long. There were twenty Oryx clan members in total, including Arjun, eleven of whom could use elemental gates. I spotted three vehicles outside the lair. Twenty-four Howlers leaned against the wall. Four fire pits. Seventeen cots. It made Aranth look like luxury.

I needed more information than I had. How large was this desert? Where did the Oryx find sustenance? Should Latona decide to mount an attack, how defensible was this cave? Not

very, was my opinion. Its only real asset was that it was camou-
flaged so well against the sand; under a sustained attack by the
goddess's army, though, we wouldn't last an hour.

"Lan?" Odessa reached for me as I stalked past.

"I don't know how well I can protect you in these sunlands."
It was different in Aranth. I knew the lay of the land by heart,
knew all the possible vulnerabilities to fortify.

"You should talk to Arjun. And Mother Salla. You worry
too much."

I looked at Noelle. "Tell me we should be *more* worried. Or
are you as calm as she is?"

"Being lulled to sleep, even as we speak," my friend said
drolly. "It's not likely that Latona will be sending anyone after
us just yet. Not when that puts her daughter—her *daughters*—in
harm's way."

Leave it to Noelle to take the rational route. In the meantime, I felt like I wanted to claw out of my own skin. Good
Mother, it was *hot*!

"How does she do it?" Odessa asked softly. She was watching Haidee. Like me, her sister was never one to sit still for
long, and she was everywhere: first inspecting the stone walls
on the other end of the cave with a critical eye, then looking through the clan's meager utensils, and now surrounding
herself with some of Arjun's brothers and sisters and gesturing at one of their pots, explaining animatedly how they could
improve their cooking time using some new improvement she
was proposing while they listened, entranced. "They have even

fewer resources than we do. She's only just met Arjun's siblings. They've been raised to despise goddesses. How can she be so . . . trusting? Optimistic? Some of them like her, already. I can tell. I envy how easy it is for her to be so . . ."

"You're just as lovable."

Odessa smiled at me, shook her head. "And you're biased." She gazed back at her sister again, a look of wonder on her face. "I have a *sister*," she whispered, sounding almost disbelieving.

"What is this?" Haidee asked, tapping on the wall. "It could help me figure out the rate of thermal conduction needed to speed up your cooking time."

"A cave?" Kadmos offered helpfully.

Haidee folded her arms and scowled at him. "I know what a cave is. What I want to know is what kind of stone these are made of. And how you were able to carve out a lair of this size for yourselves without any available heavy tools. Did you use awls? Special automata?"

The boy grinned. "Dunno about the rock type, but our clan's been blessed with plenty of Acidsmiths. Imogen and Salome melted the rocks and smoothed down the walls for the tunnels. They scour off the grime and clean out any mold we find several times a year. Keeps things neat and tidy. Don't you guys have Acidsmiths in the city?"

"Not a lot of them. Our mechanika had to improvise a lot." She glanced curiously at me.

"Where we're from?" I shook my head, still trying to towel off my neck. The heat was going to murder me long before

22

anything else could. "None who could actually use their abilities. There aren't enough stable Earth patterns where we're from to channel with. I'm guessing you don't have any Icewrights or Mistshapers or Seasingers out here, either." It hadn't stopped raining since we'd arrived at the Oryx's hideout, and a good number of Arjun's clanmates still mobbed the cave's entrance, gawking at the water gushing down. Every conceivable container capable of holding liquid, even unused pots and pans and bowls, had been dragged outside and left to collect. Now, they watched the water gather with something bordering on reverence.

"We need to find more jars," one of the girls, Derra, fretted. "What if the rain stops? What if it never happens again?"

"Can I help?" Haidee offered.

Derra froze, slight panic on her face. Likable as Haidee was, Arjun's clan clearly wasn't comfortable having one, much less two, goddesses in their territory. None of them had been outright hostile, despite Arjun's admission that they had been raised to treat them as enemies. But most did look at the girls like they were live powder kegs apt to explode at any moment.

"*We're* going to help," Arjun said bluntly, laying a hand on the goddess's shoulder. Haidee leaned back into his touch. His meaning was clear: Arjun wasn't seeking approval for his support of Haidee, so much as he was declaring it.

"I can help too," Odessa offered softly. "Where I come from, we deal with water all the time."

"Arjun said it's constantly raining on the other side of the

23

world," Kadmos said. He was the friendliest so far, and the words sounded like a tentative peace offering spoken on behalf of the rest. "With ice. I've never seen ice before."

"You're not missing out on much. Every few months large blocks of ice would drift toward our city, and we had to blast them away before they got too close." I yanked at my collar, and scowled. The heat was another thing I didn't have a plan for, and it was bothering me more than I wanted it to. I'd had no idea I was capable of sweating this much, or how uncomfortable that would be.

"It's not that bad," Odessa said mildly.

"Speak for yourself. I feel like I'm being slow-cooked over a fire the size of a lunar lake."

"Worse than being on a ship?" She was grinning. I knew she was teasing me, trying to get me out of my bad mood.

I couldn't help it; I'd thought I was prepared for almost anything the extremes of Aeon could throw at me, but I didn't account for searing heat. "Worse. I can throw up on a ship and get the sickness out of my system. There's no escaping this."

"What's a ship?" Millie asked.

"It's a bit like a rig, although it's very large and has no wheels. It takes us over water." Odessa tugged at her sleeves, then rolled them up. "What do you need us to do?"

"Derra and Mannix—those are our Mudforgers—are trying to squeeze as much water as they can out from the sand before this"—Kadmos gestured at the sky—"*rain* passes and the sun dries everything back out. But it's a lot of work for just two—"

Odessa wove Air patterns, her eyes glowing blue.

The rain around us paused, hung suspended in the air, slowly collecting into an invisible container made of wind that stretched out over our heads. "You won't have to pull it out of the ground this way," she said. "Bring out all the jars and basins you want me to put this in."

"I love her already," Mannix breathed, as the others stared at her in awe.

"Are you sleeping with Arjun, too, or is it just the Sun Goddess who is?" Imogen was even blunter. "Is it like a two-for-one deal?"

"Imogen!" Arjun barked, turning scarlet.

Haidee burst into laughter. "I'd drop a whale on him if he tried!"

"I'm not with him. I—I'm with—I'm with—" Odessa glanced at me and quickly looked down, blushing.

Imogen grinned, and whatever tension still lingered disappeared. "I mean no disrespect, Your Holinesses. I just wanted to be sure that my brother here was a decision you made out of choice and not out of necessity." She danced out of Arjun's reach, dashing outside to the sounds of laughter from her siblings.

"Sorry about that," Arjun muttered.

"It's all right. They're taking to me better than you did the first time we met."

"How exactly did you meet?" Noelle queried. "If you will pardon my curiosity."

"He tried to kill me," Haidee said cheerfully. "I changed his mind, though."

Arjun opened his mouth, let out an exasperated sigh instead.

There were fresh sounds of mirth by the entrance; the rest of the group had ventured out of the cave, and now found themselves soaked to the skin.

"That's enough," I ordered, stepping forward. "You're all going to catch hypothermia if you're not careful."

"Hypo-what?" asked Faraji, a dark-skinned boy with a mop of thick hair and an earnest face.

Right. They wouldn't know what that was. Several days ago, I wouldn't have known a barren sunland like this could exist, either. "Hypothermia. You can die from getting too cold. You can also get chills and develop problems with your breathing."

"Out of those wet clothes," I instructed, turning to the nearest Oryx clan member—Millie, who, despite the thick humidity, was already shivering. "I'm a Catseye," I began, unsure if an equivalent rank existed in this part of the world, but she looked startled, and then grateful, as she extended her hands willingly toward me. I forced warmth into her, drawing the cold out from her lungs, her sinuses, and everywhere else that could pose a problem. "You'll still need to get out of those clothes."

"No need," Mannix said, somewhat sheepishly. His eyes shone a golden brown, and droplets dripped off her, snaking out of her clothes. "I'm a Mudforger. I should have done this earlier."

The whole clan had taken to us like old friends by the time we were done. Mother Salla had once been a Devoted, Arjun said. She was the Oryx clan leader. She might have taught them to resent Latona, but that dislike didn't seem to extend to Haidee, or to Odessa.

"This is a sign, innit?" Kadmos asked. "The world really is turning."

"It's more complicated than that." Salla sounded weary, sipping her tea. "There will be more rain, and more unexpected phenomena as Aeon changes."

"Shouldn't we be celebrating?" Imogen asked. "We've got water! We won't have to squeeze every clean drop out from Salt Sea dregs anymore!"

"*Should* we be celebrating?" Salla asked Arjun. "As much as the rains give me hope, your account of your experiences at Brighthenge also fills me with dread." Her gaze moved to both Haidee and Odessa, who traded nervous glances. "I knew your mothers. It would take considerable strength to undo the chaos they caused."

Haidee raised her chin. It still felt odd to look at someone who looked so much like Odessa yet was not like her at all. "I'd like to know exactly what happened at the Breaking, for us to know if we've helped mitigate the damage or done worse. I . . ." The resolute expression on her face faltered, leaving her looking suddenly vulnerable. "I—I thought we were doing the right thing. But now Brighthenge's overrun with galla, and I know that wasn't supposed to happen. And Mother . . . Mother's convinced we've made things worse. I've never seen her this furious before, or this afraid. Did we? Do worse, I mean?"

Arjun scowled. "Don't let her words get to you."

"Too late for that. And . . . I'm afraid she may be right. I thought getting the world to turn would solve everything."

Salla smiled faintly. "Don't second-guess yourself, Your Holiness. Your actions pale in comparison to those of your elders. How much of the Breaking do you know about?"

Haidee bit her lip. "Only what Mother told me. That her sister caused the Breaking, and that she was killed in its aftermath, along with my twin."

Salla looked at Odessa. After a moment's hesitation, Odessa also nodded. "I was told the same thing, except that my aunt was responsible, and that she and *my* twin were killed."

The older woman leaned back against her seat and closed her eyes, pondering her next words. Latona and Asteria couldn't *both* be their mothers; an answer meant that one of the goddesses had been living a lie all this time. Would Asteria be capable of lying to Odessa over something this important? I thought about my relationship with her over the years, the ruthlessness she'd displayed when her position was threatened. How she frequently manipulated the Devoted into scheming against each other.

I hated that the answer was yes, she absolutely would.

Salla didn't bother to mince her words; all the better to lay out the truth without the trappings of comfort, I supposed, all the better to dissect and analyze it in its entirety. Normally I would agree, but it didn't stop my stomach from clenching when she said, "You are both Latona's daughters. It was she who was to be sacrificed before the Abyss. Asteria possessed the mark of the galla near her heart. Only the leaders knew what that meant, back then. That was how they knew it was Latona, and not Asteria, who was the sacrifice. The galla's gifts would cure Asteria's mark, but at a cost."

"The cost being her sister's life," Arjun said bleakly.

That's not true! I wanted to cry out. Asteria would have told me—

No, she wouldn't. In fact, she'd been lying to us all this time.

The goddesses' reactions were subtle enough, but still telling; a stiffening of Haidee's shoulders, and the sudden hunching of Odessa's, like she wanted to shrink into herself and disappear. I moved to where Odessa sat, kneeling beside her and taking her hand. In the brief time I'd seen mother and daughter together, Asteria had always displayed a certain detachment toward Odessa, more so than even her pragmatic personality required. It had none of the fiery anger and frustration that marked Haidee and Latona's relationship, as had been clear during the brief encounter we had witnessed near their strange, domed city in the desert.

Haidee turned to Odessa, reaching out to bridge the space between them. Odessa hesitated, and accepted her hand as well, gratitude clear on her face.

"I am sorry," Salla said, "that you were both made to suffer for your mothers' foolishness. Perhaps I should have told you all about this earlier, Arjun, but I never thought I would see both younger goddesses alive. Nor had I thought that I would ever see rain again. What do you wish to know?"

"Is that how callously people treated all the goddesses before us?" Haidee's hand, still enveloped in Odessa's, was shaking slightly. "A mark was enough to merit an execution? Didn't anyone fight for them? Were they so willing to watch them die?"

"Most people weren't even aware that two goddesses existed. Every pair of twins was separated at birth and each raised without knowledge of the other. That was the custom."

"But you knew. The Devoted who served the goddess who was to die," Odessa whispered. "How could they allow this?"

"We were told that her sacrifice was our duty. That it was the price to pay for Aeon to flourish. But many who served Latona resisted. Devika forced some to resign their service. We never heard from them again. It was her way of cowing them, we knew, so the rest stopped resisting so openly. But now . . . I wonder what truly happened to those others she dismissed."

"They should have done more," Odessa said. "The ones who knew what the ritual really meant should have done more!"

The older woman smiled faintly. "You are presuming," she said, "that those few familiar with the secret would put the goddesses's best interests before their own. I only learned the worst of it during the Breaking. The surviving goddesses often left the day-to-day administration of Aeon to the Devoted. They ruled on her behalf. In hindsight, I should have known better, should have questioned the strangeness of such a hierarchy. But I was too invested in my own comfort to protest."

Arjun swore angrily. "They could pass off the surviving goddess to the rest of the people like she'd been the only one all along, and no one would be the wiser. Those lying scum."

"Everything changed with Latona and Asteria. They found out about each other, and from that instant they broke every rule." A thin smile graced Salla's lips. "They had both snuck off to the city on their own, unaware of the other's existence, and returned together, holding hands. Devika's wrath knew no bounds, but they refused to leave each other's side."

Arjun's face was set. "So my mother was responsible for all of this."

"Your mother?" I asked.

"Devika. The leader of Asteria's Devoted," he said candidly.

The woman sighed. "She forbade the goddesses from seeing each other, yes. And when they disobeyed her, she tried to physically separate them, by sending Latona away."

"What did my father say about all this?" Arjun asked, tight-lipped.

"He had passed away when Devika was pregnant with you. He was a low-ranked Devoted, but I knew very little of him. Devika didn't like to talk about her husband. I'm sorry, Arjun. This is why I never told you much about your mother over the years."

"Did she have a Fire gate, too?" Odessa asked softly. She looked frail and vulnerable and sad, and all I wanted to do was wrap my arms around her and swear that everything would be all right, though I feared I might not be able to keep that promise.

A part of me was also furious at these people, at all these horrible decisions that had been made for the twins long before they'd even been born. Knowing that expressing my anger right now would be useless was all that kept me from punching the wall, from yelling at Salla.

"Yes," Salla answered Odessa. "She was a rare Firesmoker who could wield blue fire."

"Like me." Arjun didn't sound surprised. From the way his jaw clenched, it was almost like he was expecting it.

"Back then, those who could command blue fire were exalted above the rest. It was believed to be a sign of Inanna's favor. In Inanna's time, most served as the vestal virgins of her temple, her closest confidantes."

A loud snort came from Imogen, who was eavesdropping. "Arjun doesn't strike me as someone you'd call a vestal virgin."

"Shut up, Immie," Arjun growled.

"What I don't understand," I said, "is how Latona and Asteria went from being as close as sisters can be to attempting to murder one another."

"Neither Asteria nor Latona knew that one of them had to die. They didn't know generations of twins had come before them, or what had befallen them. They thought they were the first, that a civil war might break out, with factions springing up around each of them. I'm not too knowledgeable about the details, but the sisters had a personal falling-out, and Latona left the city, giving up all claims to rule. She was already pregnant by then. The goddess with the mark was supposed to have carried on the line, so you two were unexpected."

I frowned. "Wouldn't the prophecy written at Brighthenge have foretold all this?"

"It said that Latona and Asteria would change the world, but only in the vaguest terms. *Your* prophecy held more details than theirs."

"Who—" Odessa's voice wobbled. "Who made these predictions?"

"They've been etched within Brighthenge since Inanna's time, I'm told. Yours and Haidee's were the last of them all."

The last of the prophecies, implying that there would be no other goddesses to come after them. Odessa grew pale at the revelation; Haidee, angry and resolute.

"The Devoted under Devika planned to kill Latona and claim she had died of natural causes, hoping their estrangement would prevent Asteria from investigating too closely. Devika even tried to turn them further against each other, claiming that one twin intended to have the other killed."

"That explains the letters," Haidee said quietly. "My father realized they were being lied to."

Salla turned away. "My conscience finally got the better of me, though I had little power to stop the rites. Asteria was still too closely guarded. But I managed to send a letter to Latona. I warned her of what the Devoted had planned. She and your father rushed to Brighthenge to warn Asteria. Forgive me, Your Holinesses."

"You tried to save our mothers," Haidee said softly. "There is no fault here to forgive. Thank you."

"I told Latona not to come. We'd learned that the final galla required your father's life, and I thought it better that he stay away—though in the end, they ignored the advice. Devika's machinations had worked well on Latona. Asteria had always been more studious, more at ease with people, while Latona was awkward and preferred solitude. Devika was good at playing on her insecurities. It crossed my mind afterward that she might have deliberately caused the Breaking . . . I hoped it was not so. But when she built the Golden City and drove many people out into the desert, delighting in her power as she did, I knew. I swore I would fight her for Asteria's sake."

I squeezed Odessa's hand gently. The goddess had been quiet this whole time, looking at the floor and biting worriedly at her lip. "Are you all right?"

She squeezed back. "Mother Salla," she finally said, looking up at the woman. "If you know about the sacrificial rites, then you surely know about the ritual involving the galla."

The older Firesmoker's expression changed. "I didn't then. I was at the temple, but was not allowed to bear witness to the rite firsthand—a decision that might have saved my life. I only remember a strange light. I saw Latona stumbling into it, and then it, too, encompassed me. And then I was in the desert."

"The portal," Haidee murmured, her mechanika mind still hunting for solutions. "So many people dying—it must have triggered both portals inadvertently, without anyone meaning to. . . ." She trailed off, shuddered.

"It was whispered even back then, how those portals required human life to open. They were allegedly the portals that Inanna

34

had used to gain access to the Cruel Kingdom. None of us had ever dared try it before."

"How did you two do it?" Imogen asked the twins. "Did you just cast an incanta and command the world to start up again, or . . . ?"

Haidee and Odessa looked at each other. "I don't know," Haidee confessed. "We weren't thinking about it when it happened. We—"

"—reached out toward each other, and everything moved," Odessa said. "And the instant we touched—"

"—some strange power sparked between us, like we could do anything. We wanted to cleanse the Abyss and heal Aeon. But then we—"

"—actually felt the world quake and turn. We don't know how we know. We don't know how we did it, either. We just did. And we don't know how to replicate it."

Everyone was staring at them. "Fascinating," Noelle finally said.

"The same might have been true with your mothers. You must both try to recall as much of what transpired as you can," Salla instructed. "Perhaps the other clan elders can offer some insight."

"Clan elders?" Arjun asked. "What clan elders?"

"In the days after the Breaking, we survivors came to an understanding. We had marked out a large patch of land as neutral territory, back when we were optimistic enough to believe that the world might still be healed. Should any more extreme changes occur, we would all return. I've no doubt that the others have seen the rains with their own eyes. They will come soon enough."

"They've always hated the Sun Goddesses, too, Mother," Arjun said dryly. "I doubt they're going to welcome them with open arms."

"They must. They have just as little choice as we do."

"Why do your clans live separately, when it seems to me numbers would offer more safety?" I asked.

"Resources are few and far between here in the desert, Lady Lan. We choose to divide our people not out of hostility, but for practical purposes. But I expect them and others to arrive before the week is out."

"Clan Addax?" For some reason Arjun looked horrified.

Mother Salla's eyes twinkled. "Yes. I'm sure Lisette will be happy to see you again, despite the circumstances."

The boy coughed nervously. Haidee looked mildly curious.

"If the creatures continue to climb out of the Abyss as you say, then we must close off the gates to the Cruel Kingdom for good. Perhaps the other clans can assist us in that."

"Mother would know more than we do," Haidee spoke up.

"Not really sure she'd jump at the chance to help us," Arjun said.

"She doesn't have to. Mother kept letters that talked about the Breaking. Letters from my father, like the one I have. Maybe there's more that she's hiding."

"Are you seriously suggesting we return to the Golden City?" Arjun growled.

"It's a long shot, but it's the only option I can think of. Unless you have an alternative to offer?"

Arjun glared at her, then crossed his arms. "If you're planning on sneaking back in there, then I'm coming with you."

He'd been rather vocal about not wanting to enter the city before, but I wisely kept my mouth shut.

Salla stood. "If you'll excuse me, I must help the others—it's been a while since we've been able to store this much drinking water."

"We'll help too," Haidee said immediately. She got to her feet, Arjun following. She looked back at Odessa and then at me, her worry evident, and I nodded to reassure her that I would look after her.

"What do you intend to do?" Noelle asked me quietly, once the others had left.

"Haidee knows the lay of the land here, and I trust her to decide what's best for us. Searching for more information about the rituals does seem to be our best bet."

"Very well. I'll go see if they need another set of hands." Tact was Noelle's strongest suit. When she'd left I turned back to Odessa, who was still staring into space. I settled myself more firmly beside her.

"How are you?" I asked, letting my patterns sink into her, exploring. The shadow around her heart was still there, though not as large as it had been, and for once I was hopeful. Perhaps the other gifts she had accepted from the galla had helped to alleviate her illness.

"This was the reason Mother did nothing when the galla

first showed themselves to me," she finally whispered. "Why she allowed me to steal away on the *Brevity,* while pretending to forbid me from going. Why she kept you on as my guardian. *She went through the ritual herself.* Whatever happened at the Breaking, she knew exactly how it was *supposed* to work.

"And when she learned about us, she did everything she could to throw us together. If I gave you up, then I would be saved." Her head dropped. "She did everything she could to save my life. But she was willing to risk you for it. I'm so furious at her."

Asteria knew that Odessa loved me. Yet she had gambled with my life, hoping for the best. I should be angry, too.

Odessa laughed bitterly. "She made a mistake, though. She did it because she assumed Haidee had died, that we were the only goddesses left. I thought we'd saved the world. I thought—" Her shoulders sank. "I thought we'd made a difference. A good difference, for a change. Instead, we might have made it all worse. I was thrilled to have my sister back. But one of us might still have to be sacrificed. Maybe it should be me. It should have been me all along."

"Don't say that, Odessa!"

"How can you forgive me, after everything I've done? I took you captive against your will. I actually considered killing Sumiko, and Noelle, and the other Devoted. I *did* k-kill . . . !" She began to cry. "How can you forgive me?"

I took her gently in my arms and kissed her—lightly, content to let my mouth linger against hers with no coaxing, no

38

pressure to return it. She froze for a few moments, as if unwilling to believe I could stand to touch her still until, with a low cry, she gave in.

"I forgive you." And I forgave Asteria too, if by risking my life she had meant to save Odessa from the Abyss. But Odessa was right: Haidee was alive, and that changed everything. "I will always forgive you."

"I don't know how you can. The thought that the galla can still affect me . . ."

"When Sumiko was helping me deal with losing my rangers . . ." I stopped myself from biting my own lip, from using that pain to distract from the fresh wave of grief I always felt. It was easier now to talk about them, but that didn't mitigate the guilt. I still hadn't told Odessa everything about what happened. "She told me it would help if I could concentrate on something familiar and positive. What if we talked about the things that give you joy?"

She thought about it for a few minutes. "Marianna and Dianae."

"Who?" I'd been expecting her to recall night routines at the Spire, or a moment of affection between her and Asteria. Maybe even us.

"Marianna was bound for the Finae Islands to meet the fiancé her father arranged for her. But the ship she was on was waylaid by the pirates led by the lady captain Dianae. She'd taken up buccaneering after she was unfairly accused of the murder of . . . you're going to make fun of me, aren't you."

"Absolutely not." I was grinning. Romance novels. Romance novels were this beautiful, ridiculous little waif of a goddess's happy place. I wasn't sure I could love her more.

"I learned more about how Aeon used to be from those books, about people who could have lived and laughed and loved. I learned what summer meant. I learned about birds, and butterflies, and about balls and long dresses and dancing. I could almost imagine life like it could have been. Every story was a vow to me, that I'd one day see these places for myself. If that makes me silly—" She paused, stricken. "*The Lady's Pirate.*"

"What?"

"That's the name of Marianna and Dianae's book. I was sorting through my things earlier, and I found it." She sounded dismayed. "Apart from some clothes, that book was the only thing I was able to salvage. Why didn't I think to bring the journal with the ritual instead? I was heading into the Great Abyss; what possessed me to bring a *romance book* with me, of all things? Why am I like this, Lan? It felt like I was on the cusp of insanity then, with all the voices swirling in my head, but then I go and do something ridiculous like—"

I kissed her again, just because I could, and she sagged against me, as if her own weight was suddenly too heavy a burden to bear. It didn't matter; my arms were strong enough to carry us both. "It sounds like something you would absolutely do, and I wouldn't have it any other way." I had no answers still for so many things, but here, even in this strange cave in the middle of all this sand and heat, I could protect her. I would. "Tell me more about Marianna and Dianae, and what they framed—"

"Oh, goddess!" It was Imogen, and she sounded terrified.

We glanced at each other, startled, then scrambled toward the cave entrance and joined the others as they stared up at the sky in the far-off distance.

"What is that?" Millie gasped, arms wrapped tightly around Kadmos's waist. The rest of Arjun's siblings were terrified, clinging to each other. Mother Salla was pale, her mouth open.

"Why is the sun going down?" Imogen choked. "Is it dying? Are we going to die?"

"Is this an attack?" Arjun asked us, stupefied. His Howler was raised, but he was at a loss as to who or what to point it at. Finally, he trained it on the now bloodred sun, which was disappearing from view over the horizon. "Do we fight? How do we fight?"

I couldn't answer him, could only hold Odessa tighter with my hand on my sword, ridiculous as it was. I hadn't been under the sun long enough to know why it was waning. But the skies were turning dark above us, and I knew what *that* was. The night had been too much of a fixture in our lives for us not to know when it stared us back in our faces.

"No." Salla sounded fearful. "This isn't an attack. Aeon's turning, and this is the result. Oh, goddess. It's a sunset."

Silently, not knowing what else to do but huddle close together, we watched the sun fall for the very first time.

At least I would no longer have to complain about the heat.

41

Chapter Three

ODESSA AND THE CLANS

——————————————— ☽ ———————————————

TWO DAYS AFTER WE WERE offered shelter by the Oryx clan, three desert tribes from the Skeleton Coast arrived: the Fennec, the Dorca, and the Gila.

As the goddess of Aranth, I did what came naturally: I hid behind one of the larger sand dunes and watched them alight from their rigs. Mother was the orator, and I'd never been comfortable in crowds. Romance novels hadn't exactly prepared me for what to do in situations like this. And I sincerely doubted the clans would welcome me, even if I did know what to do.

While Mother Salla had said they were allies, the tension was obvious. Men and women nodded briefly at the Oryx mistress in acknowledgment, then turned their energies toward setting up makeshift camps without further conversation. Alliance or not, life in the desert prized caution as a survival trait. Three people I assumed were the tribe leaders sought out Mother

Salla without delay, all of them disappearing inside one of the tents without another word. Nobody paid me much attention. Even if they'd seen me, they would have thought that I was just another one of the nomads, if a little awkward.

They must have seen the sunset, too. The night had fallen everywhere. Arjun's siblings had been terrified, convinced that the darkness would be permanent. That the sun had risen again both times had yet to convince them of its now-cyclical nature, and I suspected that fear would also be common among the newly arrived clans.

For me, the last couple of days had been a blur, and the nights brought disturbing dreams where swarms of galla had converged on us; for every wave we defeated, still another appeared, stronger and more numerous than the last, and I knew with fearful clarity that they would keep doing so until we were all dead.

And then there was a shapeless void before me, of such horrifying asymmetry that it triggered my nausea just to look at it. While my friends fought the galla army, it slid toward me, enveloped in a foul miasma that pushed and prodded against my chest. *Death*, it said, reaching for the shadows clustered beside my heart, and I came awake, panting hard and relaxing only when I spotted Lan curled in her bedroll several feet away from me, sleeping undisturbed.

Now I reached up to lay two fingers against my breast, wondering. The dizzy spells and the exhaustion that often accompanied my illness had not resurfaced. I had tried to return the galla's gifts, but was refused. Was this another vision? I didn't want it to be, but it was getting harder to ignore it.

Instead, I tried to focus my mind on the details Salla had provided us about the clan meeting. The neutral ground was located several miles outside of Oryx territory, situated near several small caves along the rockier territory of the Skeleton Coast; like the Oryx clan's, these were made of what Millie told Haidee and me was limestone, proof that water had been abundant here in ages past. Some of Arjun's siblings were already on patrol duty, keeping an eye out for hostiles, and they were joined by soldiers from other clans without any discussion, like they'd trained together before.

Even that was enough to bring my old insecurities bubbling back up. What was the point of patrolling for lurking vermin, I thought fiercely, when a far worse thing stood before them? It would be so very easy for me to render each and every one of them into ashes. It could be quick and painless. Or it could be slow and excruciating. I could draw a line in the air, *tear* out their bleeding—

No. Stop it, Odessa.

They still lingered, those voices. When I forgot to concentrate I found myself falling back into old habits, into the aberrant whispers that told me I was better, that everyone around me was plotting to keep me from my birthright, those *spiteful* traitors always seeking to betray me; I should kill them before they—

Queen Rose, too, had plotters and schemers for her throne. Many at the royal court lusted for the power she wielded and sought to eliminate her with poison and assassins and war, but it was her most beloved lord, Leopold of Sa'angley, who won her heart and fought to keep her safe from—

The fiends within my mind retreated, sanity regaining a foothold. I could quote most of my novels almost from memory now. Turns out that even demons had little patience when it came to a girl chattering on about books they took no interest in. I was asserting better control than I had before, but every inch gained was a battle.

I wrapped a cloak around myself and kept my hood up; Mother Salla had no way of informing the other clans in advance that two goddesses would be taking part in this general council, and she suggested that we stay hidden until she'd made her case before the others. That meant hiding our color-shifting hair. I didn't know if any of the tribes had ties to the Devoted the way Mother Salla did, or if they would hate us on sight. I hoped she could intercede for Haidee and me, even if she couldn't for our mothers.

Our mothers. That wasn't completely true. Latona was our mother, but I had always believed Asteria to be mine. Mother Salla's confirmation had left me mercifully numb after that initial hurt. Perhaps a part of me had known all along; Asteria played the part of a parent well enough, but there had always been something between us that I found lacking, though I didn't know how to put it into words. I wasn't her daughter. She treated me more often like I was her ward.

I knew Lan and Noelle were worried about me. I knew

Haidee was too. I'd said little in the days after the revelation, was grateful no one chose to press the matter further. I welcomed my strange apathy. It was freeing, not to have to feel.

I opted not to bother Lan, who was bent over one of the newcomers, checking their pulse. Word had spread about the dark-haired Catseye and her offer to delve and heal for injuries old and new. None of the clans had natural healers, and they flocked to her care in no time. Noelle was by her side, serving as attendant. My irrational jealousy toward the tower steward, the suspicions that the galla had clouded my mind with regarding her relationship with Lan, had disappeared, but I avoided her out of shame, not knowing the right words to apologize with.

Arjun was clearly on edge; he'd perched himself atop the highest dune in the area, and occasionally pivoted on his haunches like he wanted to scan every possible direction at once. Occasionally he would stare at the sky, as if daring the night to come again. The scowl never quite left his face. He'd been in a bad mood since Mother Salla had informed him about the gathering.

Everyone was on edge. It had only been three days since Haidee had confronted her mother—*our mother*, I thought, though I wasn't ready to say that aloud yet—and I'd been tense, expecting the woman to attack us. In Latona's place, Mother would already have marched with the full might of her army, ready to attack the Oryx's lair and take Haidee back by force. Latona's odd silence brought some relief, though Haidee had responded to it with mild anger at being ignored. Kadmos and Faraji had taken to scouting near the Golden City, but had found no escalation of the military activity that had surprised us a few days ago.

Her patients treated, Lan began helping the new arrivals set up camp in her usual efficient manner, like she, too, had lived in the desert all her life. Occasionally she would glance back at me, ready to abandon them at a moment's notice if I required anything. Each time she did I would smile, wordlessly assuring her I was fine. She was giving me space without my needing to ask, I knew, but some of my old insecurities bubbled back up to the surface. What if she no longer loved me? I'd taken her, and all of Mother's Devoted, prisoner. I'd killed a man in cold blood. I'd opened my arms to darkness, invited the galla in. I couldn't be trusted, by any objective standard.

"You should wait inside one of the huts," Arjun rumbled, and I realized I'd wandered far enough from camp to be near his post. He indicated the freshly constructed boxlike tents made from tightly packed sand, shaped by clan Mudforgers. The rain was sporadic, leaving and returning at the most unexpected times, but it had finally stopped and the sun was doing its best to eradicate all previous instances of the damp. "You're not used to our weather, and even some of our most experienced can get heatstroke if they're not careful."

I wriggled my fingers at him. "I don't mind. I can make it a little cooler for everyone, if you'd like?"

"Not necessary. You'll need your strength for more important

47

things, and I've gotten used to the desert trying to kill me." He looked back up at the sky and shuddered.

"It's not so bad, the darkness," I said. "It takes getting used to, though."

"I don't know how you lived like that. I'd have gone mad. I still want to barricade the cave every time it happens. And now you tell me it's gonna happen *every twelve hours*?"

"I'm sorry."

A wry smile teased out of his mouth. "You look so much like Haidee. I still find that . . . strange, for lack of a better word."

"Is that good or bad?"

"I don't know. You're a lot more polite than she is, and I'm not used to it." He paused, looked a little pained. "Would appreciate it if you didn't tell her I said that."

"You have my word." It was easier to talk to Arjun. He didn't know me well enough to judge me, or make me think that he would. "What are you watching for?"

"Mirages."

I remembered the cloaked figure that had appeared before Latona's army shortly before the rain fell. I shivered despite the heat.

I didn't want to talk about it, but the Oryx clan had every right to know. They'd extended their hospitality toward us. "One of the gifts I received from the galla involved . . . raising the dead, much like them."

He looked back at me, interested. "I can't imagine that's a skill you'd like to have."

"I don't. But at first I thought I could . . . bring them back to life for real. I couldn't."

"If you want to know how these ones were resurrected, I've got nothing. They've been haunting these parts for as long as I can remember. We try to get out of their way. You don't get them on your side of the world?"

"No."

"Lucky." Arjun used sarcasm just as expertly as he used his Howler.

I looked back at the camp. "Do the clans make it a habit to gather together like this?"

"Last I remember was maybe ten years ago. The Salt Sea was rapidly retreating, and they were trying to come up with a fair way to ration our drinking water, or possibly dig for underground aquifers like the ones underneath the Golden City. Most clans usually go their own way. Our paths cross occasionally, long enough to barter every now and then. Most are nomads, excepting the Addax clan."

"Why?"

"They had an oasis, so their camp was the closest thing to a marketplace we had out here. If our supplies were low, they could always be counted on to have a little to spare, and there was always something we could trade. They . . ." His frown returned. "They don't have that anymore."

"Mother Salla mentioned you knowing someone from there?"

A spot of red appeared on his cheeks. "That's not important."

I giggled. I'd read enough romance to make a guess, and it felt good to laugh. "You should tell Haidee."

"I will. Just figuring out the right time." He was crimson now. I took pity on him and changed the subject.

"So it'd take something really cataclysmic for all the tribes to be willing to stay in one place."

"Yeah. The rain would have gotten everyone's attention, for starters. Mother Salla plans to wait a couple more days, see if any other clans drift in. How are you holding up?" He saw my hesitation and added hastily, "Don't answer if you don't want to."

"No, I want to. I'm scared, frankly. This is all new to me."

"If there's anything you need, you only have to ask. Can't imagine what this must be like for you."

I smiled at him. He was very kind, and I was glad for Haidee. "I'm surprised you're not freaking out more. It must feel weird to have someone show up one day claiming to be your girl-friend's twin."

He reddened again. "I'm not," he sputtered. "Haidee isn't my—well she might be, but not exactly, we never talked about—"

"Arjun!" Haidee was heading our way, carrying a contraption that resembled a large pot. Several strips of metal were hammered into a crisscrossed shape at its bottom.

Arjun sighed and looked at me. "Are you *also* a mechanika?"

"I don't know what that word means," I admitted.

"It's someone who invents things no one really asks for." But his expression was markedly different from his flippant tone. He was already smiling, the harsh demeanor he liked to fall back on thawing at her presence. It made him look younger than he probably wanted.

"It's for cooking," Haidee announced proudly as she reached us. "We won't need to fire up any stones—the sun's heat does all the work. Won't need incanta, either. Metal like this traps heat from the sun quickly, and it should cook most food in twenty minutes, tops. I've set some wooden slats here to protect your skin from burning—" She broke off. "But I can talk about it later," she added, looking guilty. "Was I interrupting?"

"Not at all. It actually sounds rather interesting. But I was hoping *we* could . . . talk? For a little while?" I glanced over at Arjun, and he nodded to indicate he understood.

I knew that Haidee had been giving me time to process everything that had happened—it was difficult, adjusting to a strange new world that was the exact opposite of the one you were used to.

But what I really wanted to do was throw my arms around her waist and not let go until we'd talked about everything. I wanted to tell her about growing up in Aranth. I wanted to ask her a billion questions about what life was like in the Golden City. There was still the problem of the Abyss and of the creatures there, but I wanted to make up for all the years that we were apart, wanted to be some kind of family with her no matter how contemptible our mothers turned out to be.

Haidee looked surprised, then happy. "Absolutely," she said, not bothering to hide her eagerness. Her hands wouldn't keep still, like she had to stop herself from throwing her arms around me, too. I knew that the thought of family appealed to her.

I just wasn't sure if she'd want to be one with me, once she knew everything I'd done.

I reached into my robes and drew out her journal. It contained all the notes she'd taken from the book she said a sand pirate named Sonfei had lent her, about the galla rituals and the lore surrounding our mutual ancestor, the goddess Inanna.

"You wrote about the radiances that the galla would bestow, along with the terrors they would impose." I closed my eyes, swallowing. "They came to me. They gave me the gift of clarity and the ability to glean brief visions of the future, but made me reckless. They gave me the ability to grow and tend to plants, but poisoned the soil in their wake. They gave me greater strength with patterns, but they also made me cruel." I hugged the book to my chest, trembling. "I accepted six of those seven radiances. I still have them. And the terrors, too. I thought they would renege on the deal and take back everything. Their voices in my head dissipated when I rejected the final gift. I *thought* they were gone for good, that I was finally free. But I'm not, am I?"

Haidee frowned. "I saw the vines you wrapped around one of Mother's cannons to disrupt its glowfires. That was one of these radiances, right?"

"Can you do it too?" I shifted the patterns around us, a variety of greens and golds that twisted into the sand until, inexplicably, a shrub sprouted by our feet. It rose higher, twisting and forming branches above us until a tree stood in its place, roughly seven or eight feet high. Thick leaves grew along its branches where I could see small, rounded fruit, ripe for the picking. But just as quickly I saw the ground around it sink, turn brown and sickly looking.

Haidee's eyes glittered as she tried to copy the incanta, knitting the same braids of color, but nothing sprouted beside my plant, for all her efforts. "No," she said slowly. "I can't. I'm not surprised, given what we already know of the ritual."

"Why can't I give them back?" It was hard not to give in to despair. "I don't want them. I never should have accepted them to begin with. I was hoping there'd be something in your notes that could help me, but . . ."

"Your mother, Asteria, would have gone through the same ritual. Did she show any similar abilities?"

But she's not my mother. Having to acknowledge that hurt, but I schooled my features. "None that I've seen. She could see brief glimpses of the future, but that's it. I always thought it was a natural extension of a goddess's abilities."

"Neither my mother nor I have any gifts for prophecy. But your mother is proof that nothing has to change. You can still use the galla's gifts to help people." Haidee looked hopeful. I had known she would be optimistic; from our first meeting she had accepted me without blame or envy. I wished I had her self-assurance.

"I still don't want it. The power—it changes you. For every

new skill I gain, there's a fresh cruelty I receive along with it. They made me selfish, and aggressive, and cold. I . . . I killed someone." The words hung heavy in the air. I waited for her to recoil, but she showed no reaction. "I wish I could say I didn't want to, that I was forced. But I wasn't. I enjoyed doing it. I don't want these *gifts*. Not anymore. They've cost me far too much, more than anything I could ever gain from them."

She knew bits and pieces of my story by now, cobbled together from what Lan, Noelle, and I myself had told her back at Brighthenge. The idea that her twin sister had killed someone should have repulsed her. It might have repulsed me, had our roles been reversed.

"Do you think we should never have done this? Tried to close the rift, tried to make Aeon right again?" The guilt had been eating me up ever since we'd arrived here.

"I . . ." She paused. "I don't know. I never realized it could go this way. I'm already exhausted at the very thought that there's still so much more to be done. But now that we're here, we have to see it all the way through. We have to get rid of the galla, of Inanna's corruption, once and for all. It's just . . ."

She looked away, as if ashamed. "Mother told me that I'd made it worse. I hate that she might have been right. But if the alternative is to accept that our world is slowly dying and we can do nothing about it . . . I reject that. I refuse to believe that our only option is to wait for death." She turned back to me. "You have the galla's gifts. Perhaps there's a way we can use that to our advantage—"

"No." I was shaking my head. "You don't know what you're asking."

"Tell me. Please."

I pointed to the ground, where the sand had blackened, the corruption already taking root. "In a few days, this will rot away, and nothing else will ever grow here. What looks to be a blessing has always been a curse instead."

"But nothing had ever grown there to begin with," Haidee said thoughtfully. "I've done research on sustainable farming, and desert sand isn't conducive to it—unfortunately. Whether it rots tomorrow or not, you've grown something in a place that would never have been able to in normal conditions, and that's saying something." Haidee's own eyes glowed as she drove terra patterns underneath the sand once more. But nothing grew, and she sighed in defeat. "I was expecting that, I suppose. I'm not the one who's been offered the galla's gifts. . . . Still, I hate failing."

"You're not worried? I could do worse. I've done much worse."

"We'll find a way." It was such a terrible promise, with nothing to back it up. But she said it with such sincerity and conviction, my eyes welled up. How could she be so confident? "I'm not our mothers. I'm not going to abandon you."

I couldn't help myself. "Asteria isn't my mother. Why do you talk like she still is?"

"She didn't need to give birth to you to be yours. I'm angry and disappointed with *my* mother, but that doesn't mean she isn't the woman who raised me and cared for me, despite both our shortcomings. It wouldn't matter if Asteria had given birth to me, either. Latona would still be my mother. In the end, that's what a parent is, right?"

I choked, caught between laughter and tears. I don't know what I was going to say when I faced Mother again, but for now Haidee was good at helping ease my anxiety. "Thank you."

"Your Holinesses." Noelle was trotting toward us, her eyes full of puzzlement. "The clan leaders are still in the tent with Lady Salla, but a few people have been understandably curious about our new botanical acquisition."

Haidee and I looked at each other. "They're going to find out about us sooner or later," Haidee finally said. "It can't hurt for them to know we could provide them with food."

I agreed. "Lady Noelle, please let them know that they are free to take as much fruit as they would like for their midday meal."

"As it pleases you, Your Holiness."

"Is she your Devoted?" Haidee asked as Noelle moved obediently away.

I thought about the people I had tried to recruit during the expedition to Brighthenge, cringed at the demands I had made of them, the loyalty I had no right to claim. "No. I don't want to continue the custom of having Devoted. But I trust Noelle implicitly. I could find no better friend." I paused. "Haidee . . . I wish we'd met under better circumstances. There's so much I could tell you about her, and Aranth. About what it's like to live surrounded by seas and storms. About Lan."

"You care for Lan very much?" Haidee asked, the words slightly uncertain, as if she wasn't sure if I wanted to talk about my relationship or keep it private.

She needn't have worried. "I love her. I could have died—or worse—during the journey here, if it wasn't for my Lan. I'd give everything up to be with her." I looked over at Arjun, who was still scowling into the distance. "And him?"

"Yeah. He's annoying and complains too much and snores too loudly and hogs all the space. And I love him."

"Snores?" My eyes widened. "You mean you've . . . you know?" Lan had propositioned me early in our courtship, long before she knew I was the goddess she was supposed to be pro- tecting. I had panicked, because all the experience I had came from the romance novels I loved, and she had assumed I knew much more. We had definitely progressed further than that since then, but were things more . . . *permissive*, here in these sunlands?

I could have been referencing other, more innocuous things, but she knew immediately what I meant. Her grin widened even as a blush papered her cheeks. "Arjun and I have done . . . things. Amazing things. Things he was insufferably smug about afterward. But, technically, yes and no. We didn't go through the whole, well—"

She didn't even need to finish the sentence. I understood perfectly. "We're the same," I admitted shyly. Weren't these the kind of confidences you would tell a sister? It was a strange com- fort, like the years spent not knowing the other existed didn't matter. It didn't feel awkward at all to be divulging secrets now.

"We didn't have much time to do more, but it felt—"

"I know. I had no idea you could—"

"Yes, and isn't it stunning how—"

"Oh, sweet Aeon, did *she* also—" She was coloring in earnest now. I was certain I was reddening in the exact same way.

"Did *he*—"

"*Yes.* He was strutting about afterward like he'd closed the Abyss himself—"

"Lan doesn't strut, but it was—glorious. I had never felt so—"

"I can *hear* you two," Arjun growled, horrified.

Haidee giggled, though she lowered her voice. "It wasn't all fun and games during our travels. He was stung by a huge scorpion. He almost . . ." Her grin faded. "He was temporarily paralyzed, but I thought it was worse than that."

I could only nod, sympathetic. Underneath her cheerful disposition was a doggedness that I recognized because I shared it; I would have fought anyone and anything for Lan, too. And I had.

"And he's still dragging his heels about sneaking into the city with me. I know Vanya can—"

A commotion rose from the tents. Mistress Tamera of Clan Fennec emerged, looking furious. She was followed by Master Lars of Clan Gila, Master Giorme of Clan Dorca, and then Mother Salla herself, lips pursed. Apparently, Mother Salla's attempts at explaining us had not gone well.

The commotion drew Lan closer; she lifted an eyebrow at me, a silent question in her eyes. I shook my head. The clans had a right to be angry. Latona had never treated the nomads well, so it was natural for their hostility to be extended to her daughters.

The group of elders stopped abruptly in their tracks, taking in the tree, before Tamera turned her ire on us.

"You've brought *goddesses* here?" she shouted. "What trick do you intend to pull, Salla? Are you spying for the city dwellers?"

"If we were working for Latona, you would all be her prisoners by now. Use your head, Tamera."

"I had not thought to believe it myself," Lars marveled, "but there are *two* of them. So it's true that the other goddess survived."

Tamera glared at us. "I was willing to ignore your former position as a Devoted because you have proven yourself a staunch ally over the years, Salla, but what possible reasons could you have for trusting these two?"

Mother Salla snorted, like it was a ridiculous question. "You want Aeon healed just as much as I do, and only the goddesses can bring that about. Look around us. Did you want to spend the rest of your life waging war with Latona over a desert?"

"The Sun Goddess didn't leave us much choice, as you recall."

"We have a choice now. They need our help. Or will you let your prejudices stand in their way?"

The other woman took off her cap, rubbing at her bald scalp. "I promise nothing until I hear what it is they want from us."

"Thank you, Lady Tamera," Haidee said.

She laughed. "Not a lady," she said, and Lan started at that. "But I will listen, even if you may not like my answer."

"I am sorry," my twin said, "that you have spent your lives out here in the desert, when my mother should have done more. *I* should have done more. My sister and I are trying to find a way to heal the breach and undo the Breaking."

"And what if that requires you to stand against your mother?"

"I already am."

"Would you kill her, if it comes down to it?"

Haidee looked shocked. "I—no. She might not listen to reason, but I won't let her harm any of you."

"And that is exactly my fear, *Your Holiness*," Tamera shot back, the title clearly meant to be an insult. "Your hesitation will mean our deaths. I cannot trust my family's lives to such indecisiveness."

A shout from Arjun interrupted us. He was pointing at a fleet of vehicles heading our way.

"Hellmakers," he roared. "Hellmakers, twenty out!"

Haidee paled.

"Another clan?" I asked, puzzled, but my sister was already running toward Arjun, the others scrambling to get into their own jeeps. Her reply drifted back to me, slamming hard into my gut once the words set in.

"Not a clan. Cannibals!"

Chapter Four

HAIDEE VERSUS THE CANNIBALS

—————————— ☼ ——————————

BY THE TIME ARJUN SOUNDED the alert I was already moving, leaving a stunned-looking Odessa behind as I tore through the sands to get to the closest rig. Arjun was already behind the wheel, readying his Howler. A cluster of gold and brown rigs sped toward us. "Clan Addax colors," he said grimly.

The blood-colored vehicles in relentless pursuit behind them, though, were most definitely not a part of the alliance.

"They're not going to make it," I muttered. The Hellmakers were too close, within firing range. They could massacre Clan Addax before any of them reached us.

Lan and Noelle made a beeline for our rig as well. "How good are you with guns?" Arjun asked them as I slid into the empty seat beside him.

"Never held one before," Noelle said calmly, "but we're quick learners."

"Get me close enough," Lan added darkly, "and I won't be needing one."

"But she's the goddess!" I heard the Dorca clan leader, Giorme, shout. "Salla, you cannot possibly allow her to fall into those men's—"

I silenced him by generating Air and Earth, throwing the concoction of patterns as far as I could. A huge cloud of sand exploded underneath the wheels of one of the cannibals' rigs. The vehicle careened wildly, the momentum flipping it sideways.

"I have to get closer!" The farther out my target was, the more taxing it was to cast. I'd learned that the hard way when I tried to fight Sonfei and his Liangzhu.

"Sounds like the goddess can handle herself well enough, Giorme!" Arjun slammed a foot onto the pedal. "Brace yourselves!" he yelled, and the rig charged forward to meet the approaching vehicles.

I didn't know if the cannibals thrived on impossible odds, or if they believed their numbers were enough to repel us, or if their hunger superseded everything else, but they showed no signs of letting up the chase. From the back seat, Noelle rose, took careful aim with one of the javelins she carried, and threw, hard. It caught one of the cannibals right through his chest. He slumped over the wheel, while his partner fought to gain control of the jeep.

"Are you a ranger like Lan?" I asked, amazed. The throw had been nothing short of spectacular.

"No," she said primly, settling back into her seat. "My mother was a lady's maid."

With his only hand still clinging to the wheel, Arjun took aim with his other arm, and fired. The next-closest cannibals' rig exploded, but the other cars deftly detoured around the burning wreckage.

Four of the five Addax jeeps shot past ours, and so the cannibals were forced to turn their attention on us instead. Only one Addax vehicle remained between us and the Hellmakers; it had lagged behind to delay the brutes, which I thought was a brave thing to do, given what would happen if they were overcome. Inside, a girl with short ash-colored hair was firing back at the cannibals with a Howler of her own, though I saw it was an older make and not as powerful as the cannibals' weapons.

The instant we drew up to one of the Hellmaker rigs Lan leaped from her seat, landing easily on the hood of the cannibals' buggy. Before the men could react, her sword had skewered the driver in place. When his passenger brought up a gun in response, she dispatched him just as easily, kicking him out of the rig with a boot to the face.

The air was saturated with fire patterns as every Howler in view trained on Lan. I pushed out with my arms, and a large wave of dust rose to deflect their shots, raining a heavy sandstorm down on them. I copied the movements of the Sand Sea that I'd observed during my long trek to the Abyss with Arjun; the way the sand there flowed and ebbed like water, the way the large, frightening creatures that lurked within would send

cascades of fine grit over us—an effective defense. The cannibals struggled, their rigs slowing to a stop as dust poured into
their engines.

But one of the rigs refused to surrender. Its occupant, a
wild-looking man with an ugly scar on his face, stood with his
Howler still trained on Lan. I realized with a start that I recognized him. He was the leader who had tried to ambush us as we
attempted to cross the Sand Sea.

Arjun had the leader in his sights. But before he could fire a
shot, a howling wind lanced across the desert and knocked the
other man out of the car, the sudden gale sweeping him a few
hundred feet away.

It wasn't my doing.

Odessa was exactly where I had left her. She was too far
away for me to see her features clearly, but I saw the rigid set of
her shoulders and the way her hands were clenched.

She was at least four hundred paces away. The immense
power it required to channel winds over such a distance would
have sapped my strength. The last time I'd tried, I'd fainted and
taken days to recover.

I watched, stunned, as she did it again, and all the Hellmakers felt her wrath. I watched them rise into the air, gasping and
choking, and I saw thick globs of sand being *forced* down their
throats. She was suffocating them.

"Odessa!" Lan screamed. "Odessa, no!"

I reached out for Odessa on instinct—a ridiculous action,
considering the distance between us—but somehow I found her

all the same, the breath leaving my lungs as my mind slammed into focus alongside hers.

I could feel her fury, and her desperation. In her zeal she'd expended too much energy, and it was a hard fight trying to reel it back under her control. The extent of her abilities frightened me. I could never wield so much strength. I knew this was the result of the galla's gifts she'd been talking about, but that didn't stop me from feeling awed, and fearful at the thought of the other things my sister could be capable of.

And envious. Oh, the things I could do, the people I could have helped, had I even half of what she had . . . !

But I pushed back those thoughts, angry that I could even think them.

If Odessa sensed any of it she gave no indication; instead, she welcomed me in. We pooled our focus together, and it was enough to dissipate the energies in the air, forcing the patterns to unravel. The winds disappeared without warning, and the cannibals dropped back down to the ground, heaving out grit, a few vomiting violently. Odessa's face was buried in her hands, and she was swaying back and forth.

Lan was already tearing through the desert, back to my sister.

"Will she be all right?" I asked Noelle, shaken. So this was the consequence of those radiances. Odessa had been gifted a greater strength in the incanta, and the ability to spin patterns in ways I'd never thought of. But there was a cost. Odessa had told me as much. It was enough to dampen my fleeting wish to have what she had.

The redhead's face was troubled. "She hasn't been herself these last few weeks, milady." I'd noticed that Noelle had a penchant for understating the obvious, but this was putting it far too mildly. "But she's trying."

The rest of the clans had caught up, their rigs pulling up beside ours. "Secure them," Tamera barked at her subordinates. "They've plagued these dunes long enough. Justice for their crimes is a long time coming."

"From what I could tell," murmured Lars, the softspoken leader of the Gila, "one of the young goddesses was well on her way to addressing that."

Lan had reached Odessa's side and was holding my sister close. Odessa's eyes were closed, but she was leaning gratefully into Lan, looking far less distressed than she had minutes before.

"Not like this," I found myself saying. "Charge them and bring them to your courts if you must, but I cannot condone cold-blooded murder on my watch."

Tamera laughed mirthlessly. "These are not your glittering Golden City tribunals, Your Holiness. Unlike the elite that make up your circles, our brand of justice does not rely on the wealth and influence of the accused."

"Nonetheless," Mother Salla said, "Haidee is a goddess of Aeon whether we wish it or not, and she shall deliver the final judgment. Chain them along the outskirts of camp, and make sure to change guard every three hours."

"Pardon me, Lisette," Giorme said politely, stroking his long, gray-streaked beard. "But where did the Hellmakers first attack you and your siblings?"

"Five, six miles from where you first spotted us."

"Interesting. We should be far from Hellmaker territory here. Their numbers have diminished considerably since we delivered our reprisals on behalf of your oasis. They may be fools, but not even fools would have risked charging at us here, given that these grounds border both my clan's and Gila territory. I've kept eyes on them since Salla told us about their attempt to muscle in on your whale meat. They've retreated out into the desert along the Sand Sea coastline ever since, living off lizards and scorpions."

I nodded in agreement. The Sand Sea had been where Arjun and I had encountered them last.

"What would drive them back here, then? They would risk the wrath of three clans alone, even without our treaty."

"A question we should ask them." The Fennec clan mistress frowned and turned to me. "You will forgive me," she said, "if I don't fall to my knees, impressive as you and your sister are. I have little reason to trust you still, but I trust Salla. If this is a trick . . ."

"It's not," I was quick to say. "I don't want to rule a broken world. I'm not even sure I want to rule at all. I just want peace. I want to bring Aeon back to what it could be."

Mistress Tamera studied me. "You seem sincere enough. Much more sincere than your mother ever was. I will believe you—for now."

"Please excuse her manners," Lars said as the older woman

walked away. "I am not fond of your mother, but if Salla vouches for you, then I will at least be cordial. I believe I speak for Giorme as well."

"You do," the other man confirmed.

"Arjun!" The girl from the last rig, the one who had been valiantly defending the rest of the Addax clan from the cannibals, had climbed out of her vehicle. Laughing, she flew toward Arjun.

"That's three times you've saved my ass," she chortled, and kissed him.

I heard a startled "Oh!" from Noelle, and something that sounded like "He's in *big* trouble now" from Faraji. Suddenly I wasn't quite as willing to show mercy to the girl and Arjun as I had to the cannibals.

Arjun's reaction would have been comical, had it been anyone else. He jumped away from the girl and held her at arm's length when she, startled by his unexpected retreat, attempted to move closer. "Lisette," he said hurriedly. "It's good to see you again." He shot an aghast look my way, clearing his throat. "Haidee, this is Lisette, from Clan Addax," he said, every word a plea.

Lisette. He'd mentioned her before, when we were driving toward the Great Abyss with little idea of what we'd discover there. He'd said she was an old lover of his, that they had broken off long ago.

From the way she'd kissed him, it didn't seem like he'd told her that, though.

"Haidee?" The girl studied me. She was pretty, I noticed

with some dismay. Her hair was even shorter than mine, cropped close to her neck. It accentuated her clear brown eyes and oval face, her light brown skin a pretty compliment to the yellows of her hair. She appeared puzzled for a moment, until her eyes stole over my colorful locks. She stood up straighter, the look of alarm on her face settling into shock and then unconcealed interest.

"You're the Sun Goddess!" she blurted out, amazed. "Arjun, she's the *Sun Goddess*."

"Yes," he said hastily, taking a small step away to avoid her outstretched hand. "This is Haidee, and she's my—well, she's a . . ."

"I'm Haidee," I said smoothly, giving her a light curtsy. "Arjun mentioned you to me," I continued, proud of how I was keeping my emotions firmly in check. "It's good to meet you."

Lisette was quick on the uptake, quick to process what Arjun was stumbling to say. She withdrew her arm, eyeing me in the careful way one might if they stumbled across a snake on the ground, unsure yet if its venom was of the poisonous variety. She came to a speedy decision, and sank into a curtsy even lower than mine was. "It's been a long time since I last saw Arjun, so I'm afraid I know very little about you beyond the stories the elders like to scare us with." Lisette hadn't been raised as royalty like I was, but recognizing jealousy transcended culture, I suppose. Not that I was *really* jealous. "I owe you both my life. I'm Lisette, mistress of Clan Addax." Her eyes twinkled. "Only friends call me Lissie, and I hope you will, too."

I relaxed, glad that we'd come to an understanding of sorts. No one bothered to tell Arjun, who continued to fidget.

"Mistress of Clan Addax?" Mother Salla echoed. "Lisette, what happened to Jassen?"

Lisette's face fell. "He died a few months ago, from the heat sickness. Barden and Esme died with him."

"Barden and Esme?" Arjun looked stricken. "I'm sorry, Lissie."

"Things have been harder since the last time the Hellmakers attacked our camp." Lisette's smile was both grim and vicious. "Should you even bother with a trial, I hope you'll let me take part—as judge, jury, or executioner. I'm particularly good at the executing part."

"Did someone *invite* the cannibals to this gathering of clans?" Noelle asked.

"Not all of the clans have been equally fortunate since our alliance began," Mother Salla said. "These cannibals used to belong to the Saiga clan, led by a man named Galon. He died only a few months after the Breaking. Without his leadership, the Saiga fared poorly, and turned to cannibalism to survive. Possibly some of its members still remember the signals, the old reminders to strike for this place after any drastic changes in the weather. There will be time enough to question them. Lisette, it is best that you and your family head to the tents we've set up on your behalf. You've traveled a long way, and you all need some much-deserved rest."

"That is very kind of you, Mother Salla, but I think there

are some loose ends to tie up first." Lisette bent down and slid a knife out from the top of her boot.

"No," Mother Salla said.

"You know the Addax's history with these cannibals, Mother. They destroyed our oasis. They have killed many brothers and sisters of mine. I demand blood on their behalf."

"Vengeance must wait. Slit their throats now, and they will provide no useful information. The world is changing, Lisette. We need every scrap we can pull out of them."

"Not while my siblings' bones still lie out in the desert."

"I am invoking the old laws of our treaty, Lisette."

Lisette glared at Arjun. "And you agree with her? You were even thirstier for their blood than I was, once."

"I know, and I'm sorry. I lost family to them, too. But Mother Salla is right. Things have changed."

"I gathered as much." The girl took a deep breath, calmer now, and slipped her knife back into its place. "We owe you and the Oryx. We'll follow your rules, just as Jassen would have wanted. But once their usefulness is done, I will ask for satisfaction." To my surprise, she clasped my hands, actually lifted one to kiss. "I've never met a goddess before, and you seem nicer than the stories claim, if you don't mind my saying so. I hope to make more of your acquaintance. For now, I have my family to see to. Clan Addax will always be grateful, Mother Salla."

"She seems friendly," I said mildly, watching them walk toward the tents. Arjun was scowling after her, a complete change from his nervousness earlier. "And what's wrong with you?"

71

"I wasn't encouraging her," he said immediately. "I didn't expect her to—"

I smothered a laugh. I would have been angrier, I suppose, if I'd seen him take any pleasure in the exchange. I wasn't used to competition; I was used to being the prize, as arrogant as that sounded. Mother often played one noble family against the other, dangling me as a potential reward for their sons. "Don't be mad at her. She didn't know about us."

"That's not the reason I'm angry with her now," he muttered. "She lost interest in me as soon as she saw you."

"Well, it's because she's honorable enough not to chase after you, knowing that I was—" I stilled. "Wait. I don't understand what you mean."

"She was *flirting* with you." He turned to me, still clearly huffy. "She's been involved with both men and women before. I know her well enough to see if she's interested in someone." He glowered. "And she better not be."

I hadn't expected Arjun to switch from nervously trying to explain his old flame, to being just as possessive as I had been. And it couldn't have helped when I burst into laughter, either.

Interrogating the cannibals took time. Odessa displayed another of those strange galla-given abilities by taking away the Hellmakers' gates, preventing them from using incanta. It had caused a stir among the other clans, and their leaders eyed us with even more misgivings. But the peace of the neutral ground held—for now.

I'm not sure I could blame them. After Odessa's handling of the ruined Saiga clan, I would have been suspicious as well. Arjun had often accused me of being too idealistic—like that was a failing!—and he certainly thought I was too trusting, especially with my twin. But from the very first instant we fell into each other's arms at the Great Abyss, discovering a connection between us that was strong enough to send the world spinning again, I knew I would protect her. No galla's gift or curse could overcome that.

Mother Salla led the inquisition, the other elders interjecting when they had their own questions. Now that they were bound and deprived of their gates, the cannibals had lost their courage, blubbering and pleading for mercy. They were clearly afraid of something, but many weren't coherent enough to offer a straight answer. Their leader, the man with the scar, continued to taunt us.

"Why do I have to answer the meat?" he snarled, baring jagged, broken teeth. "That's what you all are. All meat, all the time. You're too stringy to eat, you old hag, but you'd make good jerky. Now this one," he said, and leered at Odessa. "Good bones, all around. You'd be delicious enough to—"

Lan backhanded him across the face. The cannibal's head swung to one side, spittle flying, and Lan slapped him again. "When did they die?" she asked.

The man stared at her. "Who died? You're all going to die. My boys and I gonna feast—"

Lan swatted him again. "When did they die?" she repeated.

"Let her," Odessa said softly when Mother Salla looked ready to intervene.

"Is this wise?" Tamera wanted to know.

"Does the Catseye have experience in such techniques?" Lars asked, his nose wrinkled in distaste.

"Certainly far more than we do," Salla said with a sigh. "Let her continue. And keep Lisette and her knives away."

Every slap seemed to knock more of the fight out of him. Uncertainty bled through the arrogance, and I watched him grow doubtful, then frantic, then fearful, like every hit made him consider Lan's question with more gravity.

It took another half hour before the cannibal capitulated. By then his shoulders had slumped, a glassy look in his eyes. "Seven years ago," he said. "They took and ate her seven years ago." And he began, oddly enough, to cry.

Lan sighed and leaned back, watching him weep. "You can ask him more questions now," she said wearily. "He doesn't deserve it, but I advise you to be gentler this time. Force the questions down his throat and he'll close up again."

"What did you do?" Arjun asked curiously. Odessa had scurried forward, throwing herself on the Catseye's arm. "And how did you know about his past?"

"I didn't," Lan said, with another, deeper sigh, gathering Odessa closer. "But given the kind of life he must have led, it was likely someone he cared for had died in some terrible way. He's angry and also constantly hyperaware of everything around him, which makes him prone to violent outbursts. He uses that rage as a shield. We needed to get past it. I can't change his personality, but I can alter the balance of certain chemicals in his brain to lower his guard and make him manageable—for a while, at least."

"And you did that in increments every time you slapped him," Arjun said, eyes widening in understanding. "Pretty clever."

"You sound like you've done this before," I added.

"I've been in his place, yes." I blinked, but Lan continued on, unfazed. "A Catseye in Aranth named Sumiko helped me deal with a few things from my past. She didn't hit me that hard, but I didn't see much choice with him."

"Now then," Mother Salla said to the cannibal. "We'd like to know how you came to target the Addax clan. Have you been hunting them?"

The man shook his head.

"This area is far from your usual hunting grounds. What made you come here?"

"An accident, finding the meat." The cannibal's voice had shrunk down to a rasp. "We were already on the run."

"On the run? From who?"

"Not who. What." The man started to shake. "I saw it. A madness across the desert, lurking in shadows. A great shaking of the earth, and then something rising—high enough to mock the heavens. Dark things have come to chase us. Some of them were soot and nothingness, but among them one rose, cloaked in blue jewels, and we feared. And so we ran. We are still running. Set us free, and let us run. They will feast on the world, but at least they will feast on us last. And if you are smart, you will run, too. I know hunger. But these—there will never be enough to appease them. They are hours behind us, but when they catch us we will have nothing else but the dark. In the end, you will run. You will run, too."

Chapter Five

ARJUN VERSUS THE SHADOWS

※

"SO HOW MANY GALLA EXACTLY are we talking about? A couple of hundred? A thousand? Ten thousand? How drunk do you recommend I should be before you actually tell me the number?"

Lisette tried to sound lighthearted, but as someone who'd actually seen those sonofabitches up close I wasn't in a mood to return the banter. Haidee had closed the portal, which should have prevented them from following us. How in the hell had they traveled halfway around the world in the span of only a few days? I knew they didn't require food or sleep, but I'd never seen anything even close to resembling them out here in the desert, if you didn't count the mirages.

"I really don't know." The cannibals said the shadows had been chasing them. I don't know how many hours' head start they had on the galla, but I doubted it was a lot.

The desert still looked pristine, abandoned, like no shadows could possibly be lying in wait for us across the sands. But Mother Salla and the other clan leaders had started building a small fort around camp, in an attempt to dissuade attacks from all sides. Haidee was already trying to come up with something that could reproduce the Golden City's air-domes, and Odessa and some of the Windshifters from the other clans were aiding her. Both goddesses had added their blessings to all the weapons we had on hand, so we were at least prepared should an attack come.

"You mean, you don't know because there were too many to be counted, or you don't know because there's a chance the Hellmakers are lying?"

"I said I don't know."

"Ah." Lisette mulled that over. "So. You're quite taken with the Sun Goddess, aren't you?"

"Do you really think now is the best time to talk about this?"

"What else are we gonna do until those *things*—you call them galla?—show up? *If* they show up. I'm still not sure if those scum didn't hallucinate the whole thing. Or lie so you would take pity on them. Lars still thinks they can be saved." She fingered the trigger on her Howler contemplatively.

"You're still not allowed to shoot them, Lissie." I scanned our surroundings. No sign of galla. No sign of the Golden Army, either. If we were lucky maybe they'd run into each other instead.

"That's *Mother* Lissie to you."

"I don't think so, no."

She chuckled. "I'm not going to shoot them—yet. Stop changing the subject."

"I don't see how it's any of your business." My relief after realizing Haidee wasn't mad at me was so immense I could have spotted it from miles away. I was nonetheless determined not to let Lisette and her big mouth get me into any further trouble.

"It became my business when I made the mistake of kissing you." Her grin was wide. "Your girlfriend has a good heart, though—she didn't even attempt to set me on fire. Not like the other one, her twin—Odessa, right? I think I might prefer the girl from the night-world. Her bloodthirstiness rivals my own. How did you even meet Her Holiness Haidee?"

"On an aspidochelone."

"A what?"

"A great whale. One of the largest known. People used to mistake them for islands. They'd land with their ships and—look, like I said, it's no business of yours."

"Is it serious?" she persisted. "At least answer that."

"Yeah," I said, staring out into the dunes. "It is. Why so nosy about her? Going to try to woo her away?"

"If she were available, I would. But whatever I am, and whatever jokes I make, you know I wouldn't do that to you. I'm curious, is all. You told me before that you never wanted someone to grow old with."

Because I never thought I would grow old to begin with. "Things change."

"So they do. The world's spinning, and there's rain falling

up and down the Skeleton Coast. Two surviving goddesses have turned into four, galla are nipping at our heels, and now you're a romantic. Glad I'm a constant, at least." She hefted her Howler, squinted through the sights. "What do they look like?"

Like black holes that moved and consumed everything in their paths. Like they were made of nothing, and everything we feared. "You'll know soon enough," I said dryly.

"I'm happy for you," Lisette said. "If that means anything. You've never looked like you had anything to laugh about before, in all the years I've known you. You've always been so serious and angry. It's nice to see a little smile on your face every now and then, especially when you think she isn't looking."

I glared at her. She only grinned back. "Just stay on guard," I muttered. I knew what she was doing. We'd been far too much on edge in the hours since the cannibal's revelation, and this was her attempt at lightening the mood.

"You think she can pull some strings and get us amnesty from her mother?"

"Doubt it. She and her mother aren't on the best terms right now."

"So what you're saying is that we're gonna have another Sun Goddess *and* these demons to worry about. What's the story with the other one again? Is she to be trusted? Don't get me wrong—I'm very appreciative of how Lady Odessa chose to punish those men, but I tend to be wary still, considering that she can blow shit up so well."

"Haidee trusts her, so I will."

"You've never been this quick to take someone else's word."

"I trust Haidee. That makes all the difference." I hesitated. "I'm sorry again about Jassen, Lissie. And Esme and Barden." It was customary for the oldest member of each desert tribe to assume leadership. That Lisette was now the mistress of the Addax clan said much, and none of it good.

"Sorry enough to give me five minutes alone with that piece of shit who tried to gun down my family?"

"Lissie." The cannibals were trussed up in a solitary section of camp where they were constantly under guard. Not all of the other clans were happy with the arrangement, with some members loudly voicing their discontent, but Haidee had been insistent. For all the clans' distrust and dislike of the Sun Goddesses, I thought, they were quick to accede to her wishes. Veneration of the goddesses had been around far longer than the hatred for them; it seemed almost instinctive to obey.

Lisette laughed, though she couldn't quite hide the quick flare of pain in her eyes. "It's been a hard couple of years for us, but we're doing our best. I wish Esme could have seen the rains. She would have liked that. How do you know that scum was even telling the truth? He would have said anything to stop us from killing him."

"He described the galla a little too accurately to be making it up. Especially those blue jewels he said one of them wore." Odessa had mentioned them in particular; every gift she had received had come from a galla wearing distinctive lapis lazuli stones, as if they were marked as leaders of their own clans.

That information worried me. But from the way she'd told it, they'd never been hostile to her.

A faint whine buzzed through the air behind us, and we turned to look. A thin layer of air hung over the camp, encompassing it much like the Golden City's domes. It wasn't as thick and it flickered in and out of view a few times before finally holding steady, but it was a good replica, given the circumstances. As always, I couldn't help but feel impressed and proud of Haidee's resourcefulness.

"Your girlfriend is useful as hell," Lisette said. "I'm tempted to kneel before her and swear my undying devotion." She grinned hugely. "You better be putting everything I taught you to good use to make her happy."

"Lisette!" I barked, hoping Haidee wasn't within earshot.

Lan came trotting up, her face grim. "Odessa wants you to get ready. She's been getting visions again, and she thinks an attack could come within the next half hour."

"Visions?" Lisette asked, alarmed. "Hold up, the other goddess can see the future?"

"One of the galla's gifts, or so I'm told," I said, "but not one she can control. How accurate have they been before?"

Lan frowned. "I'm not sure. I told her I'll be joining your watch in any case. You'll need the help if she's right."

"Better tell the rest of the front guard," I told Lisette. The clans never had to fight as a single unit before, and I didn't want anyone making mistakes at this point.

"On it." Lisette slung her Howler onto her back. "If they

show up while I'm gone, leave some for me to shoot at."

"Lady Haidee said that Miss Lisette was an old flame of yours," Lan said once the other girl was out of sight.

I scowled. "We weren't ever serious—"

"Ah. My apologies. I didn't mean it that way. Lady Haidee only mentioned it to me because I asked." The Catseye was glowering worse than I was. I thought I knew why.

"Lisette was flirting with Lady Odessa, wasn't she?"

"I thought it might have been my imagination, but . . ."

"It's not. She flirts with everyone, usually when she's nervous and won't admit it. Can't blame her, though. She's been through a lot. And as for our . . . uh . . ." I knew, and Haidee definitely knew—I was pretty sure—but trying to explain my past relationship with Lisette to anyone else always seemed to put me on the defensive.

Lan raised her hand to stop me. "You don't need to explain. I know what it's like, trying to take what little pleasure you can get, when happiness is something you're afraid you'll never have the chance to find. It's the same out here in your dry desert as it was back home amid the rain and the ice. I apologize if you thought I intended to judge you—or Miss Lisette. I was simply . . . a little put out by her forwardness. Though Odessa was oblivious. As always."

I had to smile at that. Even practical, levelheaded Lan could get jealous. That made me feel better. "You've left some old loves back home too, huh?"

"Some. The last one . . . died."

"Ah. I'm sorry."

"So am I. She was one of my rangers. She was killed on my watch." Lan's voice was a little too steady to be calm, but she seemed willing enough to share. "For the longest time, I thought that refusing to talk about her death was the best way to ease my guilt, but it only made it worse, to the point that it impaired my actions. It was Odessa and Sumiko who made me see the light, made me realize bottling it up wasn't good for me. Accepting that she and my rangers are gone didn't make the guilt disappear, but it isn't as much of a burden on my mind as it once was. I cared about her, but we weren't together because of some deeper emotion. I'd lived a solitary life for the most part, and Nuala . . . made living it more bearable."

"Lisette did that for me, too." The Catseye was telling me all this deliberately, in a show of solidarity. I appreciated that. "And now here we are, in love with twin goddesses."

She laughed. "If you had a chance to do it all over again, would you still choose her?"

"I wouldn't have fought her over a dead whale, but everything else I'd do again in a heartbeat. Even that damn scorpion." I should have known the very instant I'd seen her that first time, with her stupidly beautiful hair and her stupidly gorgeous eyes and her stupidly sexy empathy for everything and everyone around her even when none of them deserved her compassion, me included. "You?"

"Wouldn't have asked her to sleep with me before we'd even had an official first date, but the same."

"Wait, what?" Odessa had always struck me as the shy, introverted type, an opposite to Haidee's more cheerful, outgoing personality. Of course, that felt like an odd thing to say after I'd seen her nearly suffocate the Hellmakers.

"I'll tell you all about it later, if you'd like." Lan pointed. "I think Odessa was being optimistic when she said the attack would come in half an hour."

She was right. I could see a seething blanket of shadow slowly encroaching over the horizon. I bit down on my tongue to stop myself from cursing again. The cannibals had been right, damn them. How had these hellspawn traveled from the Abyss so quickly? My gaze flicked through the teeming mass, seeking out the one with the blue jewels, but there was no hint of color whatsoever in that death-ridden army climbing toward us.

"Get ready!" I roared, and the other Firesmokers scrambled to take their positions, their Howlers gleaming in the sun. Out of the corner of my eye I saw Lisette climb one of the sand knolls, crouching and aiming her gun.

The whining behind us grew louder. The air-dome grew thicker over the camp, as impenetrable as Haidee was ever going to make it.

Our orders were simple enough. The Firesmokers were to fire wherever the shadows grew thickest, to take out as many as was possible in one shot. The Mudforgers had already compromised the ground around us, ready to transform it into quicksand at a moment's notice. We'd already pulled all the rigs back into camp; our strategy didn't require them, but in case the worst happened and we needed to run, we'd kept them close. I was hoping it wouldn't come to that.

Odessa emerged from camp and trotted in our direction.

"What's she doing?" I demanded.

"She thinks she can still control some of them." Lan didn't sound too happy about it. I assumed she and the goddess had argued, and that the Catseye had lost.

I could hear howls rising from one part of the encampment, where the cannibals were rattling their chains and crying out in fright. Trash as they were, I couldn't blame them for fleeing this.

Odessa reached us, her brow already creased in concentration. Lan touched her arm, and I could feel warmth from patterns I couldn't see, spiraling out from them both as she slowly added her strength to the goddess's, followed shortly by crackling energies.

"Don't shoot until I say the word!" I called out. To my shock and delight, the black throng seeping toward us was slowing down, almost to a complete standstill. It was working. I didn't know how Odessa was doing it, but she was controlling the shadow mob.

It struck me then, the immensity of the power she could wield—the power she could so easily turn on the rest of us if she wanted to, had she not been on our side.

I could hear the cheers as the others noticed, and I spotted some starting to lower their guns. "Keep them up and focused!" Lisette roared from her nearby dune. At the same time, Odessa gasped.

I saw it, too; within the swarm, a hint of blue, faint enough that I had to screw up my eyes to see it clearer, to make sure it wasn't just a reflection of light hitting the sand. The huddled shape that bore those jewels was smaller than I'd expected; the size of a child almost, shriveled up and hunched over, inconsequential compared to the demons around it, if not for that sparkle of color in its fist.

Odessa screamed, backing away, her eyes wide. She jumped in front of a startled Lan, her arms spread wide. "No!" she shouted. "I rejected you! I won't let you have her!"

Her focus was broken. The army of shadows skittered forward again, ready to consume, bearing down on us at incredible speed.

"Now!" I shouted, and punctuated that order by firing right at that grotesque shadow-infant. It disappeared before I could hit it, but my flames took out a hefty portion of the horde. The rest continued to surge ahead, ignoring the other explosions as more Firesmokers shot into the crowd.

"Get back into camp!" I yelled at Lan, already starting the retreat myself. The demons were moving too quickly, caring nothing for their casualties. "Mudforgers!"

The ground surrounding the campsite shimmered, decayed into darker shades of brown. It caught the first wave of shadows, the creatures sinking quickly down, limbs clutching desperately at nothing. It took the second and third waves too, and by the time the seventh and eighth had staggered over, we had already retreated back behind the air-dome. Though I wasn't sure how long it could hold.

"I rejected it," Odessa sobbed. "I don't want this. I don't want it!"

Still puzzled, I looked to Lan.

"It wants her to trade my life in exchange for its last gift," she supplied. "She refused."

Ah, right—Haidee and I had first met them right after she'd rejected it the first time, and a giant-ass demonic incarnation of Inanna had come climbing out of the Abyss to protest her decision. But how could the Catseye sound so composed?

A scraping noise made me look up. A part of the air-dome had opened up, and Haidee had climbed on top of the tallest sand-tent we had, up high enough to poke her head out of the barrier. She raised her hands, and a sandstorm rose up in response, sweeping across the desert and taking out another huge swath of the monsters.

I heard a shriek. The cannibals' prison was along the edges of the dome, and one of them, in a fit of panic, had rolled too close to the barrier. The shadows had reached the blockade, clawing at the shield and battering down the already-thin layer from sheer numbers alone. A cluster of them overwhelmed the dome long enough to rip a hole in the layers of protection; I saw some of the Windshifters working hard to put it back up, stronger than before—but not before the unlucky prisoner was dragged away, still screaming even as the darkness rose up and overwhelmed him. My stomach churned.

The shadows returned, tearing another hole, but Lisette had quicker reflexes, aiming and firing a well-placed shot through the gap before any of the shadows could get through again, blasting a knot of them to smithereens.

Another tornado swept through the right flank of the invaders, but there were still far too many. The other clans had followed Lisette's lead, taking up positions around the weaker points of the air-dome and firing at the creatures struggling to get in. Odessa had recovered, and the monsters' attacks slowed as she fought to gain back control, though it was clear the effort was sapping quickly at her strength. I knew Haidee must be tiring as well.

I was considering pissing my pants when a fresh wave of tornadoes tore through, annihilating more groups of shadows. The stunned look on Haidee's face told me this wasn't her doing.

And then I saw them.

There were about two dozen in all, and that was frightening enough. I'd never seen more than one at the same time, never realized that they could gather like this, as if they too could congregate and strategize even in death. The mirages all looked the same from my vantage point—the same cloaks and hoods covering their faces, each one silent and imposing. As we looked on, one of them raised their hands, copying Haidee's gesture, and another sandstorm swept through the horde, destroying every shadow it came into contact with. When the dust cleared, the mirage responsible was gone, its energies used up in the assault, sacrificing what life it had left to aid us.

Yet another sandstorm raged in from the opposite side of the neutral grounds, but this one came with lightning. The bolts tore through the rest of the galla, efficient in their ruthlessness. The hooded figure responsible was dressed differently from the other mirages—a golden cloak that showed none of the wear and tatters of the rest, though it also wore a hood.

Two more attacks and soon the sands were clear of the last of the enemy. Noelle and the others now had their weapons trained at the new threats, fearful despite their help. In all the years I'd lived here, none of those mirages had ever come to our assistance. It was difficult to feel grateful now.

One of the mirages drifted forward, its hooded face turned to regard Haidee, who was still standing on top of the sand-tent, her mouth open. It bowed—bowed!—in her direction, and the rest of them copied the gesture.

And then, all at once, they were gone, like they had never been there to begin with.

All that remained was the golden-robed mirage, the air around it still charged with crackling electricity. It shifted, and this time I saw a few locks tumble out from underneath the hood, saw the colors shift from red to green to white. Haidee gasped.

"Mother?" she cried out, but more sand whirled around the remaining figure until, when it finally abated, she too, was gone.

Chapter Six

'LAN ON NEUTRAL GROUND

—————————— ☾ ——————————

IF ANY OF THE CLAN leaders still held doubts about either Odessa or Haidee, those were long gone now. The sight of the mirages bowing down to Haidee, and Odessa's efforts to control the galla, had convinced them that to have two goddesses by their side was a better alternative than any scenario without.

Haidee, on the other hand, was despondent. "Why would she aid us, but then leave without saying a word?" she cried. "What was the point?"

"The point was to save you." Arjun sounded hesitant, unwilling to defend Latona's actions if he could help it.

Haidee set her jaw. "If she thinks I should feel grateful, I'm not. I'm not listening to her until she tells me she's willing to sit down and talk. Not if she wants to make amends without listening to what I have to say."

Sumiko was the one who specialized in analyzing behavior,

but I had to agree with Haidee's assessment. Still, I thought my Catseye friend would have said Latona's actions were a good sign. The Sun Goddess had been willing to set foot outside her city. She wasn't as detached from all this as her daughter thought she was. But Haidee had refused to say another word on the subject, though she still seemed set on returning to the Golden City to hunt for more information about the Breaking. I didn't want to think about that possible reunion.

The rest of the day cycle had been dedicated to rebuilding the camp, working to enforce the air-dome above us, and setting up more fortifications in case any more galla came calling. I tried my best to be helpful, healing whatever old injuries I could coax the clans into admitting. It felt important to establish as much goodwill among them as I could.

The cannibals were no longer antagonistic. They all fell into nonsensical babbling and prostrated themselves each time either goddess walked past their pens. Their newfound piety kept them out of further trouble, at least.

"Those mirages know something we don't," Haidee insisted, pacing the ground before us. In contrast, Odessa had been silent ever since the galla's attack on the camp, content to pore through her sister's notebook detailing every piece of information we had gleaned from Brighthenge. "Why would they show up and save us?"

"Jesmyn's mirage led us most of the way through the Sand Sea," Arjun reminded her. "She was the reason we both decided to set out in the first place." He paused. "And even before that, she had already saved me from the Hellmakers once."

"Maybe if we collared one of them we could get more answers," Haidee said, scowling.

"Jesmyn's mirage never gave us any answers. Just pointed us in the right direction and stayed far away; we couldn't even get close to her."

Haidee sighed loudly, then resumed her pacing. "They know something. What about the galla? Why attack now? Was Aeon's turning a catalyst?" She paused, as if struck by an idea. "Is this what Mother meant when she said there would be repercussions? What does she know that we don't?"

"'The world torn asunder,'" Odessa said. "'Night and day rule from their two thrones. Where the darkest hour and the brightest light meet, the Hellmouth shall be crossed by she strengthened under the gift of day, by she liberated with the gift of night. And the world is whole again.' That's what it said on the plaques at Brighthenge, right?"

Our discovery of those texts had sent a chill through me. Within Brighthenge, that strange temple that bore witness to the Breaking, were passages commemorating Haidee and Odessa's deity-ancestors. But the fate of only one twin was emblazoned on each stone memorial; the other had been sacrificed to the Abyss, and therefore had no achievements to honor.

"I agree. Latona knows something," Odessa said. "Devika must have told her about our prophecy. If only more books had survived. . . ."

"You a scholar, too?" Arjun asked.

Odessa coughed. "I—I don't know if I would call myself a scholar, but I tend to read books in which learning to pick out the subtlety in context is encouraged."

I thought about the numerous romance novels Odessa had in her room, the armloads of volumes I'd seen her carry around back at Old Wallof's bookstore, and the few she'd thought to smuggle along during our mission to the Abyss, and grinned silently to myself.

Haidee sank to a crouch, hands on either side of her head, eyes closed as if in agony. "There was another letter from Father," she said, anguished. "I read it once, but Mother burned it to prevent me from finding out more. The Devoted were trying to play one sister off of the other, even then. . . ."

I understood Haidee's pain, and also her frustration. The only people who knew what had happened were their mothers. But I doubted Latona or Asteria would ever humor us with the truth.

"There was one other book that I remembered reading from her collection. It had no title, but I would recognize it if I saw it again. Something about that night-and-day passage . . . The more I think about it, the more certain I feel that I've read something similar to it before, and it has to be in one of those books. I'm going to sneak in, find those books, and then sneak out again."

"Like hell you are," the Firesmoker sputtered.

"Got any other bright ideas? We're working with missing information. I'd like to fill in those gaps if I can, and if anyone can successfully infiltrate the Golden City it's going to be me. I'm a mechanika. I helped maintain those air-domes. I know the weaknesses to exploit."

"That would have been very useful to us years ago," Lisette said, poking her head inside the tent. With her were Mother Salla and the rest of the other clan leaders, all solemn. Salla had already assured us that they didn't intend to kick us out of camp, but I felt myself tense up all the same, expecting the worst.

"We've come to an agreement," Tamera said curtly. "We will work with you, because that increases our own chances of survival."

"But . . . ," Arjun muttered, low enough for the older woman not to hear.

"But," the clan mistress continued, "there is every reason to be wary of the abilities you both display—abilities on a scale we have never known to be possible. Mother Salla says that the galla can corrupt even a goddess, that they can make her turn on her own people at a whim. The Saiga clan have much to answer for, but it could easily have been us choking on sand, were you inclined to direct your anger in our direction. I apologize for being blunt, Your Holiness, but how can we know that you would not do the same to us if we incur your wrath?"

Odessa gazed back at the woman placidly enough, but it was difficult for me to contain my anger at their disrespect, after everything she'd done for their sake. When my goddess finally spoke, it was a gentle murmur, calm and pleasant. "You won't," she said.

"Lady Odessa—"

"Would you like me to lie to you? When I first received these gifts I was not in control of myself, not knowing how much they could affect me. Do you know how difficult it was to reclaim my sanity? To pull myself back from the point of no return? Even as I speak now, they're in my mind; enticing me, telling me that I will suffer no consequences, whatever I do."

"Odessa—" I began.

She shook her head. "I have to be honest, Lan. I'm a guest in their territory, and I owe it to them to explain all the dangers. I don't want to be cruel. I want to rid myself of these gifts, but I'm afraid that I can't. If anything goes wrong—I won't mince words. If I cannot pull myself back from the brink, then you must kill me."

"And I'll kill anyone who tries!" I snarled.

Odessa turned to me. "Lan—"

"I can bring her back," I continued, ignoring her. I knew that everything she said was the truth, but I could not stand by and let her put herself at risk. "I've always known how to bring her back. Let any consequences fall on me, but I swear to you all, here and now—I won't let her go that far."

Silence trailed in the wake of my words. "I'll vouch for Lan," Haidee said agreeably. "And I need Odessa here, or we'll all fail. I can't do this without her. You know that, don't you?"

Odessa looked back at her. "I know," she said, sounding tired. "But we have to prepare for the worst."

"We'll find it in the city. I know it. I don't know what Mother has planned, but I won't let her stop me from finding out the truth."

"You're something, you know that?" Arjun said gruffly. "Nothing seems to faze you."

Haidee skipped toward him, gave him a playful peck on the mouth. "We're just that good," she said lightly, then skipped over to where the crowd gathered. Arjun grumbled at that, but the smile remained on his lips, his gaze adoring as he watched Haidee.

"Haidee's right," I told Odessa. "I won't have you second-guessing yourself. Come with me for a moment."

"Where are we going?"

"The elders may not be keen on us, but there's another clan we can sway to our side, if you'll help me."

The cannibals were surprisingly quiet, most flat on their backs and staring aimlessly up into the sky. They scrambled to their knees when Odessa approached, several pressing their foreheads against the sand. Their leader, the one with the scarred face, froze, staring fearfully at her.

I stepped forward, and he shrunk even further back, a hand rising to cover his face as if expecting me to slap him again.

"Get up," I barked, grabbing him by the shoulder and hauling him to his feet. I'd told Odessa that I would do most of the talking, which she agreed to with some relief.

"There will be no more attacks on this camp by any of you," I said. The sweet round fruit we'd gathered from Odessa's tree broke apart in my goddess's hands, blades of Air slicing them into halves. The cannibals followed her movements, knowing that those sharp winds could just as easily slice through their throats if they made the wrong move. "Her Holiness Odessa saved your lives, which means you are now hers to do with as she sees fit. You will obey her, or I will personally toss you out into the desert without any food, water, or rigs. With Her Holiness, you will no longer have to hunger. You will no longer have to hunt. But you *will* be her weapons. Fight for her, and I will see to it that you will always be fed. Do we have an understanding?"

The leader watched her, something almost like admiration in his gaze, and nodded.

"Swear to her. Swear it on your beloved's grave."

He wet his lips. There were tears in his eyes. "There was no grave, milady, Your Holiness. But I swear! Feed us, and I swear it on what'll be left of my bones!" The others began to yell and clamor, taking up the same rallying cry, making the same macabre oaths.

I took the rest of the potatoes from Odessa, tossed them into the crowd. The men snatched them up, gobbling hungrily, still sobbing.

"How did you know they would agree?" Odessa asked.

"You did most of the work for me just by standing there."

"What did he mean when he said that there was no grave?"

I closed my eyes. "That's not important."

"Don't shelter me from bad things, Lan." Odessa's voice was pleading. "I've had enough of that from Mother. Please."

"Her body was"—I took a deep breath—"consumed. He said as much. And as far as I know, they're the only cannibals out in that desert. Arjun would have told us if there were more clans like them."

"You mean . . . ?" Horror gripped Odessa's expression.

"I don't know who it was that killed her, but I know he was forced to—either by someone else, or because he had no choice. These poor boys—they're just as much a victim of the desert as anyone else. That's why they chased everyone else down, even when the odds were against them—because they knew they'd have to kill another of their own if they came back empty-handed. Oh, Odessa. . . ."

It was too late. She was already tearing up. I tugged her to one side while the Hellmakers feasted, and kissed her, hoping that would stop the flow.

"I'm all right," she whispered. "I needed to know, even if it makes me cry."

"You're a better person than you know. You're not cruel. Nothing will make you be cruel."

Shadows flitted across her pale eyes. "You don't know the voices in my head."

"Odessa . . ."

"I'm not afraid for myself," she said. "I'm afraid of the seventh galla. I saw it there among the horde, in those blue jewels I've come to hate. I'm afraid it might make me do bad things I don't want to, just like that Hellmaker. And Haidee—Haidee can help me chase away the urges. *You* can help me chase away the urges. I'd rather die than lose you."

"That's not going to happen." It was my turn to take her into my arms, knowing full well I might not be able to keep that promise. "I swear it."

Chapter Seven

ODESSA AT THE GOLDEN CITY

——————————— ☾ ———————————

LADY LISETTE HAD VOLUNTEERED TO infiltrate the Golden City with us, and Arjun had some problems with that.

"Have *you* ever been inside the Golden City?" Lisette had asked Arjun archly. "You don't know anything about the city, either."

"No, but I've got more reasons to go than you do." I knew he was suspicious, and for good reason. But Lisette didn't strike me as the malicious sort, and she had always been polite to me, even playful.

Oddly enough, Lan appeared to share Arjun's skepticism, becoming a little more watchful when the other girl was nearby. "It's normal for me to be mistrustful," she'd grumbled when I'd asked, though she wasn't as vigilant with the other clan leaders. Noelle had only laughed when I'd pointed that out, told me not to think about it too much.

I felt more than a little restless. In the two days following the galla attack, Lan and I hadn't had much time alone. Haidee and I were finalizing plans with the clan leaders, building up the camp defenses and planning our infiltration into the city. Meanwhile, Lan and Arjun were busy patrolling our territory, guarding the border against any ambushes by the Golden army, or galla if more should come. They also planned on sending scouts to the east, to search for more of those strange mirages that had come to our aid.

Haidee was adamant about making the infiltration attempt as soon as possible. I could understand her desperation. We still didn't know what had truly happened at the Breaking, and the Golden City was the only place we knew to look for answers. There were indications that their army had resumed their mobilization, but I didn't know if they planned on attacking us. I'd pointed out again that Latona had aided us the last time, but Haidee had scowled. "She thinks I'll capitulate if I owe her enough," she'd said, and that was that.

"One of the goddesses must remain with us," Lars suggested. "It's a risky undertaking, and it will be a huge blow to us if Latona succeeds in capturing you both."

"No," I said immediately. "I have to go with her." I didn't want to be somewhere safer while she was risking her life.

Lisette was insistent. "I can sneak in just as quietly. I'm a good shot." The Howler she carried made a rough, grating sound as she shifted the canister into place. "You'll need more than one gunner if you're gonna mess with those Silverguard lunks. I'm one more person to watch Their Holinesses' backs."

"There are far too many of you to be an effective scouting party," Tamera argued. "You'll be discovered quickly enough."

"What about the darkness?" This was from the cannibal leader. The dishonored Saiga clan now had freer rein of the neutral grounds, though most stuck to their side of the camp, well aware of the others' dislike of them. The Hellmaker had ambled nearer, not hiding the fact that he was keen on eavesdropping.

The Fennec clan elder stared at him. "Pardon?"

He shrugged. "Attack the city at night. The meat guarding the gates will not be prepared for the dayless hours, and they will not be as organized."

"He's right," I said. "How many we are will matter less under cover of darkness. I should know, I've lived with the night all my life. I doubt that any of Latona's guards are handling it well." The others, Tamera and Arjun included, still had stunned expressions on their faces, as if they'd never considered the idea before.

"We may have to rework some previous strategies," Tamera muttered.

So despite Arjun's objections, we were six when we finally set out at nightfall—Haidee and I, Lan, Arjun, Lisette, Noelle. Haidee claimed she knew a way to sneak back into the Golden City without anyone being the wiser. "Is that how you snuck out in the first place?" Lan whispered as we crouched behind some dunes, watching a group of Golden army soldiers making their rounds just outside the dome.

Haidee shook her head. "Friends of mine helped me escape. They don't know I'm trying to get in and I can't let them know from out here, so we'll have to do this the hard way."

"If we can even get close enough to the gates without them noticing," Arjun said, and grunted. No area of the dome was left unattended for long; men strolled past us every two minutes, so we had little time to act. We *could* probably take them all out, but it wouldn't be quiet, and their fellow soldiers would notice their disappearance. It would be only a matter of time before we were caught.

"I think Lan and Noelle can take out some of the guards without anyone else noticing," I said softly. "Just give us the signal."

Haidee waited until another soldier had walked past us, then crept out. We followed her to a spot far enough from the main gates to be unobtrusive.

I'd never been this close to the air-domes before. Curious, I reached out to touch the shield that had kept the Golden City standing and protected for years. It felt solid enough underneath my fingers.

"That's what they're supposed to look and feel like." Haidee's eyes were already glowing—she was channeling like a Shardwielder, fire-gate users who could control terra patterns. I watched them burrow into the thick barrier, slowly dissolving its surface. "The dome is made of densely packed Air and Fire patterns. At the right temperature, they can form this kind of steel-like glass. I'm simply reverse engineering the process by removing the Fire patterns so it reverts back into sand. With a shield of this size and scope, there'll always be tiny bubbles in the surface, flaws in an otherwise sound—"

"You do know you don't have to tell us every step of the process?" Arjun reminded her gently.

"Speak for yourself, Arjun," Lisette breathed from behind me. "I'm entranced by her narration."

"Shut up, Lisette," Arjun growled, and frowned at me when I giggled in spite of myself.

Haidee ran her hands down one section, fingers sinking into a depressed spot. "I might need some help," she told me.

"Just tell me what to do."

"Better make it soon," Lan whispered. "I hear someone coming."

Lisette was already drawing her Howler, setting her sights toward the sound of footsteps crunching lightly against the sand, accompanied by a bright light drawing nearer. As soon as the man rounded the corner, she shot him.

Her Howler made no sound. Neither did the soldier, who promptly dropped to the ground. The light incanta he'd been channeling fizzled out.

Both Noelle and Lan were on him in an instant, grabbing him by the feet and dragging him behind the dune where we'd been hiding. Arjun rounded on Lisette, furious, but she lifted her hand, anticipating his anger. "It's a paralyzing dart. He won't be able to move for a good three hours, which should give us plenty of time."

"Paralyzing dart?" Arjun looked mildly terrified. I remembered what Haidee had told me about him being stung by a giant scorpion en route to Brighthenge, rendered immobile and helpless to do anything but hope Haidee, thinking him dead, wouldn't accidentally bury him alive.

"There are more than a few snakes' lairs in our territory. Milana's taught a whole generation of kids to milk the poison out of their fangs. It's been of use to us in the past." Lisette frowned. "You all right? I'm sorry I didn't tell you about it. It's not something that would come up in regular conversation."

"It's nothing." Arjun had broken out into a mild sweat, and it wasn't because of the growing cold that came with the night. "Just warn me next time."

Lan and Noelle trotted back over the dune, Noelle now wearing the soldier's uniform. "Might help us avoid attention," she said with a shrug.

I hesitated, then reached out and took Haidee's hand. Perspiration beaded Haidee's upper lip as she concentrated, her eyes lit with a silver glow. I focused on taking as much moisture as I could out from the air, focused on taking the heat around us away and lowering the temperatures in the same way I would fix the dykes around Aranth. Ice slowly gathered around the edges of the hole Haidee was painstakingly boring through the dome, keeping the sand from re-forming.

Even with the galla's gifts, I struggled. It took much more energy to squeeze out moisture from these sunlands, much less create ice from it, even at night. Water patterns were common in Aranth, but even the recent rainfall hadn't been enough to restore them to this parched desert. Lan realized this; she gently brushed the back of my neck with her fingers, and I felt the familiar warmth of her even as the glow of Aether patterns swirled around me.

"Thank you," I whispered, and the Catseye rubbed her thumb lightly over my collarbone in response.

Two more guards ambled along and were promptly ambushed, and two more sets of uniforms were added to our collection, before we finally drilled a gap wide enough for all of us to steal through. Once inside, I allowed the ice to melt. Haidee reconstructed the glass, leaving no trace of our intrusion behind.

"That's a good trick," Lisette said, impressed. "But how did you create the ice?"

"I drew moisture from everywhere I could, and lowered the temperature." I was exhausted. Lan was already looping an arm around my waist, like she would carry me if it came down to it.

"The Citadel is that way," Haidee said. "But we need to take a detour to the North Tower first." She pointed toward a dilapidated-looking, top-heavy structure that looked like it had been cobbled from random spare parts, then held together by spit and sheer force of will.

"What's in there?" I asked.

"My friends." Haidee grinned. "Having the mechanika on our side will help us bypass some of the security protocols at the Citadel."

"And how do you know they're going to be on our side?" Arjun grumbled.

"They helped me escape the first time. I'm sure they'll see things my way."

The mechanika of the Golden City did not, in fact, see things Haidee's way at first. We'd barely slipped inside the tower when alarm bells sounded—a horrifying jangle of noise. I found myself staring down the barrel of the largest cannon I had ever seen. "Don't take another step," warned the stressed-looking man behind it. "Or I'll smoke you!"

"Yeong-ho?" Haidee didn't even look fazed. "Yeong-ho, it's me! Where did you find the cannon?"

"Your Holiness?!" Other faces peeped out behind Yeong-ho, all dirty and smudged from the heavy smoke lingering in the air. The whole place was shrouded in darkness, save for a few paltry orbs of light floating above us. Wheels and cogs of varying sizes turned and creaked, many of them larger than my head. And this was the place Haidee spoke of lovingly as her home? It made the Spire look like a luxurious palace.

"It's a long story. We need to sneak into the Citadel without anyone else knowing."

"Absolutely not," the man said immediately. "Are you aware of the chaos you caused by running away, young lady? Night has returned! Night! Her Holiness Latona had her hands full calming everyone down. Nearly started a riot! A mob tried to force their way in here, like this was all our fault! And your mother's furious! She upended the whole city trying to find you, combed the desert for miles around. If she'd known Jes and Charley had abetted your escape"—he turned to glare at a couple of his sheepish-looking charges—"she would have thrown them in the gaols! Or worse! And so I had to lie! To Her Holiness! It's a wonder she believed me, and that I haven't been imprisoned myself!"

"This is important, Yeong-ho! I've returned from the Great Abyss! Night has returned because the world is turning aga—"

"What? You've been to the Abyss?! Haidee, what exactly is it that you—"

And then Yeong-ho stopped and stared, because I had stepped forward, the light from the orbs falling on my face. One of the other mechanika emitted a high-pitched yelp, and another swore, his fingers curling tighter around a large wrench.

"Did you bring a mirage into the city, Your H-holiness?" Yeong-ho stuttered. "I know you've been curious about them in the past, but I never—"

"I brought my sister," Haidee said. "My sister, Odessa, who Mother said had been dead all these years. Do you understand now? Mother has been deceiving us this whole time. The world is turning, but monsters are still pouring out of the Abyss. Aeon's healing is incomplete, and the secrets are in her study. We must get into the Citadel, and I know you have the key."

"I must inform Her Holiness that you're in the city," Yeong-ho warbled. "I can't disobey her again, Haidee. I can't."

Lan turned to Haidee. "If I may?"

"What are you going to do?"

I spoke up, knowing what she was about to do and hoping the mechanika wouldn't panic. "She won't hurt him. I swear it."

Haidee looked a little agonized, but nodded. Lan stepped toward Yeong-ho.

"Sorry, pal," she said, giving him a friendly pat on the cheek. The man's eyes widened, glazed over. The Catseye caught him easily. "I only put him to sleep," she said, before the other mechanika could react. "Your goddess, Latona, isn't willing to listen to us, and time is something we can't afford to spend. Will you help us gain entry to this Citadel of hers, or would you guys like to take a nice long nap, too?"

"Lan!" I exclaimed.

"Please," Haidee said softly. "You know I wouldn't ask this of any of you if it wasn't important."

The three mechanika exchanged glances. "I have the key to the postern," the woman finally said.

"Charley!" one of the men said, sounding shocked.

"I believe Haidee. And you saw the rains coming down just as well as I did, Jes. I've never seen that much water in my whole life. And then there's all this darkness. Tell me that's normal."

"But how do we know we can trust the rest of them?" The tallest mechanika eyed us with suspicion. "Did your sister do all this?"

We had, technically. "It's more complicated than that," I said instead.

"Do you need a hostage?" Arjun asked. "I'll be your hostage. You know what that is, right?"

The boy froze, horrified. "Y-yes, but I don't—"

"It means," Arjun barreled on, because his patience was obviously running thin and Haidee wasn't going to like it if Lan knocked out the rest of her friends, too, "that if any of the others harm your goddess, or if they do anything to indicate they've lied, then you're free to kill me." Calmly, he slid a knife out from his boot and extended it to the mechanika, hilt-first. "Here you go. Cut my throat if you need to, right about here." He drew a line across his neck. "I keep the blade good and sharp, so you shouldn't have any trouble."

"Wait," I said, alarmed, not really sure if he was serious.

"I'm not—" the other boy quavered.

"Arjun—" Haidee began.

"If taking me prisoner helps you agree, then that's what I'll do. I'm one of the desert riffraff your goddess has been at war with for most of our lives. I'm the enemy she keeps your dome up for. I never liked Latona. Still don't. But Haidee's different. I'll protect her any way I can. You're her friends. You've known her longer than I have. Why can't you trust her?"

"You don't even know us," the second boy sputtered.

"But I know Haidee," Arjun said, "and that's enough for me. Let them in. There's more at stake here than either you or me."

"I feel like you should have led with this instead of threatening them into taking you hostage," I suggested, unhelpfully at this point.

"I might not have thought this completely through, yeah."

"Did you really do that?" the girl asked Haidee. "Did you bring back the night?"

Haidee looked down, guilt crossing her face momentarily before she straightened to return her gaze. "I did. For better or for worse, we did. My sister and I did. And that's why we need to act immediately."

The taller boy frowned; gave in. "We don't need a hostage. Give them the key, Charley. Haidee, I don't know what's going on, and I don't know if this is the right thing to do . . . but your friend is right. I don't know what the Mother Goddess intends, but if I had to bet between her and you, I'd choose you every time."

"Thanks, Jes." Haidee's eyes had gone very soft. "And Arjun. Thank you."

Arjun grinned. "Thank me as soon as we're out of here."

Once all the misunderstandings had been put to rest—much like the mechanika they called Yeong-ho, who now snored on one of the benches—I allowed my curiosity to get the better of me. I stopped by one of the heavier wheels, watching them shift and click into place. So this was how the Golden City worked, I thought. The grinding metal made an intimidating noise, cogs turning in place or combining with others to create a revolution of gears, like they were all small, spinning worlds of their own.

Was this how Haidee had lived? Exploring these little worlds, making sure each one ran smoothly? I could see why the thought of fixing Aeon might appeal to her; the thought of it no longer spinning, like a cog out of place, would have been too alluring not to try to solve.

The closest I'd ever come to an act of rebellion, Lan and smuggling my way onto the *Brevity* aside, was escaping into the city to buy romance novels. Meanwhile, Haidee had been having all sorts of adventures—exploring the desert on her own, conducting experiments among the mechanika here. Why wasn't I as brave?

Would I have been more like my twin if I'd grown up in the Golden City along with her? More outgoing, more adventurous? Would Lan have been attracted to that girl?

"I helped," Haidee said, popping up beside me. She sounded proud. "Yeong-ho was the architect of it all. He taught me everything I know about building things."

"I wish I was as resourceful." It didn't feel like I'd done much for Aranth in comparison. I'd always been too sick to be let out of the Spire. Not for the first time, I wondered what more I could have done for my city if it hadn't been for my illness.

"You told me about the Banishing," Haidee said stubbornly. "That must have taken a lot of strength, to keep your home from being overwhelmed by the ice. Don't sell yourself short."

I smiled at her. "I guess I'm a little jealous. You had freer rein here than I ever did."

My sister ran her fingers along the edges of an unused gear leaning against the wall, sounding wistful. "My cage might have been a little bigger than yours, but it was still a cage."

I couldn't argue with that.

Charley had volunteered to come with us, while the others tended to their sleeping comrade. It was a short walk from the North Tower to the Citadel, with half of us in army uniform and the other half wrapped in cloaks the mechanika had supplied for us, hoping the strange mishmash wouldn't arouse curiosity. Looking above us, I could see dark clouds gathering in the sky again. I caught Lisette and Arjun staring as well; they were still unused to the sight. "This is normal for when it's about to rain," I tried to assure them. It was the truth; this was common in Aranth, where the storms were even more relentless. But the sudden swirl of heavy mist reminded me of the fog that marked the edges of the Great Abyss. I took *that* as an omen, but kept that fear to myself.

The citizens of the city, at least, were staying inside; the streets were devoid of light, save for a few flickering orbs from inside windows. It was obvious that no one here had ever experienced the nighttime before, and they'd been woefully unprepared when it came.

We huddled at the back of Latona's tower as rumbling sounds emanated from the sky. Charley took out an oddly shaped lever from the knapsack she wore and slid it into a small hole on the door. She fiddled with it for several seconds. There was a tiny, precise click, and the door swung open.

"That didn't seem like a lot of fuss," Lisette remarked.

"It's tied to an alarm system we invented. If you don't have the right key and you force the door, it'll alert all the guards within distance." The girl peered cautiously inside. "Stick close, Your Holinesses. If anyone approaches, please let me do the talking."

It was larger inside than it looked on the outside. Lights flickered overhead—giant balls of Fire interlaced with Air patterns, larger than the ones at the mechanika's tower. There were far more rooms here than at the Spire, and almost everything appeared to be made from what Haidee admitted was gold, much to my shock. Mother didn't have as much of a taste for opulence as Latona seemed to.

"We had to use every bit of iron and steel alloy we could find for fortification," Haidee said, somewhat defensively. "We control the gold mines to the north, but the metal on its own is too soft to stand up to stress, which doesn't make it as good for forging weapons or constructing towers."

"Weapons and towers to fight against the desert clans, right?" Lisette asked coolly.

Haidee faltered, but it was Arjun who responded, in a voice too even to be truly neutral. "She has as much right to defend her home as we do. She doesn't view us as the enemy. She never did. Took me a while to figure that out."

Lisette looked at him, slightly disapproving, but let it drop.

We bypassed the throne room and edged along the shadows toward Latona's private study. I worried that the goddess herself might be there, but Haidee was confident she wasn't. "I know her habits," she said. "She won't be there at this hour."

As it turned out, she was right. Lisette and Lan posted themselves behind the door to keep lookout, while Haidee all but ran to her mother's desk. "She hid all her books and tomes in here the last time I got nosy," she said eagerly as she opened drawers and compartments. I wandered toward the bookshelves. There were not as many volumes as I expected—perhaps two dozen at best; books were harder to come by here in the desert than they were in Aranth.

"What should we be looking for, specifically?" I asked as Noelle followed my lead.

"Anything that talks about the ritual, or about Inanna or any of the other goddesses." She paused. "And anything to do with the sacrifice," she added, quieter. "Any documentation about goddesses who'd been sacrificed, in particular."

I paused. In Haidee's expression I saw the reason for her nervous tittering, her unusual spastic energy. She was terrified about what she might find, just like I was. She was the one prophesied to die, and we might discover there was no way out of it.

"Sacrifice?" I heard Lisette ask Lan. "What's that about?"

"Long story," my Catseye replied, "and best told after we return to the neutral grounds."

For the better part of an hour we searched; I was slower at it than Haidee, but Noelle was skimming faster than even my twin could. Just as we finished going through all the books in the study and I'd worried we'd found nothing, it was she who let out a soft cry of victory, rising to her feet with an open book in her hands. "You both need to read this," she said, sounding hoarse.

Haidee and I crowded around her, looking down at the page:

At the first gate, sacrifice your clarity for prudence.

At the second gate, sacrifice your courage for caution.

At the third gate, sacrifice your harvest for healing.

At the fourth gate, sacrifice your regrets for mercy.

At the fifth gate, sacrifice your arrogance for modesty.

At the sixth gate, sacrifice your dominion for self-control.

At the seventh gate, sacrifice all for happiness.

The similarities to the rituals I had gone through were too much of a coincidence to ignore.

"I almost didn't read this," Noelle confessed, flipping the book over to show us *Meditations for a Proper Life* lettered on its cover. "But I remember my mother having several of these—required reading for a lady's maid like her—and it made me curious."

"I never did bother to open it," Haidee said, wincing. "Self-improvement books were never my preference. Bless your mother for knowing better, Noelle."

"Why are the galla rites in a self-improvement book?" I asked, my heart pounding.

"It's not even good guidance," Lisette said with a frown, reading through the text. "Sacrifice all for happiness? Who would do that?"

It was my turn to wince.

"The author states that her advice was inspired by a passage from another book, called *The Ages of Aeon*," Noelle said, scanning the page. "I am sorry, Your Holinesses. It doesn't explain much beyond this."

But a look of agony was stamped across Haidee's features. "*The Ages of Aeon*," she echoed. "*The Ages of Aeon*. I know I've heard it somewhere, but I don't quite remember the—"

She straightened up, her hands falling back to her sides. "Vanya!" she exclaimed. "He owns a copy of that book!"

"What makes you think he'll be of any use?" Arjun growled.

"It's a start. It's something, at least!" But then her face fell.

"Infiltrating the Arrenley residence might be harder than sneaking into the Citadel. I don't know much about where they're—"

"Lord Vanya Arrenley?" Charley interrupted. "Lord Torven Arrenley's youngest son?"

"Yes," Haidee confirmed, surprised. "Have you met him before?"

"No. But I do know that you won't have to break into his home to steal anything."

"And why's that?" I asked.

"Because the Arrenleys have been living right here in the Citadel ever since you left." The mechanika beamed at us. "The elder lord and his youngest son, anyway. Whatever book you think they have, you can probably filch it from them tonight."

Chapter Eight

HAIDEE IN THE CITADEL

———————— ☼ ————————

CHARLEY DIDN'T KNOW WHERE IN the Citadel Vanya had been housed, but I thought it likely we'd find him in one of the guest chambers a couple of floors above us. Getting in would be the problem; the Arrenleys were the most prominent noble family in the Golden City, and they brought their own armed guards everywhere they went.

"Why are they staying here?" Arjun asked as we crept up another flight of stairs, as if finding the Arrenleys within reach was a personal affront.

I was busy mapping out the Citadel in my mind, trying to figure out the safest route, but I wasn't distracted enough to miss his undisguised jealousy. It made me feel exasperated and strangely exhilarated, an unusual, giddy combination. "It's not uncommon for Mother to invite some of the lords to stay at the Citadel, but I've never heard of anyone staying for this long." I turned to Charley. "Are you sure about this?"

The girl nodded. "Yeong-ho said that Lord Torven frequently complained about the lukewarm water piped in for his baths. He demanded that he make them cooler."

"He's living in the hottest part of Aeon, but lukewarm water is still beneath him?" Lan murmured.

"Piped in?" I echoed, not sure what she meant. "They want you to go through all that trouble to pipe in water for a wash-basin?"

"No, Your Holiness. He had a new porcelain bathtub installed. I think he built wider pipes to funnel into that."

"What?"

"We didn't put it in for him. His lordship brought his own mechanika. Yeong-ho was the only one he'd talked to, and the boss was practically seething when he returned. Said it was unnecessary, but they overrode his protests."

"He added in his own *bathtub*?! *Changed* the pipes?"

"Haidee, hush," Arjun hissed.

"I don't even have a bathtub *of my own*." I was seething. "We had to conserve resources, especially with the Salt Sea receding so far. And Lord Arrenley has been wasting water on *baths*?"

"Save your anger for his son, Your Holiness." Lisette peered out of the doorway, and frowned. "If we're able to get to *any* of your Arrenleys. This floor is crawling with soldiers."

"I'm not sure we can search every room here and not sound the alarm," Lan said.

"Where are the pipes located?" Noelle asked. "Do you build

them inside the walls, or run them through each floor?"

I thought about that. "Through the floors."

"This isn't the time to be admiring the tower's plumbing, Noe," Lan growled.

"I'm not. If the Citadel is structured the same way as the Spire in Aranth, then that can work in our favor. Lady Charley, did Yeong-ho know where they added the new pipes?"

"On this floor, actually. Lord Arrenly summoned him because Yeong-ho had designed a small container that could collect water to help with the aquifers. Lord Arrenley wanted one—so when his lordship turns on the pipes he doesn't have to wait long for the tub to fill, I guess."

"There you go," Noelle said. "Follow the path of the pipes, locate this container, and you'll find out where they're staying."

"I'm not sure we've got time to break down the walls to see where the pipes lead to," Lisette objected.

"We don't have to," Odessa said, a small smile on her face. "I can locate the water's path. I can detect where the highest concentration of it is collected, and go from there." She laid a hand against the floor and closed her eyes, but not before her irises sparked a bright blue. "Let me try."

There was silence for a few minutes. Lan watched the soldiers' movements carefully. "Their rounds are too random," she muttered. "I can't track their schedule, like the guards outside the dome."

I watched Odessa, felt what few water patterns were in the air shift and pour into the wall beside us. "There are two rooms," she finally said, her eyes opening. "The first room is at the center of this floor, and the second beside it."

"Now that we know where we're supposed to sneak," Arjun said, "how do we get past all these guards?"

"I have an idea. None of you make a sound when I do it." I looked at Odessa. "I'll need your help again. Does the sky outside always cloud over like this when it's about to rain?"

Odessa nodded. "Once enough clouds gather, it never takes long. Do you want me to—"

"Yes. I'll take care of the lights, but we have to—"

"Concentrate it around the tower so the focus will be on—"

"—the lightning. Oh, that's a good idea."

"That's amazing," Lisette marveled to Arjun in a loud whisper. "How long have they been able to do that?"

"As long as we've known them. Which is a few days. What are you two going to do?"

But my sister and I had shut our eyes, focusing on the patterns around us.

It was . . . strange. To know what she intended to do, for her to know what I intended to do, all without words. And every time we strengthened this odd link between us I always felt . . . at peace. More assured than I had ever been. And I knew she felt the same way.

A sudden streak of lightning illuminated a window, the flash dangerously close. There was a loud crash of thunder before the whole floor plummeted into darkness.

Charley gasped loudly, but her cry was lost over the sounds

of panic as the soldiers crashed into each other in the sudden darkness. I could hear someone shouting orders over the din, though the continuing noises indicated no one paid him any attention. The men had never encountered total night before. They'd spent their lives learning to cope with the constant sun, and now they were deprived of even that.

A second bolt of lightning raked through the sky, even closer than the first and, though I was expecting it, the following roar nearly ruptured my eardrums.

"Hell and sandrock," Arjun swore, jumping.

We opened our eyes at the same time; mine, I knew, glowed red from my fire-gate, while Odessa's burned water-gate blue. "I can lead everyone to the room," I said, "but we might have to take down a couple of those soldiers along the way. The darkness should help disguise our presence."

"Leave them to me," Lan said grimly.

It was even easier than I'd hoped. Whoever was in charge had reined in most of his subordinates, yelling at them to keep to their posts. Nobody paid any attention to us as we stole through the corridor. Every time a soldier drew too close, the Catseye simply reached out and grabbed them by the arm. It was over quickly; the men remained standing when she took her hand away, muscles locked and eyes wide with fright, unable to cry out. Lan's eyes were bright giveaways in the gloom, though, and she kept her head lowered, cloak pulled tightly about her.

Finally, we stopped before the two rooms and I paused. Which would be Vanya's? Mother usually put the younger guests closer to the middle, but the older Arrenley was an arrogant, selfish ass who considered proximity to Mother an indication of his higher status.

"Well?" Lisette demanded nervously.

I came to a decision. "This one," I said, and laid my hand on the door farther away.

I was right; the figure on the bed lay unmoving, blissfully unaware of our presence, and slimmer than Lord Arrenley's imposing bulk. I slid the door shut quietly behind me and gestured at the others for silence, though I could see that it was unnecessary. The loud snores coming from the sleeping boy were testament to that.

I manifested my own orb made of light and approached the bed, but Lisette was already there, drawing a knife. She ripped off the blankets and had the blade pressed against the poor boy's neck before he had come fully awake.

"Wait!" I gasped.

"Wh-what's going—?" The boy's eyes grew large as he took us all in, was smart enough to shut his mouth at the telltale prick of sharp steel against his skin.

"I'm not going to hurt you," Lisette whispered, sounding cheerful despite the situation. "I don't *want* to hurt you. I'm going to remove my weapon, but if you scream I have no qualms about slicing you from ear to ear, then gutting you besides. Do you understand?"

The dimple at the boy's throat moved as he swallowed, then nodded.

"Vanya," I said, holding back a twinge of guilt. Of all the suitors Mother had foisted on me, he had been the most respectful, the only one I actually enjoyed talking to. "I'm sorry to have to come to you like this."

"Your Holiness?" The boy stared. "Where have you been? Your mother's about ready to tear the dunes apart—"

"And I don't intend to face her just yet," I interrupted. "Not until I've got what I'm looking for. You told me once that you had a book called *The Ages of Aeon.* Do you still have it?"

"Well—er, yes. But it's not with me at the moment. It would have been more prudent to find me in the morning instead of seeking me out in the middle of the night with . . ." He eyeballed the rest of my companions, remained at a loss to describe his dismay, and forged on. "I understand that our engagement relaxes certain protocols, but I don't think Her Holiness would appreciate—"

"Our what?" I burst out, just as Arjun butted in with a more aggressive, "You *better* not have just said *engagement.*"

"Your mother planned to make it public soon," Vanya said, obviously taken aback by the poor reactions to his announcement. "I . . . I thought you were willing to—"

I was furious now. I could find no evidence that Mother had fretted over my absence beyond feeling humiliated that I'd escaped her. It felt like she'd only used it to further her own goals, taking advantage of my inability to protest her schemes. She *knew* where I was now. She'd helped us fight off the galla, but then she'd taken her leave without a word, when I had wanted nothing more than to have her stay. It only told me she wasn't ready to listen, was only going to save me as long as she could continue to gain something from it. She still thought I was going to crawl back and beg her forgiveness. "I will not be honoring any engagement that Mother made on my behalf," I snapped. "All we need is that book, and we'll be out of your hair. Please tell us where it is."

"Father has it in his possession. I can ask him—"

"No. He can't know we're here."

Vanya looked even more at a loss. "Your Holiness, I can't go against my own father. He's in charge of the safety of the Golden City now. That's why we're here at the Citadel."

"Do you remember anything about the book? You mentioned a few details to me the first time we talked. You said it had some information about rituals and the Cruel Kingdom in it."

Vanya gazed up at the ceiling, frowning. "Yes, but only generalities. When a young goddess comes of age, she takes part in a ritual where she renews her vows to sacrifice herself for Aeon should it be necessary. But when twin goddesses—Her Holiness Latona and her sister, Asteria—were born, a schism grew between them. Asteria brought about the Breaking as a result, and turned mad in the aftermath. Her Holiness had to kill her to save what was left of Aeon, though that also resulted in the death of one of her own twin daughters." He looked puzzled. "But surely you knew that already."

I did. That was the lie we'd been told all our lives.

"That's almost verbatim what we were taught back in Aranth," Lan growled, annoyed by the young man's certainty, "save that it was Latona who destroyed the world and Asteria who was forced to stop her."

"And what about the Cruel Kingdom?" I persevered.

Vanya was eyeing Lan nervously. "It said the goddess Inanna had descended into its depths to bring back her lost love?"

"Is that all the book talks about? Nothing else about Inanna? This is important."

"One epic does wax on about an entrance to the under-world." I bit back a gasp at that. "But I don't see why this is so important that it cannot wait a few hours. It's a book of poetry, not of history, and I'm sure the author took creative liberties."

"And you're an expert historian?" Lisette asked sarcastically.

The lordling stared at her. "I don't have to prove myself to you, whoever you are. I've studied Aeona and a few other old languages. I've translated two books. I know more of history than almost anyone else in the city. *The Ages of Aeon* is a rare prize only because works of fiction are hard to find. A copy of *The Book of Small Myths*, for example, was the only one of its kind and fetched a commanding price last month, and also *A Natural World* before that. But they're stories for children. What is so important about a volume of—"

"Can't you see the darkness outside? Didn't your father think you important enough to tell you what's happening? The world is *turning*. The rains are only the start of it. The book is more than just of poetry. Tell us where your father keeps it."

Vanya paused. "I . . . I don't . . . know."

"You had it with you at Mother's throne room, where I first met you."

"I'd borrowed it without Father's permission. He took it from me that day when he found out, and I haven't seen it since."

"What?" I was stunned. "You were reading it right out in the open. Your father and the counselors were right there!"

"I was reading a different book then. I switched when they moved to your mother's inner sanctum. Father had no idea." He looked mortified now. "I wanted to impress you. I heard that you were an avid reader, and Father guarded the book zealously. He's had it for as long as I can remember—I doubt even Her Holiness was aware he had a copy. He refused to let anyone so much as touch it. I only knew it was a rare find. I . . . thought it would help you take more notice of me."

"You blithering ass," Arjun muttered.

"Vanya," I said. "I would be very much impressed with you now, if you would tell us how to get our hands on the book. You have no idea of its importance to us."

"I . . . I can try, but I can't guarantee a—"

"I think not, my boy," a cool voice interrupted. "The goddess Haidee has been stripped of her authority, by her own mother's decree. You are not going anywhere, and neither is she."

I could feel currents of Air tighten around my arms and midsection, pulling taut and rendering me immobile. I heard startled yelps and curses as the others were subjected to the same treatment.

The door opened. Lord Arrenley stood in the entrance, soldiers on either side of him. Several of his men had bright, pale eyes, revealing their Windshifter abilities. The lord's own unringed brown gaze surveyed us calmly, and a smile quirked at his lips. "I didn't expect Your Holiness to find allies among the desert tribes. You are quite the resourceful young lady."

"I'm still your liege and your goddess," I told him angrily. "You will stand down this instant and let us go."

"That's not quite accurate, my dear," he said. Lan grunted as someone took her sword away. "It is Latona who I serve and obey. It would be best if you keep still"—he nodded at both Arjun and Lisette, who were also being divested of their knives—"and come quietly with us. I can at least promise that you will be treated well, though Lady Latona must pass the final judgment for your companions."

"No," I snarled. "I am done with having to obey her, Lord Arrenley. Get out of our way, or I will *make* you move."

"Brave words, Your Holiness, but hollow. Not even you can shake free of these restraints."

He snapped his fingers, and some of his soldiers stepped forward. "Do not harm them. Take particular care with Her Holiness, and the other young lady with similar features. If any of your friends so much as twitches, or if you choose to channel even the weakest of patterns, I will have no compunction slitting one of their throats in retaliation."

I gritted my teeth, testing my bonds. They were wrapped too tightly for me to struggle free, and the soldiers wore gloves that prevented their bare skin from touching Lan's. "Don't struggle," I told the others. Arrenley was not the type to bluff.

"What did they want, Vanya?" the lord asked.

Vanya hesitated, looking beseechingly at me. "They wanted a book," he said, miserable. *"The Ages of Aeon."*

"And what is so important about this book that you would brave infiltrating the Golden City for it?" Lord Arrenley's smile had too many teeth in it. "Surely, Your Holiness, anything of note that you find there should be relayed immediately back to your mother."

"There's no reason for me to tell Mother anything." I was reaching for the patterns without thinking, and realized Odessa was doing the same. Something brushed against my mind and I realized it was hers. Our incanta flowed together with ease, in much the same way they had when we bored through the dome to sneak into the city, but we stopped short of channeling for fear Arrenley might follow through with his threat. *Could she sense me, too?* "She lied to me. She's lying to you all now. There is more to the Breaking than what she told you. Did she talk of Aeon turning again? Of night finally falling on this side of the world? Did she tell you that was why there is rain in the desert for the first time in over seventeen years?"

Arrenley didn't even blink, though I saw some of the soldiers behind him stir uneasily. "Were you anyone else, your words would serve as evidence of treason. We are here to serve at Her Holiness's pleasure. She has kept us alive and well all these years, and we see no reason to doubt her. You, on the other hand, have been quite the thorn in your mother's side these last few weeks. Disappearing without warning, only to arrive in the company of desert traitors." His eyes gleamed. "If anything, Your Holiness, I would say that the rebels are trying to cause a schism between you and your mother, to divide you and weaken you long enough to take the city."

"That's not true!"

"It doesn't matter," Arjun said heavily. "Nothing you say will change his mind. He'll only invent some new inanities, and blame us for all of it."

Lord Arrenley bowed to me. "I'm disappointed in you, Your Holiness, but you have my gratitude. It's been a while since our gaols were occupied. Perhaps some of your friends can even be persuaded to talk."

"Father," Vanya said nervously. "Haidee has nothing to do with—"

The older man cut him off abruptly. "I'm even more disappointed in you. The goddess appears in your quarters and you don't think to alert us? I'm surprised they've kept you alive this long. I would have struck you down in their place."

Vanya paled. "Father—"

"I burned the book on the very day you stole it. I'd planned to send what's left of it as an engagement gift when Haidee returned and made your betrothal official, as a reminder not to disobey me again. For your sake, I have decided not to inform Her Holiness of your foolishness here, though I very well should. You once said that you wished nothing more than to follow in my footsteps, to immerse yourself in learning about the city's infrastructure to prove yourself ready for governance. You expressed interest in Haidee, and I believed you would make her a good match. But if you are going to bend over to cater to the whims of a woman, even if she is the goddess of this city, then that makes you too spineless for politics. Aeon favored me with two better sons, at least."

"Father . . . I tried my best to live up to your—"

There was a loud slap. Vanya stared up at his sire from his position on the floor, his cheek already bruised.

"You'll live," Lord Arrenley said coldly. "I cannot say the same for these desert scavengers. Take them away."

One of the soldiers grabbed Lan's arm. She pulled back, and he slapped her hard across the face. "Don't fight, and this will be easier on you," he barked.

Oh no.

I turned to Odessa, opening my mouth to tell her to do nothing, only to realize that it was already a lost cause. Her eyes glowed a bright pale before bleeding into strange hues of reds and yellows. I reached out again, desperate, wanting to reforge our mental link, knowing I could help to calm the rage she'd inherited from those terrible gifts—but I reached her too late.

Lightning filled the room. One bolt blazed in and struck the soldier who'd hit Lan, squarely in the chest.

There was a brief, stunned silence. And then the man toppled over, dead, with his clothes on fire.

Chapter Nine

ARJUN IN FLIGHT

⚬

THE BONDS AROUND LAN DISSIPATED, and she sprang forward, taking out the next closest soldier with a swift punch to the face. With the other hand she latched on to Lord Torven Arrenley's neck, and the stunned expression on his face disappeared, his eyes closing as he dropped to the floor.

I was moving almost as soon as she did, swinging my Howler and striking two more guards down. The rest of the soldiers turned their own guns in my direction, but a sweep of Haidee's arm sent a small hurricane through the group, throwing the rest of them outside the room.

Lisette slammed the door shut. "We better get out of here, and fast," she said nervously. "At this rate, we'll be better off dead than prisoners."

Noelle moved to the fallen lord, checking his pulse. "He's fine," she said, while the boy named Vanya made choking, frantic sounds. "Lan merely put him to sleep."

"Who are you people?" Vanya whispered, staring at Odessa and seeing her clearly for the first time. "Who are *you*? You're not Haidee."

"Any ideas on how to proceed next?" I asked. "I don't think jumping out the window and falling hundreds of feet down is an option any of us want to explore."

I could no longer ignore the smell of burnt flesh, and I looked down at the smoking pile of what remained of the man Odessa had killed. The soldier was beyond recognition now; his skin warped and burnt off, smoke still rising from the corpse.

"I called down lightning from the sky and killed him," Odessa said, in a daze. "Not even Mother would dare."

"Odessa?"

"You killed him!" Lord Vanya was still suffocating on nothing, staring down at the body in horror.

"Let him be the last person killed today," I said crisply, deliberately forcing away the part of me that was still horrified. Lisette was right: we'd be better off dead if they captured us at this point.

No. They'd keep Haidee and Odessa alive. The rest of us—

But the thought of them hurting Haidee sent fury rising to the surface, and I had to fight for calm. The soldiers in the room were out cold, and the ones behind the door not an immediate threat. No one else ought to be killed. As long as nobody else pissed Odessa off.

"Odessa?" Lan's voice sounded tentative.

133

"I'm sorry," the girl said, though I'm not quite sure she meant it. Lan had reached her side, looking worried. Odessa smiled at her, but it was the smile of someone who'd had too much codrum and gotten themselves drunk.

There were no sounds behind the door, which was suspicious enough on its own. I didn't doubt that they were still there, keeping the wooden frame between them and the goddesses' lightning, but also waiting for another opportunity to attack.

"Odessa?" This time it was Haidee. "Odessa, look at me."

She did, and whatever they wordlessly shared with each other finally snapped her out of the fog she was drifting in. Her gaze shifted down to the corpse, anguish finally dawning.

"I think we can get us out of here," Haidee said, and gestured at the window.

"The fall would kill us," I objected.

"It won't, but I need Odessa's help. Odessa?"

The girl said nothing, her eyes still round with guilt.

"No, Odessa." Lan forced her chin up, forced the girl to look at her instead. "No," the Catseye echoed, her eyes sparking with silver and gold hues again. "Odessa. *Untamed Wildness*. Tell me about it."

I had no idea what she meant, but Odessa blinked, finally snapping out of it. "Lady Carmela and Santiago, the first mate," she said faintly. "They were stranded on an island together."

"Good. I want you to think about their story until we're out of the Citadel. Just as soon as you're done with Haidee. Do you know what she's asking you to do?"

A nod.

"Are you sure she's all right, Lady Lan?" Haidee asked anxiously.

"She will be. After you help your sister, Odessa, I want you to focus on Carmela and Santiago again, and let me handle everything else and get you out of the Citadel. Will you trust me to take care of you till then?"

"Always," the goddess whispered meekly. She allowed herself a quick shudder, then turned to Haidee. "I'm ready."

I saw ice creeping up the window from outside the glass, solidifying against the sill. The twins concentrated again, and the ice extended outward, until it had formed a thick, glassy sheet sliding down to the ground on a giant incline.

Haidee wasn't as versed in manipulating ice or water, just as Odessa wasn't as strong in fire. But when the twins came together like this, it didn't matter.

"Wait," Haidee said. I saw a strange spark ignite between them, watched as the patterns changed and glittered, adapting to more unspoken commands. The sheets of ice tilted further, no longer a slide plummeting down sharply, but a gently sloping curve that would allow us to travel down it with minimal injuries. "It's all about the angles. If we left it that way, the speed we'd travel as we descended might kill us."

Expending that much energy had still taken its toll on Odessa, and she was breathing hard. Lan scooped her up in her arms, ignoring her protests. "However strong you are, creating that much ice is still going to take a lot out of you," she said bluntly. "Especially out here."

135

"I can walk on my own," Odessa countered feebly.

"So you say," the Catseye replied, looking like she would carry Odessa into old age if she could get away with it.

The air shifted again. It didn't come from either Haidee or Odessa. At the same time, a peculiar screeching sound echoed across the whole city, and it was most definitely not the thunder.

Noelle pointed out the window, where another portal had shimmered into being out in the desert, so large that it was visible from where we stood. I swore, expecting a swarming mass of galla to climb out of the gateway. How had they learned to open the gate?

The answer to that came quickly enough. People streamed through the opening instead, adding to my shock. Even from this distance, I could see the banners they carried fluttering in the wind, blue and white.

"Aranth's colors," Odessa gasped. "Mother's here?"

Lan opened the window and stuck a foot out, placing the toe of her boot against the edge of the ice incline and staring grimly down at the drop. "Your Holiness, how certain are you of your calculations?"

"I'm pretty sure." Haidee's eyes glittered, and winds swirled around the icy incline. "I'm creating buffers to slow us down, just in case." She turned to Vanya. "Please come with us," she said.

I hated it. I *knew* this was important. Didn't stop my selfish ass from not wanting him anywhere near Haidee.

"The book might have been destroyed, but maybe you can

still remember information that could help us," she continued. "Please, Vanya."

The boy hesitated, then shook his head reluctantly. "Your Holiness, I cannot leave my father."

"You don't owe him your loyalty. He treats you terribly."

Vanya's hands trembled. "I cannot leave, Your Holiness. I am sorry. I can't."

And just like that, I was pissed for a completely different reason. The hell kind of husband was he going to be if he couldn't get out from under his father's thumb long enough to help the girl he was betrothed to?

"We *really* need to go." Lisette glanced back at the door, where the sound of an ax and the sight of splintering wood told us we didn't have long to wait. "Want me to clobber him over the head? He looks light enough to carry."

"What?" Vanya sputtered.

"No, Lisette. He's told us everything he can. I've already asked too much of you, Vanya. Thank you." Haidee turned and, before any of us could protest, jumped out the window.

"Haidee!" I swore, dashing toward it and watching her slide down with little incident. I could hear her loud whoops of mingled exhilaration and fear as she skidded to a halt at the foot of the tower.

This girl!

"Lan," Odessa whispered, but the Catseye was already lifting her up, poised to follow Arjun. "Carmela and Santiago," the Catseye reminded her.

"I'm sorry," Vanya said again.

"So are we," Lan said, and leaped. Lisette, Charley, and Noelle scrambled in after them.

"You're a fool," I said. I had half a mind to grab the fool and drag him kicking and screaming out the window with me anyway, but I was pretty sure Haidee, who was honorable even at her own expense, wouldn't like that at all.

"I can't go against my father," the boy said, agonized. "He has his faults, but . . ."

"And that's what's wrong with you lot. You don't realize that you owe him fucking *nothing*. They're the reason we're in this hellhole, and you're too blind to see that he only cares about himself." I placed a foot against the sill. "You don't deserve her."

"And you do?" Realization dawned in his eyes, that gut instinct flaring when they know they've got a rival. He was quicker on the uptake about this, at least.

"No. But of the two of us, I'm the only one jumping out this window for her." I spun around and, just to prove my point, pitched myself out the sill and onto the ice.

Haidee's trajectories were sound, but I kept up a steady stream of swearing just to keep in practice as I hurtled down the sculpted ice. The winds slapped at my face, but they prevented me from speeding down so fast that it would be fatal. Haidee had angled the end of the sheet slightly upward, so I could slide off and land safely on my feet without stumbling, without breaking stride, as I took off running after the others.

Haidee skidded to a stop, frantically signaling at us to hide behind one of the buildings. "We can't go out this way," she whispered.

The gates were opening. Regiments were already lining up, streaming out of the city to face the invaders. Odessa clutched at Lan. "Do you think Mother will fight them?" she asked.

Lan's eyebrows drew down; she was clearly too tired to hide her worry. "I don't see how Asteria has a choice."

"I have to confront her."

"Odessa—"

"It feels like it's been years since I last saw Mother. Everything I've discovered about her since then makes her seem like a stranger to me now. But I need to talk to her. I need to hear the truth from her own lips. I want to hear her admit I'm not her daughter."

"I know she owes you an explanation. She owes everyone." Lan sounded hoarse. "But not now. Not while we've got the city already against us."

"We'll need to sneak out the way we came in," Haidee said matter-of-factly. "Too much activity here. Once we're done, Charley, tell Jes and Rodge to—"

The mechanika hugged her without warning. "I know, Your Holiness, and I will. We're just all so glad you're all right. Even Yeong-ho, if he's too grouchy to say it."

Haidee's eyes filled with tears. "Charley, thank you. Tell everyone I'm so sorry."

"Just happy to serve, Your Holiness." The mechanika was

also tearing up. "Don't forget us while you're out there. Maybe when your mother calms down, you can come back."

The goddesses wasted no time carving a fresh hole in the sand-dome so we could escape back out into the desert. The portal had disappeared, and the two armies had stopped two hundred paces or so away from each other, waiting for a signal from their commanders to attack. Asteria's army was noticeably smaller than Latona's, but I knew that didn't necessarily mean they would lose, if Odessa and Lan were right about her.

"We have to go, Your Holiness," Noelle said urgently, but Odessa was rooted to the spot, unable to tear her eyes away. So was Haidee, her face white.

Because Latona was standing right there at the front of her army in all her self-righteous fury, bolts of lightning sizzling behind her. And across from her, on the other side of the field, was her twin sister, the patterns flying around *her* made of the same volatile, destructive energy.

We were in so much trouble.

Chapter Ten

'LAN AND THE DEMONESS

― ☾ ―

IT WAS ASTERIA WHO CAME striding forward first. I didn't know what to expect, but even I would have had trouble telling the goddesses apart if she wasn't wrapped from head to toe in furs and Aranth colors, her hair as wild as the gathering storm above us.

I saw more familiar faces emerge from Asteria's camp, as other Devoted scrambled to defend their position. Filia, Halida, and Miel must have forgiven Gareen; all were laboring to erect barriers of Wind around their group. Slyp, Merika, and the rest of Odessa's faction of Devoted were working side by side with Gracea's faction. I hadn't expected this alliance; the original Devoted had been abusive to the new recruits. The latter had retaliated with extreme prejudice once Odessa had given them the power to fight back.

But much to my shock, I saw other citizens from Aranth as

well, all scrambling as far away from the goddesses as they could. They were ordinary people from the city, neither Devoted nor soldiers. Why had Asteria brought them here?

Was it possible that they were here as a show of good faith, to negotiate a cease-fire with Latona? The older goddesses had each thought that the other was dead for almost twenty years. Surely they could put aside their differences, at least for the moment?

That hope faded as soon as Asteria opened her mouth. "Latona," the goddess said, in a terrible voice that was just as loud as the thunder.

Latona didn't even bother with a greeting. A bolt of lightning streaked down toward Asteria. Odessa cried out, the sound lost amid the rain, but her mother extended an arm and plucked the light out from the very air, the ball sizzling in her palm. Haidee gasped.

Asteria had gone through the galla's rituals herself. I knew that now. But I'd never seen the extent of her abilities before. She'd never had cause to display them so openly, beyond the Banishing.

Latona's eyes blazed with barely suppressed fury. Asteria matched her stride for stride, until they were both several yards away from their respective armies, staring at each other, close enough to touch.

It was an unnerving sight. Side by side they looked so much more similar than their daughters, down to the way they wore their hair, which glittered with the same shifting colors.

"I see you survived the Abyss, dear sister." Latona was full of venom.

"You left Farthengrove to save my life, didn't you?" Asteria's voice was more tempered, but I could hear the same fury. "It would have been a shame if your efforts had gone to waste."

"I should never have tried to rescue you. I should have let them throw you down into the chasm, let the demons consume your soul for all of eternity."

"You brought him to Brighthenge. I begged you not to. His death is on your conscience as much as it is on mine."

"He tried to protect you!" Latona all but screamed. "He loved me, but he loved you, too, even if it wasn't in the way you wanted! And you killed him!"

"You knew I was full of the galla's spite. You knew I wasn't myself!" Asteria shouted, her temper now rising to match her sister's. "I *begged* you not to bring him to Brighthenge!"

"Did you really think he would listen? Did you think he would agree to be left behind with the world falling apart around us?" There were tears trickling down Latona's face. "I couldn't stop him. And you—you *knew* what was going to happen. You *knew*! And you didn't care!"

"He was never in danger!"

"Liar! You loved him! The final galla required his sacrifice!" Latona was raging fire and brimstone.

"He was never in any danger! But you never trusted me enough to believe me, even then! I wanted you both to be happy! I didn't ask to be saved!"

"Maybe what you wanted all along was to see him dead. If you couldn't have him . . . !"

"How dare you accuse me of that." Asteria had gone quiet. It was a bad sign.

I tugged at Odessa. "We have to go." Both older goddesses were too caught up in their past resentments to care that their fight was putting their daughters in danger, but I knew that there was no point in trying to make them see reason today.

"I've never seen Mother cry," Haidee whispered, shaken. "I can't leave her like this. What if Asteria—"

"We have to go!" Arjun interrupted, echoing my words.

"You claimed you would let him go. That you would see us happy." The lightning was now sparking around Latona, kicking up dust everywhere it sizzled into the sand. In contrast, clouds gathered above Asteria, and for the first time since arriving at the Skeleton Coast I felt a genuine chill, a promise of frost. "Was naming your city after him evidence you were ready to give him up, Asteria? Was this your way of ruling over him, even after his death?"

It was Odessa's turn to gasp.

Asteria didn't answer. Instead, icicles shot up from the sand, sharp-tipped stakes heading straight for Latona.

The other goddess shattered them with her bolts. She threw more lightning at her sister, and Asteria parried with blocks of ice erected before her like shields. Neither of the armies were willing to engage, both withdrawing to a safer distance while the furious goddesses traded elements, each doing their best to kill the other. In their rage, the sisters made no distinction between friend or foe. I saw soldiers on both sides blasted with lightning, impaled on icicles.

But creating this much ice in a place that had very little water to begin with was taking its toll on even Asteria. The cold spikes she wielded were shorter and brittler than the large stalagmites she could summon with ease to strengthen the ice walls in Aranth. But Asteria had always been quick to adapt; when another of Latona's lightning strikes blazed her way, she responded with one of her own. Patterns of concentrated, immeasurable energy crackled against each other, and despite the distance I could feel the hair standing on the back of my neck. There was too much magic here. It was only a matter of time before one of them would truly be hurt.

"Stop," Odessa whimpered.

"We're too damn close to the fight!" Arjun was yelling now. "We need to get back to the rig!"

"What if they kill each other?" Haidee cried. "We can't—there must be something—"

"Stop!" Odessa shouted.

Arjun and I traded glances, and a quick flash of understanding. We were both in love with fools of goddesses, it was plain to see, and the best thing we could do for them now was to haul their asses away from this place, as fast as we could carry them.

"Put me down!" Haidee squeaked as Arjun slung her over his shoulder.

"Once we're out of here, sure. Lan agrees."

"You weren't even talking!"

"The two of you communicate just fine without words," I

said, as I hoisted *my* goddess up in the same way. "I'm sure the ability transfers to your consorts."

"This is a completely illogical hypothesis!"

"No," Odessa said, and gasped, staring past me. "Oh no."

I didn't know who the hell the apparitions were. Somewhere in between the flashes of lightning they had suddenly appeared, and one look told me they weren't human. They were almost translucent, like someone had drawn outlines of their shapes but had forgotten to fill them in with color. And yet their features were cast in a peculiar sharp relief, standing out despite their gray, ashen forms.

"Are those mirages?" Lisette gasped.

More figures had manifested around the dead Devoted, ones that I'd never seen before. They wore similar clothes, albeit designed in a different style, much more in keeping with what rangers from Aranth wore. Their cloaks were thick and furred, with swatches of colors lining their hoods. Unlike the other mirages they did not hide their faces underneath their cowls, so I could see them clearly: an older man, two young girls, a youth.

I didn't want them here. I had hoped against all odds that they had found their rest back at Brighthenge. I knew it would gut Odessa terribly, seeing them again. I knew the guilt she harbored, knew she had blamed herself for their deaths. I'd done the same, but I never had to deal with my rangers' ghosts like Odessa had to deal with her dead Devoted.

The specters remained still, content to watch the scene

unfold. Both Asteria and Latona had reined in their tempers, neither willing to attack the new obstacles in their path. Arjun and I resumed dragging Odessa and Haidee away, using their temporary truce to flee undetected. It was a wise decision; I could see more clouds gathering around them, the rain falling harder just as the wind picked up, telling me that this was only just the beginning of an even worse storm to come.

"Where there's mirages, there'll be sandstorms!" Arjun yelled. "Let's move!"

He was right. A sandstorm came spinning out of nowhere, almost on top of where the undead had gathered. Odessa made a startled sound, but I refused to set her down. "There's nothing we can do for them."

"I resurrected them. They're still my responsibility!" Odessa was actually crying now. "Cathei, Nebly, and Salleemae gave their lives for me. I can't leave them!"

"I'm sorry, Odessa. Let them go."

"I can't! Mother's *here*. Out in the open, without the Spire and the city of Aranth as a shield, and this is the only time I'll ever be able to tear out her secrets, everything she kept from me since the day I was born!" Odessa jerked out of my grasp without warning. I stumbled, and she ran.

"Odessa!"

Haidee flipped herself over Arjun's shoulder, landed on the ground, and ran for her twin, and we had no choice but to swear and follow after.

Asteria stopped at Haidee's cry, and so did Latona. The latter had had days to adjust to her youngest daughter's presence, but her eyes were a mystery as Odessa approached. It was easier for me to read Asteria, for all her reticence. At the fore was relief, in a softening around her eyes.

But all she said was "Do not intervene, Odessa."

"You're not my real mother." The words came almost like a physical blow, and Asteria visibly recoiled from the truth of it.

"Yes," she said, after an eternity in between breaths.

"Why?" Odessa sobbed. "I trusted you. I believed you. Why did you lie to me?"

"I would have lied to you for the rest of my life," Asteria said, with a frankness that startled me, "if it meant you would get better. You grew sicker by the night, and I was desperate. Look at you now. Stronger than I remember, and with the galla yours to command. The galla's gifts made *me* stronger. I knew they would do the same for you."

"You allowed her access to the galla?" Latona snarled. "What have you done, Asteria?"

"I saved her life, Latona. Your daughter's life."

Latona snarled, the gates in her eyes a crimson red.

"Mother!" Haidee took one more step toward Latona. "Please, stop."

The clouds dimmed, and the rain slacked off. For a moment, it felt like the whole world had stood still. Like it was taking a breath, holding it in.

But then it let go.

The earthquake was immense. Fissures rose from the earth,

cracks lancing across the ground. Fine sand cascaded into bottomless chasms, and I had to dance out of the way to avoid a sudden tear that ripped through the ground under my feet. It had not come from Latona, or from Asteria; I saw the twin looks of shock on their faces as they too fought to regain their balance.

There was a roar behind me. I turned—and saw one more impossibility, one more horror.

This was the nightmare that had haunted me for months. I thought our distance from the Abyss would keep us safe—that it could appear now at will, even this far away, was terrifying. Surely nothing this massive could assume corporeality in just a blink of an eye.

And yet it was here, looming above us. It was a human-shaped tower with hands that looked harder than stone, and shadow-feet. There was the suggestion of a large head, but I could make out no features in that impenetrable face. Its arms and torso seemed to lengthen upon command, which meant there was no one here who wasn't within its reach. Something glittered upon its brow: a dark crown fashioned from blue gemstones.

Daughters, it said, and I screamed.

Madi's body, ripped apart. Yarrow before the edge of the Abyss, violently cut in two. Cecily on the ground sobbing, her tears no defense against the shadows that eventually consumed her. Merritt and Nuala, their lives hanging on a choice that I never made.

We had faced it at the Great Abyss. It was easier for me on

the second visit; I knew what I was going to find there, and my fears for Odessa were stronger than even my terror of it. When we had made our escape through the gateway, I thought we would be free of its grasp as long as we remained outside its territory.

And now it was here. The distance from the Great Abyss to the Skeleton Coast was not a barrier to its hunger. The corrupted goddess Inanna seemed formed from smoke and fog, as if she was composed entirely out of penumbra.

In the early days of my recovery I had hallucinated its shadow, convinced that it would find me anywhere: within the city, along Aranth's borders, even on the first night I was to protect Odessa. And now that fear was coming true.

It had no mouth, but a low, dreadful sound emanated from within it—a haunting moan that sucked out all other sound from the desert.

The war between Latona and Asteria was forgotten. As one, both goddesses turned to face the new threat. For Asteria, defense came in the thick slices of Air curved like daggers, hurtling to embed themselves deeply into the monster's torso. For Latona, it was the fires of the desert: thick bursts of glowfire, aimed high to explode against the shadow's chest. The giant shadow staggered, but continued to move.

Much to my horror, it was heading directly toward me. Though it had none, I swore I could feel eyes on me, a peculiar hunger that did not require a face to convey. I took a step back, away from Odessa, and its face turned to follow my path, ignoring the goddesses' assault.

"Stop!" Odessa cried out.

"It's not like the galla," I whispered, trying to curb the fear in my own gut. I had escaped death that first time, and it was coming for me now, to complete its collection of dead rangers. "It won't obey you."

Unexpectedly, the shadow reeled back, its arm caught in a sudden conflagration of blue flames. Arjun stood on top of his rig, smoke still rising from his Howler as he whipped more Fire into the cylinder, the tip glowing a bright blue as he prepared to shoot again.

"You will not!" Asteria roared, and more ice raked the creature, shattering parts of it with sudden bursts of hail. It should have been a mortal blow, yet it reconstituted itself quickly, the holes and punctures closing up as we stared in horror. I retreated again as it continued its inexorable trek toward me, a hand already reaching out in apparent eagerness.

"Get the goddesses on the rig," I ordered Noelle, and took off running in the opposite direction.

I knew I couldn't outrun it. I didn't have much choice. I could give or take life at a touch if I wanted to, but I had no defenses against something that wasn't even alive. Inanna's corpse had no life for me to manipulate.

"No!" Odessa cried out, but the shadow took no notice. All I could hope to do was put as much distance as I could between myself and the others.

Its arms shot out, faster than I could run, and every part of me tensed up, expecting white-hot pain through my body any second—

A volley of blue fire consumed part of its arm again. The limb broke away from its body, crumbled into ashes. Arjun was breathing hard, readying his gun for yet another shot, but he would soon reach his limit.

And then *another* stream of fire, the flames every bit as blue as Arjun's, soared through the air from Asteria's camp, taking out the creature's other arm.

"I'm glad to see you unharmed, Lady Lan," Janella said, as the flames around her fingers died down.

That was a lie: She had encouraged Odessa to give me up to the Abyss, to fulfill the last of the rites. The smile she bestowed on me was bereft of sincerity.

But her flames were as azure as Arjun's. She had not manifested that ability during our journey.

"Stop," Asteria ordered. She channeled her own flames at the creature, and Latona joined her. As their attacks intertwined, the fires turned just as blue as Arjun's and Janella's.

A sudden burst of light glanced against the side of the behemoth's head, crushing part of its temple. I growled as another of Asteria's Devoted came into view, a woman with long hair and a self-important expression on her face.

"Gracea," Odessa said stiffly. The Starmaker nodded briskly at her in acknowledgment, then hurled more lightning at the creature.

"A friend?" Haidee asked.

"Not the word that comes to mind, no." Emboldened by the fire's effectiveness, some of Latona's soldiers began channeling the same; soon there were streams of patterns hurtling from both Latona's and Asteria's camps, briefly united in their attempt to take down a more immediate threat.

It was still the blue flames that dealt the most damage, and as another cobalt flare enveloped the demoness, a low, stunned cry from Arjun alerted me to the mirages, four in total. They had drifted closer, and whatever their intention, I realized it was not to attack us. Their focus, too, was on the Inanna-demoness. One of them—a figure in a dark blue cloak so painfully similar to the ones we wore in Aranth, similar to those of the dead rangers we'd found during our journey to the Great Abyss— lowered its hand, smoke rising from its fingers.

There was a shimmer in the air, and more specters drifted forward; first Salleemae and Graham, and then Nebly and Cathei. I heard Odessa gasp.

And for the first time, the shadow paused. It inclined its massive head toward the eight wraiths that blocked its path. But it made no move to pass whatever unseen blockade the specters had set up.

The ghosts of Salleemae, Nebly, Cathei, and Graham pulled away from the rest. Patterns warped around them, churning into white-hot heat.

"No!" Odessa cried.

They turned their heads in my goddess's direction. I thought I even saw Cathei smile.

And then the sandstorm they had generated tore through the desert and punched a hole through the demoness. When the winds cleared, they were gone.

I could practically taste the strength of all the spells in the air, glittering and thick on my tongue. The magic came from everywhere—from the lingering energies of Odessa's undead Devoted, from the desert mirages, from the bristling patterns that Latona and Asteria hurled, from the added firepower of Arjun and the other Devoted and soldiers as they continued to pummel it with shotbursts. It came from Haidee and Odessa, each looking up at the giant with a determined expression on her face, both steeped in magic and strange patterns that were unfamiliar to me.

Odessa took Haidee's hand. "You're *not* taking her," she said. And then both their eyes changed, the gates within them flaring into a myriad of colors.

With their sacrifice, the Devoted specters had weakened the creature. And now thicker, heavier blue flames enveloped the monster until it was a giant ball of writhing fire that scorched the skies and blackened the sands around it. Even in its dying throes it did not stop moving. As the rest of it succumbed, darkness turning into embers into ash, it continued to reach out for me. It fell to its knees and strained in my direction, the tips of its fingers mere inches away, each easily larger than my head, before the last of the fires turned it into powder, the wind carrying the rest of its remains away.

Where it had stood, only one peculiar shadow remained: one that was no bigger than a child, with something that glittered in its hand. I saw Odessa look at it, fear and hate at war in her gaze.

"I refuse!" she shouted.

A breeze rippled through the shadow, and it was gone before I could blink.

I sank to my knees; breathless, grateful, guilty that I was still alive. My legs felt like water. I couldn't stop shaking. "All good," I whispered to myself, trying to believe my own words.

The quiet didn't last long. There were the telltale clicks of several dozen Howlers locking into focus, a sound that echoed on all sides as Mother's soldiers and the desert clans leveled their guns. Asteria's followers responded with the gates in their eyes glowing, ready to channel the elements.

This was bad. Any unexpected twitch could set off the first shot, and I knew there would be no going back after that. The Devoted were at a disadvantage, being the fewest in number; I despised nearly half of them, but I didn't want to see them gunned down, either.

"Stand down," I ordered, because somebody had to say it. Nobody listened. Everyone was waiting for somebody else to acquiesce first, and none of them intended to be that person.

"Stand down," Haidee said, louder.

"Stand down," Odessa echoed.

Her voice was softer, but with her words came a shift in the air.

And at her call came more shadows. Some crawled out of the fresh cracks on the ground, or detached themselves from the silhouettes across the sand, or slipped in with the rain. Now the power had shifted to our side, the soldiers and Asteria's Devoted and the desert clansmen less certain about pulling their triggers.

"Stand down," Odessa said again, and this time they did. Asteria's people no longer surrounded themselves with shifting patterns. The army lowered their rifles.

Odessa let out a small, shuddering sound. The galla wavered and vanished. Their disappearance didn't stop the two groups of people from looking at Odessa like she was about to sprout two more heads. The desert mirages simply stood there and said nothing, content to observe.

Asteria rounded on Latona, her eyes still aglow from barely contained magic. "What trickery was that?" she hissed.

Latona shook her head. "That was not my doing."

"You saw it! We are four goddesses, standing in one place. Why would it choose to attack one of *my* people?"

"Mother," Haidee pleaded. "We need to put aside our differences. We have to—"

But Latona deliberately turned her back on her daughter, as if she couldn't bother herself with a reply, and I saw the entreating look on Haidee's face fade away, cold anger taking its place.

"Odessa!" I heard, and turned to see my goddess staggering, her skin ashen and her hand clasped over her chest. I was by her side in moments, my hand against her face, willing strength back into her. Color bloomed on her cheeks and she took a deeper gasp of air. "Lan," she said, and smiled up at me.

Asteria rushed forward, but drew up short when Odessa put out a hand to stop her. "Stay away. I don't want to see you again."

"Odessa—"

"You schemed to send me thousands of miles from home, to

face horrors beyond my imagining at the Abyss. You didn't care that I would lose my mind and my love in the process."

"Odessa," Janella began smoothly, moving to rest her hand on my love's shoulder. "You're not well. You must get yourself assessed by Sumiko, ensure that—"

"Don't you dare touch her." Janella had orchestrated so many deaths during the journey. She'd sabotaged the *Brevity*, killed Cathei and Salleemae when they'd found out. She sacrificed Lorila and Tamerlin without thought to open the portals back into Aranth and the Golden City. How much of it did Asteria know? How much of it had she approved?

Janella straightened, the smile on her face sickeningly false. "I was merely worried, Lady Tianlan."

"You caused more pain to us than my sickness," Odessa snarled. "Does Mother know even half of what you've done?"

"I made my case before her. Gracea can attest to that. Her Holiness agreed that I only did all I could to ensure you were safe, and that her instructions were carried out as closely as I could manage it."

I glared at Gracea in disbelief. Was she so enamored of her position that she would agree to anything to keep her hold on it? She looked away again, and the guilty expression on her face answered my question.

"You were sick," Asteria said. "And I was desperate. I believed Brighthenge housed the spells needed to purify you. What else could I have done?"

"There were no spells, Mother. No medicines. Only demons. And you knew it. I'm surprised you even decided to leave Aranth, given your preference for putting other people at risk in your place."

Latona stiffened at the name, but Odessa seemed not to notice. "Who did you place in charge of the city? It can't be Gracea; I see her right behind you."

"Odessa." There was an odd note in Asteria's voice, a strange thread of pain I'd never heard from her before.

Odessa's expression changed, from angry to wary. "Mother. Why did you leave Aranth? What happened to it?"

The older woman said nothing. Odessa wavered, and I held her more tightly. "No." It was a tiny, hurt sound. "*No. I'm going to save everyone. I can't do that unless there's a home to return to. You said you would save Aranth. I wanted to join the expedition because I *knew* I could save Aranth. Aranth isn't gone. It's not. *It's not!*"

I turned to where the people from Aranth were gathered. I saw Mistress Daliah, and several of the orphaned children she cared for. But I didn't see Old Wallof, the bookstore owner. Frantic, I scanned for more familiar faces, and found very few. Was this everyone Asteria had brought from our city? Had she moved the others somewhere safer before arriving at the desert? Or were they all she was able to save?

I heard a loud gasp from Haidee and saw her face turn pale, a hand over her mouth. "Did we do that?" she whispered as Arjun, carefully stone-faced, moved to stand beside her. "Did we . . . ?"

"Do you see now?" Latona grated. "Do you finally understand?"

"Surely you are the last person to lecture so freely on consequences," Asteria said icily.

I could do nothing but stand, helpless, as Odessa wept in my arms. Asteria hadn't come to the desert to declare war on Latona. She was *fleeing* the waters and the ice she could no longer control, trying to save what was left of her people. I remembered that vision I had shared with her, of the city being swept under the waves. Was that the consequence of what Odessa and Haidee had done at the Abyss? How many had Asteria been able to save?

I wanted to grieve, but couldn't find the words. It felt like the last several months had been nothing but an endless flow of tears.

"You knew the secrets of the portal," I said, trying to change the subject, refusing to let my mind dwell on this new, horrifying reality. "I realized it the instant I saw that Janella knew how to use it. There were other shrines. Other portals."

"Yes. Sister temples to Brighthenge. During Inanna's time, they were used by the goddess to travel quickly from one end of Aeon to the other. I was well aware of its purpose, but it had never been used in my lifetime, to my knowledge. Not until the Breaking."

"Why did you force my team into that months-long expedition when we could have arrived there sooner? Why did you make me go through that *twice*?" I balled my fists, unable to keep the rage out of my voice. I'd come to terms with Asteria's willingness to sacrifice me to save Odessa, but it had never occurred to me until then that she had also decided to sacrifice my rangers.

"It wouldn't have worked."

"How can you be so sure?"

"*It wouldn't have worked*. And even if it had, you've seen for yourself what opening that portal entails. Your team died for you to glean that knowledge. I am sorry about them. But would you have made a different decision had you been in my stead?"

"I would have," Odessa said. "I would have told my daughter the truth. Not pretend everything is normal like a coward, just because you couldn't stand to face the wreckage of what you two had done."

"Odessa!" Asteria gasped.

"Odessa!" Latona cried out at the exact same time.

My goddess was still grieving. Tears had tracked wet paths down her cheeks, and more shone in her eyes. But even in her despair, she was refusing to bend. Only her shaking hand was the telltale sign she was close to breaking.

I took it without asking. I wanted to weep, too, but I knew it would change nothing. Instead, I gathered every calm thought I could muster, every wordless comfort, and willed it through my touch, warming us both. Catseyes can't heal broken hearts. They can't cure grief. The best I could do was show her I loved her, send her every Aether pattern within reach.

Her fingers tightened around mine. One stroked lightly against the back of my hand.

Haidee rounded on Latona, eyes flashing brightly. "You hid too, didn't you? You constructed another city in the desert, put a bubble over it so you wouldn't have to hear the sounds of people dying outside. It doesn't matter which of you is our real mother. It doesn't matter that you've been living a world apart all this time—*you're both the same.* Neither of you could face what you've done, and you wound up doing more harm to Odessa, and to me—more than her illness ever could."

"You will cease this nonsense, Haidee," Latona said. "Come back to the city with me—you and your sister. None of Aeon's demons will reach either of you there. I have always protected you—"

Haidee cut her off. "Your *protection* is the reason we are here, Mother. If you'd thought to put more effort into undoing the Breaking than you have into shielding me from it, then maybe we wouldn't be in this position."

Latona's nostrils flared. "I did what I thought was best for you!"

"And look at us now! Is this what you think is best?"

"Haidee. Let's talk about this back home. Please."

"No, we won't. Odessa's right. You were afraid, too. We all would have died out eventually. We would have run out of water. And somehow, *somehow,* the two of you still thought hiding was the better option. And I can't forgive either of you for it."

Latona stared back at her daughter, too furious to be coherent. But I could see the guilt there too, mixed in with the anger. I looked past her, to where Gracea stood. The Starmaker caught my gaze, flushed, and looked away.

"I don't want anything else to do with you. If you're not

going to help us fix the world, then Odessa and I will do it ourselves." Haidee turned.

"Go back to your camps and go back to pretending the world never stopped turning," Odessa said. "Let's go, Lan. I'm tired."

"Lan." There was a fury in Asteria's voice still, but it was tempered by something close to uncertainty. "Like it or not, Tianlan, I am still your liege. You and Odessa must come back with me. We can still heal her. *I* can still heal her. Lan—"

But I too turned away, scooping Odessa up like she weighed no more than a bundle of leaves, my steps steady and sure as the distance between us and the older goddesses widened. My shoulders were braced, expecting her to demand more, use her incanta to compel me to return—and I was surprised when she did nothing, and let us leave.

"Is she all right?" Haidee asked worriedly once they'd caught up to us. I placed Odessa carefully inside the rig; she looked exhausted, and my heart twisted. We'd said very little to Haidee and Arjun about the extent of Odessa's sickness. A quick check told me that the darkness clustered by her heart had not grown in size, which was small comfort.

"She will be." I sounded tired as well. It seemed like the only way to heal Odessa was to have her go through the galla ritual. It was hard not to sound despairing.

"I'm not giving up. And neither should you."

"Odessa's first vision was of Aranth being overcome by waves," I said hoarsely. "She predicted that one day the ice dams we built around Aranth would no longer be enough to shield us from the storms and the waves. That eventually all would be overwhelmed by the ice. Asteria foresaw that, too. But I always thought that future would be so much further away. I . . ." My voice deepened, broke. We no longer had a home to return to. I didn't want to think about the number of casualties. Far too few people had arrived here with Asteria. "How many was she able to save?" *And how many did she sacrifice?*

"I'm so sorry, Lady Lan."

"Let's get out of here first," Arjun said. "I don't want to stick around long enough to see that Inanna-shadow resurface."

It was only after he'd started the car and we were moving that I gave up resisting, and looked back.

The older goddesses were talking. From where I sat I could tell it wasn't cordial, though they were no longer throwing fire and lightning at each other. It was Latona who backed away first. I saw her mouth form words as she hissed something at Asteria, though what she said I never knew. Then she turned to issue orders to her generals, who started their withdrawal from the battlefield, marching back into the dome.

Asteria watched them leave. I could do nothing but watch her figure grow smaller and smaller, until she and the rest of her army were lost among the endless sand.

Chapter Eleven

ODESSA IN PREPARATION

———————————— ☾ ————————————

THE FIRST THING I DID upon returning to camp was to climb out of the rig and stumble a few feet away so I could empty the contents of my stomach onto the ground.

"Odessa!" I heard, and then felt a warm touch along the nape of my neck as Lan lifted my hair, keeping it free from vomit as I continued to puke.

Learning Aranth's fate had made me ill. I no longer had a home to return to. The rogue waves that plagued the city had finally succeeded in sweeping away everything I loved, and all that was left of my people were here, stranded in the desert. What good was being able to see into the future if I could do nothing to prevent it?

And the man I had killed at the Citadel. The stench of him still filled my nostrils, and I could do nothing but breathe in the decay, even many miles away. I could still taste the soot, the smell of burnt flesh rising from the body, and my guts twisted.

He was going to hurt Lan, something inside of me whispered. *It was his fault. Not yours. Never yours. You were only protecting the one you love. Only a warning, to all who dare hurt you. They will never harm Lan, because they will fear you. This is good, Odessa. This is* good.

Was that a smile on my lips? No. *No.* I shook my head, rejecting the idea, forcing myself to be repulsed by the thought.

But surely I was a terrible person. Since emerging from the portal I had given little thought to the undead Devoted I had left behind at the Great Abyss. I had assumed, with my rejection of the galla's final gift, that they too would be gone, their souls released back into wherever souls were supposed to return to.

I was wrong.

Salleemae, Cathei, Graham, and Nebly—men and women who died for me. I had thought giving them back some semblance of life would save them and ease my guilt. I was wrong there, too.

And they died for me again.

And Mother. Despite my anger and my hurt, I'd had to stop myself from weeping, from running into her arms. I missed her, even after everything. A part of me wanted to believe I could still return with her to Aranth, pretend like nothing had ever happened. I didn't mind the shadows in my chest. I didn't mind performing the Banishing along Aranth's shores for the rest of my life. That part of me wanted a return to the way things were: listening to the rise and crash of waves from my room in the Spire; sneaking out to hunt down bargains in bookstores; kissing Lan.

But all these were no longer possible. And it was my fault. It had always been my fault.

"I failed, Lan," I whispered once my bout of nausea was over, wiping my mouth. "Our city's gone. We have no choice now. I . . ." I could not stop the tears from falling.

"Shh," Lan murmured, and I found myself against her chest, weeping into her shirt. She stroked my hair. "We're going to get through this."

"How?" I sobbed. How many of them had died because of what I had done? Mr. Wallof and his bookstore had been my sanctuary away from my responsibilities. I might have hated the restrictions of the Spire, but it had been the only home I'd ever known. Why couldn't I have done more?

"Odessa," Lan said, and her touch was a warm jolt to my system; I felt the patterns summoned from her aether-gate gathering in my mind, slowing down my racing heart, making it easier to breathe so I could whittle my guilt down into smaller portions to deal with one at a time. "We're allowed to grieve."

Haidee had a much different approach. A concentrated ball of Air gathered in her palm, and she released it with explosive fury. A tornado hurtled through the sandscape, tearing toward the horizon, where it eventually disappeared from sight, leaving grooves in the ground at least three feet deep.

"Nothing's changed!" she roared out into the desert, her anger even more powerful than the hurricane she'd unleashed. "She hasn't changed! The world's falling apart all around us, and she's still selfish enough to do nothing about it! I hate her!" She flung a second tornado, then a third. "I hate her so much!"

Lisette started toward her, but Arjun held up a hand. "Let her get it all out," he said calmly.

Haidee and I gave ourselves several more minutes to unburden our anger, our anguish—me through fresh storms of weeping, Lan holding me close, and Haidee carving through more dunes until her rage had passed.

We both knew what our mothers' reactions would be.

It's just that we loved them too much not to hope that they could change for us. Even if they never did.

Finally exhausted, Haidee knelt beside us. "Odessa. I'm so sorry. When Aeon started moving, I thought—I had no idea that your home would be—" She choked on the words, sounding stricken. "I'm so sorry."

It was easier to alleviate someone else's pain than face my own. I forced all my feelings away, tucked them into a little corner of my mind. I had to take action. I couldn't allow myself to wallow in more misery. "Help me save everyone else," I said.

Haidee gripped my fingers tighter. "I swear."

The tension was palpable by the time we had all disembarked from the jeeps. One of Arjun's clan brothers, Kadmos, waved to us as we arrived. "We caught more intruders," he announced excitedly.

"Intruders?" Arjun echoed. "Cannibals again?"

"No, they said they came a long way from the east. Beyond even the Sand Sea." Kadmos sounded awed. "Their leader said they know you, and that you could vouch for them."

Arjun stared at him, puzzled at first. And then his face fell, into an expression that lay at a juncture between angry and resigned. "Oh, hell," he said. "Of all the hundred blasted sands of hell."

"So you do know them?"

"Unfortunately."

"Wait," Haidee said. "Surely he doesn't mean—"

"Yeah, he does. The damned sand pirates are here again."

The Liangzhu tribe were seated on the ground, divested of their weapons. Mother Salla, clan leaders Tamera and Lars, and a dozen guards from several other clans stood watch over the group. The tallest of the captives, a bald man with an eye patch, waved cheerfully at us. Arjun groaned.

"It is very good to be seeing you again!" the bald man called out happily. "We are, alas, having trouble explaining to your fellows that we are friends and do not wish to bring trouble."

"What are you doing here, Sonfei?" Arjun asked wearily.

"Do you know these people?" Mother Salla demanded.

"Yeah. They aided us on our way to the Abyss. Let them go. Give them back their gear." Arjun looked like it physically pained him to have to say the words.

"You have all our thanks," Sonfei continued merrily, as the guards proceeded to do just that. "Your Holiness, you are looking as beautiful as ever. It is a pleasure . . ." His voice trailed off as he took me in. "Wait. Why are there two of you?"

"This is Odessa, Sonfei," Haidee said. "And these are Lan

and Noelle, her companions. They came all the way from the other side of the world."

The smile slid off Sonfei's face. The other Liangzhu had quieted, staring at Lan.

"Is there something wrong?" I asked tentatively.

"Your hair. Your face is like Haidee's. You're—you're of her family. Asteria's family. She was—we were—" Tears ran down the man's face, to my shock. "You are alive? Is *she* alive?"

I wasn't sure how to break it to him. Mother had never spoken of a Sonfei, but that wasn't a surprise. She'd spoken very little of her past. "Yes. She's well, and she's here in the desert, but she's not at camp with us."

Sonfei rose to his feet without another word, and stalked some distance away. A few of his clanmates murmured among themselves, a couple standing to follow him.

"Did I say something wrong?" I asked. "Did he dislike Mother?"

"I think it was very much the opposite," Haidee said carefully. "And from what I could glean from previous conversations with him, your mother didn't reciprocate."

"Oh." *Mother had a suitor?* "I'm sorry to hear that."

"He will return when he has taken a better hold of his emotions," one of the other Liangzhu told us. She was a woman only a few years older than us, with a shaved head and a scar on her right cheek. "My name is Bairen. We left after the first nightfall, and traveled across the Sand Sea to find you." She shuddered. "Have you ever seen such darkness, listened to the silence that descends with it? Sonfei came striding out of his tent, hollering that the goddess had succeeded and that we must aid her. And so here we are, offering our help. And we come with gifts."

"There's no time to be trading any—" Further words stuttered on Lan's lips as she took in the monstrous carcass the other Liangzhu were dragging in behind them. It reminded me of some of the sea creatures that hunted in Aranth's waters. This one appeared to be made from rock, though from the chopped portions I could see what looked like red meat inside of it. It was easily twenty feet long, built like a giant, sentient piece of hemp rope. It was also headless; the Liangzhu had no doubt deemed that part inedible and lopped it off before seeking us out. I was grateful for that; some details I would rather not know.

"Food," Bairen said proudly. "Even with the size of your camp, its meat can be feeding all of us for many weeks to come. It is this we offer, to soften the blow for the bad tidings we must bring."

"And what bad tidings are those?" I asked warily.

"The creatures of the chasm have begun to move, Your Holiness." The woman shivered. "A demonic exodus be rising from the east, like a foul wave. In time, they will overrun the world and be consuming all in their path."

"But we've already defeated the swarm," I gasped. "We just stopped it only hours ago."

"I do not think that the demons are the same ones you faced. They would need to have overtaken us to attack your camp, and so we would not be alive right now to tell you so."

"So what you're saying is that there's *another* swarm heading our way?" The dreams I'd had of the galla attacking us. Were they more visions?

Bairen glowered. "The one we saw looked to span almost the length of the Abyss. I predict that they shall reach us by the next day's cycle. We must band together. Stay strong together." She looked at Lan. "You are Liangzhu as well." She sounded stunned.

Lan blinked. "I am, yes."

"I had never expected to see another outside of our clan. You do not know our happiness now." Bairen took Lan's face in her hands. Her voice trembled. "Your parents have gone, yes?"

"Years ago," Lan said quietly. "I've no other relations."

"You are part of ours now. I am glad to see you finding family with the goddesses, but I hope you will have room for another."

"Thank you." There was a hitch to Lan's voice, and my heart went soft.

Mother Salla looked aghast. "If what you say is true, then we have even less time, as I feared. Once your leader has his emotions under control, you are invited to join us inside, to discuss what our next steps shall be."

"When we saw the winds pick up and the storms darken, we thought we were witnessing a second Breaking in the process," Tamera sad tersely. "Every time Latona and Asteria meet, it is always at the rest of the world's peril, it seems."

"Four goddesses all in one place," Mother Salla said grimly, "and two at war with each other. Did you find what you were looking for?"

I shook my head, dejected. "I'm sorry. It seems the book we were after had been destroyed by one of the lords of the city."

"At least Latona and Asteria will be more invested in taking each other out before they concern themselves with us," Lan said. "Let them fight each other, while we concentrate on healing Aeon."

"But what if Latona injures Mother?" I didn't want either of them hurt. There'd been far too much bloodshed already.

Lan managed a quick smile. "They had several opportunities to kill each other, but they didn't. I know fighting, and I know what Asteria's capable of. She could have gone for the jugular many times and taken Latona out, but she didn't. Latona was the same. They're angry at each other, but I don't think either one actually wants to see the other dead, no matter how loud they've been screaming. Let them work their frustrations out. They hadn't seen each other in close to eighteen years, and that's a lot of pent-up anger to fester."

"Are you a general yourself, Lady Lan?" Lars asked politely. "It seems you're very familiar with the arts of war."

"I . . ." Lan hesitated, a sudden anguished look on her face. "No. I don't have the qualifications to be a general."

"Mother asked you to protect me," I reminded her gently. "She trusted you and knew how good you were. You're more than qualified for anything."

Lan smiled at me. "And you're far too biased to make that call."

"You know I'm right." I took a deep breath. "I'm still mad at her. I don't know how to make her care about Aeon more than she hates her sister. It's like Father and I are the only ones who matter to her now, and he's been gone for years."

A frown marred Haidee's face, disappearing just as quickly.

I caught it all the same. "And what's that supposed to mean?"

"Asteria might have been fond of our father," Haidee said somewhat evasively, "but to name a city after him . . . that doesn't seem appropriate."

"She didn't know your—our—mother was still alive. And it's just a city. She can name it however she wants."

"If I named *my* city *Lan*, I know you'd have a problem with it just as much as I would if you'd named yours *Arjun*."

"You're making my mother sound worse than she is!"

"And you're dismissing the feelings of mine!"

We scowled at each other, arms folded across our chests; a near-mirror image, I was sure.

"Odessa. Haidee," Noelle said gently, always the peacemaker. "Your biases are showing. There's enough blame between them both for the Breaking. Who started it is a moot point. We need to know how to restore Aeon. Anything else is inconsequential in comparison."

She was right. I took a deep breath, and saw Haidee doing the same. "I'm sorry," I mumbled. "I didn't mean to demean your mo—our mother—Latona."

"I'm sorry, too," Haidee said, in the exact same embarrassed tone. "I know they haven't always been good parents—but they're the only ones we've ever known."

"Well, *I* am sorry that you were not successful in finding what you needed in the dome," Giorme said. "Though I had always thought it a long shot. There is, however, a new concern about you two."

"What is it?" Lisette asked.

"The other leaders have voiced concerns that your loyalties may be compromised." The man still somehow managed to make that sound apologetic.

He gestured at one of the tents. "Let us discuss it inside. The wind is picking up, and I've never relished the scraping of sand against my skin."

Haidee and I exchanged glances, not liking the sound of that one bit.

"Do I need to be in on this meeting?" Arjun demanded. "I'm pretty good at yelling."

"More likely you'll be bored five minutes in," Haidee told him. "I'm sure we can handle it. I'd feel safer with you out here."

"I'll go see to the patrols," Arjun relented. "And if we finish early, it should only take about five seconds to march in and tell them to quit bullshitting around and listen to you."

"Feeling confident, aren't we?"

He grinned. "Well, I did somehow manage to find myself a goddess. That takes a lot of humility." He leaned close and kissed her. Haidee responded with enthusiasm, all but jumping into his arms. I blushed, and turned my back so they could have some privacy, though it was clear this was the furthest thing from their minds. "I'll come wait for you outside the tent," Arjun managed to say, a little short of breath, once they'd broken apart.

"You know," Lisette chuckled, after he'd left and we started heading for the leaders' tent. "I wish I'd met you before Arjun did. I'm a bit envious."

Haidee blushed. "I'm sorry. I think you're very beautiful. But . . . well . . ."

"You don't explore the same paths I do. I understand. Too bad for me," she sighed, then eyed me speculatively.

"Tear those thoughts away from her," Lan said calmly from behind us, "because I *will* fight you, and you *will* lose."

Lisette laughed. "All right, Catseye. I know when I'm beaten."

The tent we entered was the largest within the neutral territory, with Stonebreaker patterns coating the outer canvas to ward off the sun's heat. In lieu of chairs we sat in a circle on small mats that had been brought out for that purpose. We now hosted members of clans Gila, Rockhopper, Fennec, Addax, Sidewinder, Ibex, and Pronghorn—and the Saiga, if you counted the cannibals. The Ibex clan master, Alonzo, bowed his head sadly. "We were over twenty tribes when the desert first came to be," he said. "And now we are less than half that number. A hard life. An even harder death."

They all listened intently while we relayed what had happened back in the Golden City, and gasps rose all around when Haidee described the Inanna-demoness, and the fight between Latona and Asteria.

"They will kill us," Rockhopper clan master Minh proclaimed fervently. "But what can we do? We could barely fight off Latona's fury before, and now there are other monsters to deal with."

"Lady Lan believes fighting each other will keep Latona and Asteria's attentions away from us, and I agree," Mother Salla said. "But the galla are an even greater problem."

"Where did they come from? Why only now?"

"Aeon turns," Lan said softly. "I have reason to believe that is what triggered their attacks."

"Is that why Latona and Asteria chose not to put Aeon back in order?" Noelle asked. "Is it possible that they knew this was going to happen?"

Tamera looked at us. "Your Holinesses. It may be that we will still have to wage our own war against Latona. She has made no secret that she despises us, and would eradicate all the clans if she could. And Asteria's arrival only adds to our worries. This is why many prefer that the two of you be removed from our plans, if not from the neutral grounds altogether."

"Haidee and Odessa are trying to help us, and you know that!" Lisette interjected.

"Yes, but their objections are valid. It's reasonable to assume that a young goddess would choose to side with her mother even after everything. You've only known them a few days, Lisette. Lady Haidee has spent all her life within the Golden City. Such bonds are hard to break. You've known Lady Odessa even less."

"I'm not going to kill Mother," I said angrily. "And I'm not responsible for my mother's actions. If anything, *we've* had to clean up *their* messes."

"Most people here find it hard to separate us from them," Haidee said quietly. "We're goddesses. Goddesses broke the world. Nobody thinks much about the nuances when they're angry."

I looked at her, wondered how it must feel to be reviled your whole life for something you didn't do. As sheltered as I'd been, I'd had my people's support. "That still isn't an excuse."

Tamera snorted. "I have a duty to protect my clan. I would be a fool to believe you would come to our assistance if you had to choose between us and your mother."

I shook my head. "I would put myself in harm's way first. But Lan is right. I would much rather that we ignore them both altogether, and instead concentrate on other options."

"They will have their hands full with each other," Haidee agreed. "We should put our efforts into untangling what we know of Brighthenge and the rituals."

"According to the rituals of Brighthenge," Tamera said stiffly, "all it takes to revive the world is the sacrifice of one goddess."

Haidee and I froze. Tamera might only have said it to prove a point, but it was a threat all the same.

"All our troubles began the day we attempted to force such a sacrifice," Salla said sharply. "Sacrifice one now, and you will have three angry goddesses to contend with."

"I have no intentions of performing such distasteful rites. But the others are aware of them, and it will only be a matter of time before that stirs up more resentment. You may be goddesses, but you're both woefully naive to think that this will pass without bloodshed."

"Are you saying that sacrificing another goddess would stop

this . . . invasion, and return Aeon to what it was before?" Minh asked.

"There will be no more sacrifices," Mother Salla thundered sharply.

The Rockhopper clan master spread their hands. "It was only a question, Salla."

"Let us start with what we already know," Ilenka, the Sidewinder mistress, said. "What are these portals that you mention, Your Holiness? A method by which the goddesses can travel from one end of Aeon to the other?"

"I never knew they existed until I reached the Abyss," Haidee admitted. "I originally thought they were only accessible from Brighthenge, and that they led to only two destinations—one back here to the desert, and another to Odessa's city. It explained how the two goddesses were separated during the Breaking. But now I'm not so sure. Asteria could not have traveled to the Great Abyss this quickly in order to access the portal found there—which means there must be some way to access it from Aranth, the city she founded. And there must be a way to access Brighthenge from here, too."

"Wherever that is," Giorme said, "it would be near Asteria's camp, in the territory the Aranthians currently occupy. We would need to get past them if we think to use it."

"Aranthians," Lan echoed, slightly bemused.

"Was that the wrong term to call your people, Lady Lan?"

"No. It's just that we never thought to define ourselves with any terms before. We thought we were the last humans on Aeon.

178

There were no other groups to distinguish ourselves from."

That was true. I'd always thought we were the last settlement on Aeon. It seemed inconceivable to me then that there was any human life beyond the storms and the monsters that purportedly roamed the lands outside of our territory.

"Would it even be possible for us to access the portal?" Tamera asked. "Or are the goddesses the only ones capable of such travel?"

"We can use it without requiring a goddess's aid," Lan said, expression suddenly wooden.

"Lan," I said softly.

"How can you be so sure, Lady Lan?" the Fennec clan mistress wanted to know.

"Because I went through that portal on my own, once. A few months ago, Asteria tasked me to lead a team to the Great Abyss, in an attempt to learn more about what had transpired during the Breaking. Asteria had thought to see if the temple still stood, believed there were secrets there we could benefit from. I know now that she lied. We reached the edges of the Abyss, but we were beset by creatures made of shadow, and my whole team was killed. The demons there spared me, sent me back through that very portal to report to Asteria, likely to lure Odessa into their territory. The blood they spilled, it . . . activated the portal."

"Good Mother." Haidee put her hand to her mouth, stunned. The elders said nothing, but sympathy was evident on their faces. "I'm so sorry."

"I'm sorry, too." Lan's voice was still unusually blank. Wordlessly, I scooted closer, looped my arms around her waist. This was another guilt I hadn't known was mine to bear until recently: that my mother's single-mindedness had put Lan through so much, all because of me. I wished I could take away her pain, bear it for my own. "A sacrifice is required to open the portals each time. The galla are not very particular about who."

"And if Asteria opened a portal from Aranth to travel here," Noelle added bleakly, "then she has no qualms about doing some sacrificing herself. We must be very careful, milady. Asteria has never been predictable, but I have never known her to be deliberately cruel until now."

"Then let's talk about what we do know." Haidee laid her journal at the center of the circle. She had written down every name, riddle, and observation from our time at Brighthenge. She had even sketched out a very crude layout of the temple, trying to remember every detail, no matter how small or trivial it had seemed then. "I've been looking through this, but I can't determine what might be important. I hope you will help and find something I might have missed."

"There is no one alive among us who bore witness at the heart of the Breaking, or even to the sacrificial ritual that had been practiced for generations before, save for the older goddesses themselves." Valaria, the Pronghorn clan mistress, leaned back, frowning. "Mother Salla was the only one within close proximity of the calamity, but even she was prevented from viewing the rites in person. It will be difficult to find the essentials in something of which we have so little knowledge."

"That is not true," a voice said. Sonfei entered the tent, grunting as he found an empty place between Lan and me. The man's eyes were slightly red, but he was almost back to his jovial self. "Like your Mother Salla, I was also present when the Breaking took place. Naturally, I too was banned from seeing the ritual myself, but I will do my best to tell you what I can be remembering."

"I will help," Mother Salla said. "Perhaps another point of view will help refresh my mind."

"I remember you, now that I think about it. Your hair was longer then, and dark, like the blackest of nights. You looked very different."

"So I was." Salla sounded surprised. "I do not resemble the woman I was then. I doubt anyone would recognize me, had I any contemporaries still living. I am sorry that I do not remember you."

He laughed. "You would not have known me then as I look today. I had hair and both eyes then. I was young and naive. I was a visiting noble from Liangzhu, there to pay my respects to the goddess on behalf of my king, only to discover that there were two of them. I . . ." He faltered, then soldiered on. "I fell in love with your Asteria during my visit. I believed she was not completely immune to my affections, but . . ." He bowed his head sadly. "I was mistaken, for she loved Aranth, a merchant's son, though he had no titles or rank to his name. I was told that the rites were conducted to restore Aeon's beauty. But I did not know then that it would involve sacrifice. By the time I learned that Asteria was in peril, it was already too late. If I had known there were other ways . . . I'd like to believe that I would have done something. I *know* I would have."

"Was Aeon dying, even then?" I asked.

"The people prospered and flourished, but at the height of their wealth they became too careless with nature's bounties. They neglected the soil and the waters, contaminated them with their waste and their leavings. The rot would increase. Crops would begin to die. The ritual rejuvenated Aeon and cleansed the world once more, so we could prosper and flourish and repeat the process all over again. Most of us thought it was simply the natural way of things."

"We could have prevented this?" This was from Lisette. "There was another way to save Aeon without pissing off the goddesses? And all it required was *not* to live to excess?" She turned on Salla. "You were old enough to remember. *You* were one of the Devoted. Why didn't you do anything?"

"Because I," the older woman said, "like most everyone else back then, never realized that the worst could happen, until it happened."

"They lied to us," Ilenka muttered. "We trusted them with our lives, and they *lied*."

I only nodded. This explained the Devoted's entitlement, the stories Haidee told of the excess within the Golden City. Old habits died hard. "Was there any truth to what Mother said about medicines to be found in Brighthenge?"

Mother Salla frowned. "There was talk of a secret within the temple where one could achieve immortality—which always seemed odd to me, as not even Inanna was supposed to be eternal. Perhaps Asteria referred to those rumors."

"I should have known that it would take more than a simple ritual to heal Aeon," Sonfei said. "I knew about those endless loops of prosperity and ruin. If I had been smarter then, perhaps I could have realized that there was something more sinister behind the rites, that it was too good to be true. . . ."

Mother Salla patted his hand. "It is easy to believe we could have done better after hindsight. Let us do what we can now."

Together, Sonfei and Mother Salla went through Haidee's notes and drawings while the other clan leaders discussed how best to make and distribute copies.

"You have a good eye, Lady Haidee," Sonfei said. "The sketch of Brighthenge—this is how I remember it. Asteria bade me to wait here." He pointed at a spot inside the shrine just by the entrance.

"And I waited here, with my colleagues among the Devoted." Mother Salla's finger rested in the middle of the temple, near the large plaque dedicated to Inanna that adorned most of one wall. "I was not permitted access to the inner chambers."

"And where are these inner chambers?" Lan asked.

"Here." Mother Salla's finger moved again, tapping at the innermost wall farthest from the entryway. "Asteria, Namu, and Devika entered a small enclosure here. It leads into the heart of the chasm. Jesmyn and another Devoted from Namu's sect followed them in."

I frowned, trying to remember. "I never saw that wall.

There was too much debris. I didn't think there was anything else behind it."

"It all happened so quickly." Mother Salla closed her eyes. "I knew the instant the ritual failed. The mountain behind the shrine was split into two from the force of the patterns. A fissure formed on the ground, widening to become the Great Abyss. Had I been standing closer, I would have fallen—as many of my fellow Devoted did." Pain streaked across her creased face. "But then there was a flash of bright light—and I found myself in the desert, alone."

"I remember much the same," Sonfei said. "When the ground first cracked open, I rushed to the inner temple, wanting to rescue Asteria, but it had been caved in. So I ran outside, intending to circle to the back of the shrine—only to find myself staring into the yawning Abyss, which was growing by the second. I could do nothing but retreat. I thought she was already lost. There was no bright light for me. We fled the place on foot."

"Was Latona or my father there?" I asked intently.

"Both," Sonfei said, his face falling.

"They dashed past us right after the ceremony began, into the inner chamber before we could stop them," Mother Salla said. "The Breaking happened a few minutes after that."

I looked up to ask another question, and froze.

The tent disappeared. Everyone around me was gone.

I was back at the Great Abyss, staring wordlessly as an army of galla, twice as many as the last one we fought, filled the landscape from horizon to horizon. They were streaming out of the chasm, scuttling out into the wildlands. They were coming for us, I thought, panicking, even as the Inanna-demoness, reconstituted and showing no signs of the damage we had wrought upon it the day before, lifted its head out from the Abyss and looked at me—

Lan caught me before I collapsed. "Odessa?" She paused in astonishment when I began to cry.

"Another glimpse of the future," I choked, my vision still fresh. "They're coming. They'll come tomorrow, and the day after that, and the day after that."

They would come for her, and they would come for us, I knew that now. Every day of the rest of our lives they would come, until we were dead, or until Aeon was destroyed—or until I gave Lan up.

And I was never giving Lan up.

I thought I had no tears left to give today, but the tears came all the same.

Chapter Twelve
HAIDEE AND THE AGES OF AEON

———————— ☼ ————————

"YOU'RE BEING RIDICULOUS," LAN GROWLED. We were all in the hut assigned to Odessa; away from prying eyes, my twin tended to be a lot more expressive, more demanding about what she wanted than when we had a larger audience. Lan had refused a place of her own and slept outside Odessa's hut instead, despite Odessa's growing unsubtle attempts to woo her inside.

Odessa placed her hands on her hips and tried to look intimidating. "I'm being cautious. If there's any chance that the demoness can re-form and return here it would be best to keep an eye on you. If galla are going to attack just as I fear, I'm at least going to make sure that you're safe."

"I can take care of myself!"

"Really? Against a fifty-foot shadow? One that took two whole armies to bring down the last time?"

The Catseye glared. My sister glared right back.

"All right," Lan allowed, leaning back. "But I don't need bodyguards looking after me. In case you'd forgotten, *I'm* the bodyguard. What are you smiling about?"

It was good to see a grin on Odessa's face; I knew the last few days had been particularly exhausting for her, and her latest vision hadn't helped any of our nerves, least of all hers. "Now do you see why I always balked at being kept inside the Spire?"

Lan sighed, long and loudly, then raised her voice. "I'm not going anywhere. I will allow a total of two"—she paused to glare past the entrance of the hut to where several clan members were waiting to guard her—"people to keep watch by my side, and that's going to be Noelle and Arjun. Put the rest to better use around camp."

The men and women standing outside heard her. They paused, looking uncertainly at each other, and then back at Arjun for confirmation.

"Arjun has other duties," Odessa pointed out.

"I don't mind," he said easily. It was his turn to receive a glare from my sister, which he ignored. "You can all leave for now," he called out to the others. "Tell Kadmos to relieve the patrols every three hours instead of four. We'll need everyone well rested once Their Holinesses decide what to do next."

"Arjun!" But the men were already retreating, obeying his instructions. The scowl on Odessa's face grew more pronounced, along with the smile on Lan's. "Thanks, Arjun," the Catseye said.

"I'd balk too, if I were in your place. And if you'd been in mine, you would've gotten me out too, right?"

"In a heartbeat."

The two lummoxes grinned at each other. I rolled my eyes.

"You're crankier than normal," Odessa complained. "What were you doing with the other Liangzhu last night?"

"Nothing." A pause. "They drank," Lan admitted. "I had a little too, to pacify them. Even in the sunlands, they've managed to find a way to distill alcohol."

"*The sunlands* sounds a lot more romantic than things actually are," I murmured.

"Alcohol, you say?" Arjun looked amused.

"Strong enough to punch through a devil whale. Good, though."

"I meant what I said," Odessa swore. "I'm not letting you out of my sight."

"Of course," Lan said, oddly compliant.

"I'll protect you."

"I know you will."

"Are you patronizing me?"

"Never." Lan bent forward and kissed her. Odessa let out a muffled squeak, but showed no signs of pushing her away or breaking it off.

"I think we should leave them alone," Arjun suggested. There was a decidedly hungry edge to their kiss, like it had been simmering for days and was just about ready to bubble over.

"We're going," I said, like either were even listening, and Arjun and I snuck out as quietly as we could.

The clan soldiers were still milling about outside, probably waiting for Arjun to change his mind. I looked at them, and felt a flash of anger at Lan's situation. It wasn't fair that she had to fear for her life like this. It wasn't fair for us, either. Why did we have to deal with something we'd had no part in? I didn't want to have to clean up Mother's messes. Odessa shouldn't have to deal with *her* mother's, either. And yet, here we were.

But even as I asked the question I knew what the answer was. We were the last line of defense. If we failed, the whole world was doomed.

It wasn't supposed to be fair. Wishing for fairness didn't give us leave to abandon our duties.

I was the goddess meant to be sacrificed. I had forced myself not to dwell on that, though knowing the demoness could leave the Abyss and hunt us made me even more fearful of what was to come. I didn't want to think about my death. The best way to deal with it was to figure out a loophole, not allow myself to be frightened.

And Lan was supposed to be sacrificed, too. Generations of goddesses before us had to deal with the exact same thing. But if there was a way to break the cycle, we would find it.

"Is it wise to leave them?" I asked. "They're obviously under a lot of stress, more than anyone else here. They're the ones stranded thousands of miles from their home." A home that they no longer had.

The guilt returned.

"People deal in different ways," Arjun said, his own voice odd. "They haven't had much chance to be alone since arriving. They need something familiar to hold on to."

We hadn't had much chance to be alone since arriving here, either. I remembered our time at the abandoned village close to Brighthenge, the way we'd been all over each other like we were afraid of getting caught, like our time was limited. Neither of us had known how much things were going to change, that privacy would not be a priority. He'd been very good at not pushing it, at not letting us be selfish.

Still. He *had* promised. And I was under a lot of stress, too. Thinking about him was always a nice distraction, and I seized on the opportunity.

"You told me there were other ways to be alone out here." I was trying to sound seductive. Or at the very least, flirty. Or was I coming off as pushy instead? Was this how you were supposed to woo a lover? I had no idea what I was doing.

I must have done part of it right, because Arjun's breath caught, and the look he shot my way was anything but innocent. I was reminded immediately of his expression back at the spring, at his harsh, raspy groan of relief when I'd tried to massage the stump of his arm. Of the house where we'd taken shelter, of the canopy he'd stretched over the makeshift bed and the things we'd done there.

"Are you sure?" How could anyone's voice go that impossibly deep? I could feel its timbre all the way down my back. "Because I know a place."

"Very sure," I whispered, my heart a constant hammering against the anvil of my chest, and watched his eyes darken.

Somebody yelled his name, and then Lan's. Arjun sighed, and the moment was gone. "What is it now?" he muttered. I could already see Lan stepping out, looking just as disgruntled as he was.

Some of the Fennec and Gila nomads were dragging two boys over toward us. Both were already bound in rope; one wasn't putting up much of a fight, allowing himself to be led, and the other wasn't struggling to get free so much as he was protesting the situation. "You can't treat me like this!" he sputtered. "Unhand me this instant! I'm under the protection of Her Holiness, the goddess Latona!"

That was the wrong thing to say when surrounded by men and women that same goddess had declared war on, so it was fortunate that I recognized him quickly. "Let him go!"

Arjun groaned again—this time out of exasperation.

Lord Vanya brushed the dirt off his trousers—a futile effort, since we were all but surrounded by dirt—and straightened his coat, though the effect was marred by the fact that he was also sweating heavily. He had gone out into the desert dressed like he was attending a debutante ball, all fitted up in heavy wool and shiny leather. In another hour the sun would have baked all the water out of his body, and he would have perished of thirst.

"Get him something to drink," I commanded. One of the men looked dubious, like they thought it would be wasted on him, but another sharp look from Arjun sent him moving.

"Ah, the city lordling with the degenerate father," Lisette

greeted sweetly, toying with her Howler. "Why aren't we shooting him yet?"

"You can't!" Vanya squawked. "I'm demanding sanctuary!"

"You can't *demand* sanctuary, you buffoon."

"Lisette," I interrupted. "Please."

The girl scowled. "First your sister defends the cannibals. Now you're welcoming entitled Golden City nobles into camp. These aren't the reinforcements we had in mind."

"Lisette," Arjun said.

She sighed noisily, and put away her gun.

The other boy smiled sheepishly back at me as a Fennec clan member took off his cap, and I realized she wasn't a boy at all, but Charley.

"What are you doing here?" I exclaimed, quickly untying her hands before sweeping her up in a hug.

"Escorting the lordling across the desert—and hoping we'd find you soon, because he has not shut up for one second since leaving the city."

"I had to," Vanya said, coughing through parched lips. "I had to find Her Holiness."

"Depends on why you're looking for her," Arjun scowled. "You rejected her offer to come with us."

"I changed my mind." One of the clan members arrived with a cup of water, and the boy wasted no time gulping the liquid down gratefully. "I had to come here. Miss Charley can vouch for me."

"I wouldn't *vouch*, per se," the girl demurred. "But he's got something important that I think Her Holiness ought to know."

"That's for me to decide." Still, I was impressed. As clever and as witty as Vanya had been, and as much as I did like his company in the short time I'd known him, I knew how much he, like every other noble in the Golden City, enjoyed their creature comforts. They didn't think about the strain on resources it caused for bathtubs to be installed at the Citadel for their pleasure, for them to demand that cool water be made available at all times. They didn't give much thought to those who had to go without. "Lord Vanya, it's a long journey from Mother's palace just to find me. You made it clear that you weren't interested in going against her, or your father."

"I had to. I've only just realized—" He paused to gape at Odessa, who'd emerged from her tent and come trotting toward us, her face awash with curiosity. Vanya's room back at Latona's Citadel had been shrouded in darkness, his nerves further aggravated by the fearful storm and tested to their limits by his father's sneering contempt. It was only now, with the sun sharp against my sister's face and no shadows in the way, that he finally saw her clearly.

"You really do look so much like her," he choked out.

"I'm her twin," Odessa reminded him gently. I suppose she'd had to deal with nobles like him in the past, too. "We're supposed to look like each other."

"You killed one of Father's soldiers."

Lan growled, but Odessa remained calm. "I felt like I didn't have much choice."

"Her Holiness Latona said you were dead."

"Her Holiness Latona doesn't know everything that happens in Aeon."

"Why are you really here, Vanya?" I demanded.

"I found it!" As soon as his hands were freed, Vanya dug into his coat and produced a book that had clearly seen better days; its pages were frayed and torn along the edges, and there had been attempts to repair the cracked cover, though these were only partially successful. The spine had been reinforced with thick, solid strings stitched into the leather, clearly newer than the book they held together—the work of some craftsman experienced at preservation.

"*The Ages of Aeon*," Vanya said hoarsely. "I brought it for you."

I stared at him.

"It's why I brought him here," Charley added helpfully. "Jes wasn't sure about him but Rodge agreed with me, and Yeong-ho we couldn't tell because he would be honor-bound to tell Her Holiness Latona if he'd known, like he told you. I thought that if Lady Haidee risked getting caught in the city to look for it, that it had to be more important than anything."

"Thank you, Charley," I said, hope blossoming in my chest. "Vanya, your father said he destroyed the book."

"I knew he was lying the instant he said it. Father would never destroy something he thinks he can use as leverage. And I—" He gulped. "Her Holiness Latona doesn't know he has it, either. I'm sure of that, too. That made me all the more convinced it wasn't just a book." He held it up before him like a shield. "I can't go back to the Golden City. Father would never forgive me. I want to claim sanctuary in exchange for this. I want you to swear it, that you'll protect me."

"Why help us now?" Arjun asked bluntly. "You were so keen on doing your best not to incur your father's wrath, even when he thought you were worthless."

"Arjun!" I admonished.

"No, he's right," Vanya said, looking like it killed him to admit that. "I've never gone against Father's wishes in the past. But I haven't done much to curry his favor either, especially in light of my other brothers—they've led prestigious careers more to his liking. It's why he'd been grooming me to be Her Holiness's consort. I would become his direct conduit to Haidee and ruling the Golden City, a position even more illustrious than being part of Latona's trusted counsel. But I'm taking a stand now. I have to."

"You're still not being entirely truthful," Arjun accused. "If you want to help as much as you say you do, then you'll stop keeping anything from us. How do we know you're not setting us up for a future ambush?"

Vanya stood straighter, spots of color on his cheeks. He pointed to Arjun. "I came here because of you."

"What? Me?"

"You told me that I didn't deserve Haidee. That I was always going to choose my father over her. But I don't want to. I want to be worthy of her, too." Vanya straightened his shoulders.

"And it's more than that. I know Haidee wants to save Aeon, and I do, too. It just took me longer to realize what I had to do. You can't—you had no *right* to mock me for not making the right decision after you waylaid me in my own rooms and assaulted my father's men, without giving me any time to think things through. I spent the whole of yesterday agonizing over why I should remain loyal to him if he's keeping everyone else from the truth."

"And how do you know what he's hiding?" Lan inquired.

"Because I've actually read *The Ages of Aeon*. Of all the books he's accumulated over the years, that was the only one I was forbidden to look at, which made me even more determined to read it. But I've always treated it as fiction. I never thought it could have talked about real events."

"If the book is as important as your father thinks it is, then what's to say that they aren't going to come after it—and you—now?"

"Because the goddess Asteria has been delaying our forces, Lady Lan," Charley chirped gleefully.

"What?" Odessa cried. "What has Mother been doing?"

"Disabling our jeeps and caravans, to start. They hobbled all the rigs under the cover of another storm."

"She's whittling down every advantage Latona has by delaying their next confrontation," Lan said grimly. "Asteria has the smaller army, so she wants to choose the right moment to face her. Ensure an even fight."

I shared a worried glance with my sister. Neither of us

wanted another battle between them. "Or maybe she doesn't want to confront Latona at all," Odessa said.

"I . . ." Vanya faltered. "Is the woman out in the desert really Asteria? Latona's twin? She destroyed the world and caused the Breaking, didn't she? They said she was dead."

"I wish," Lisette muttered. Something in the desert had caught her attention, because she had taken out her spyglass and was raising it to her eye.

"They both broke Aeon," I found myself saying. "I know the stories Mother spun to convince you that she was right and Asteria was at fault, but I assure you they're equally to blame. And Odessa and I are determined to fix their mistakes."

Vanya stared, not quite ready to believe me just yet, though I could see he was desperately trying to. My heart went out to him. He'd turned against his father for the first time in his life, committed himself to an undertaking that would ruin everything he'd built his life to achieve, and all for principle. He'd told me once that as my consort, he would trust me to rule the Golden City, would defer to me in matters he had little knowledge of. He'd spoken true.

I wasn't interested in pursuing a relationship with him, but I didn't want to reject his affections in front of everyone. He deserved to hear that in private. "Vanya, do you recall anything else that mentions a ritual? Or anything that refers to Inanna by name?"

"Yes." He riffled through the pages. "I've noted a few passages of that sort before. Here is one:

"Suffer the truth within the quiet temple.
Take the stone, and venture down into the kingdom
to face Ereshkigal's discontent.
Test your worth; offer
to her, Inanna's immortality.
She will grieve endlessly for the sister
who slumbers in the house of the dead,
but her tears will save us all.

"And until the Gates of Death and Life intertwine,
Love continues to be the toll.
And she will pay with a half-life.
She will pay."

"Wait!" I scrambled to my feet and practically ran to my tent, where I kept all my notes on Brighthenge. "That last part was written on one of the plaques at Brighthenge," I said triumphantly when I returned, flipping the pages until I'd found what I needed. "On the monument that talks about Odessa and me. But everything before the line 'Test your worth' wasn't written there. Neither was 'And she will pay with a half-life.' So either a transcriber made a mistake in your book, or . . ."

"Or," Odessa finished for me, "it was deliberately omitted at Brighthenge."

Vanya held out *The Ages of Aeon* to me. I took it, cradled it protectively in my hands. "I'll read everything," I swore. "And I'll figure it out even if it takes me the whole dayspan." I stepped forward and kissed Vanya chastely on the cheek. Arjun made a grumpy little sound, but I didn't care. "Thank you. You risked everything to come here. You will always have my friendship for that."

Vanya's smile wobbled at the last sentence. "I only want what's best for you, milady. My admiration for you is—"

"You could have sent Miss Charley over with the book," Lisette interrupted, still squinting through the glass. "What use do we have for a spoiled lordling out here?"

Vanya glared. "I've been trained with the use of guns, and I'm a good shot with a Howler myself."

"There's a huge difference between an actual moving target and the little clay pigeons you amuse yourself with in your father's backyard."

"I don't know how good a shot he is, but he definitely can't go back to the city." Charley skipped toward the rig they'd driven in on and grabbed at the tarp that was covering the back seat. "Even if Lord Arrenley forgave him for stealing the book, I don't think he'd forgive his son for all the weapons he stole—"

"Borrowed," Vanya gasped.

"Stole from him," Charley insisted. "That's how I knew he was serious about coming here."

Arjun harrumphed. "I don't think a few trinkets he brought along are going to change any—"

Charley whipped the covers off with a flourish. Sunlight gleamed on several dozen top-of-the-line Howlers, sleek and oiled and ready for combat.

"Hell," Arjun rasped, mouth agape.

"There's a chance we might be needing them soon," Lisette said, lowering her spyglass. "I found something."

"The galla?" I asked, already feeling sick.

"Only marginally better." Lisette pointed. I saw a dark figure standing in the distance, with dark blue robes and a heavy hood that obscured its features. I heard Arjun draw in a sharp breath, his hands forming fists.

"There's what looks to be a mirage hovering just outside our territory," the Addax clan mistress said, "and I don't think it's here to say hello."

Chapter Thirteen
ARJUN AND THE MIRAGES

I WAS TWELVE YEARS OLD when I saw my first mirage. Millie had come barging into the cave fresh from patrol, white-knuckled and pale, yelling about how she'd seen one of the desert ghosts prowling the sands and it hadn't seen *her* but *she* had most definitely seen it and she'd finally understood what it felt like to be cold for the first time in its presence and basically she wouldn't shut up about it.

Naturally, being twelve—only two years since I'd been deprived of a hand and still feeling pissed over the loss—I demanded to see it for myself, as if weird desert phantasms couldn't technically exist until I'd witnessed them with my own eyes. I was also irrationally put out at Millie for having seen something I hadn't yet, given how smug she was about it.

Mother Salla had decided to turn it into a learning experience for the rest of us because she knew we were gonna sneak out and see the mirage for ourselves, her foresight being one of the reasons she was our leader.

As it was, our first mirage sighting was almost our last, because Kadmos panicked and tried to shoot at it when it drew too close. He was punished with scrubbing all the sand out from our rig after the mirage sent an unexpected sandstorm our way. We were lucky. We'd heard stories from other clans about people losing their lives inside one of those mirage-powered hurricanes.

But willfully seeking out something that could potentially kill you because of misguided curiosity was a personality flaw of mine.

This time it was the mirage who'd come to our camp. It stood several hundred paces away. From my vantage point, it was nothing more than a black spot in the distance—too far away to see what it was doing there.

But I knew it was watching me.

I'd already spent hours trying to ignore it. I continued to patrol territory. I stood guard over more meetings where Mother Salla and the other clan leaders argued about strategy, about what to do should either Latona or Asteria attack us. Odessa's prediction that the galla would be coming again had us all on edge, worrying about when and where they would strike. Clan meetings had started devolving into arguments and shouting matches about whether or not Haidee and Odessa could be trusted, whether or not the galla really *were* coming or if this was the goddesses' ploy to keep us dependent on them. After marching angrily out of one meeting I decided I'd rather devote my energies to defending camp.

The number of patrols in the desert now were thrice what we would normally send out. Maybe people were just as frustrated at the clan leaders as I was. Or maybe they believed Odessa anyway, and were simply waiting for the hammer to fall. People snapped at each other for no reason; unexpected fistfights broke out.

I tried to cope by scouting out the borders of the Golden City, watching for any hostilities breaking out between the goddesses. I stood over dunes for hours at a time, keeping watch.

But even when I couldn't see it, I *knew* the mirage was there. Waiting.

"Would you like someone to try again?" Lan asked tentatively. Now that Haidee and Odessa were busy seeing to the camp defenses, were too busy trying to prove to some of the still-wary clans that they weren't the enemy, Lan and I had been spending more time together on guard duty. I liked her. She was a practical, no-nonsense woman, as well as a damn good fighter and healer. She was devoted to Odessa, which meant that, by extension, she was also looking out for Haidee. I suspected she was doing the same for me. That was fine, since I'd been returning the favor.

"That's a nice offer, but we both know it's a futile one." Sonfei and his people had made an attempt to approach the apparitions with their rigs; the mirage had simply flickered out of view, reappearing only after they'd left, to resume its silent scrutiny of me.

We'd spotted a few more of the specters shortly after we'd returned from the Golden City, drifting along the boundaries of neutral ground, but never straying too close. The mirage that had sent us on a chase halfway around the world, Jesmyn, had evaded us in almost exactly the same way.

When the specters appeared near camp the first few times they drove many people into a panic under the mistaken belief they were galla. It took several tense minutes to convince the clans these weren't the enemy, but the revenants' presence wasn't doing us any favors. We were tense enough as it is.

The mirage lingering near camp right now had red piping on its hood. Mother Salla herself had told me that only Firesmokers wore those colors.

I didn't want it here. I was supposed to be watching out for galla like everyone else was doing, not getting distracted by my mother's ghost.

And that was what pissed me off the most. *You almost single-handedly destroyed Aeon because killing a goddess was easier than—I don't know, planting some fucking trees to keep the world from going to shit, maybe, and now you're looking at me like all this is my fault?*

"You do know that it wants to talk to you, right?"

I scowled into the sand. "You don't seem worried that there's a ghost haunting us."

"None of us think it's here to harm anyone. It's not like there are monsters out there explicitly singling *you* out to hunt, so you should be safe." Lan couldn't say the same for herself, but her smile was wry, a shade self-deprecating. "Gallows humor,"

Mother Salla had called it. Joking about death to ease the fear of it. She looked down at the flask she was holding and took a sip, making a face.

"What's in that?"

"The Liangzhu's booze. Bairen said it would help ease my nerves. You stayed with them before, she said." She lifted the container back up to her lips. "Ever tried it?"

"They distill it from deathworm piss, so I've never had the urge to," I said, and watched her spit out a mouthful, choking and gasping. I thumped helpfully at her back until she stopped.

"Ughhh."

"Sorry. Thought you might want to know."

"Would have preferred to have known that earlier, but thanks." She glowered at me. "And you don't need to play bodyguard for me, either."

"Sure." The rest of clan Oryx was never far from the Catseye; my brothers and sisters kept their distance, knowing Lan's reluctance, but we were just as stubborn as she was.

"You shouldn't have to. I can take care of myself."

"Can't hurt to have backup. Bring it up with Odessa."

"You talked to Odessa?"

"I figured you'd try to dissuade us and say it wasn't worth it. So if you're going to lodge a protest, I'd suggest bringing that up with her, not me."

She frowned at me. I wasn't even bothering to hide my grin. "I thought you said you would bail me out, make sure nobody's following me around."

"In your place now, I'd be crapping my pants every other

hour. We haven't known each other that long, Lan, but did you seriously think we'd abandon you at this point? Haidee would kick my ass."

"You can't possibly—I knew the risks going in, but I can't allow any of you to bet your lives on this."

"This is all on a volunteer basis. We've all fought worse odds before."

"But not for me!" Lan's voice rose in a panic, the usually composed Catseye more distraught than even I thought she'd be. "I don't want anyone else in danger just because I was—I was—"

It was Noelle who broke in, gently laying a hand on Lan's arm in comfort. "You know you're not responsible for what anyone else chooses to do. Remember what Sumiko said?"

Lan had started breathing easier before the steward had even finished. "To focus on the choices I make instead of what others decide. But . . ." She exhaled. "All right. But don't do anything rash."

"When have I ever?" I asked, pretending to look hurt, and was relieved when she finally smiled.

"I'm going to take a leak, and then check on Odessa. Do I need company even for that?"

"Nope. Leak away."

"Hope I didn't insult her," I murmured to Noelle once the Catseye had left. "I figured she wouldn't approve, but she sounded odd. . . ."

"She isn't used to being fought for, Sir Arjun," the girl said sadly. "She still bears some guilt over her rangers."

"Guilt over . . . oh." I wanted to kick myself. Of course. Hadn't she mentioned that she'd lost her whole team to the galla, and had been the only one to make it out alive? "I didn't mean to make it sound like she—"

"She understands, but that doesn't make it any easier to process."

"What do you plan to do about her?" Haidee asked, coming up behind Noelle and nodding at the mirage out in the desert.

"Nothing. We've got galla to worry about. She's not worth another thought."

She looked worried. "Arjun. I know I'm the last person to rise to her defense, but . . . she's still your mother, after all. Maybe she's here to help us? She did the last time."

"She chose her duties over me when she was alive. Don't think that's gonna change now that she's dead."

"But she could. She might tell us something important."

"Nothing new with the book?"

"A few more passages matched those at Brighthenge. Nothing else has jumped out at me so far yet. Vanya was right. I could have easily dismissed the book as nothing more than a collection of rambling poetry. None of the poems make much sense on their own. I need some rest and fresh air to clear my head. Are you going to stare at her forever?"

I stood up, aimed my Howler. The shot wasn't as loud or as strong as the ones I've fired before, but it packed a powerful enough statement. The sand beside the mirage exploded, dirt and grit raining down, but still the damn ghost refused to budge.

"What are you doing?" Haidee gasped.

"Maybe you're right. Maybe it's about time I did something about her. Maybe I've got a few questions of my own." I hadn't told her what Jesmyn had said to me, either. Not yet. "I'll chase it in a beat-up rig again if it means getting something out of it."

"Tamera might not appreciate us leaving our posts," Noelle pointed out.

"We're not leaving our posts, we're relocating. The mirage is lingering by that big ridge half a mile out that'll give us a better view."

"Well, we won't be using any beat-up rigs to get there," the goddess said cheerfully.

"We?"

"I'm coming with you." She glared at me. "No complaining."

"So will I," Noelle said.

I raised an eyebrow.

The steward smiled and shrugged. "I am occasionally useful."

"I bet," I conceded, remembering the excellent javelin throw she'd made against the Hellmakers.

"Besides, if it tries to run away, I've come prepared," Haidee continued. "I made some small changes to one of the Oryx's jeeps yesterday."

The "small changes" Haidee referred to were heavy steel plates affixed to the front of one of the rigs to serve as either a heavy shield or a battering ram depending on the situation. "Small changes" were heavy-duty tires ringed with the same

Earth-armor patterns used to coat our clothes with, for the wheels to gain better traction against the sand and improve their average speed. "Small changes" were higher-powered engines that absorbed water from the air to keep it from overheating.

They were gorgeous.

"And you finished all this in *one* day?"

"I had help." Haidee sounded defensive, as if I was gonna yell at her for making more modifications. "I've got Charley here now. And Imogen and Millie are both great mechanika—they knew how to work to the specifications I had in mind. Lady Noelle made for a rather excellent assistant, too—though she says they don't use many jeeps in Aranth because it's too dangerous to venture out of the city. Lan and her rangers used a couple when they were scouting, but they're not as—"

"I'm not mad," I said. "I'm the opposite of mad. In fact, I wanna come over there and kiss you before you get too technical again."

Haidee turned red, cast an agonized gaze at the other clan members around, who were most avidly listening in. "I . . . I would like that, but there are people—"

I kissed her, cutting her off short, because when you live in a cave with over a dozen people, privacy and embarrassment lose a lot of value. I ignored the giggles and the whoops of encouragement, but Haidee was pure scarlet by the time we ended it. "I—I'm going to go look over the engines one last time," she stammered, and practically fled.

"You weren't that bold back when we were going out," Lisette drawled once Haidee was out of sight, looking amused.

"I'm not sure 'going out' is the aptest way to describe our relationship."

She nodded. "True. I've never really felt like I wanted to tie myself down to anyone. I don't know if I should envy you for finding someone."

"You, regretting something? Doesn't sound like you at all."

Her brows knitted. "I'm not regretting. Just wondering about the what-ifs." She grinned. "I'd say you got the better deal in your arrangement. She seems a lot more useful than you, objectively speaking." She looked over at Noelle. "Would you like to commiserate my lack of companionship with me?" she asked flirtatiously.

"I'm afraid I have little interest in romance or sex myself," the steward replied apologetically.

Lisette sighed. "Why are all the pretty ones always unavailable?"

When they heard what we were planning, Kadmos and Faraji offered to tag along, too. So did Sonfei. "Have you milked any more deathworms?" the man asked cheerily, clambering into the back seat.

"Thankfully not." Haidee was still doing some last-minute checks underneath the rig's hood.

"A pity. That blue fire of yours would be attracting all such creatures for miles, I am sure. Ah, but if the rains keep up, perhaps it will not be necessary. Though not even the rains can compare to the pure taste of a deathworm's stomach-water."

"Deathworms?" Lisette had been initially intrigued, and then more appalled the closer Sonfei got to finishing his sentence.

"It's a long story," I said shortly.

Another giggle rose from Haidee, which she quickly stifled.

It was a short ride, but we saw plenty of new phenomena out in the desert. We crossed beneath a cluster of dark clouds not far from camp. It was a strange sensation to ride through that quick spurt of rain and emerge on the other side of it with the sun just as hot as ever. Noelle wordlessly passed out clean rags for us to wipe with. She had been some kind of domestic back in Aranth, I remembered, though I wasn't really sure what that meant. A quick glance at the sky revealed an odd ring circling around the sun that seemed to be made of light—similar to the rings around a person's irises that proved they could channel incanta. "They feel like they're made of ice patterns," Haidee said, squinting and no doubt already planning how to study it later. "How curious."

There were other mirages littering the area. Some drifted along with our rig for a while, never moving closer, only to shy away and disappear behind a sand knoll. Others stood still and watched us pass.

"Do we try to approach them, too?" Haidee asked.

I shook my head. Only one mirage could give me what I wanted.

"Do you really want to know about the role your mother played in all this?"

"You wanted to know about what *your* mother had done, right?"

A pause. A sigh. "Yes. But you shouldn't have to learn of it this way."

"She knew everything. She's guilty of this whole mess. She's part of a past we need to know more about." I took a deep breath and stared straight ahead. "Would I have been a Devoted, you think?"

"What?"

"If the Breaking never happened. I was the son of a Devoted and had a fire-gate, so it stands to reason I would have followed her path. Would I have caught your eye if I was an ass-kissing subordinate instead of a desert nomad?"

"There's no reality that I can comprehend where you're either an ass-kisser or a subordinate."

I had to grin. "Wouldn't have minded, you know. Being a Devoted. If it meant I was still protecting you somehow."

A warm glow lit her face.

Another mirage materialized out of thin air, tailed us for a few minutes, then winked out of sight again.

"It gives me the frights, just looking at them," Sonfei said with a shudder.

"You never encountered them where you and the Liangzhu tribe lived?" Lisette asked him.

"No. For the longest time we thought we were the only ones who had survived the Breaking, and saw no others for years."

I shrugged. "Must be something here in the desert bringing them to life. Some of the ones that showed up during your mothers' fight were resurrected by Odessa. Do you really think she's to be trusted?"

"Arjun!"

"I know you're attached to your sister, and I like her. But you can understand why I'm asking." Watching the cannibals choke in midair had been disquieting. She'd killed a man by sending lightning down from the sky. What would stop her from doing the same to us if she lost control? "No offense to your liege, Lady Noelle."

"None taken," Noelle said, troubled. "And I doubt she would, either. But I wish I had the answers for you, milord. I do know that Lady Lan is a calming influence on her. She has shaken off corruption many times solely for the Catseye's sake."

"So what you're saying is that none of us should piss Lan off."

"I wouldn't need a galla's influence to be seriously pissed off if someone harmed you," Haidee said.

I laughed. "That's the best compliment you've ever given me."

"You have every right to be worried. But I trust her. And she has me now, too."

I stepped on the brakes, the rig skidding to a halt in the sand.

The mirage—my *mother*—hadn't tried to run. She hadn't moved at all. She was only a hundred or so feet away, observing us underneath that red-marked hood.

Sonfei muttered a series of epithets. For someone who lived in an isolated tribe across the Sand Sea, his words were startlingly creative.

"Are we going nearer?" Lisette asked. "Because if you say we are, I would like to make a protest."

"None of *you* are." I got out of the jeep.

"What are you doing?" Haidee protested.

"Stay here with the others. Don't argue with me."

Haidee scowled at me, but Noelle spoke up. "He has a good point, Your Holiness. If anything happens, you'll be in a better position to defend him from here."

"If *anything* happens, I'm going to run over that mirage myself," Haidee snapped.

I leaned over and kissed her. "Thank you."

"You'll still need someone with you," Kadmos argued.

I thought about that. "You and Faraji. Stay twenty feet away from me at all times. I don't think it's going to attack me, but I can't promise the same for either of you."

"What exactly are you going to do, brother?" Faraji asked.

"Just having a friendly mother-son talk, Faraj. It's been a long time coming." I began my trek toward the figure, both Faraji and Kadmos falling into step behind me.

My eyes never left the Firesmoker mirage. Its features were still obscured by its cowl, just like the rest of its undead brethren.

Horrifyingly enough, Jesmyn had no head when she approached me at the edges of the Sand Sea. What was I going to find underneath my mother's cloak?

I stopped, barely two feet away.

"Mother?"

The mirage was silent, like it couldn't even bother to acknowledge the son it had abandoned. That ticked me off.

"You knew, damn you. You hid the truth from Latona and

Asteria. You helped cause all this."

Still nothing, but I fancied some of the other specters wandering nearby stirred at the mention of the goddesses' names.

"You deliberately played them against each other. You and every Devoted before you had been doing that for generations. You were supposed to be protecting them, not killing them!" I didn't know I was yelling until I was, letting go of all the pent-up emotion I'd been keeping inside since learning she'd had a hand in the Breaking.

Still it said nothing.

"Mother Salla said you recorded Haidee and Odessa's prophecies. You *know* how to fix Aeon." Taking hold of all my courage, I reached out to grab it by the cloak.

It spun to face me, and I lost all ability to move. There was darkness behind its cowl, nothing to tell me that it even had a face.

If any other gods or goddesses were still out there listening, *Please oh please oh fucking please, don't make me look at my own mother's headless corpse.*

I am sorry, it said, in a voice that I knew only I could hear.

"That's not good enough!" I was still too angry. "Devoted like you killed goddesses for *centuries*! Can you bring them all back with an apology?"

Thankfully, no light could pierce through that hood. This must be what Odessa meant when she described an endless night. **Arjun**. A skeletal hand reached up to linger at the edges of my headwrap. **My Arjun. Cross the circle of dead. The**

stone will light your path. The stone will show you your way.

But first, you must die.

Images coursed through my head, so quick and fleeting that I had no capacity to comprehend any of them until it was over. When I came to, I was flat on my back, gasping up into the empty sky.

The sand was softer than I'd expected it to be, until I realized it was Haidee cradling my head in her lap, her worried pale eyes looking down at me. The relief on her face was apparent when I groaned.

"What happened?" she whispered, pushing a canteen of water against my mouth.

"I don't know just yet." My lips felt dry and cracked, and I drank greedily, gratefully. That done, I took a glance back at the mirage. It continued to regard me detachedly. "I told you to stay behind," I grumbled weakly.

"She did," Noelle said. "Right up until you fell."

"I'm fine. I've just got a splitting headache." With Haidee's help, I eased myself into a sitting position. "They're guarding something."

"I would imagine. I thought we were here to find out what."

"No, I mean they're guarding the location of something."

"Where?" Haidee looked around. "There's nothing else here for miles."

"I saw it. A temple. A smaller one than Brighthenge, but even more ornate. You're going to have to tell Vanya to look up more passages in that damned book. Tell him to look for something about a room, red with the blood of treasures. And a—" I squeezed my eyes shut, trying to remember more. "A stone. The answers to life and death that lie inside a stone."

"You sound like one of those mysterious prophecies you all go on about," Lisette said.

"Like hell I'm a prophet." But I didn't like where this was going, either.

Haidee had risen to her feet, staring hard at the mirage. Before anyone could stop her, she marched right up to the ghost and deliberately placed her hand on its arm.

"Haidee!" I groaned, scrambling to my feet.

"I don't see any visions. Either she chooses the people she allows to see them, or . . ." She looked right at the darkness hidden under the cowl, unafraid. "Please, if you still have any love for Aeon, I beg you. Tell us what to do to set things right again. Is sacrificing either myself or my sister truly the only way?"

A shudder ran through the mirage. It caused a ripple, spiraling out and affecting the other mirages in turn. I felt the hairs on my neck stand again.

Slowly, the mirage lifted its arm, and I saw to my revulsion that there was no skin left on it, only bone and muscle. It pointed.

I saw it, then. Another blanket of darkness, coming up on the horizon—faster than anything I'd ever seen. I swore, scrambling to my feet. This was the moment we'd been dreading for days, and now that it was here it had still somehow taken us by surprise.

"Move!" I yelled at the others. Lisette was already reaching over to gun the engine as we began to run back toward them. They were too close. So close that I wasn't sure we could get away, even at the speed of a jeep.

I heard a scream behind me. I turned and saw Faraji being thrown to the ground, soon lost from view as the galla swarmed over him.

I was shouting, though even I couldn't make sense of what I was saying. I turned back to help him, saw Kadmos already ahead of me. The Howler was in my hands and I was firing, blue flames consuming the demons wherever they landed.

A howling wind tore through the bulk of the shadows, and many of the galla were tossed away, shredded into ribbons. The swarm retreated, and a second mirage channeled its incanta, the sandstorm it manifested slicing through the creatures even as the mirage itself slowly dissolved into the air, its energies expended.

Kadmos reached Faraji, hoisting our brother over his shoulder. With Haidee pushing the closest of the swarm away with winds and me firing everything I had into the ones that escaped her grasp, we all managed to pile into the rig, Sonfei lifting Faraji into the back seat while Lisette took the wheel, sending us speeding away from the thick of the swarm, wheels throwing up clouds of sand.

Another mirage's sandstorm took out another swath. It was enough to make our escape, but not enough to completely stop the tide. We would still have a fight on our hands when we reached camp.

I turned my head one last time and saw my mother, staring out at us from the distance before the hard winds shielded her from our view.

"Shit," Noelle gasped, as our jeep drew closer to theirs. I'd never heard the steward curse before.

Faraji wasn't breathing. Sonfei was hard at work pushing air into his lungs, but even I knew it was a hopeless cause long before he finally stopped, looking sad. Kadmos was already crying.

"I'm sorry," Haidee whispered. "I'm sorry."

I couldn't answer her. There *was* no answer. All I could do was cradle Faraji's bloodied head in my lap, and weep.

Chapter Fourteen

'LAN AMONG PROPHECIES

—————————— ☾ ——————————

HAIDEE WROTE IN LOOPS AND whorls. Her handwriting was neat and tidy and easy to read, and in many ways it helped highlight the differences between her and Odessa. Her pencraft flowed and skated across the parchment, the roundness of her letters pleasing to the eyes, her *o*'s properly curved.

Noelle told me that she used to berate Odessa—gently— on her penmanship; my goddess's words scratched at the paper like hens, vowels shaped like dying declarations and consonants made of hurried slants. She was too eager to put her thoughts down on paper, Noe had said, and her hand couldn't quite keep up with her thoughts. A minor distinction when taking everything else into account, but it made me feel better. Haidee and Odessa were alike in so many ways, but many other things set them apart, too.

I wasn't one to complain, though. My handwriting was even

more atrocious than Odessa's, much to Noelle's despair. Still, I felt restless. I was used to action, to reacting. Sorting out the words of long-dead people wasn't my forte.

None of this was my forte: the desert, the clans, the changing weather. That was what frustrated me the most. I didn't want to be stuck in some strange new territory with no concrete plan. I didn't know anything about the sunlands. My brief time inside the Golden City hadn't given me anything but a general idea of how their security worked. I hated knowing less than the others, and it didn't matter that they'd spent their whole lives here when I hadn't. It made me feel like I wasn't doing a very good job of protecting Odessa.

Everyone was restless. Many were still distrustful of Odessa and Haidee, and also unnerved by the thought of more galla coming to attack camp. People were carrying their Howlers with them everywhere, ready to defend themselves at a moment's notice. Some had, in their frustration, even pulled their guns on someone else. A few injuries were reported, though thankfully without any casualties, and I decided then that it would be best to keep Odessa out of view. I wasn't very good at research, but staying inside meant she'd be safer.

A loud slap broke through the quiet. Odessa looked dazed; her hand still hovered below her face, a red mark on her cheek from where she'd hit herself. Across the room, Lord Vanya Arrenley looked up from his own papers with startled concern.

"Odessa?" I swallowed the instinct to scold her, to demand

that she stop harming herself, knowing well enough that this wouldn't make things any better. I'd struggled to make peace with my own demons, and it had been uphill work; Odessa had to contend with both that and actual devils.

My touch soothed, as always, though it never healed to the extent I hoped it would. I could feel the patterns knit around the black spot by her heart, felt it shrink just enough for me to relax, but I knew I couldn't remedy the ones that had taken root in her head. "What are you doing?" My knuckle grazed her bruised cheek.

"Sorry," she mumbled. "I know I promised, but . . ."

"Is this the only way to stop those thoughts from intruding? Thinking about your books isn't enough?"

"The books help, but every now and then I require something more . . . robust. It's a far better alternative to just throwing myself into the Abyss."

"Odessa."

"I'm sorry. I don't know why I said that. I'm very tired." There were dark circles under her eyes; they'd grown the last couple of days. Sleeping was hard enough, especially when there was a sun in the sky now. But her exhaustion was more than just the difficulty of adjusting to the cycle of light. Sometimes she would wake up in a cold sweat, grabbing blindly for me, in a panic over dreams she couldn't remember.

"Is Her Holiness all right?" None of us quite knew what to do with Vanya. I had been expecting more demands from the lordling, considering his father's entitlement. But he had made no complaints about his new surroundings, was content to stay in his little corner reading every bit of information we had regarding the Cruel Kingdom, distilling it into summaries he could explain to the clans. Nobody had thought to inform him about Odessa's struggles with the galla; it was a conversation for later, though *later* was vague at this point.

"I'm all right," Odessa insisted. "My apologies, Lord Vanya. If you find anything of note, please let us know."

"I will, Lady—uh, Your Holiness, I mean."

"Do you want to take a break?" I asked her.

"No, I'm almost done with Haidee's notes. I can rest after that."

"Odessa . . ."

"I promise I'm fine." She smiled at me, and that was genuine enough. "Reading actually helps distract me. I wish I'd thought to bring along my other books . . . but this is almost as good. Haidee has been very meticulous with her notes. She's listed every scrap of text we found at Brighthenge, including those strange eulogies for the goddesses and the complete Inanna's Song. Remember this one? *A demoness is what men call a goddess they cannot control.* Those are the same words I saw scribbled on the margins in one of Asteria's books, the volume I brought along with me when I snuck aboard the *Brevity*. Something about the passage has always struck me as odd."

"How so?"

Odessa pointed at the text comprising Inanna's Song, which I'd read countless times by now:

A demoness
Is what they call
A goddess
That men
cannot control

There is no shame
In goddesses falling
Into the Abyss
When they find new purpose
In rising up
As darkness

Praise the women who fly
And fail and succumb to
Night;
Death sustains Inanna,
Who is One and Whole,
Who sacrifices her life into the Below
To save her life in the Above
Who is the sacrificed and the sacrificer,

The demoness and the goddess
Are one and the same
And both shall rule the heavens
And the Cruel Kingdom
As two, but One

As the enduring Above,

So shall the Great Below.

"There are some differences in the wording from the passages we'd seen in Brighthenge, but it's obvious that they're both talking about the same thing. And this stanza jumps out to me in particular: 'There is no shame in goddesses falling into the Abyss where they find new purpose in rising up as darkness.'"

I shuddered. "That's Inanna, then."

"I wish I still had that book. I left it at camp at the foot of the Great Abyss, before I ventured out into the mists with Lorila and Tamerlin—" She stopped, stricken.

I knew why. Lorila and Tamerlin had never made it out of Brighthenge. Janella had murdered them to open the portals; we'd found their remains afterward. With the galla approaching, we'd had no time to give them a proper burial.

I could feel my own palms start to sweat as more faces flashed across my head: Nuala, Wricken, Aoba, Madi, Yarrow . . . so many more people dying without the honor of a funeral.

I forced those thoughts away, with much effort. It was easier to nowadays, after Sumiko's help. Their ghosts were easier to ignore when I could focus on Odessa's troubles instead of mine.

"It could still be there, abandoned for all I know, since the others returned to Aranth, after . . ." Odessa looked down. "After Janella's betrayal."

Janella. It was hard to bite back my anger, the way she'd stood with Asteria against Latona and brazenly inquired after

Odessa like she was never at fault.

"Saffra and Gareth," Odessa said.

"Who?"

"Saffra and Gareth. *Her Majesty's Knight*. Saffra, mourning her rejection by her protector, was told a story by her nanny about a goddess who had constructed a man out of clay; he was a replica of a lover she had once lost. But no matter how much she tried, the patterns couldn't breathe true life into him. He would forever be something not quite human, unresponsive to her affections. Saffra's nanny wanted to convey that, like the clay-man, Gareth could not accept her love, because he was a ruthless man, not quite human himself."

"But they overcame the odds and lived happily ever after, anyway," I guessed.

She smiled, though that turned into a scowl as she glanced down another page. "'Test your worth; offer to her, Inanna's immortality.' It doesn't make sense."

"Very little of this does."

"No, I mean these two lines in particular. Inanna didn't have immortality. That was the whole point. The only constant was death, or so all the legends stated."

"Is Her Holiness a student of literature?" Lord Vanya asked, catching the tail end of the conversation. "It appears to me that you have a very keen grasp of elegiac poetry such as this."

"I read a lot of romance novels," Odessa said, straight-faced, and Lord Vanya blinked. "You told me before that works of fiction are rare in the Golden City. That's quite the opposite where I grew up. We were abundantly blessed." A swift tremor stole along her mouth; she was thinking about the lives lost at Aranth. I covered her hand with mine and my aether-gate flared, hoping to soothe her.

"Romance novels," the lordling repeated, in the tone of one who has found a new species of insect he didn't particularly want to learn about. "I was referring to books that talk of the political and social—"

He broke off. Odessa was looking a little murderous.

"I'm sure they're very good books, Your Holiness," he hastily amended.

"You learn a lot of nuance with romance and other fiction. You should try it sometime."

"I hope there will be an opportunity to, in the near future." He sounded more genuine there, at least. "May I assist in your analyses? I've had some experience in this area."

"Are you a scholar yourself, Lord Vanya?"

"Not in any official capacity, I'm afraid. I have a penchant for old languages like Aeona, and I have read every history book in the family library. I would have liked to dedicate my life to academic pursuits, but my father said it was a fool's profession. That there was nothing to study after the Breaking but sand." The lordling's face fell somewhat at that admission.

"I am very sorry that you are estranged from your father," Odessa said as gently as she could. "It could not have been easy to make the choice to come here, and we cannot thank you enough."

"I am glad I can be of use, milady. I should have made that choice earlier, when I had a better chance to prove my mettle."

A wistful look crossed his face. "Her Holiness Haidee, and that other desert nomad. How long have they been . . . ?"

"Any questions about Haidee would be best addressed to her, I think," I said carefully. "I wouldn't dare to claim any knowledge of—"

"She loves him, Lord Vanya," Odessa broke in. "And if you've come here with the intention of breaking them apart, then you will have to answer to me, regardless of your help with these passages."

"Odessa."

"He deserves a straight answer, Lan. I don't want him relying on false hopes, especially when we owe him our gratitude. I learned that the hard way during our courtship, remember? I wasn't as forthcoming, and tried to pretend I was someone else so that I could avoid the consequences a little while longer. I've always regretted it. I am sorry for being so blunt, milord, but I think you have the right to know."

"Thank you, Your Holiness." Lord Vanya had recovered, though his face was still scarlet. "I bear them no ill will. I have no claim on Lady Haidee. We had only met twice before. I had every expectation then that we would marry, but my disappointment is no one's fault. And it does not change my desire to help you two."

"You're a good man, Lord Vanya." Odessa clasped his hands and beamed at him, which made him redden all over again. My girl looked too much like her twin for him not to be reminded of that fact. "Have you any guesses with regard to *The Ages of Aeon*?"

He took a deep breath. "I have a few theories. Do you mind if I take the lead?"

"Please do."

His first instructions were to place the passages we'd found within *The Ages of Aeon* side by side with the one we had found in Brighthenge. I read through the one he singled out, a passage differing significantly from what we'd read at the temple:

Test your worth; offer

to her, Inanna's immortality.

She will grieve endlessly for the sister

who slumbers in the house of the dead

but her tears will save her sister;

but her tears will save us all.

"This one sounds like it might be referring to a solution. Was Inanna originally immortal, but gave that up after entering the Cruel Kingdom and failing to save her consort? Or something else? And how does one sister 'grieving' save us?" Lord Vanya paced the ground, still talking animatedly, his gestures matching his rising excitement. "How can one sister slumber in the house of the dead, but still be saved? And there's this final stanza:

'And until the Gates of Death and Life intertwine,

Love continues to be the toll.

And she will pay.

She will pay.'"

"That doesn't inspire much confidence," I said.

"I would disagree. Learning what these Gates of Death and Life are and how to control them could possibly nullify the need for sacrifice. To sacrifice one's love was the final demand of the galla's rituals, correct?"

"Who told you that?" Odessa gasped.

He grinned. "I'm cleverer than I look, Your Holiness. I've read Lady Haidee's notes, and secrets are difficult to keep in this camp, I've found." His smile disappeared. "My apologies. I didn't intend to make light of it."

"None taken. But I'm not sure what the Gates of Death and Life are, myself."

"Is it a reference to us Catseye?" I asked. "We can both heal and hasten death—though I imagine the answer isn't as easy as that. Is it Odessa's ability to bring back some aspect of the dead?"

Lord Vanya looked helpless. "That's about as much as I can glean from these texts, Lady Lan. We're already speculating a great deal as it is."

I scowled. "Then what good is all this, then?" I wanted to be out somewhere, fighting something. Even if it was that accursed shadow-goddess. I felt useless here.

Odessa was also frowning. "Haidee mentioned something about the Gate of Life after we arrived here. It was in one of our ancestors' journals."

I glanced down at the rest of the strange poem. It wasn't much, but Lord Vanya's analysis was enough to spark hope.

The Cruel Kingdom, I knew now, referred to the under-world where the dead and other strange things lingered. It was where Inanna had descended, in a bid to find her lost love, though she returned to Aeon without him. The mentions of "two, but one" made me think of the fact that there was always a pair of twin goddesses in every generation.

I looked through the rest of Haidee's notes; none of the other goddesses' plaques had talked about them crying for their sisters, although the sacrifices had been successful, as far as their Devoted were concerned. Each pair of goddesses had been sequestered in their own little bubbles, growing up without ever knowing their twin.

"Would the mirages have something to do with this, do you think?" Odessa asked softly. "I—I don't know what they are, really, or if they're the same as my—"

Shouting rose from outside, interrupting out conversation. "Galla on the dunes!"

I dashed out of the tent to the roar of engines, spotted Haidee, Arjun, and the others heading to us in their rigs. Something was wrong. They all looked panicked.

Sonfei and Lisette were struggling to lift Faraji's prone, bloodied body out of the jeep, and I was moving before I knew it, by their side as they lowered him to the ground.

One look told me all I needed to know.

"Arjun," I said, but the boy was already stomping away, unable to even look at his brother's still form. With a heart-wrenching cry, unable to fully articulate his grief, he spun, aimed his Howler into the distance—where I saw, much to my horror, a new wave of galla arriving, a swarm almost twice the size of the one we'd faced before—and fired. A mass of moving shadows promptly disappeared as the sand around them exploded, and then burned.

"What happened?" Odessa asked, eyes round with fear. "Did the mirages attack?"

"No," Haidee said, looking drawn. "They tried to help."

"Their help did not be coming soon enough." Sonfei all but snarled; angry, fearful.

A mad scramble ensued as others saw the approaching horde and ran for their nearest weapons. "Bring him to our hut," I told Sonfei, who was now carrying poor Faraji, and drew out my sword.

There was another loud roar; the sound of a Howler firing. I saw a fireburst arc through the air, disappearing from view.

It was a stream of blue fire, and it wasn't Arjun's doing.

And then I heard a new voice rising out of the din. It belonged to no one in camp, but I recognized it all the same.

"Fire at will!"

I looked at Odessa, and we knew.

Janella.

Chapter Fifteen

ODESSA AND JANELLA

☽

THERE WAS NO TIME TO demand an explanation. No time to question why Janella had appeared at camp with many of Mother's Devoted, defending us like she'd never betrayed Lan or me before. The horde of galla that had once more appeared over the horizon was closing fast.

The air-shields were already up. We'd learned from the last fight, and now there were small pockets within the barriers for Lisette and the other gunners to position themselves behind, ready to return fire. Janella and her team were outside the barricade, retreating as the galla drew closer. Her Howler retorted again and again, sending wide swathes of azure flames into the thick of the shadow-army. The galla were most susceptible to blue fire, I remembered, but Janella was the only one of Asteria's people capable of it.

Sharp icicles stabbed their way through some of the fiends,

brutally impaling most and freezing the soil for yards around us. This wasn't Haidee's doing, judging from the startled look on her face. It wasn't mine. No one I knew back in Aranth had been strong enough to do this. Nobody but . . .

My gaze swung to one of the fighters at the back of the pack, standing alone. Ice glittered around her, solidified into more spikes that sprung forward and skewered more of the monsters. I nearly stopped breathing.

"Odessa!" Haidee called, and I snapped to attention. More than enough time later. More than enough time to ask Mother what she was doing here.

My hand brushed Haidee's, our fingers linking. I willed my thoughts somewhere fierier, hotter, and I felt her do the same.

The area around the neutral grounds exploded into flames, creating a fiery moat that prevented the galla from pushing forward. They slowed down long enough for the others to pick them off with more firebursts. Sonfei and the Liangzhu were summoning heavy gales of wind, channeling air patterns above the creatures and bringing them down with enough force and weight to crush them. We kept up the wall of fire, burning our way through as many of the galla as we could, our minds and thoughts so intertwined that it was difficult to remember we had ever been two people instead of the one that we were now.

"Lower the shields to my left," Haidee shouted, "and bring them inside."

"But they're Asteria's—" Lars, the Gila clan leader, began to protest.

"Asteria's or not, they're helping us, and I'm not going to let them die!"

The shields shimmered briefly, and Janella stumbled inside, gasping and smiling widely. "You have my thanks, Your Holinesses," she purred, then lifted her Howler to send another barrage of shots through, taking out several galla.

"You and I will have a reckoning after this," I hissed.

"As you wish, Your Holiness."

Daughter.

I froze. Haidee had reverted to using fire patterns like they were glowfire, tossing balls of flames into the densest part of the army. She showed no signs that she had heard it.

Daughter.

From behind the army of shadows a dark figure unfurled and stood.

Daughter, Inanna repeated a third time, the crown on her forehead blazing brightly, socketless eyes burrowing into my soul. *There will be no suffering. You are welcomed here.*

I knew what she wanted. I could see them lurking by her side—seven galla in total, all shining with sapphires.

She would retreat if I accepted them all, I knew. She'd take the shadow-swarm with her. Retreat to the Great Abyss and stay there until another day came, with another generation of goddesses. Everyone else in camp would be saved from her wrath. Everyone else in Aeon.

Except Lan.

"No!" I screamed into those shadows, into that grotesque form.

Her reply was fierce, unyielding.

The world went dark for a few brief moments, and when I came back to it I was screaming.

I wasn't alone. Haidee was on the ground as well, her hands clutching at her head, pain stamped across her features. I dimly realized that the connection between us had been severed, ripped away. Had Inanna done this?

Everywhere hurt. Everywhere was agony.

Inanna struck again, and this time I saw her tear through the surface of the air-dome the way a sharp claw might rend cloth. Our protection wavered, right on the verge of disappearing, and with it our chances of surviving.

With a cry, Haidee held out her hands. The dome turned opaque as hardened earth began to clump against it. I knew the risk she was taking—the added terra patterns would make breaching the shield harder, but the added weight could also cause it to collapse quicker. I tried to reach out to my twin again, intent on reestablishing our connection so I could add my strength to hers, but only encountered a wall of white-hot pain that sent me back to the ground. Haidee collapsed too, as the same bolt of agony hit her.

"Your Holiness!" I heard. I lifted my head and saw Slyp bracing himself underneath the dome's center, eyes flashing green as he continued what Haidee had started, shaping the terra patterns around the dome to stabilize it. Bergen was beside him, his gates flaring just as brightly as he followed the older man's lead. "Your Holiness," Slyp panted. "Please find yourself somewhere safer."

The demoness continued to slam the full force of its strength against the barrier. Slyp grunted as debris rained down on them with every blow.

I could feel Haidee reaching out to me again, and the both of us staggering back when a fresh bout of hurt rose up between us, making our heads spin.

Several more blows sent cracks forming along the dome's radius. The men grunted, trying to keep it upright, but the demoness was too strong. She tore a hole through the barrier, and the galla were quick to stream through the opening. "Retreat!" I heard Mother Salla roar out, but the order only sent a chill through me. Retreat to where? We were surrounded on all sides.

A series of high-pitched screams rent the air, and the Hellmakers threw themselves on the invaders, shouting and shooting and hacking their way through, buoyed by a sudden ferocity that stunned me. "Protect Their Holinesses!" their leader roared.

Arjun dropped down to one knee, eyes glowing red and his Howler trained on the demoness. Blue flames shot out from his gun again, aimed at the sparkling jewels across Inanna's brow. They hit their mark, but did little damage. Still racked with grief, he loaded, fired again, loaded, fired again, without pause.

"There's more here than there were the last time," Lan hissed.

"Just means we gotta shoot faster." Arjun focused again, and the incanta he was sending through his Howler flared brighter. Beside him, Janella did the same, her own eyes burning red as she built up the patterns in her own Howler, the gun steaming with blue-wrapped smoke.

They both fired at once, and both aimed true. Blue fire blazed forth and turned the demoness's lapis lazuli gems into ashes, and the giantess's form staggered back. I heard a shout from Mother, who had been biding her time, allowing her ice to warp around the demoness; higher, stronger, thicker. And when she finally attacked, it felt like the whole world shuddered in recoil.

Ice enveloped the creature, freezing it where it stood. Janella shouldered her gun, aimed, and fired one last time.

The demoness shattered, dissolved into tiny, frozen crystals.

Low moans spread among the army of shadows, as if they sensed their mistress's defeat. In another instant, they too were gone. All that remained was the seventh galla, staring back at me with its lapis lazuli clenched in its palm.

"Never," I snarled at it, and then it was gone.

A faint cheer rose up in camp, though the sounds were muted, exhausted. We weren't without casualties. I could count at least six dead, and just as many injured. Arjun exchanged a few swift words with Haidee before heading to the tent that housed his brother's body, not bothering to hide his anguish. Haidee watched him go, her grief obvious too.

The cannibals were hard at work. One of their own lay dead on the ground, and they were busily kicking as much sand as they could over the prone form.

"What are you doing?" Lan snapped at them.

"Burying him," the leader said matter-of-factly.

"I'm sorry he's dead, but—"

"No. Not sorry. He died happy, knowing we do not eat him. You feed us. That is why we can bury him and not feed. Do you know how precious, this gift you offer? We understand the respectability of graves now." He turned to his men. "Honor her!" he shouted.

The Saiga clan roared in unison, groveling on the ground before me despite my protests, despite the tears that threatened to overwhelm me.

One of them had died for us, and they called it an honor. I didn't want that. I didn't. . . .

Lan sighed, resigned. "Tell your men to take your comrade's body and bury him *outside* of camp, not within it."

Noelle sank down to the ground, weariness in every gesture. "We can't do this every day."

She was right. A vision rose in my mind again; a fresh new swarm, in even greater numbers approaching camp just as the sun began to set. Inanna would never stop sending her hordes until we were completely overwhelmed. I fought hard not to be sick at the thought.

"You can't," Janella agreed calmly, setting the butt of her gun against the ground. "It would have been so much easier, Lady Odessa, if you'd given Lan up to the Abyss like I asked."

Immediately two dozen Howlers were trained at her face, gates flaring and running the gamut of colors. Janella only laughed, adjusting her robes—robes worn by the Devoted, I saw, with the red piping along the hems that marked her as a Firesmoker. It had not taken long for Mother to invite her spy into the Devoted's official ranks. More fool I, who'd activated her fire-gate in the first place. How could I ever have thought her meek and unassuming? "You cannot fault me for speaking the truth, Your Holiness."

The other Devoted gathered around her, careful not to make any sudden movements lest the clans open fire. My stomach twisted at the sight of them—Slyp and Filia, Bergen and Jeenia and Holsett, and so many others.

I couldn't look at them. I had destroyed Aranth. I was the reason they were in this desert, fighting demons.

"Why are you here?" Haidee demanded. "Why did you help us?"

"Because as far as I'm concerned, we share a common enemy—the demoness of the Abyss. Blue-fired Firesmokers are rare enough as it is. Neither of us on our own will be sufficient to withstand her next time, Haidee. But our chances of survival increase if we work together. Ah, there you are, Lan," she purred, as my Catseye and Noelle drew closer, both looking exhausted. "I'm delighted to see you looking so well. The fresh sun seems to have invigorated you."

A growl rose from my throat before I could stop myself.

"Did I say something?" Janella asked, looking over at Noelle.

"Drop dead," the steward responded calmly.

Janella chuckled, then transferred her gaze back to me. "Your mother is worried about you, Your Holiness."

"She was never my mother," I shot back, ignoring the brief spasm of pain that gave me.

"And you don't know how sorry I am for that."

I went numb. Tamera had already shifted targets from Janella to Mother, and most of her clanmates did the same.

Mother looked terrible. She looked older and grayer, lines around her eyes and mouth that hadn't been there before. Occasionally a faint tremor would seize her shoulders, and her back was bowed. I was stunned. She was almost a different person, far from the cool, self-possessed woman I'd last seen standing in Aranth's harbor.

There was a gasp from Mother Salla. "Asteria. Your Holiness . . . I never . . ."

A faint smile graced Mother's face. "Salla. How wonderful to see you again. I am glad to see you looking well. Of all the Devoted you were the kindest to me." She looked at me. "We have to talk, Odessa. I understand that your friends might not appreciate my presence in their camp. We can return to ours if you'd like."

"I'm staying right here," I said.

Slyp and Bergen looked at each other, shuffling their feet nervously. The other Devoted looked just as uncomfortable.

"Your Holiness," Slyp said guiltily. "Your mother granted us amnesty. She's right—we cannot be fighting each other. She— at the Great Abyss, she—"

It hurt to look at them. To see that they didn't blame me for wiping out Aranth.

"Whatever you think about us, Your Holiness," Janella interrupted, "you must set it aside for the sake of these people who chose to follow you. The shadow-armies grow stronger with every day cycle that passes. Her Holiness Asteria is offering you all sanctuary with her. Together, we will be strong enough to defend from the next attack."

"Haidee ought to make the final decision," I said stiffly.

Janella's smile grew. "You defer to your sister, then?"

She has none of your strength. She has none of your power. You made her, and you could break her. Strike her down before Mother, prove that you are the one true goddess—

No.

The urge passed, and the voices drifted away, and I breathed easier again. Lan looked at me questioningly, knowing by some sixth sense what I was going through, but I schooled my face into impassiveness.

"All I need from you, Mother," I said, "is to tell me how to save Aeon. If you won't do it, then let it fall to me."

"The sacrifice . . . ," Mother began.

"Anything but that."

"I don't know any other way, Odessa. Why did you think breaking the world was the choice we made?"

"I won't sacrifice Lan!"

"I never accepted that final gift, but the Abyss's mark left me all the same. Perhaps the same can happen to you, too!"

I paused. Mother might have rejected the galla, but that hadn't saved my father. Didn't that fulfill the seventh galla's requirement, even if she hadn't been willing?

"Come back to our camp, you and Haidee. We can figure this out together."

So not even Mother knew of another way. I tried not to give in to despair. "No. Not unless you revoke Janella's authority and keep her under guard."

"I can't do that. We need her still."

"Did you know what she's done? You condone her actions?"

"I confessed everything, Lady Odessa." If I hadn't known Janella for what she truly was, I would have actually thought her contrite. "I did what I thought I could to save your life. Her Holiness commanded me to ensure an easy transition of the galla's gifts to you, even if you were unwilling. I am sorry about the others, I truly am. But the whole expedition would have turned on me had they known."

"I should strike you down this very second." The voices were right in one thing; I had given her a fire-gate, and I could take it away. That was the only time she had ever shown me genuine emotion—the tears that I thought were for her chance to rise from her lowly position and make something more for herself. I now knew they were from realizing she would be able to wield the cudgel herself in a far crueler manner than even Gracea had.

"You will do no such thing, Odessa," Mother said sharply. "I have forgiven Janella for her actions, distasteful as they may have been. She was desperate. I was—"

"If you were so willing to kill your own people to ensure my safety," I shouted, "then why didn't you simply open the portal from Aranth and enter Brighthenge yourself? One life would have been an easier choice!"

A shudder racked Mother's form. "I can't—you have no right—"

"Your Holiness," I saw Catseye Lenida glide forward, place her hand on Mother's bare arm. Mother froze, then slowly relaxed.

"Your Holiness"—the Catseye nodded at me—"the journey has been exhausting for your mother. I must ask that you postpone this conversation for another time."

"What happened?" There was something they weren't telling us.

But the suggestion that she was somehow weak made Mother's shoulders stiffen, the old flinty spark returning to her eyes. "My offer to your group stands," she said, her old arrogance back at the fore, "You have tonight to think it over. I will send some of my people to you tomorrow, and we can determine our next move."

"Asteria?" Haidee's voice was soft, unsure. Mother glanced at her, and her eyes softened. "Yes, Haidee?"

"We . . . if you are to help us, we need both you and my mother on the same side. Help us convince her that there's a bigger world beyond her city that needs saving."

Mother paused. "I am open to whatever overtures Latona wishes to make," she finally said, "though I won't hold my breath. She thought I would sacrifice Aranth to earn that last gift. I could never—Aranth wasn't—"

"Asteria?"

Sonfei stood behind us, the yearning on his face painful to see. "Asteria," he echoed, taking a few shaky steps toward her. "I never dreamt—I had always hoped that you would—"

244

Mother had been frozen to the spot, her face even more ashen as she stared at Sonfei. But when he moved toward her, she turned away quickly. "Leave me be, Sonfei."

"I cannot. Asteria, please. You cannot know how much I have wished to see you—"

"I have no wish to see *you*." She inclined her head and the others gathered around her, some of them looking apologetically back at us as Mother led them away. Only Janella remained behind. Sonfei lifted a hand, his throat working as if about to call out after her a second time. Finally, he let his hand drop instead.

"You must be more considerate of Her Holiness's feelings, Lady Odessa," Janella chided. "You don't know how much it took out of her to come here."

I wanted to strangle her. "I can still take your gate away."

"You need me, Your Holiness," the girl said cheerfully, flicking her fingers to summon a tiny blue flame. "You may not think so, but I am fond of Her Holiness. All I do is for her sake. And yours, even if you may not appreciate it. I am sorry that we weren't able to resolve our differences before we parted ways. Sumiko sends her regards, by the way."

Lan froze. "Sumiko?"

"She is eagerly waiting for word from me, and hopes you will accept Her Holiness Asteria's offer. She would be quite inconsolable if anything prevented my return. The journey to the Great Abyss left her quite distraught. I worry she might do something rash."

"If you hurt her—" Lan snarled.

"I said nothing of that sort. If anything, you've all been threatening me. I wouldn't want Lady Haidee to think poorly of me."

"I trust Odessa and Lan," Haidee said coldly. "I have no reason to trust you."

"Too bad, Your Holiness. I'm the only one who can tell you everything Asteria knows about the Breaking. Everything she is ashamed to tell you."

I was astounded. *Ashamed?* That didn't sound like Mother at all.

Janella sighed at my expression. "Yes, ashamed. You shouldn't have done it, Your Holiness." She sounded almost scolding. "There was a reason why Asteria thought it would be safe for you to go to the Great Abyss. The galla never would have caused you harm, as long as Aeon didn't turn. For Aeon to flourish, a goddess must be sacrificed. Latona and Asteria refused, so Inanna sent the galla to collect her due. The twins' instinctive response was to stop the world from spinning. To buy themselves time. Asteria believes that, anyway, though the solution escapes her even after all these years. Their sabotage kept Inanna from claiming a sacrifice, but it kept Aeon from flourishing, too. But now that the world turns? Well, Inanna wants what she's owed. Did you think it would be simple? Heal the breach, and things will go back to normal?"

Both Haidee and I flinched. "And if we return to the Abyss to undo what we've done?" Haidee ventured to ask.

"I'm not quite sure Aeon can survive coming to a standstill

246

a second time, Your Holinesses."

I gritted my teeth. "Is Aranth truly gone?"

"What remains of the city lies under the waves now. Asteria had no choice but to open a portal to save everyone that she could, lest the water consume the rest of us."

I knew how I looked, knew there was a smoothness to the expression on my face that was too artificial for my liking. I didn't want to think about my city. I didn't want to think about my people's last moments. When I finally forced myself to speak, the words came out slow and measured, as I weighed the gravity of each one before I shaped them aloud. "How many died?" I tried to recall the number of our people I'd seen out in the desert. Did those numbers match up to half of the population? A quarter? Less than even that?

Janella hesitated. Her smugness disappeared. "Enough. As I said, Asteria saved all that she could." She sighed. "At a great cost to her. You were right. She had no desire to return to Brighthenge. She was . . . afraid."

"Mother? Afraid?"

"Even goddesses know fear, Your Holiness. And the Great Abyss had taken away almost everyone she had loved. Or so she thought."

"And Mother couldn't tell me this herself?" How cold I sounded to my own ears. I could almost believe I didn't care.

"Your mother is too busy protecting what remains of your people against her tyrant-queen of a sister to assuage her daughter's tantrums, Odessa." I froze. "She is not interested in a war on two fronts; her hands are full enough with Latona's army.

You, she feels, would see things her way. She is taking a chance that Lady Haidee would be more amenable to an alliance than her mother. Or will you fight Aranth's survivors now?"

"Odessa would never go against her own people," Haidee snapped.

"I imply nothing of that sort. Although it would pain the citizens of Aranth to learn that Asteria's daughter had turned against them in favor of a horde of desert barbarians, wouldn't it?" Janella smiled, all teeth and artifice. "Did you know the original Devoted intended to tell Asteria that Latona passed away from natural causes? Her body would have been thrown into the Abyss at the completion of the rites. Asteria would have been asked to give up Aranth's life for the seventh gift."

I'd never met my father, but the callous way she referred to him, like he was nothing more than fodder for the ritual, made my blood boil. "And the gifts that she did accept?"

"Those disappeared after the Breaking. Only her visions remain—many goddesses have had that gift, though the galla's radiances give them more accuracy. Personally, I believe that these gifts disappeared because her responsibilities have now been passed on to you. But saying so makes her angry, and so I do not mention it in her presence."

"You know far too much about my mother, even for a spy."

Janella shrugged. "Would it surprise you to learn that my mother was a Devoted? A minor one—a documentarian. I was old enough to remember her stories."

"Monsters," Lan growled.

"Latona was ambushed at Farthengrove; she killed her assassins, and she and Aranth raced to Brighthenge to warn Asteria of what Devika had done. I can only imagine what happened next. The galla arrived to claim one of them, and in the ensuing battle, Aranth was killed; grief drove both goddesses to blame the other; in their anger, they stopped Aeon from turning. Perhaps Aeon's split symbolized their own estrangement."

I nodded slowly, saw Haidee doing the same.

"Latona had brought her babes along; foolish, I suppose, but after the attempt on her life she was convinced that you and Haidee could not be entrusted to anyone else. Latona's side of the Abyss was swarmed and overcome, and Asteria believed her sister and Haidee were lost. She only managed to rescue you."

"So that's the only way to truly heal Aeon? For me to sacrifice Lan?"

"And to sacrifice me as well?" Haidee asked softly.

"Asteria of all people understood. She gave you the choice to sacrifice Lan. You may not believe me, but I suspect she knew you would take after her and refuse the final gift. She believed your rejection would change nothing for Aeon, which would continue as it was, frozen. But she thought it would heal you."

"And what does she expect me to do now?" I demanded. "Fight Haidee like she probably did Latona? That's never going to happen."

"Never is a long time to be certain, Your Holiness. So many things can still happen." Janella bowed to us. "Lady Lan. Lady Haidee. Lady Odessa. Thank you for your hospitality. I suggest joining forces before the next onslaught. I will return on the morrow to help facilitate." Janella drew her red-trimmed cloak around herself, glancing at some of the clan members who had come to watch them. "How noble you all are," she called out gaily. "So many of you who continue to die willingly for the goddesses' sake. A pity that neither are willing to do so for you."

With a loud curse, Arjun stepped toward the other Firesmoker, but the damage was done. With another laugh, Janella left, the faint mutterings of the crowd trailing in her wake.

"We'll need to find a way to open the portal back to the Abyss again," Lán said quietly, "but without taking another life. We need to find that final galla."

"I won't, Lan!" I exploded furiously. "I won't sacrifice you!"

"You may have to, regardless of whatever Asteria hoped. Too many lives have already been lost when it could have just been mine. You can't look at these people and tell them my life isn't worth it, Odessa."

"Or mine," Haidee said softly. "The galla will grow stronger with every defeat. We staved them off today. We can probably stave them off tomorrow. But how much longer after that?"

"If you're going to throw yourself into the Abyss," Arjun threatened, coming up behind us, "I'm jumping in right after you."

"Arjun!"

"How are you gonna stop me? I told you I'd follow you wherever you go." His eyes were red from weeping. "I'll cross whatever circle of dead that mirage was talking about, or descend into the Cruel Kingdom myself, if it comes down to it."

"Stop it!" I cried. "Stop talking about sacrificing yourselves. Stop saying you're all leaving me. Stop saying your lives have no worth to me just because they have none to you!"

That gave them pause. "Odessa," Lan said softly.

"I'm tired, Lan. I don't know what the galla want me to do. I don't want them to *tell* me what to do." This was all my fault, and everyone was to suffer for it. Lan had forgiven me. How could she forgive me? "I'm trying, Lan. I'm trying so hard. I don't want to hurt anyone else."

"We'll need to move." Lan cast a glance back at the crowd. "Our presence isn't exactly appreciated at the moment, I think."

"Odessa," Arjun said, hesitant. "You said that you could—bring people back from the dead. I wondered—if you could—"

"I'm sorry," I said helplessly. "I can't. They—they don't come back the right way. It will look like Faraji, but it won't be him. I don't think you'd want to see that."

"Can't—can't you try? Maybe it could be different. Faraji's a tough bastard, he'd shake off any—"

"Arjun." Haidee took his face in her hands, pressed her forehead against his. "Please don't do this to yourself," she begged.

A pause. Arjun closed his eyes. "Yeah," he rasped. "You're right. I don't think I could bear that. Shouldn't have asked."

"Excuse me." There was a strange expression on Lord Vanya's face, his eyes screwed up like he was struggling to recall something else. "*The circle of dead.* Why does that sound—where did you hear that?"

Arjun frowned. "From—well, from the mirage. What are you—"

But Vanya was already making a beeline for his tent, looking determined.

Lan hugged me, pressed the palm of her hand against my temple. She was warm and light and as steady as a heartbeat, and her touch melted away some of my anxiety. Her presence was enough to ease my pain, made me feel like I was worth the effort. "The galla will attack again, if Odessa's visions and the last few battles were any indication," she said. "We need to find out when and where they'll come again, if we're to have a chance. Let Noelle and I put our heads together, think of something."

"You were supposed to protect Faraji!" a voice cried behind Haidee. Imogen's hands were clenched so tightly together she was shaking. Kadmos, Derra, and Millie stood with her, the latter sobbing on Kadmos's shoulder. "You promised you would!"

"Immie . . . ," Arjun began helplessly.

"Imogen!" Mother Salla said sharply, her own eyes still wet.

Imogen turned and fled. Arjun moved as if to follow, but then paused, resigned, as he caught sight of others looking our way, resentment and suspicion and distrust clear in their faces.

"I *should* have protected him," he muttered. "She's right. I should have."

"She is right," Haidee agreed, voice down to a hoarse whisper. "I should have done more. I chose to put everyone in danger. But the fault is mine alone. Arjun . . ."

"Your H-holinesses." Vanya was back, and his hands were

shaking. "I might have found something."

"What, another poem?" Arjun snapped.

"'When the dead find words, the goddess and the Devoted son will meet atop a fish not a fish, on a sea not a sea. It is she who travels to the endless Abyss, and it is he who guides her. When the galla comes, the ranger shall protect the goddess. It is she who travels to the endless Abyss, and it is she who guides her.'"

Arjun's head swiveled toward the lordling, an incredulous look on his face. "How did you know?"

"Is the passage familiar to you?"

"That's how Odessa and I first met. Mother Salla recited those words verbatim to me weeks ago. She said it was one of many predictions my mother made about Haidee and Odessa." Arjun halted, his face suddenly stark white. "Is this my mother's book? Are these a collection of prophecies she foretold?"

"I'm not familiar with prophecies in general," Vanya said. "But it confirms the link between this book and Brighthenge. You also asked me to find another temple that might have been dedicated to Inanna, one that contains the healing spells both Lady Lan and Lady Odessa had asked about in the past. Well, I think I found it."

Chapter Sixteen

HAIDEE AND THE CIRCLE

---- ☼ ----

"I ALMOST MISSED IT," VANYA continued, pacing the ground in the erratic, pent-up way he did when he was excited about something. "Most of the other poems—I'll refer to them as poems for now, to simplify things—don't refer to Inanna by name, and even Brighthenge is rarely mentioned. The only reason I paid attention to this one is because it mentioned the Abyss. And then there was that whole 'sea that's not a sea' reference that I thought could be the Skeleton Coast. Mother Salla has been helping me look through the rest. . . ." He trailed off and looked to the Oryx clan leader.

"A few sound like things I'd heard Devika cite before," Mother Salla conceded. "But I wasn't privy to all the prophecies she made."

It sounded promising, at least. "And what of the other shrine?"

"Cross the circle of dead," Vanya began, reading from the book again:

"Where endless rock follows endless sand.
Where blue shines brightest; let it show you the way
to where Ereshkigal's temple waits within.
Take water from where your eyes cannot see—'"

"I understand nothing about this," Lisette interrupted. "What's an Ereshkigal? Is that the name of Inanna's lost love?"

But Arjun had gone even paler. "Cross the circle of dead," he repeated. "My—the mirage said that. And something about a room, red with the blood of treasures."

He sat down heavily on the ground, hands fisted in his hair as he squeezed his eyes shut, agonized. "What the hell did it say again? A temple. 'The answers to life and death lie within the stone.' And other things. 'The stone will light your path. The stone will show you the way. But first—'" And then, abruptly, he fell silent.

"Arjun?" I sat in front of him, placing my hands on his knees and waiting for him to finish.

"That's it. That's all I can remember." A pause. "Where is Faraji?"

"They're . . . bathing him," I said softly, tentatively, not sure how I should phrase it. "Your brothers and sisters are attending to him." I didn't want to hurt him more than he already was. The other clans were treating him coldly because he'd defended us ever since we'd arrived, like he was to blame for our presence. I could understand their distrust of me and Odessa, but

Arjun was one of them. He didn't deserve their anger.

It wasn't fair. It wasn't *fair.*

His head dropped. His thumb stroked at the side of my hand. "What the hell does all this mean?"

"I don't know," Mother Salla said softly. Her own eyes were red-rimmed. Only an hour ago she had thrown herself across Faraji's body and cried. I'd watched her adopted children gather around her, grieving, and stepped outside, unable to bear their agony.

"These mirages . . ." Odessa bit her lip. "They seem to have more agency than . . . those I've raised from the dead. What if there's something out there sustaining them? Something we can't see, at least at first glance?"

"A temple?" Lisette asked dubiously. "You think this poem is saying there's a temple out there that we don't know about?"

"'Endless rock follows endless sand.' Do any of the clans know a place like that?"

Tamera frowned, scrutinizing the ground. "Yes. We've taken cursory patrols there, but I've always warned my people never to stay long. The area *is* full of rocks in that part of the coast; not even the hardiest scorpion or insect could thrive there. On the two or three occasions I've roamed the area, I've seen derelict ruins, crumbling structures fallen beyond repair. None of them ever resembled a temple to me."

"Clan Addax are settlers more than nomads like the others," Lisette said. "But I heard stories of that part of the coast from the clans who'd visit us. It's the hottest and driest part of the desert."

"My experience is the same," Lars confirmed, and a few of the other elders also murmured their agreement. "There is nothing of value in that region. We never lingered long."

"So no one's ever seen this supposed temple?" Noelle asked. No one answered. "For all we know, it could have been destroyed during the Breaking."

"How sure are you that it's a *temple*?" Lisette asked Vanya.

"The topography could have changed by now, of course. It will require exploring the area in person."

"What guarantee do we have?" Lisette asked.

"This is all speculation, so I can only make a hypothesis on—"

"That's not what I mean. Forgive me for still being skeptical, but I still don't know if I believe a Golden City lordling would willingly leave his comfortable life to betray his father. It sounds more feasible that the same lordling, who has never shown an inclination to get out from under his father's thumb until now, is doing Arrenley's bidding to mislead us, sending us to comb through a dangerous part of the coast as a distraction."

"Lisette!" I cried.

"It's my life on the line too, as well as those of my clan. He ought to offer us more proof beyond just claiming that he wants to do the right thing."

"But it's not fair to—"

"No, Your Holiness," Vanya responded hotly. "Let me answer her. What's wrong with wanting to do the right thing? Regardless of what Lady Haidee feels about the matter, it is my duty to see to her safety!"

"Oh, really?" Lisette sneered. "All this for love? I don't believe that."

"Maybe you can't because you've never cared deeply for another person in your life."

Lisette's eyes widened, anger standing out on her face, but before she could respond I intervened. "There's more to it than just Vanya's word."

"I won't stand here," Vanya sputtered, "and allow you all to blacken my—"

"I'm on your side, you lout. Remember what you said about this book back at the Citadel? You said your father guarded it so closely that even Mother wasn't aware of it. How did you know that?"

The boy paused, considering. "The volume was in his study once, when Her Holiness paid us a visit. I saw him deliberately take the book from his shelves and hide it in a drawer before she entered. He never said anything to me about it, but it made me wonder about the book, why he'd been so keen not to let her see it."

"Have you ever known your father to have taken expeditions out into the desert?"

"Do you really think the lord disloyal enough to conduct his own investigations without his liege's knowledge?" Mother Salla asked.

"I . . ." Vanya straightened his shoulders. "If you're asking me based on what I know about my father, then yes. Father always wanted to rule the Golden City himself. That was why he was so invested in my engagement to Lady Haidee."

"Are you suggesting that he's been to this temple?" Noelle asked. "That he also interpreted the passages in this book, and knows where it's located?"

"I don't think so. If he'd found anything there, he would have acted on it." Vanya turned to me, looking alarmed. "Are you going to tell your mother? I didn't tell you this to strip my father of his position."

"Mother won't take very kindly to it. And quite frankly, your father's not my favorite person right now." Mother had always kept everyone at arm's length, including her private council. Maybe that had led her to keep her distance from me, too, even if she didn't realize it.

"Any landmarks that could lead us to this temple may be long gone themselves," Giorme pointed out. "We could be searching for months."

"Would Lord Sonfei and his people be familiar with some of these landmarks?" Noelle asked me.

"I don't think so. Their territory lay beyond the Sand Sea." I didn't want to approach Sonfei yet. The poor man was deliberately keeping himself apart from the others following his confrontation with Asteria, and it was clear that he wanted to be left alone for now.

"Are there any other parts of the book that mention the Cruel Kingdom in any way?" Arjun asked.

"There's the Corridor of Yearning."

"The what?"

"The Corridor of Yearning, where those who had been greedy in life were encased in stone, with only their hands free

259

to cling and entreat passersby to join them. And the Gorge of Wrath, where penitents who'd succumbed to rage were punished to fall forever." Vanya caught Arjun's blank stare. "The Cave of Realities? Sinners are tortured with their worst nightmares. Or the Sands of Punishment. And then, of course, there's the Path of Regret, where you're condemned to spend eternity with your greatest guilt, but I don't know if that comes after the Corridor of Yearning or the Gorge of—"

"Hell and sandrock, Arrenley. Is this what you think the afterlife is gonna be like for you? You've got some sick, twisted mind—"

"It's supposed to be *everyone*'s afterlife! Goddesses may be able to enter the Cruel Kingdom, but mortal souls must endure several areas of hell before they can even reach the kingdom's entrance. It's what parents use to scare unruly children. You've never heard of the stories? My brothers and I learned them almost from the cradle. They're why I initially dismissed the *Ages of Aeon* as a work of fiction."

"I never had a cradle, much less bedtime stories," Arjun said flatly.

The lordling looked suitably chastened. "Well, that's all the book says about the Cruel Kingdom."

"I have an idea." Odessa had been quiet for most of the gathering, but now she stood.

"What do you have in mind?" Lan asked, rising to her feet as well.

"You said none of the clans are familiar with the area. But

it seems to me that at least one clan has roamed most of the Skeleton Coast."

We received hard stares from numerous clan members as we made our way to the other side of camp, and more mutterings trailed in our wake once they realized where we were headed. The initial awe many of them had felt for Odessa and I had long since been replaced by suspicion. I wasn't sure I could blame them. I might have felt the same had I been in their place.

"A thousand curses on Janella," Lan muttered. "She knew what she was doing."

"I hope you know what *you're* doing, Odessa," Arjun said quietly. "Nobody's in a good mood right now."

The cannibals' leader, the one with the ugly scar on his face, sat up as we approached. "Your Holiness," he groveled.

"I could have let you burn till there was nothing left of you but ashes," Odessa told him coolly. "All your life you roamed these deserts seeking food and pleasure, but now you will have purpose. Swear to obey my sister and me, and you will never need to hunger."

The cannibal's eyes flicked back and forth between us. Maybe he was waiting for me to side with her, or make a statement of my own.

"Disobey," I added, hoping I sounded just as threatening. "Disobey, and I will kill you myself." Lan was right. I had to trust Odessa.

Anyone else would have been afraid of such an ultimatum.

But the Hellmaker's eyes grew bright, the expression on his face adoring.

"You and your Saiga brothers know the desert better than anyone else here," Odessa said. "There are questions I would like answered. In your wanderings, have you ever come across a small temple?"

There was a moment's pause before the man shook his head.

"There is a section of the Skeleton Coast, I'm told, that is mainly of rock and hard sand. How well have you explored that area?"

He wet his lips. "Ground's too hard for much, but you can find enough scorpions and lizards to feast on underneath the rocks if you look hard enough."

"Anything that might resemble a circle of dead?"

A shudder went through him. "The ghosts?"

"What ghosts?"

"They stand there sometimes without moving, in a circle. We run when we see them. I don't think they would taste like meat."

My hopes lifted. Finally, a breakthrough. "Will you lead us to them?"

The cannibal stared back at me, and then let out a quick bark of laughter. "Do I have a choice? But I like you. I like her. She gave us food when others would kill us. My belly is full. We will lead you to the spot, and may the Good Mother help you with what you find there."

"Swear it to me," Odessa said. "Swear it to me this instant."

"They're not likely to uphold any of the oaths they make," I warned.

"Because no one's ever treated them like they could." Odessa crouched down so she was eye-to-eye with the Hellmaker. "What's your name?" she asked.

He trembled now, his arrogance disappearing. There was a sheer look of amazement on his face, like he couldn't believe anyone had even asked. "I—" he faltered. "I don't remember."

"Before the dayspan is through, you shall all find yourselves names. You will then tell them to me. I want to know them."

The knot on his throat moved up and down as he swallowed, then nodded.

"They'd never even given themselves names?" I heard Lord Vanya whisper behind me in disbelief.

I knew why. You didn't name your food. Arjun teased me often about my penchant for name-giving, but there was a promise in every one I bestowed. I never named anything I ever wanted to harm. The Hellmakers couldn't even guarantee that to their own brethren.

"I will swear. You make our stomachs full." He saluted us with a clenched fist over his heart, and his subordinates followed.

"Tomorrow," Noelle said.

I frowned. "We won't have much time before the next attack."

"I'm not sure we should set out now, given the circumstances." Noelle's tone was hushed, almost reverent. "Look at that."

I stared. The sun was sinking behind the sandscape, fading into the next nightfall. But beneath it was another, even more stunning sight.

I saw the waves before I realized they were water. From a distance they glittered, as they washed through the terrain, stealing across sand and rock that had not known water for decades. The Sand Sea moved like this, the grains of sand so small and smooth they mimicked an actual sea.

But this wasn't mimicry. This wasn't sand.

There were shouts from the other clan members as they too poked their heads out of their tents to gape. As the bright ball of the sun gradually disappeared from view, a glitter of stars replaced it, shining down onto the waves.

"What is that?" Noelle asked.

"It's water," Lisette whispered. "The Salt Sea is returning."

Chapter Seventeen

ARJUN AT MIDNIGHT

———————— ☼ ————————

BOTH NOELLE AND MOTHER SALLA advised caution. The sea was still miles away, though clearly visible from where we stood. In what remained of the daylight, Tamera had sent some of her clan to gather water, though if the dead aspidochelone Haidee and I had found was any indication, the Salt Sea could still hold its share of monsters. But being in close proximity to so much water had eased some of the growing hostilities, and for now, that was good enough.

Tomorrow, after the sun rose, we'd be leaving this place. We'd be leaving the graves of Faraji and the many others who'd lost their lives in the last raid. Immie had wept throughout the short funeral, though my other brothers' and sisters' eyes were dry. "He wouldn't have wanted us to be sad for him," Kadmos said quietly, though his own eyes were hooded with sorrow.

I didn't cry, either. Grief had hollowed out my chest. There was nothing left in me to weep.

"You can bring him back, can you?" a voice said, and I saw Immie approaching Odessa. "You said the galla's gifts let you bring them back," she begged. "You can do that, can't you? Faraji believed in you. He thought you could save everyone. Can't you do it for him? I won't ask anything else from you, I swear!"

Odessa stared helplessly back at her. "I'm sorry. I—I shouldn't. He won't be the same person. He—"

"So? You're the goddess! You're supposed to watch over us. You're supposed to keep us safe! So many people are dead now because they thought you could keep them safe!"

"Immie!" I shouted, but the girl was already running away. The rest of my siblings trailed after her, none of them looking back at either goddess.

"Haidee," I began.

She shook her head sadly back at me and looped an arm under her twin sister's. *Later*, she mouthed, pale eyes glistening as she steered the guilt-ridden Odessa away, Lan swiftly following after them.

I'd sat by Faraji's mound after that, for as long as I could.

The clans had agreed to depart at first light. "If these day and night cycles continue as they are now, we'll start seeing more lasting effects on the weather," Vanya explained. "As the colder winds shift back east, there'll be more rainfall, which should replenish the Salt Sea and give rise to even more—"

"Why are you like this?" Lisette asked.

"I'm an avid student of history. I've read enough treatises from scientists of old to make a valid—"

"That's not what I mean. How can you remain so positive even with"—the girl waved her hand to indicate the darkness surrounding us—"all this. Hell, Vanya, we just buried some of our people. Even in your well-defended city there were casualties."

"I can't do much about that, can I?" The lordling looked down at the pile of papers in his hands. "I'm sorry about the friends you lost today. I know I'll grieve for any I've lost, should I ever return to the Golden City. I'm not like you. I've never been given much to do back home. I've never been considered important enough for most things. But I can actually be useful here. I can help change things. I know I can."

"You're a strange person, Vanya Arrenley," Lisette said softly, her eyes unreadable. "Admirable. But strange, all the same."

"Still feels like we're taking a big risk for some prophecies we still don't know are true," I muttered, though I already knew the hypocrisy of my own words. I'd had less to go on when I first agreed to travel with Haidee. Still.

"We have all the confirmation we need," Sonfei pointed out, gazing up at the stars blanketing the sky. They glinted down on us like diamonds, a wealth of light not even our earthly greed could corrupt. Sonfei was not quite over Asteria's dismissal of him, but was trying to sound upbeat despite it. "You believe your mother's words, and they be fitting the passages the Arrenley boy here has found. It is more than ample."

"It's not," I snapped. Sonfei always had that uncanny habit of singling out exactly what was pissing me off.

He nodded sagely. "You don't want to be responsible if it is a red herring, yes?"

"A what?"

"A red herring. It is a tasty little fish common in the waters before the Breaking. But in my time, it was also used to call something that may mislead others. And so you do not want to be a red herring."

I glared at him.

He remained unruffled. "If you and your mother are wrong, then so what?"

"You act like the fate of the world doesn't rest on this being right."

"We have had the worst already happen, did we not? You will be forgiven. Both Haidee and Odessa will be forgiven by your family, even though they act like they will not. It is not your fault if you are wrong. I have been wrong many times, and sometimes it isn't my fault, either. Right now, we are alive. We might not be tomorrow, or the day after that. We be doing nothing wrong to take risks, to fight for the moments worth having." He stood up, stretching. "The Liangzhu and I will be moving around camp, to comfort their fears and tell them that change is sometimes good. See? I, too, am a positive man."

"Much as he gets on my nerves at times," Lisette said, after he'd gone, "he's right."

"You're not the one with the undead mother."

"Arjun Revenantson. Got a nice ring to it."

"Screw you, Lisette."

She chuckled. "Haidee might object."

The mood was somber. Most were still wary of the dark and so remained in their tents, with a few nearby caves repurposed for shelter to accommodate everyone else. The restrictions against the cannibals had eased on Odessa's orders, including more rations of food and water. If they were to be the key to finding this temple, then they would need their strength, even though having to rely on them irked me.

Odessa was staring out at the sea, her face wistful. I wondered if it reminded her of the home she'd lost.

"I'm sorry about my siblings," I began.

She turned to look at me, shook her head. "They're mourning Faraji. There's nothing to be sorry for. I would have done the same in their place."

We fell into a comfortable silence. A few clouds marred the starlit sky, dark and foreboding, an indication it might start raining again before long.

"They sacrificed goddesses," Odessa finally said, "because it was easier than protecting the land. Easier than watching over the seas, the forests. With every death, the world was renewed again—with few repercussions for them. They were complacent, and then they were greedy."

I agreed. Hadn't Haidee talked about the mechanical marvels lost since the Breaking? She'd talked about the difficulties of purifying the air within the Golden City without poisoning their citizens, about rationing the water provided by their aquifers. What had the people of the past been able to build without those restrictions, knowing they could spread as much poison as they wanted? Knowing that the death of one goddess was all they needed to start over, without ever paying the price themselves?

Very few of those past achievements had survived. Most of those people hadn't survived, either.

"Then let's make sure the next time's gonna be different," I said, wanting to hope, so much that I was aching from it. "Our turn now."

She smiled at me. "Thank you. I'm glad Haidee has you." She cupped her hands, and a plant grew out of the sand before us, eventually depositing a heavy, spine-covered fruit into her hands. "I'm going to give this to Lan. She hasn't eaten much today."

I found Haidee talking with the lordling, Vanya, when I returned. Her back was toward me, but I could see the earnestness on the boy's face, the infatuation that he couldn't completely hide, and my stomach worked itself up in knots.

I knew that he and Haidee had a shared history. I hadn't known that her mother had arranged an engagement between them in her absence. I was confident enough in Haidee's love for me, but I had to hesitate. If by some miracle we were successful, Haidee could return to her old life in the Golden City, and all the luxuries afforded to her there—including a devoted fiancé. I couldn't offer her any of that.

My first instinct was to linger. The second instinct soon overrode the first; I shouldn't be listening in, if I claimed to trust her. I turned to leave, only to find Lisette blocking my path, a huge grin on her face.

She grabbed my shirt and dragged me behind a nearby dune, shushed me when I made an indignant sound. "You're too noisy. We won't be able to hear what they're saying."

"This isn't any of our business," I hissed back.

"You've always been so noble, Arjun, but I don't trust that man. I still think he's an agent for his father. Better to apologize to your girl later than be betrayed and not see it coming, don't you think? He might be convincing her to turn on us."

I scowled. "Haidee wouldn't do that."

"Shush. They'll hear you if you try to leave now."

"—can't believe this," Vanya was saying. The dolt had finally discarded his woolen coat in favor of an undershirt and a thin cloak. "You're the queen of the Golden City! A goddess! Why are you choosing to remain here with these desert people, in these . . ." And here he scrunched up his nose in horror. "You can be afforded more protection in the Citadel! The galla can't get to you there! There isn't even any plumbing here!"

"Why protest now? This never concerned you before."

The lordling wilted. "I may not be able to return to the city, but now that I've taken better stock of the conditions here, I'm worried for *your* safety. It's obvious how some of these clans don't want us around. I can hear them muttering when they think no one else hears. I don't want to be caught in the middle of a mutiny."

"That's my problem to deal with. And there are more things to life than good plumbing, milord. I've crawled through air vents and hammered out pipes as a mechanika. I rode halfway around the world in a rig I modified myself! Don't you see? I don't have to be in the Golden City to be a goddess! The citizens there aren't my only subjects!"

"But don't you want to return when this is over?"

"I . . . don't know. The more I learn about the world outside, the less inclined I am to remain inside the gilded cage Mother built for me."

"Would it be so bad?" Vanya persisted. "You don't have to be outside the city to rule over the people beyond it. You'd have the backing of the whole council, and all the influence and power they can muster. Out here you have nothing but scarce resources, a few dozen men and women for security, and barely a tenth of the authority your mother wields. I want to find this temple and the secrets of Brighthenge, but I'm also thinking about what happens after."

"Are you asking me to return to honor the engagement Mother made with you and your father? Do you think returning to the Golden City will make me change my mind?"

Vanya's lips thinned. "I would be lying if I said I didn't want it. I . . . Haidee, from almost the moment I first laid eyes on you, it was like someone had cast a spell over me. The city needs you more than you think they do. You have to convince Her Holiness to see things your way. I'd hoped that in time, you'd come to feel the same way for me that I feel for—"

"No, Vanya." Haidee cut him off, though her voice was unexpectedly gentle, even sad. "I'm sorry. I won't ever feel the same way. I'll always be grateful that you chose to disobey your father, but you cannot use that as a weapon to make me honor an engagement I didn't want."

The boy shook his head. "I came here because my father was in the wrong, and I believed you when you said you wanted to save Aeon. I would never use this against you. I only wish . . . But it's Arjun that's keeping you here, isn't it?"

"He's one of the reasons, yes." Haidee's expression had gone very soft, a smile on her lips, and my heartbeat quickened. "I love him. But even if I'd never met him, I would have rejected the engagement. I want to choose my own partner, on my own terms. I won't allow Mother to control my life any longer. If you still wish to go, I can arrange to bring you safely back to the Golden City."

Vanya laughed then, bitter. "I burned all my bridges when I made my decision, Your Holiness. I left a letter to my father explaining exactly what I thought of him—words I'd never had the guts to say to his face. Whatever your decision about the engagement, I have no plans to return."

"What a load of crock," Lisette said, very loudly.

Haidee gasped, and Vanya rose to his feet, alarmed. Lisette strode forward, and I groaned. "You're an unmitigated liar," the girl began heatedly, showing no embarrassment at all that she'd been eavesdropping.

"I said nothing untrue," the boy protested.

"You claimed to have cut all your ties to your father, took steps to ensure you would no longer be welcomed back. And yet here you are, enticing Lady Haidee with the possibility of returning so you can rule by her side. Who do you intend to fool? You're either a spy for your father, or—"

"How *dare* you insinuate that I would do something so dastard—"

"—you've gotten cold feet, overwhelmed by what you've done, so you're talking Lady Haidee into returning so you can get back into your father's good graces—because that is the only scenario in which he could welcome you back."

"I will not stand here and allow myself to be insulted by an unprincipled nomad who's never known responsibility for anything bigger than herself," Vanya said stiffly. "If you'll excuse me, Lady Haidee."

"You're going to have to apologize to him," Haidee said once the boy was out of earshot.

"Me?" Lisette looked surprised. "It was a statement of fact, Your Holiness. He does not have the temperament to be out here in the desert. The sooner he returns home, the less of a liability he becomes for us. We got everything we needed from him."

"That doesn't matter," I groaned. "Of course he doesn't have the temperament; he's been sheltered and pampered his whole life. I'll be the last one to admit it to his face, but he had some gumption, defecting. Of course, it was only after his father called him worthless, but . . ."

"Why are you of all people taking his side?" Lisette accused. "Isn't he your rival?"

"Vanya would only be a rival if I reciprocated his feelings," Haidee said. "You really must apologize, Lisette. It takes courage to defy everyone and everything you've known, to do the right thing like he has."

Lisette threw up her hands. "Fine," she grumbled, stalking away. "Although I don't see why I turned out to be the villain in all this."

"Should I be angry at *you* for listening in on us?" Haidee asked me.

I cleared my throat, prepared to blame everything on Lisette. "I was against it, but she was persistent about her suspicions."

"And do you always go along with everything she suspects?"

I abandoned that plan. "No," I admitted. "It's just easy for her to rile me up whenever you're involved."

"Are you saying you don't trust me?" But she was smiling.

"We haven't had the chance to be alone much these days, what with everything else, so I wasn't very happy to learn he was trying to wheedle you back."

"He's feeling panicked. So was I, on the way to Brighthenge. It always feels intimidating to defy a parent. He'll get over it. And we're alone now, aren't we?"

"What?"

"I said, we're alone now." She took a step toward me. Her smile grew wider. "Wasn't that what you wanted?"

The skies chose that moment to open up. Haidee gasped as

water rained down on us—a full-out storm instead of a light shower.

"Better find somewhere dry," I said gruffly. I could see the others retreating back into their tents or the caves appropriated for their use, leaving only the few scouts on duty.

She tugged harder at my arm. "My tent's all the way on the other side of camp. I know a place no one else is using. We can wait out the rain there."

I let her lead me to a large, roomy cave, dry and equipped with the bare essentials: a woven blanket, covered pails of clean water, small sticks for fire. "Look at that," Haidee whispered as she pointed into the distance, her voice awed.

A thunderstorm loomed over the horizon; far enough away not to be worrisome, but near enough that we could bear witness to its fury. Lightning crackled and zigzagged through the air, and I could see Fire patterns spiraling out from it, arching up, dazzling, into the night sky. I could only imagine what Haidee must be seeing. "It's beautiful," she whispered.

"Yeah," I echoed, staring at her, at the way the light was flickering across her face, casting a soft, pretty glow. Her hair moved against the air in shades of pink and gold.

She turned to me and smiled again, and I couldn't resist.

I missed her. Missed the way her mouth felt against mine, the way her body curled into mine like we belonged. Missed the choked breathy sounds she made when I dared to do more, missed her hands fisting in my hair when I drew her down. She was a safe shore to steer for after Faraji's death, and being here with her reminded me that this sadness, too, could pass. The ground was hard against my back, but she was warm and inviting above me, and that was all that mattered.

"I've been thinking about this," she whispered against my neck, "ever since the village."

"Are you sure?" I owed her so much more than this. She deserved more than a rickety bed among ruins then, and she deserved more than a cave in the middle of nowhere now. She deserved more than just a promise to love her always. But she'd left her glittering city for me, because there was nothing good enough for her there, either.

Maybe she saw something worthier in me instead. The realization humbled me.

She lifted her head to look down at me, a glorious picture. The sporadic flashes of lightning cast her in an ethereal light—surely Inanna or one of her ancestors had been worshipped in the past as a deity of beauty, too.

"I've always been sure," she said, and leaned down to kiss me again.

Afterward, she curled against me, idle fingers tracing a path down my chest, grazing my stomach. The rain was falling harder, but the cave was warm enough that our bed of discarded clothes and our body heat gave us all the comfort we needed. "Do you think they're going to wonder where we are?" she asked.

"Not if they know what's good for them," I rumbled, and

she laughed. "Most are scared enough of the night as it is, and the Salt Sea's return has shaken them. They'll probably search for us after the rain lets up."

"Good." She threw an arm over my waist. "I wish we could stay here forever."

I wished that, too. Wished the goddesses could stop Aeon from spinning again, wished they could stop the hours and the days so we could have all the time in the world. I could almost believe that I could spend the remainder of my days here, with nothing but Haidee and the rest of my life to cherish her.

You will die for her one day, Jesmyn's ghost had told me.

But first, you must die, my mother's shade had agreed.

Fingers brushed against my mouth. "You're frowning," Haidee said. "I don't like that. What are you thinking about?"

I smiled, and caught her hand. "Nothing at all."

There was the sound of rain slapping rhythmically against stone. Thunder roared somewhere overhead. Here in this moment, it was easy to believe nothing else mattered but us.

Chapter Eighteen

'LAN AND THE FORGOTTEN SHRINE

—————————— ☾ ——————————

I NEVER THOUGHT I'D BE so happy to see so much water again; it stunned me how calm the Salt Sea was when compared to the raging ocean that surrounded Aranth. Though everyone was dismantling the campsite, eager to be off as soon as was possible, I saw several clan members, including Tamera, pausing in their work to watch the waters, awed.

But there were far too many changes. Far too many things that could go wrong simply because the world we'd known was no longer the world we saw. And it was making me nervous.

The Salt Sea was not as impressive as its name implied. It was gray and brackish, no more than half a dozen feet deep at the first three or four hundred paces, and Tamera's scouts had found nothing living within those boundaries. But it was water, and out here in the sunlands that meant life.

Janella had returned, as she'd promised, with several Devoted to accompany us. There would be four dozen or so jeeps in total. The bulk of Asteria's followers, including the goddess herself, were to remain behind at their camp near the Golden City, while several soldiers handpicked by Asteria had come along with the Devoted, ostensibly for backup should the galla swarm strike again. Arjun and Janella were our only Firesmokers capable of blue flames, and one of them had to stay behind to shore up defenses.

Our alliance was fragile; the clan leaders were still suspicious of Asteria and her soldiers. I was wary, too, because she had placed Janella in charge of accompanying Salla and the other clans back to Asteria's camp. I found no reason to trust the girl, was dismayed my liege would persist in this. The other girl knew of my dislike and kept her distance.

There was no guarantee that we would ever find this strange temple, having nothing to rely on but Vanya's interpretation of the passages, the Hellmakers' dubious knowledge of the area, and Haidee's unshakable will. The cannibals' presence still put the other clans on edge, though for the moment the Saiga clan were on their best behavior. Odessa had gone so far as to give the gate-users among them back their abilities, and their response had embarrassed her. Every Hellmaker had fallen to their knees before her, chanting exaltations. They appeared genuine; being provided for was obviously a novelty to them, and one they relished.

The rains had finally let up, giving way to what seemed like another long bout of sun. Charley, who was polishing one of the rigs, looked up and gasped. I did the same, and spotted a bridge of color lancing across the clearing sky, the view so unexpected that many others stopped and stared and pointed, their amazement greater than it had been at even their first glimpse of sunrise.

Mother Salla was unperturbed, a rare smile on her face. "A rainbow," she explained. "Sometimes they come as a storm clears."

"It's just like Their Holinesses' hair," Charley marveled.

Odessa reached up self-consciously, combing through her locks. Their colors shifted to mimic the variety of hues above us, almost instinctively. "It's beautiful. I'm going to treat this as a good omen for the day ahead."

Arjun and Haidee trotted toward us. I took note of the rumpled state of their clothes, the wild arrangement of their hair, the way their hands were constantly reaching out for each other, lightly skimming across skin, wanting some evidence of the other's company. I smiled. At least there were two people in camp who'd had a good night.

Odessa looked at me, and then at Haidee. Her sister blushed, and my goddess giggled.

I waggled my eyebrows at Arjun. The grin he shot my way was almost bashful. "Had to find shelter from the rain," he said.

"I'm sure you did." I would have offered him some of the Liangzhu's deathworm piss-wine, but the girls were watching. It was nice to see him sounding more like himself again.

"I'm still not sure setting the cannibals loose was wise,"

Arjun grumbled to Haidee. "You do remember that the one with the scar tried to eat me, right? And tried to eat you too, now that I think about it."

"His name is Bull," Haidee informed him.

He sighed. "Naming them again?"

"They named themselves this time. They spent a good part of the morning yelling their names out just because they can." She sighed. "This is a good thing, Arjun. With names, they can finally start remembering that they're human, too, and not just meat for emergencies."

"Where's Lord Vanya?" I snapped. The boy, I was told by the other camp dwellers, was not an early riser, but he knew today was important. We absolutely had to return before the next wave of galla arrived.

"The proximity of the Golden City should afford us more protection, even if Latona refuses to aid us," Mother Salla said. "But Tamera has asked to join you."

"Well," Arjun began diplomatically.

The Fennec clan mistress actually smiled. "My people are the ones most familiar with the area, after the . . . Saiga men." She grimaced at calling them by their clan name. "Perhaps I have grown too cynical, but this seems to me a very long shot. And yet we have little other recourse."

"There is much knowledge to be had in books, clan mistress," Odessa said softly. "People remember. People write things down, in the hopes of enlightening the next generation. I hope everything we have learned from this particular book will be enough to return things to their proper course."

"And what is the proper course, Your Holiness? Do you intend to bring back the old glory days where the goddesses ruled and the Devoted ran the cities? To repeat their mistakes all over again? I am old enough to remember what those days were like. Perhaps I am not so eager to put my life back into the hands of those who destroyed the world in the first place."

Both Haidee and Odessa met her rebuke with implacable calm. They stood side by side, one with her darker skin and short bob, and the other fair-complexioned, with hair coiled into a loose tail that trailed down her waist. When one spoke, it felt like the other did, too. "We aren't eager for those days ourselves, if those stories are true," Haidee said. "We don't know what the answer is yet, clan mistress—"

"—but we do know that we and the goddesses that shall come after us can no longer afford to stay sheltered and ignorant, as our predecessors had been," Odessa continued. "That much we can promise."

The older woman shook her head in wonder. "Perhaps there is hope for us still. But the future is still some long ways away— as is this alleged temple."

"We'll find it," Arjun rumbled. "I wound up traveling halfway around the world with Her Holiness on gut instinct, and I was right, wasn't I?"

Haidee blushed again. Odessa laughed, a welcome sound.

Lord Vanya finally arrived, bright red and fumbling. I was about to reprimand him for oversleeping, then paused. There was something odd about his appearance. The lordling's usually painstakingly neat clothes were uncharacteristically rumpled, and tufts of dark hair stood up from his head. His embarrassed demeanor I presumed was for his tardiness, until Lisette sauntered up.

The pretty girl was practically purring. There was an extra bounce in her step, and she looked like she had stolen the choicest parts of the meat Sonfei had cooked that morning without anyone the wiser. In contrast, her normally messy shirt and breeches had been carefully smoothed out, and the well-polished Howler slung over her shoulder gleamed, slick with whale oil.

Arjun looked at them and groaned. "You didn't."

"It has nothing to do with you," the young clan mistress said glibly, breezing past them toward one of the jeeps. "You should be thanking me for distracting him."

"I—" Vanya stammered. "I wasn't—I didn't expect—I had a—"

Sonfei, who had been checking the wheels of his own rig nearby, began to laugh uproariously.

"They didn't!" Haidee exclaimed, her eyes wide. Odessa clapped a hand to her mouth before a snort could escape.

"Oh, they did," Arjun said darkly. He looked to the lordling, who was still trying to find words, and took pity on him. "The best way to go about this," he said, clapping the noble's back, "is to enjoy the moment for what it is."

"I wasn't thinking," Lord Vanya managed to squeak out.

"That's often the case, yes."

The cannibals occupied three of the two dozen jeeps. They took the lead, careening on ahead; their driving was just as haphazard as everything else about them.

"Full bellies keep them under control more easily than any chains can," Sonfei observed. He and a couple of the Liangzhu made up another rig; the big man had insisted on accompanying us from the very start, but directed the rest of his clan to go with Mother Salla and the others to Asteria's camp. "We are good at extracting water out of everything," he boasted, his vehicle keeping easy pace alongside ours as we tore through the sands. "In our home we have taken water out of everything to survive; from the smallest particles of sand, from the very air, from the monsters that prowl the Sand Sea, from the deathworms. If there is anything to siphon out of this desert, then my Mudforgers will find a way."

"I'm sorry," said one of Tamera's clanswomen, a fresh-faced girl named Cailin. "Did you say *deathworms*?"

Sonfei responded with a lovingly enthusiastic and excessively long description of the creature in question. The roar of the engines was no match for the sound of his booming voice, and by the time he was done, most of the others wore a faintly greenish cast. Cailin herself looked like she'd regretted asking before he was even halfway done. "I miss them," the man said sadly, like he was talking about beloved pets. "It is true that they be gigantic parasites with razor-sharp teeth, but they be helping sustain us for all these years. They be admirable, noble creatures."

"You were at the Breaking when it happened, weren't you?"

another Fennec clan member asked. "Did you escape through those strange portals too, like Asteria and Latona?"

"No. We fled as the mountain broke into two, away from the shadows that swarmed the chasm. We ran as far as we could, but we not be running far enough; the world warped and twisted all over, and we saw the corruption set in, even hundreds of miles away. We saw the ground spit up sulfur and acid like poisonous fountains. We saw the trees decay and rot down to their cores. The Sand Sea was a new phenomenon then; the strange magic from the Great Abyss corrupted it long before we arrived at its shores, and it be turning the life-giving waters into churning gravel." His eyes grew distant, and I suspected he was thinking again of Asteria.

My curiosity got the better of me. "I worked for Asteria for almost all my life," I said slowly, trying to figure out the right way to phrase my intentions without giving offense, "and I never heard her mention your name. She doesn't talk much about her life before Aranth."

Sonfei nodded. "If I may?" he asked, and before anyone could answer he immediately vaulted off his jeep to land in the empty seat beside mine, his eyes aglow from his air-gate. "I do not be blaming her," he said, lowering his voice and ignoring the annoyed yelp from Arjun as he fought the wheel to adjust to the new unexpected weight. "She must be having a lot of trauma to unpack, and it is easier, I think, to ignore me than to address it head-on. It is the same whether you are a lowly Liangzhu or a noble goddess. Did your parents tell you much about us Liangzhu?"

"No. My father was gone before I was even born, and I never knew much about him. My mother I recall dimly, but she died of a lingering sickness before I was four years old."

"Tianlan means 'blue sky,' did you know?"

"Yes. A little ironic, considering I'd never actually seen one until a few days ago."

"A name is an important thing. To a Liangzhu mother, a name is not given because of what she sees around her, but what she sees in her child. And Asteria . . ." He paused, his gaze fixed on one of the sand dunes before us, his face a forlorn sight. "Asteria wanted to have a child. But it meant nothing, when she couldn't be with the one she loved. She fought with Latona before her twin and her husband, Aranth, departed for Farthengrove. She cut them off, told them never to return. It be easier for her to staunch her wounds than wait for them to heal with time."

"I'm sorry," I said. Odessa was silent, her head tilted to one side, listening. But her pale eyes were glittering, like she was holding back tears.

"It is what it is. That I am not the one for her does not mean that I love her any less. If she can remember me with fondness one day, then that is all I will be hoping for. It is a Liangzhu problem, to love too fiercely." He grinned. "Is she your *yexu* yet?"

I felt my face flame.

"Do not be so shy about it, Tianlan. There is no shame in wearing your love with pride."

"She does." Odessa curled an arm around me, smiled back at Sonfei. "I'm her *yexu*."

He chuckled. "The little goddess is, at least, more forthcoming. Celebrate happiness wherever you can. It is a good code to live by, even when living in a desert of shifting sands."

"Asteria is still here," Odessa said. "Will you take the chance as well?"

Sonfei froze. "That is very different. You saw her rejection of me, little one."

"You said yourself that she cuts people out of her life so she won't have to care too much. Mother has been lonely for a very long time. I think it would be good for her to see you again, to help her remember the better times."

"You are a very idealistic lady."

"And very forthcoming about it, as you said."

"An asset. I do not know what I will do when I face Asteria again. But it eases my soul very much, to know that she is here."

A very different conversation was taking place in one of the other rigs to my left, one composed mainly of long silences. Lord Vanya had not been happy about being placed in the same vehicle as Lisette, who was behind the wheel, and he'd buried his face in *The Ages of Aeon*, refusing to raise his head. Lisette kept sneaking glances back at him.

Noelle, who was unfortunate enough to be sitting with them, cleared her throat. "You're supposed to let us know if we've passed any landmarks."

"I know," came the muffled response from behind the pages. "But I'm not very familiar with the lay of the land, either."

"You weren't familiar with the lay of the land last night."

Lisette seized upon Noelle's words to reach out to Vanya again. "But you did quite well, if I do say so myself."

The figure behind the book slunk down farther.

"Do you want to talk about it now?"

"No."

"I promise to be gentle. Not at all like—"

"Good goddess, woman!" Lord Vanya roared. "I don't want to talk about it, least of all with you!"

Lisette sighed, then fell silent.

"Thank you," Noelle murmured, speaking to no one and everyone at once.

"Serves her right," Arjun muttered, pulling slightly away from the other rig so the words didn't carry over the wind.

"Arjun," Haidee chided.

"She's used to being the center of attention, to getting her way. Vanya's stumping her."

Our hope of finding landmarks, it seemed, had been too optimistic. The springs that could have marked the route had long dried out, and though we spotted a few broken, crumbling structures along the way, we could ascertain no recognizable shapes.

"This is where the going gets rougher," Tamera told us. "The sands peter out here, and the rocks make it harder to drive. Hopefully our rigs will not suffer too much from the shocks."

"The shocks?" I echoed.

"The constant pressure coming from underneath the ground

causes small explosions," one of Tamera's clanmates informed us. "The whole place appears to be made of flat rock, and stress from the Breaking has caused it to shift and fracture constantly. The movement isn't strong enough to cause injury, but it can be alarming if you're not used to it. And loud."

We stopped to rest two hours in. There were now more rocks here than sand, and we wanted to get our bearings before we moved on. Sonfei's Mudforgers squeezed out as much water as they could from the air, and we dined on fruit and dried meat, took turns keeping an eye on the Hellmakers and watching for any suggestion of the galla's presence. Lord Vanya was studiously avoiding Lisette, who was now clearly irate at still being ignored. The cannibals, without any prompting, set up their own camp separately from ours, perhaps sensing that they were not yet forgiven, though they still groveled happily whenever either Haidee or Odessa walked by.

The twins spent a couple of hours talking quietly, their hands linked as if their need to maintain physical contact was paramount. I understood; there was a powerful connection between them that transcended normal relationships. By all accounts, Asteria and Latona's own closeness had been just as strong at their first meeting, which was why their falling out had been particularly devastating. I didn't feel jealous; to be threatened over their obvious bond felt like refusing to accept a part of who Odessa was.

"What do you think they talk about?" Arjun asked. "Half the time they finish each other's sentences anyway."

"From the way they're sneaking glances in your direction now, I have a pretty good idea."

He actually blushed. "Yeah? You're telling me you haven't fooled around with her yet?"

"We've done plenty. But I'm not going to push her for more. Not when she's dealing with so much."

"I can understand that. How's she holding up? Can't be easy, especially with the galla."

"She's doing well. I don't think I would have done as well as she has. I don't want anything to happen to either of them." I loved Odessa. Arjun loved Haidee. We both knew what the stakes were.

He nodded. "Then we just gotta make sure, right?"

The ground grew harder and more jagged when we resumed driving, and we were forced to slow down as the rigs' wheels grated over broken stones, jarring us from our seats with growing frequency. Our sightings of broken statues, the ruined foundations of what might once have been cities, and other detritus grew more frequent. But the cannibals never faltered, heading unerringly west, and we followed.

Hissing noises sounded nearby, and Tamera cursed loudly, swerving wildly to the left as the stones underneath her jeep slid against each other with harsh grating noises, large cracks opening between them. We drove as fast as we dared, avoiding the steam that rose up from the fissures. Thirty paces away, the rocks broke apart with a loud bang, an unseen force from below spitting them up into the air.

"Like I said," Arjun grumbled. "Not too dangerous, but they don't help us go any faster."

It was another hour before we finally caught sight of the mirages. There were a dozen of them in a close circle—a literal interpretation of what *The Ages of Aeon* had described. They remained unmoving. It unnerved me. Not even their cloaks were being picked up by the wind.

"That's more than I've ever seen in one place," Lisette said. "Is Her Holiness Odessa right, that something here is animating these ghouls, somehow?"

There was no trace of a shrine here either. Only one small statue stood at the center of the mirages' grotesque gathering, weathered from age. Its head and parts of its face were gone, but one arm was raised, pointing ramrod straight in our direction.

"It's got a female figure," Noelle whispered. "Just like that statue back at Brighthenge."

No temple.

But there was a pool.

The statue stood in the middle of a small pond of water. Water that was physically impossible in the driest part of the Skeleton Coast.

Tamera made a sound of surprise, taking a step closer to the circle.

"Wait!" Haidee ordered.

"There's a reason they're circling the area like this." I took a tentative step toward the mirages. None of them looked up at us. Arjun moved even closer, eyed the distance between them

292

and us. "Step into the circle," he instructed Bull, who was watching him a little more expectantly than he should.

The leader held back. "What?" he asked, with a startling nervousness he'd never displayed before.

"You look a little too expectant for me not to think you're waiting for something to happen." Arjun aimed his Howler in the man's direction. "Either step into the circle, or spit it out."

"Wait!" the cannibal squealed. "There are traps hidden beneath the surface!"

"What traps?"

"The traps that be killing these poor fellows," one of Sonfei's people, Oda, spoke up. He pointed to something on the ground, half hidden by the sand. To my horror and disgust, I recognized it as a grinning skull, bleached by the unending sun. Farther on, I saw a partially concealed corpse; there were no predators about, so it lay rotting with nothing to disturb its remains. Its clothes were blackened.

"You're all going to describe to me in painstaking detail what these traps are," Arjun said, "if you don't want us using any of you to spring them."

"We don't know!" another of the cannibals cried out. "There was a flash like lightning, and then the meat was dead, burning. We ran."

Noelle bent down and picked up a small rock. Hefting it expertly, she threw it in the direction of the shrine—

—and it felt like the whole world had caught on fire. We dove to the ground as flames lashed out, engulfing the stone and dying out almost as quickly as they had begun.

"What . . . ," Arjun said, spitting out sand. "What the *hell* was—"

"My apologies," Noelle said. "There are no winds in these parts. I wondered if any errant movement would serve as a trigger. It seems that these mirages are marking the radius of where it becomes dangerous for us."

"They're actually *warning* us of these traps," Tamera sputtered. "Protecting us!"

"I cannot walk on air to access it, then?" Sonfei asked.

"If you don't want to share the same fate as the rock I threw, no."

Haidee shivered. "How do we get past it?"

"Let me figure something out," I said. "The rest of you keep your distance."

"I'm not going to let you do anything dangerous, Lan," Odessa said fiercely.

"I don't intend to do anything dangerous. But of all of us here I'm the one with the most experience taking stock of strange territories." The clans knew the sunlands better than I did, but exploring unknown terrain was *my* specialty, and I was determined to be useful. "Trust me."

She took a deep breath. "I do. Please be careful."

I gave her a quick kiss, then began to circle the mirages. The sand within the radius was far too pristine, marred only at the points where the unfortunate corpses lay. There were half a dozen bodies that I could see at a glance; soldier's uniforms on some, raggedy clothing like the Hellmakers' on others.

Halfway through my survey, a sudden flash of light caught my attention. I looked up, and nearly fell over.

The eyes of the half-destroyed statue stared at me, a dazzling bright blue.

The others wasted no time copying my route, after I'd explained. "I don't see it," Odessa said, puzzled.

Arjun positioned himself in the exact spot where I'd been standing, and muffled a curse. "I can only see it when I stand at this point," he said tersely. "What kind of trick is this?"

"Wait!" The agonized cry came from Lord Vanya. "'Where blue shines brightest; let it show you the way.' That's what the passage meant!"

"But that means nothing," Tamera scoffed.

"Noelle," I said. "Fancy you could put your stone-throwing abilities to the test again?"

Noelle bent to retrieve another rock. "Where do you want it, milady?"

"Imagine a straight line between Arjun and the statue. Toss it anywhere within that path."

Noe's aim was true. The rock sailed in a perfect curve and landed in the sand within the mirages' circle.

Nothing happened. The sands didn't catch fire; the stone landed unmolested.

"As long as you keep a direct line of sight to those glowing blue eyes," I said, "then you can enter the circle without harm."

"A rock is one thing," Arjun said, "and a human body is

another. I can fight almost anything, but hell if I can walk in the absolute straight line this requires."

"I can try something," Odessa said, taking Arjun's place, "but I'll need some of your water rations, and Haidee's help." She looked over at Haidee.

"I understand," was the prompt response. "And I can use air patterns to pack in the sand from either side, so it's as straight as we can manage it."

I offered Odessa my flask. Her and her sister's eyes glowed, one a bright amber and the other a silvery gray, and a thin wall of wet, tightly packed sand slowly rose on either side of the line I had indicated, bordering the safe path leading into the shrine. The mirages on either side of it didn't even budge.

I took a step into the circle. Odessa cried out, but nothing else happened. I took several more steps, not stopping until I was halfway through. "Well," I said, not bothering to hide my relief. "That was a rush."

"Please tell me what you intend to do before you actually do it," Odessa yelled at me.

I grinned at her. "Why does it feel—colder in here?"

She stared at me, eyes widening, then turned to face the statue. Her eyes glowed, just as blue as the figure's.

Something rippled through the air surrounding the statue, the effect much like that of a reflection on a lake disturbed by some idle hand. I crouched down, expecting the worst, but the ripples only extended outward, until they wavered and vanished. The statue was still there, but a temple now loomed behind it: smaller than Brighthenge, propped up by columns on three of its four sides, with the fourth on the ground, broken up into pieces.

"I wrung the water out of the air," Odessa breathed.

"A mirage," Haidee gasped at the same time. "A true mirage—an illusion of the desert; a displacement of light that can be distorted by colder air as it descends. Leeching the water out broke the illusion."

We all looked at each other. "'Take water from where your eyes cannot see,'" Vanya repeated shakily.

"Hell," Arjun said, and I agreed.

Chapter Nineteen

ODESSA AND THE TRIALS

———————— ☾ ————————

NOT EVERYONE WOULD BE ENTERING the temple. Tamera and her clan were to stand guard outside, partly to keep an eye on the cannibals but also to alert us of any more hostiles. The cannibals were happy enough to remain behind, clearly wanting nothing to do with the place. From the outside, it looked to be no bigger than my room back at Aranth—

I stopped, forcing myself not to think about Aranth. My city was gone. There was nothing I could do about it. Moving forward, protecting what people I had left was the only option I had—

But even that was deceptive. We realized as soon as we crossed the threshold that no shrine existed within; only stairs that led further underground, further into the unknown. Should galla descend on Tamera and the others, we might not even be able to hear them. Should *we* encounter any threats, they might not be able to hear *us*.

"It explains why they chose to build a shrine here, of all places," Noelle noted. "The layer of hard rock above would make this an ideal place for secrets. Any artifacts stored here could last longer away from the sun's heat."

"At this point," Lisette grumbled, "I wouldn't be surprised if the artifact was Inanna's bleeding heart, considering the ways this place has already tried to kill us."

"Stay with Tamera," Arjun told her. "You aren't used to closed, dark spaces."

"Neither are you. If you can do it, so can I." She paused. "I'd appreciate some light, though. A *lot* of light."

Lan took the lead over my protests, arguing that she had the most experience with unknown terrain—true enough, but that didn't mean I liked it. Sonfei and two of his Liangzhu, Pai and Oda, also accompanied us.

The corridors were dark and smelled moldy, but no other traps had lain in wait for us so far. Our progress was slow but steady, with my Catseye stopping to inspect nicks in the walls and floor in case they were trigger mechanisms for snares. Haidee and I reached out with our gates, trying to feel for potential threats, searching for anything that felt atypical: unnatural concentrations of metal, for example, or areas of unexpected heat in the otherwise cool surroundings.

"Be cautious," Lan said. "The path widens from this point on, so I want you all to stay close. Try to step exactly where I go."

"Water," Arjun said.

"I have some to spare," Haidee offered.

"No, I *hear* water."

"That's impossible," my sister said, shocked. "This is the most arid part of the Skeleton Coast."

But I already had my hand pressed against the wall, concentrating. "You're both right," I gasped, repulsed. "It feels like there's a large stream up ahead, but at the same time it's—*not* a stream at all."

"And if that's water," Lisette said grimly, "then it's shining a lot more brightly than any I've seen before."

Lan cursed, coming to an abrupt stop. "Stay back!" she ordered.

It was my turn to gasp. Flowing perpendicular to us was a river. But there was something peculiar about the way it looked; a glimmer to it that I've never seen in the seas of Aranth, a bright waxiness that clung to the sheen on its surface.

"That isn't water!" Haidee cried out. "It's quicksilver! Don't fall in!"

"Does quicksilver occur naturally underneath rocks like this?" Lisette demanded.

"Not at this concentration," Lord Vanya whispered. "But the Golden City maintains some quicksilver mines—Father owns one, in fact. Finding a natural deposit isn't a surprise, but not in liquid form like this. This was deliberately planted here."

"But for what? Is it another trap?"

"Quicksilver has a greater density than most liquids," Haidee said. "The cooling system inside the Golden City is run with it in place of water. You could technically walk on quicksilver, if you don't consider other factors."

"What other factors?"

"Quicksilver has little surface tension. You're more likely to fall down when you try to stand on quicksilver, and walking would be all but impossible. It's also toxic when ingested in large amounts. So are its fumes."

"Not just in large amounts," Lan confirmed grimly, her eyes glowing ivory and gold. "They've added something else to this river. I can literally see the poison running through it."

"Great," Arjun said. "What you're saying is we can't stay here long or we'll die from poisoned fumes, and we can't go across because contact might kill us."

"We do not be needing to walk *on* water." Sonfei's eyes flashed white, and unseen winds lifted him off his feet. "I will be back." He was off before anyone could stop him.

"Let him," Haidee sighed. "He's very bad at following orders, anyway."

"Somebody went through all this trouble to construct these traps," Arjun said. "What is it they're keeping here that's so important they would kill to protect it?"

"My father kept this a secret from Her Holiness," Lord Vanya said quietly. "Maybe he knows something we don't."

"You're hiding something else," Lisette told him.

"What?"

"Your lower lip juts out when you're keeping something back. I think it's adorable."

Vanya, who was doing exactly that, glared. "I saw some of the corpses as we were entering the shrine. Some of their clothes resembled those that my father's soldiers wear."

I recalled the state of some of the corpses, half-hidden by

the sand. Lord Arrenley's soldier had worn similar colors in the Citadel, before I'd struck him with—

No. Stop thinking about it, stop thinking about it, stop thinking about—

"What was the book you were reading, the first time we met?" Lan asked calmly.

"What?"

"The book you were reading, when I first saw you at Old Wallof's bookstore. What was it called?"

"*The Queen and Her Hunter.* Eric the Huntsman and Queen Rahne." She knew. She knew what I was thinking somehow, and she was helping me keep my sanity. I felt my heartbeat slowing down as I focused. "He was poaching deer—that's an animal with four legs—in her forests, and he chanced to see her riding with her lady's maids. It was love at first sight."

"How appropriate, then. I was hunting through books when I looked up and saw you."

"I wish I'd told you who I was from the very start." I still hadn't completely forgiven myself for lying, for the fallout that came after.

She planted the tiniest of kisses on my mouth. "That's in the past. And I can't deny that I don't regret everything that happened afterward."

Sonfei soon returned, looking triumphant. "There is an ending to the endless river," he informed us. "It is perhaps over a mile out, nearer two, before you can find dry ground by the giant's face."

"By the what, now?" Arjun asked.

"A giant's face, carved into one of the walls. I look at it as proof that we be following the right path."

"I don't really want to know why there's a giant's face sculpted into an underground cave wall," Lisette said.

"Let's worry about that once we get there." Arjun scowled. "How do we get across? I'm not a Windshifter or a Skyrider."

"Perhaps we can squeeze the poison out?" One of the Liangzhu, Pai, asked, her eyes glowing amber. Terra patterns burrowed into the quicksilver, but kept constantly sliding away from the liquid, like it was too slippery to find a firmer grip. "The poison is too bonded to this peculiar liquid. It would take hours to separate."

"Ice?" I wondered.

"No," Lan decided. "Freezing this whole river would tire you and Haidee out too quickly."

"It is a good thing, then, that I am here with you," Sonfei said. "I shall carry you all across."

"All of us?" Arjun asked skeptically.

"Perhaps not all," he conceded. "I am strong, but I have limits."

"I can carry maybe two others," I said.

"As can I," Haidee spoke up. "Though it will be rough going."

Sonfei was an adept-enough Skyrider that he could lift Vanya, Lisette, and his two clanmates easily into the air. I was able to do the same with Lan while Haidee took Arjun, and then we divided Noelle's weight between us. I'd never had to carry anyone else this way before; pulling Lan back into the

Brevity when she'd fallen off the ship, when the devil whale had been stalking us, was the first time I'd ever made the attempt. But Lan smiled at me as I lifted her up, trusting even now.

"I wanted to sweep you off your feet," she whispered. "Not the other way around."

I yearned to kiss her, but I didn't want to distract myself, especially since I was starting to feel the strain. "Time enough for that later," I whispered back.

Slowly, we pushed ourselves through the air above the flowing quicksilver river. Sonfei had promised no more than a couple of miles' work, but when you're carrying your body-weight plus someone else's, two miles felt like forever. My strength was waning, but I only tightened my grip around Lan and Noelle—I would fall in first before I would ever drop them. Even now Lan was still at work, using her aether-gate to draw as much of the exhaustion out of me as she could.

"This is hard work," Haidee grunted. Arjun had his arm around her waist; I knew he trusted her as much as Lan did me, but the look of terror on his face wasn't going away.

"Draw closer to me if you can," Lan said, "and I'll see what I can do to ease the pressure. The same goes for you, Sonfei."

"My thanks, milady," the man said. "And perhaps you would also extend your healing to Lord Vanya, who be looking close to a heart attack."

"I'm not!" The lordling was adamant, though his insistence didn't bring much color back to his face.

It was when we were rounding a bend that we finally caught

sight of the giant's face that Sonfei had told us about. It was hor-rific. The image of a woman's face glared back at us, grotesque snakes frozen mid-writhe, spiraling out around her face as if they were living hair. The mouth was open far too wide to be natural, and sharp teeth jutted out from the opening.

"I'm assuming this is Inanna," Noelle said. "A chthonic depiction of her, at the least."

A sinister rumbling echoed through the cave, growing louder by the minute. "That doesn't bode well," Sonfei mut-tered. "Let us pick up our pace, ladies."

The sounds grew louder, and it was Lisette who first spotted the projectiles from above. "Move!" she shrieked at us.

Arjun didn't have time to grab his Howler; eyes glowing red, he simply pushed up at the incoming projectiles with both hands. A wall of intense blue fire burned through the arrows heading our way, the high heat enough to turn them into ashes before they could reach us. "I don't mean to sound ungrateful," he yelled, "but we better move faster!"

My breath left me in pained gasps as I struggled to push us quicker, harder. I could see the dry bank looming in front of us, a sign that we were almost at this strange river's end. Lan said nothing, though the warmth I could feel coming from her hands increased, forcing strength back into my arms. Sonfei was grunting hard, the winds around him yanking his passengers forward several feet at a time in short, quick bursts. Haidee's face mirrored my own exhaustion, while Arjun scanned the space above us again, bracing for another assault.

The next wave came when we were almost at the end, our strength nearly gone. With an inhuman roar, Sonfei pushed out with one massive arm, throwing his clanmates onto the safety of solid ground. With another yell, he drew back the other, prepared to do the same with Lisette and Vanya.

More sharp projectiles hurtled down toward us. Arjun blanketed the empty space above us with a fresh wall of blue flames, but this time a few snuck past his defenses. Sonfei cried out in pain as one pierced through his hand, his concentration broken long enough for him to falter, the winds around him giving out.

I grabbed him as he toppled past me, almost from instinct, and the additional weight made me scream in agony and sent us dangerously close to the quicksilver's surface. I heard another cry of pain as Haidee caught Lisette, struggling valiantly to keep her up, but neither of us were quick enough to catch Vanya, who fell right into the river.

"No!" Lisette lunged down, her hands plunging into the liquid, at the spot where he'd disappeared. Haidee groaned, but managed to keep her aloft as the other girl continued to dig frantically until, with a shout of victory, she found the lordling's arm and fished him out.

Sonfei had recovered; pulling free of my grasp and gritting his teeth against the pain, he flung both Lisette and Vanya onto the bank, where the other Liangzhu caught them. He dove and landed beside them with a grunt, hand wrapped around his other wrist where a five-inch arrow lay embedded at the center of his palm.

We dropped to our knees a few feet behind them, caked in sweat and exhausted beyond measure. Lan was by Vanya's side in moments, checking the unconscious boy for signs of life.

"Is he dead?" Lisette asked, pale and tight-lipped.

"He's breathing, but he's ingested some of the poison." Lan pushed down on the boy's chest, and I watched as Aether patterns entered his body, slid down the length of him. "Turn him over to one side," she commanded, and the Addax clan mistress complied, rolling him toward her. Almost immediately Lord Vanya's eyes flew open and he began to choke, coughing up huge globs of silver liquid. Lan pounded him on the back for a few minutes until he stopped gagging, then forced him up into a sitting position. "I think I've gotten everything out," she pronounced.

"One of you should bring him back," Lisette insisted. "He'll be useless here. Surely the other clans can—"

"No," Vanya said, still coughing. "I'm not heading back."

"You oaf! You're in no shape to—"

"Lady Lan said she got everything out, didn't she?"

"It doesn't matter," Arjun said heavily. "We don't have time to bring him back."

"You're heartless," Lisette accused.

"I'm not leaving," Vanya said stubbornly, still the color of candle wax.

"My apologies for interrupting, ladies and gentlemen," Noelle said quietly. "But we must focus on the present if we all are to get out of here alive. It appears to me that this statue hides another entrance."

"Haidee. Odessa. Can either of you sense what's behind it?" Lan had moved on to Sonfei. The large man barely winced as he sent sharp Air cutting through the arrow, as close to the skin as was possible, and hissed softly when my Catseye pulled it out in one quick movement.

Haidee and I were reaching out for each other before I'd even realized it; Haidee's other hand was pressed against the cave wall, while mine was braced on the stone beneath us. As one, our minds burrowed through the strange limestone rocks, toward the faint pulsing we could detect behind the stone face —only to come upon a strange resistance, preventing us from going further.

"There's some odd incanta shielding whatever it is behind this statue," Haidee said. "We can't break through."

"There are two holes on either side of the stone woman," Noelle observed. "There are dark stains around each opening. It could possibly be old blood. I'd advise caution."

"I'm not going to stick my hand in there," Arjun muttered. "I don't have any left to spare."

"There are *two* holes," I pointed out, already angling toward the one on the right.

Lan grabbed my arm. "What are you doing?"

"I would have thought it obvious."

"Odessa—"

"I can do this."

Lan paused and nodded. "I'm staying beside you, just in case," she threatened.

I grinned, because that was exactly what I'd expected her to do. "Of course you will. Haidee?"

"I'm ready when you are."

"Haidee—" Arjun began.

"Trust us?"

The boy exhaled. "Yeah. Always."

Despite our confidence, I could sense the same worry I felt emanating from my twin sister as we both approached. I let my terra-gates flare, let the patterns wrap around my hand and arm, shaping them into the hardest barrier I could manage, and could feel Haidee doing the same. We both took a deep breath at the same moment.

"Ready?" Haidee asked me.

"Yeah. One—"

"Two—"

"Three!"

We both plunged our hands in, and I steeled myself for anything, including pain. I felt something shift behind the stone, a strange pressure building up and then slamming down on our Stonebreaker-protected fists, but I didn't feel so much as a sting.

A light shone out of the carved woman's eyes, that shade of blue I had come to hate. There was a faint whirring and a *click*, like something had locked into place—or like something had been unlatched from the inside.

And then, with a heavy, grating noise, the stone face slowly swung inward.

Chapter Twenty

ᴴAIDEE AND THE STONE

——————— ☼ ———————

WHAT I SAW INSIDE TOOK my breath away.

We found ourselves within a large expanse of cavern—much bigger than the passageway we had just gone through. It was a few hundred feet high, almost as tall as the Citadel. But the immensity of this hidden chamber was not the most surprising thing about it.

The cave was filled to the brim with glittering treasure. Chalices and jewels carpeted the floor, and stacks of coins several feet high were piled against the walls. They were all dusted with a bright red powder that did little to diminish their shine. I was used to the opulent displays of gold in Mother's throne room at the Citadel, but they were nowhere this impressive. They were dazzling to the eyes, intimidating in their richness.

"Amazing," Lisette breathed, her eyes round with stunned delight. She took a step toward the the nearest chest.

"Red with the blood of treasures," Arjun muttered.

I crouched down to peer more closely at the red gold. I'd never seen this kind of substance before, wondered if I could get a sample to study once we returned.

"Wait!" Lan warned sharply before I could reach my hand out. "Don't touch anything!"

"But . . ." Lisette cast a yearning glance at the gems littered around us.

"I've read enough medical treatises to recognize cinnabar. It's toxic to the touch, and even a whiff of it can be poisonous. Tread carefully and try not to breathe in too deeply. I can purge it from your body if necessary, but let's not get to that point."

"Right," Lord Vanya agreed with a shudder.

"There are enough riches here to fund several large cities for years," Sonfei said. "Why would anyone be going through all this trouble to coat them with such foulness?"

"Whoever did this could afford to waste all this gold." Noelle carefully prodded at a coin with her foot. "This was created as a warning."

"I don't think most people know what cinnabar is," Lan said. "They wouldn't know not to attempt to steal these."

The steward nodded. "I know. The cinnabar is punishment for any would-be robbers, but I also think this treasure is here as camouflage. Someone wants us to focus on the gold, and not on whatever it is they're distracting us from. There's a smaller alcove up ahead. Let us hope the air is less toxic than it probably is here."

The smaller enclave we stepped into was bare, and fortunately absent of any more of the cinnabar powder. A small altar stood at its farthest wall.

"No telling what other traps lie in wait here." Arjun's flames glowed brighter as he turned to examine the walls.

As one, Odessa and I dropped to the floor, placing our hands on the surface and letting terra patterns spread out underneath us as, we probed for hints to what lay underneath. "There's something strange by that altar," Odessa finally said, frowning.

"Another barrier," I grumbled, none too pleased. Whoever had constructed this place hadn't made it easy for even us goddesses to solve its mysteries. But why? "We can't seem to penetrate that, either."

"Let's stay clear for now, then. Look." Arjun raised his arm higher. "There's writing here."

It was an understatement. As it turned out, carved text dominated the cave walls, accompanied by large-scale drawings. I focused on the first of them, which depicted a youth being pulled down a dark hole by shadowy hands, his arms raised beseechingly toward a woman. The latter, garbed in ceremonial robes, was reaching out desperately toward him. The colors had faded over time, but there was no mistaking the hues of her hair.

"Inanna," Odessa gasped. "And her beloved."

Arjun moved to reveal the next illustration: now there were two girls with the same multitoned hair, opening a portal before a monument that looked eerily similar to the one at Brighthenge. "Twins?" he questioned. "Are these Inanna's daughters?"

"No," Lord Vanya said, reading the text underneath the first painting, etched into the hard rock. His eyes glittered with excitement. "This is written in old Aeona. I can interpret it for everyone—" Without waiting, he began:

> "*A demoness is only a goddess*
> *That men cannot control;*
> *They could not control us.*
> *And lo! She pays for my sins.'*"

He moved to where Arjun stood, underneath the twins, still translating.

> "*My sister, who loved me dearly.*
> *We descended to the world below*
> *To steal immortality from the Cruel Throne*
> *And return my beloved to me.'*"

"What sister?" Arjun asked, but nothing could stop Vanya at this point.

> "*Seven gates we traveled through,*
> *Our Devoted guarded every doorway*
> *A radiance at every door, the price for passage*
> *Accept this gift, I said, and grant us entrance.'*"

"A radiance," Odessa echoed, staring at another depiction of the goddesses, the two girls passing through seven arches. People I assumed were their Devoted were stationed at every archway, their weapons raised and ready, facing strange galla with blue jewels fused to their bodies. Odessa took one look at them and shuddered.

The next work repulsed me, though I couldn't explain why. The goddesses now faced a gigantic, nameless void. The artist was a master at their craft; the demon the twins confronted had neither shape nor symmetry, and was an inky, indescribable abstraction. But something in that absolute blackness made me suddenly afraid.

"'The last gate demanded no gifts
Instead, it led us to the foot of
a decayed throne
a decayed horror

Within the kingdom, it waited
It sent fires, and we overcame
It sent pestilence, and we overcame
It sent demons, and we overcame'"

The next painting made us all gasp. One of the goddesses was being overwhelmed by shadows with twisted talons and horrendous maws. Her mouth was open, her arm reaching back as if to beg her sister, but the other goddess was running away, not even looking back.

"'And finally, there lay a jewel
shining on a throne
You may take this immortality, It said,
but for a price.
The price was my sister.
The price was my sister,
and I took the stone,
and fled.'"

"Inanna has a *sister*?" Arjun growled. "Are you translating this accurately?"

"I know what I'm reading," Vanya said, in no mood to be lectured at.

> *"'I repented; but, as with all gates, what was once*
> *opened to two, remains forever shut to one;*
> *The Cruel Kingdom, fat and heavy with my sister's soul*
> *Brought Aeon to blossom as her brideprice.*

> *"There is a hole inside me*
> *where my sister's love used to be.'"*

Odessa gasped, a hand fluttering to her own chest.

The next painting depicted the goddess on her knees and weeping, while the world behind her flourished and people celebrated.

> *"'Let the bravest of my daughters*
> *return this stone to that spiteful Kingdom;*
> *Place immortality into Its heart*
> *and bring her the freedom and peace I could not;*
> *And may they learn to love*
> *their sisters better*
> *A demoness is only a goddess*
> *That men cannot control;*
> *Remember Inanna and Ereshkigal*
> *When you rule your kingdom.*
> *A half-life is better than*
> *No life at all.'"*

"This was the answer all along," I whispered. Inanna and Ereshkigal had originally sought out immortality, at the cost of Ereshkigal's life. Unable to access the kingdom again without her, Inanna had written this strange riddle, hoping one of her descendants could finish what she couldn't. Here lay the reason the people of Aeon had been killing their goddesses almost from the very beginning. The Devoted then had come close to losing both goddesses to the Cruel Kingdom, and they were resolved never to do so again. Sacrificing one was infinitely better than losing two.

Odessa and I stared at each other, awed. We should have known Inanna had also been a twin. Why hadn't that ever crossed our minds? Why did we think Inanna would be any different from us? It felt *right*, that she would be just the same as us.

"Inanna had a sister," Lan said, stunned. "In hindsight, we should have realized. . . ."

But I was already a step ahead. "The shadow wasn't Inanna, either," I said weakly, and saw Lan's face turn from shock to horror once she realized what I meant. "It was Ereshkigal." Of course. Why would Inanna implore us to save her sister, and then return as a terrifying demon to stop us from doing exactly that?

"And because of the sisters," Odessa said softly, "one goddess from every generation since has been sacrificed."

"But why didn't she just return and save her twin, if she regretted it?" Lisette asked.

"'But, as with all gates,'" Noelle quoted, "'what was once opened to two, remains forever shut to one.' Sounds like you need two goddesses to open any portals into the Cruel

Kingdom. She *wanted* to return. But with her sister lost below, that was no longer possible."

"And so the people discovered how to bring prosperity back to Aeon," Lan said darkly.

"How cruel," Oda muttered. "They treated their goddesses like cattle, fattening them up for slaughter."

"So it's true?" The anguished cry came from Odessa. "That's all they wanted? Rather than do the work to keep Aeon fruitful and flourishing, it was easier to kill us instead?"

I hugged her, sharing a worried look with Lan. If not even Inanna could undo sacrificing her sister, then what hope did we have of avoiding the same fate?

No. There had to be another way.

"Someone better tell me what 'Place immortality into Its heart' means," Lisette demanded. "Is Inanna buried here?"

"I doubt that this shrine would be booby trapped only to protect paintings on walls. Inanna would have wanted her descendants to know about this." This was our whole history laid bare before us. They called Brighthenge our temple, but this small and forgotten grotto was our true link to our first ancestress, personal and private and tragic. She was a goddess, but in this nameless shrine she was human, with faults and regrets just like the rest of us.

"Maybe," Sonfei said grimly, "whatever is hidden here is more important to protect than even the truth."

"I suspect it's got something to do with that altar over there." Arjun glared at it. Fire sparked along his fingers. "Let me try some fire incanta on it."

"You absolutely will not!" I barked. I could still feel that strange barrier emanating from it. "What makes you think that will even work?"

"You needed mastery of a water-gate to enter the shrine, and air-gates to pass through that river of quicksilver. You used Stonebreaker barriers to clear the third trap, and that requires terra-gates. I'd say you need a Catseye and therefore an aether-gate on hand too, to protect against the cinnabar. Whatever's going on with that altar, I *know* it's going to require fire-gates."

I hated that he had a point. "Odessa and I can use fire incanta, too, so I don't see why the responsibility should fall solely on you."

He flashed me a cocky grin. "Because I'm expendable. And I'm not trying to sound arrogant, but if we need a fire expert, that's me."

"He be right," Sonfei said. "The deathworms go crazy with desire over him." His two fellow Liangzhu murmured their agreement.

"You're not helping me, Sonfei." Arjun crouched down, staring intently at the altar.

"What are you doing?" Lisette asked.

"Waiting. With Fire patterns, there's always something that gives them away, no matter how well a trap is hidden. Some shift in the air that tells me there's a spark lying in wait, or heat I can sense in a place where it shouldn't be." His eyes narrowed, before a smile suddenly flitted across his handsome face. "Ha. Found it."

"Wait!" I yelled when he began walking toward the altar. I hurried after him. "There may be other—"

The sudden conflagration knocked me off my feet. Flames erupted around the altar, abruptly hiding Arjun from view. I screamed and scrambled forward, but my fears were unfounded. Arjun's blue fire spiraled out from the burning floor, and he emerged, coughing slightly. He raised an arm toward what remained of the flames, concentrated, and the rest died down just as quickly. "Flammable air," he confessed, waving away the smoke. "I've encountered natural pockets of it in the desert before, though they don't make it to the surface often. There must be some hidden contraption here that spews it out. If it spreads too far it could bring the whole place down, so I ignited what I could find, cleared it out in one go—"

He grunted when I nearly knocked him over, gluing my mouth to his. "I want to throttle you!" I squeaked, my pitch climbing with my frustration. "Through our entire trek to the Great Abyss, you were constantly on my ass about thinking before I acted, about never knowing the dangers, about *not getting into more boring overly complicated technical details because you can barely follow them*, and now you . . . !"

With a laugh, he kissed me back. "You must be rubbing off on me. One of us had to risk it, and I was the best bet. I won't do anything rash now, if you'd like."

"I would very much like," I snapped fiercely, and then kissed him again.

"It's not over yet," Lan cautioned, approaching the altar much more slowly than Arjun had, because unlike him she was actually competent and more considerate of Odessa than he was of me. She pointed. "I knew it couldn't be that easy."

There was something mounted on the altar. In any other situation, the device would have thrilled my mechanika-loving heart. Small interlocking gears held it together, each piece so precisely machined that it fit perfectly against the rest. Why was it here, in a clear position of importance?

I took a step toward it and immediately had my answer. I reeled back from the heavy concentration of patterns I could feel emanating from within. *This* was the barrier Odessa and I had sensed earlier, the one we could not push through.

"What do the instructions in *The Ages of Aeon* say about this?" Noelle asked Vanya.

"Something about unlocking the Gates of Life and Death, I believe."

"Wait." It felt like the solution was there, hovering at the tip of my tongue, if only I could pull myself together enough to think. I knew nothing about the Gates of Death, but I was familiar enough with the Gates of Life. Nyx, my ancestor, had described her attempts to resurrect a bird using that very term, though she had not been specific as to the process.

But I had failed because Nyx possessed the Gate of Death, like Odessa. It was her sacrificed twin who could command the Gate of Life, and so it must be *that* ability I wielded. Hadn't I used it to close the portal that brought us back to the Golden City?

I came to these conclusions the instant Odessa did. We turned to each other, our eyes shining.

"The four trials we needed to pass to make it this far," I breathed. "Water, Air, Terra, Fire—"

"Five," Odessa pointed out. "We needed a Catseye's aethergate to purge the cinnabar."

"Five trials. A group with varying gates could pass these tests, but if the traps' creator wanted to ensure that only a goddess could overcome them all—"

"The Gates of Life and Death—"

"But not one without the other, so they would have failed to—"

"Unless they had received the gifts, which meant they were aware of the ritual—"

"They're doing it again," Lisette complained.

Odessa and I blinked at each other, realized she was right, and giggled at the same time. "We know what we have to do," I said. "Or we think we do, at least. We're going to open this box."

"With what?" Lan asked.

"Us. Just us." My grip on Odessa's hand tightened. "Brace yourselves. We don't know what's inside it."

This was the knowledge that Nyx had lacked. Like Odessa, she had taken in the galla's gifts, which was how she was able to bring dead things back to life, or a form of it, in the same way Odessa had been able to resurrect her Devoted. That was the Gate of Death. Without it, I could not revive whales, but without my Gate of Life, the people Odessa brought back were only a different kind of dead.

I channeled all five gates. Then I channeled their respective patterns all at once, too. Fire, then Water. Air. Terra. Aether. I'd tried that in the past once, out of curiosity, but none of the patterns had ever worked.

Odessa watched me carefully, then did the same—only differently. It was like she was creating a mirror image of what I had done, channeling from the opposite direction.

Together, we funneled our combined energies into the odd contraption.

For a few seconds, nothing happened. And then it began to glow. As we looked on, lines formed along its surface, blue and green and amber and red and white blending together as it shuddered, like something within was desperately trying to break free.

It exploded.

We all dove to the floor as a bright light illuminated the cave. I braced myself for anything, everything—earthquakes, fires, the walls collapsing. There was only silence.

I lifted my head.

And found myself staring straight into Inanna's immortality.

It was a simple gray stone, smooth but without any artificial polish. There was nothing else to distinguish it from any other rock I'd ever seen.

All this trouble, for something so . . . plain?

"It's a rock," Arjun said, his voice next to my ear and stating the obvious, as always.

Odessa's disappointment mirrored my own. "That's it?" She sounded incredulous, if a bit muffled from her position on the floor. She was half buried under Lan, who, in a moment of unnecessary heroism, had thrown herself over my twin in a bid to protect her. "We went through all this trouble, and that's it?"

"Let's take a closer look." I poked Arjun in the ribs because he, too, in a moment of unnecessary heroism, had thrown himself over me. He grunted and moved, and I sprang to my feet. "At the very least, this should be the last of the tests."

"It's a rock," Arjun said.

"You've mentioned that, yes."

"It's a damn *rock*. Did we just nearly kill ourselves over a damned *rock*?"

"I have to agree with him on this one," Lan said. "Have we considered the possibility that an enterprising thief may have swapped this out for the real thing eons ago? That's what I would have done."

"I'd almost forgotten that you used to steal things," Odessa said, a little more admiringly than one would expect.

I drew nearer, peered down. It still didn't look like anything special. "Vanya, does the book say anything about how to harness it?"

"Not that I've found, Your Holiness. I don't think anyone who's ever lived, excepting Inanna herself, knew the process."

"Figures, I guess. No one's ever gotten this far." Very lightly, I touched it with the tip of my finger.

Pain exploded through me. At the same time, visions spilled into my head, too quickly and too furiously for me to try to shut them out.

A woman with my hair and my eyes, smiling at me.

The same woman calling out to me for help, as the darkness curled up around her, sliding over her mouth, silencing and suffocating, until she was swallowed up by a—

A stone cradled in my shaking hands, the glow weak and flickering. What have I done, *I whispered.* What have I—

I was on the ground, cradled in Arjun's arms. I blinked, the cave coming back into focus.

"What happened?" Arjun's face was gray with worry.

"The stone kept the Cruel Kingdom in balance," I croaked. The words spilled out in a jumbled rush, desperate to be said. "When Inanna stole it, it required something else in exchange. So she sacrificed Ereshkigal. The rituals were created to pacify Ereshkigal. If she couldn't get Inanna, she would take her descendants instead. We must return the stone to the Cruel Kingdom and restore the balance, so we can free her soul."

"And how do we do that?"

"A sacrifice." I hiccuped, on the verge of crying, though I don't know why. "One final sacrifice."

"Take a deep breath," Arjun said sternly. "You can tell us everything when we get out of here."

"Knowing how even touching this stone affected Her Holiness, how shall we be intending to bring it out of the shrine?" Sonfei asked.

"I have an idea." A new voice sounded from the cavern entrance, just before the inner chamber, and a curse issued from Arjun's lips before I'd even registered that the voice belonged to Lord Arrenley. "Perhaps it can leave the shrine under my care."

"That is true," Janella sang out, stepping out from behind the nobleman. "There are so many options, if you care to think about it."

Chapter Twenty-One

ARJUN AND THE BETRAYAL

——————— ⚬ ———————

WE WERE SO GODDESSDAMNED SCREWED. Arrenley had brought reinforcements at least three times our number, and they barred the only way out of the shrine. I'd never trusted Janella from the moment she first arrived, not to mention her history with Lan and Odessa, but this was a new low. Odessa looked stunned; the Catseye, furious beyond belief.

"Does Asteria know you're here betraying her?" Lan snapped, drawing her sword. "Or are you simply looking out for yourself, as you've always done?"

"She and Latona were being obstinate," Janella said with a small shrug. " I've found some of Latona's council more amenable to an alliance, however."

"You've done your job, Vanya," Arrenley said. "Now take the stone and bring it to me."

I threw a furious glance at the lordling. "So this was all an act?" I'd done my best not to murder him the hundred and eighty times I could have whenever he'd acted the fool, because Haidee had said to trust him. And all this time he'd been planning on betraying her!

But the boy was shaking his head, taking a step back rather than toward his father. "I was never in your employ, Father! I sought Haidee out of my own volition!"

"Has the desert heat addled your brains, boy? We prepared for this. You were to present the book to them, to lead us to this—"

"He's lying!" Vanya's confused, horrified anger couldn't be a performance. "We discussed nothing! I tried to convince you to forge an alliance with Haidee and her people, but you called me a fool and refused to broach the topic again."

"You *are* a fool," Janella drawled. "Your father is giving you a chance to return to him, without Latona ever knowing of your betrayal. And you're too much of a twit to take it."

Vanya paled. "I made my choice. I'm not giving you anything."

"We don't want a fight," Arrenley said, threatening just that.

"Neither do we, but we're leaving. You'll be returning to the Golden City empty-handed." I aimed my Howler at them. I could feel sparks in the air as dozens of people's gates opened at the same time, until we were all training weapons at each other.

There was no alternative. The only option was to fight our way through Arrenley's men, or . . .

I cast a quick look at the ceiling. How far underground

were we, exactly? The stone-hewn stairs had made for a long descent. . . .

"I'm almost impressed," Haidee said curtly. She'd recovered somewhat, had sat up beside me. "What happened to Tamera and the others?"

Janella smiled. "There's a battle being waged above our heads at this moment, Your Holiness. Your desert nomads fight well, but it's only a matter of time before we gain the upper hand. We must thank you; I'd been puzzling out how to breach the entrance to the shrine without losing any more men, and you were kind enough to do that for us, along with dismantling the other traps we've encountered here. The only real difficulty was that fascinating river of mercury, but I brought enough Windshifters to compensate."

"How did you know we were here?"

"Your clans have very impressive rigs, Your Holiness. They leave unusual patterns of Fire in their wake—very easy to spot. My scouts avoided the patrols you put out and followed some distance behind." She grinned. "Lord Arrenley knew of this temple for years. His men had mapped out this side of the desert, but they could never figure out a way inside. Nor did he know what it contained. What a pleasant shock, to learn where Inanna's immortality had been lying all this time. We are most appreciative of this new information."

Vanya had gone still. "You let me take the book. You let me leave. You thought the goddesses would succeed where you couldn't."

"Miss Janella and I came to see the advantages of mutual

cooperation shortly after our lieges' fight. Did you really believe I would foolishly leave the book unguarded in my study shortly after finding it in your room? I knew you were far too enamored of the goddess for your own good." Arrenley turned, admiring the cave paintings. "It would come as a shock to her, to learn her ancestors were not as fervently worshiped as she believes. Most books that survived the Breaking portray Aeon as a utopia, where no one wanted for anything. That was not always the reality."

"A utopia where all you had to do was kill a goddess every now and then," Haidee said.

Arrenley nodded at Sonfei. "He looks old enough to have known that."

"I know now, standing before the truth written on these walls," Sonfei said. "But I never knew then. I never knew that the goddesses had always been twins. Aeon had always been bountiful, but in cycles. A few decades of peace and prosperity, followed by a gradual decline. Crops failing. Earthquakes. An excess of rain in one area, and an excess of drought in others. But it would always recover before the worst could happen. I didn't know it was because of the sacrifices. Until the Breaking."

"Aeon, as my father told me, had an unquenchable appetite for goddesses. The Devoted soon learned to use that for their own interests instead." Arrenley shrugged. "Power is a bad habit. Goddesses like your mother, Haidee, thought the best of people when it was easier for them to be the worst. Why work when a deity's blood can replenish the land and seas? It was a contest among some of the Devoted, I'm told, to see what they could destroy in their greed and gluttony, before the death of a goddess made things right again."

"You are horrible," Odessa whispered.

"It was not I who made the world, Your Holiness. I only live in it."

"Right," I said, not bothering to hide my disgust. "Poor you, only living in a world where you'd give up your own son for immortality. Unfortunate that there's only one stone, and neither of you look like you're used to divvying up the spoils."

"There are other ways to share," Janella said smoothly. "Hand over the stone and you shall see for yourself."

"Can we?" Lisette muttered. "Hand over the stone? Or touch it, even?"

I bent down and snatched the stone that had previously fallen from Haidee's grasp, before she could muster a protest. Whatever it had done to her had no effect on me.

"I overheard Lord Vanya talking about the verses on these walls; may I offer an opinion?" Nobody answered her, but Janella continued on anyway. "My mother's hypothesis, you understand. If Ereshkigal had to suffer the eternal darkness of the Cruel Kingdom, then she was determined that the twin who had betrayed her share the same fate. Once she had realized her sister's soul was more important than her lover's life, Inanna attempted to make amends, only to learn that it could not be unmade; the only way to undo Ereshkigal's corruption was to forfeit both the stone and her own life."

She chuckled, without mirth. "Inanna was a coward. Of course she would hide the stone, would hope instead that one day, one of her own bloodline would find the courage she never had, to stop her sister's malice. Of course she would demand more from her descendants than she herself would ever give. The true deception is believing that the goddesses are better than us simply because of the nature of their birth."

"We are wasting time," Lord Arrenley said, and gunfire rang out.

Noelle, who had shoved both Lan and Odessa to one side, fell down with a grunt—she'd been hit. Oda toppled over as well, but the rest of the fireshots dissolved against a barrier that Odessa had quickly erected. The goddess's eyes were shining so brightly her pupils were no longer visible. The air before us blurred and whirred, churning up dust as more projectiles glanced off it, mimicking the Golden City's protective dome.

"You will submit to us sooner or later," Lord Arrenley said. "We outnumber you, and the only way out of this shrine is through us."

"Then through you it shall be," Lan said, grim satisfaction in her voice. She was crouched over Oda, a hand pressed to his forehead. Noelle had already sat up with a grimace, cradling an injured shoulder, but otherwise appeared all right. "You could have waited for us to leave this shrine to ambush us. I think neither of you wanted to risk it. You couldn't predict what the goddesses were going to do with anything they found."

"Clever as always, Lady Tianlan," Janella mocked.

"I saw it," Haidee whispered.

"Don't try to talk," I warned, trying not to let my own hands shake as I touched her face. "You went on a hell of a ride back there. Don't think too much about—"

"But I can't not think about it. I saw *everything*. That stone isn't just Inanna's immortality—it held all her knowledge. I know how to enter the Cruel Kingdom. I saw Ereshkigal. She was—"

Her grip on my arm tightened. "She's dying!" she cried out, in pain. "She's been dying every day for an eternity. And the only way to bring Aeon back is to find someone to take her place."

The ground shook. I thought it was Arrenley and Janella's doing at first, but they looked just as confused as everyone else.

Haidee clutched at me. "We have to leave," she said in a panic, staring over my shoulder. I'd never seen her so afraid before. "We have to leave right now. They're coming."

"What's coming?"

But the shadows lengthening along the cave floor answered my question. The altar was visibly shaking; as we watched, it split down the middle as cracks appeared underneath the stone ground, widening into crevasses. We all scrambled back as a fresh sinkhole appeared before our eyes, leading down into an impenetrable blackness.

And then, to my horror, a large, bony hand reached up from within that dark pit, followed by another. The creature that slowly pulled itself out was one of unspeakable horror: a rotting corpse, strands of hair hanging sparsely against a decomposing face, weathered skin stretched tight from malice and cruelty. What few teeth it had left were brown and broken, its skeletal jaw pockmarked with bits of blackened flesh. Its eyes were gone, but within those black sockets something malevolent peered out.

And it wasn't alone.

"We have to go!" Sonfei yelped as galla slithered out from the new chasm, an army of them skittering across the wall, up into the ceiling. Odessa's barriers flickered, weakened as she turned to face the new threat. One of Arrenley's men fired another shot directly at her. Lan lunged forward, and her cry of pain was loud as she took the hit in her goddess's stead.

"No!" Odessa screamed, the sound loud in the cavern, and Noelle rushed over to the fallen Catseye's side. "She's breathing," the girl reported, though the obvious fear overriding her usual composure spoke volumes. "Scatter projectile. It hit her arms and stomach, but nothing fatal. She's bleeding badly, though, and we'll have to move her quickly. Odessa—"

But the goddess was no longer listening. I could see her rage in the Fire patterns around her as they erupted into a fiery, white-hot heat, and Haidee was in no shape to rein in her sister's fury.

A blaze took out the unlucky gunner, the flames burning too hot and too quick for him to do more than call out his shock before his ashes crumbled down at Arrenley's feet. Lightning lanced through a couple more soldiers, striking the walls and crumbling chunks of stone. If the temple had been stable before, that was no longer the case. We had to leave.

But rather than heed the warning and retreat, the lord barked out more orders; his men turned their attentions to the goddess, guns raised.

"Stop!" a voice rang out, and Vanya was pointing his Howler at his father, finger already on the trigger. "If any of your men fire again," the lordling said, his voice giving away his fear as it shook, "I'm going to shoot you."

Behind us, Sonfei and Pai were fighting the galla, and Lisette was shooting at where the shadows were at their densest. Despite their efforts, the army pouring out from the hole showed no signs of slowing down. Was this the next wave of galla due to attack, or something else? Were Tamera and the others fighting them aboveground, too?

And then I realized that it didn't matter. We would be overwhelmed soon. And with Arrenley and his men blocking the exit, there was nowhere else to go.

Arrenley laughed, full of derision. "Do you think you have the guts to actually shoot your own father?" he taunted. "You haven't the courage, boy. You are nothing but a—"

Vanya shot him. The lord gave a stunned gasp, his hand clasping at his thigh, sinking down.

"You'll live," Vanya said coldly, in the exact same tone Arrenley had used on him back at the Citadel.

"What are you doing?" Lisette asked when I rose to my feet, holding Haidee securely in my arms.

"What I have to do." Haidee was incapacitated, Odessa too distracted by Lan to think rationally. The only options were to rush Arrenley's men—which would only kill us quicker—or . . .

"Haidee," I said, trying to keep my voice low and soothing. "I want you to reach out toward the cave ceiling and figure out which part of it's the thinnest. Then I'm going to blast through the rock. Haidee?"

She blinked at me, her eyes still unfocused, but I could detect a glimmer of recognition there. I repeated my request, and kissed her forehead. "Haidee love, we're not getting any younger. The way things stand, we might not get any older, either. Please."

She took a deep, shuddering breath, her eyes falling shut. "There," she whispered, and I saw something spark against the darkness above us, a marking point for me.

"Thanks." I pointed my Howler at the spot, pushing everything I had into the gun, until it overflowed with Fire. "Hold on," I said, and aimed.

The ceiling exploded outward, and warm sunlight spilled into the cavern for the first time in centuries. I could see the sky, and maybe it was because we'd been down here longer than we wanted, but it was even bluer than I remembered. "How far can you throw us?" I yelled over at Sonfei.

The big man looked puzzled at first, until he glanced up. "I am strong enough. I will toss you all out, without a problem."

"Send me first," Noelle said. "I can assess what the situation is like outside."

"You're injured, too," I protested.

"It's only a flesh wound. This is nothing to me."

I could believe that. Noelle crouched down at Sonfei's instructions. The Liangzhu man had clearly done this before. "We will put buffers around the ceiling, so you can expect to land safely above," he told her. "Still, it might be jarring your first time. Are you ready?"

"Do it, Sonfei."

With a fierce howl, Sonfei's eyes flared, and Noelle was launched nearly a hundred feet up into the air. His aim was true; she passed directly through the hole I'd made in the ceiling. I saw her shove her spear into the ground, stopping her momentum and allowing her to roll to safety. *What the hell kind of training do tower stewards undergo on the other side of the world,* I wondered.

"We're clear!" I heard her call down to us. "Tamera and the Saiga are holding against Arrenley's men!"

Sonfei's companions followed shortly after, and then Lisette and Vanya together; the boy hung on for dear life, screaming as they hurtled through the empty space, until he was promptly caught by Noelle and some of Tamera's people.

I turned to Odessa next. The goddess was still holding on to Lan's unconscious form, still scouring both the galla and Arrenley's men in deadly fire. She had destroyed many of the shadows, but the men were seasoned fighters and were retreating behind the enclave's entrance, out of her reach. "We have to go," I said, adopting a sterner tone with her than I had with Haidee. "Lan needs treatment."

That brought her back to her senses. "Yes." Odessa's face was streaked in tears. She glanced back at the men, and I could have sworn there was a tiny, vicious smile on her face as she took in their dead and wounded. "Yes, let's go."

Sonfei was still strong enough to toss both Odessa and Lan up at the same time—a good thing, because the goddess showed no inclination to let go of her injured Catseye. That left Haidee,

Sonfei, and me. I was about to suggest Sonfei send us off in the same way, when a sudden earthquake nearly knocked us off our feet.

The hole underneath the shrine was growing, the ground no longer able to bear our weight and the growing number of galla filling the cavern. We were slowly being backed into a corner. A terrible cracking sound echoed above us; the rest of the ceiling was also collapsing. The whole structure was falling apart.

"Now!" I yelled at Sonfei. With a shout, he propelled himself up into the air, and I felt Air incanta seize both me and Haidee along with him.

A surge in Fire patterns caused me to look down. I saw death blazing toward us in a wrath of flames that, if it reached us, would not leave much of us to bury.

With a loud curse, I shoved Haidee into Sonfei's arms, and spun around to face the new threat.

There wasn't time for my Howler, so I used my limbs instead. The heat was unbelievable at this proximity; I would have been burned alive had I been a regular Firesmoker. I kept my grip firm on the stone still in my hand and shoved back against the patterns, stomping out the blue flames with my will before most of them got too close.

But one got past me, caught Sonfei on the shoulder. His concentration broke, and I fell.

I knew how to roll and bear the brunt of a fall from great heights, but this was too far. The crack of bone in my ankle as I struck ground knocked the wind out of me. I groaned in pain, forced myself up to one knee, trying to keep as much weight off it as I could.

Janella was waiting. "A pity," she said sweetly, her Howler leveled at my face. "I was hoping the fall would have killed you if my flames didn't. Give me the stone."

"Over my dead body."

Her smile grew. "That can be arranged," she said, and fired.

I was already moving before she'd pulled the trigger, swinging my own Howler up so that its barrel struck her in the face. Her head whipped back, and then it was my turn to fire. She caught the flames in time, grinned as her fingers closed, extinguishing them entirely. "That won't work on me."

"You're mad. The cave is *collapsing*." She had to be. Even Arrenley's men were gone, carrying their injured leader away.

That only made her laugh. "What does that matter when we've got *immortality*, boy?" She punched me hard in the face, and grabbed for the stone in my hand. I kicked at her, and we wound up tumbling across the floor. *I'm going to die here*, I thought. *There's no exit, and the damn demons are surrounding me, and I can't—*

I swung my Howler again, and it caught her hard across the midsection. She went down, and I scrambled up, biting back a cry at the sharp pain running up my leg.

"Arjun!" I heard someone scream. I looked up and saw Haidee's face, her eyes wide. Air spiraled from her fingers, reaching out to yank me up to safety. I reached toward her, relief breaking through.

And then more pain punched through my side. I staggered, clutched at my chest, and felt sticky warmth leaking down my shirt.

"You're not going anywhere," Janella panted, and pulled her knife out of me. I fell, and she reached past me, to pluck up the stone that had fallen out of my grasp.

And then, with a gasp, she reeled away.

The mirage hadn't been there a few seconds ago. Blue smoke steamed from underneath its cloak, and it watched as Janella screamed, her hair and scarlet-piped cloak aflame. She lashed out, but my mother said nothing even as Janella's fires surrounded her. For the first time, she lifted her head to look at me, and I saw the faintest glimpse of a rosebud mouth, startlingly dark eyes, and hair as stringy and black as my own.

Arjun, she said, and the flames swept through her.

I could hear shouting above us, but that no longer seemed to matter. With the last of my strength, I lunged and tore the rock from Janella's grip. At the same time, I planted my Howler right between her eyes.

"You're not going anywhere!" Janella had been horribly burned, her face a mask of rage, hands still reaching up for the stone I'd reclaimed.

"*We're* not going anywhere," I corrected her, and fired.

And then the ground beneath us gave way, and we were falling.

Chapter Twenty-Two

'LAN'S REGRETS

—————————————— ☾ ——————————————

AWARENESS RETURNED IN FOLDS, IN shades of white. As my vision cleared, I found myself stretched out on the ground, my head in someone's lap. There was a throbbing pain on my right side. There were sounds that made me think of stones grating against each other, followed by a heavy *thump*.

I tried to sit up, was immediately pushed back down. It was Odessa; her face was tear-stained and blotched, eyes red from weeping. "Don't move, please," she begged. Noelle appeared beside her, and I realized only then that my arm and side had been heavily bandaged.

"Why is it so bright?" We were in a cave; that was the last thing I remembered. Someone had aimed a gun at Odessa, and I had moved to . . .

"Please." Odessa's voice sounded so raw. "We need to get you back to camp, and you should lie still."

We weren't at the neutral grounds. We weren't on any of the rigs. "Why"—my lips felt parched, but I persisted—"aren't we doing that right now?"

A sob was her answer. There was something else she wasn't telling me—something far worse than even my injuries. I fought the dizziness and raised my head.

Haidee had stripped out of her mechanika jacket and was down to her undershirt. She gestured, and chunks of detritus rose from a hole before her. She flung them dismissively to one side, echoing the thuds I'd heard earlier.

She did it again, and then again. Her pale eyes were blank, her movements almost mechanical.

Sonfei was by her side, using his own air-gate to help, assisted by a few people from other clans. The Liangzhu man was openly crying. The rest watched Haidee with a mixture of fear and helplessness; even Tamera looked drawn, sympathetic. Lisette was bereft of her usual snark, pity evident in her gaze. It was clear even she had been weeping.

I sat up anyway, waving Odessa's protests away. "Was there a cave-in?"

Noelle was silent, arm freshly bandaged and face downcast. Vanya was fidgeting with his fingers. Everyone watched Haidee like she was a powder keg ready to explode, and Arjun . . .

Arjun . . .

"No," I whispered.

"You need to lie down," Odessa insisted, her voice raw.

Haidee tossed away more debris.

"How long has she been doing this?" I asked quietly.

"Almost two hours," Noelle said, after a pause.

I didn't need to ask her why nobody had tried to stop Haidee. If Arjun was underneath all that rubble, he could not have survived. But that would mean nothing to someone desperate for proof.

"Arjun and the stone are gone," Noelle continued. "I saw them fighting over it, and saw them both fall—him and Janella."

I knew what she was saying—that Janella, too, was dead. The ground had given way underneath them, and no one could know who had gained the upper hand in those final, horrifying moments. But the loss of Inanna's immortality paled in comparison to the loss of Arjun.

Finally, *finally*, the goddess had hauled most of the wreckage out. We found ourselves staring down at what was left of Inanna's shrine—but there was no trace of the chasm that had opened up at the rocky cave floor below us. The altar still lay in shambles, but the ground before it remained intact. It was like we had all hallucinated the ravine the demons had crawled out of. The fight had also demolished the ceiling over the adjoining chamber, where the cinnabar-dusted coins and jewels had been stored. Those, too, were gone. The gorge had claimed those treasures also before, inconceivably, closing back up.

"Haidee," Odessa said.

Her sister didn't answer. Her hands were clenched tightly and I could see patterns wrapping angrily around her fists, sparking against each other.

"Haidee." Odessa laid a hand on her arm. "Haidee, we have to—"

"We need to search the rest of the caverns," Haidee said crisply. "The other areas appear to be intact. He could have retreated back to where the river of quicksilver flowed, maybe all the way to the stairs back at the entrance."

"Haidee—"

"We'll need some buttresses to stabilize the walls, but that shouldn't take longer than an hour to set up. The Stonebreakers should be able to construct something adequate for our purpose."

"Haidee—"

"Some of Lord Arrenley's men might still be skulking about. The hole must have been an illusion, just like the temple oasis. I'm sure he's wandering around down there, irritated and—"

"Haidee!"

The Sun goddess fell silent, shoulders rigid.

"Haidee, I'm so sorry."

"I won't leave him, Odessa!" Haidee snapped. "I thought him dead once, and I'm not going to make that same mistake again! I'm not leaving until I see his body!"

"Haidee—"

"This would never have happened if you had better control!"

Odessa looked like she'd been slapped. I jerked toward her.

Haidee realized she'd gone too far. She turned away. "I can't leave him," she said hoarsely. "I can't. What would you have done if it had been Lan, Odessa?"

"I would have done everything in my power to rescue her. But he's not here, Haidee."

Odessa's twin paused, nodded decisively. "You're right. I'll need to go after him."

She jumped into the hole, her terra-gate shimmering. The cave floor broke apart, the bedrock shattering beneath the force of her will.

But Odessa had anticipated her move. Haidee stopped, suspended in midair, only halfway down. "Let me go, Odessa."

"What do you intend to do?" I cried out.

"The Abyss closed up after him, so all I need to do is break it open again. I'll punch my way to the center of the world if that's what it's going to take." She lashed out, again and again, and the ground rocked from her fury. But all she uncovered were more layers of stone.

The goddess was past caring. She tore through the slag, digging deeper.

"I know how much you love Arjun, Haidee." Odessa was crying. "But I can't let you do this."

"I'm the Sun Goddess!" The ground splintered, fractured, burst. "I can do *anything*!"

"You can't. *We* can't. Our strength is finite, and you'll die at the rate you're going. You've seen the paintings. You've read Inanna's instructions. She couldn't put the world back to rights because she needed her twin. *I* need my twin. We can't heal Aeon without you. Please, Haidee."

Haidee had stopped struggling but her eyes remained closed,

desperate not to listen. She said nothing as Odessa pulled her back up into the desert.

"I am so sorry, Haidee," Odessa said again.

"You can't tell me you wouldn't do the same thing." Her twin sounded so impassive; her voice used to always be so warm.

"I know. I would have done exactly what you did. And I . . ." Odessa's voice broke. "I would have lashed out at you in much the same way, I think. But I would also hope that you, had you been in *my* place, would have stopped me from doing more harm to myself. Reminded me about our duty to everyone else."

Haidee stared at her for a long moment, her face a study in detachment. "Duty," she echoed. "Inanna said to take her immortality and journey to the Cruel Kingdom, didn't she?"

But the stone was gone along with Arjun, and no one wanted to say that out loud either, for fear of making things worse. There was a cold fury to Haidee now that I'd never known her capable of. I remembered Odessa's white-hot rages when she'd been in the grip of the galla's influence, compared them to the icy, almost inhuman goddess now standing before me. No monsters were influencing Haidee now. Haidee, who had always been so cheerful and happy and hopeful.

"Duty," she said. "I'll do it for duty."

It almost felt like we'd lost Haidee, too.

We were quiet on the ride back. Noelle had taken over the driving in Arjun's place; seeing someone else behind the wheel only drove his absence further home. Haidee sat in the back seat.

345

Her eyes stared out, unseeing. Odessa sat beside her. Something had passed between the sisters, unseen, and I feared, irreparable. This felt like the first break in their relationship, and I didn't know how deep that fracture went.

This was not how I wanted to enter Asteria's camp, where tensions were already running high. Odessa was in no shape to face her mother. Haidee was in no shape to do anything. I had no idea how Asteria would react to being told Janella was dead.

That turned out to be the least of our worries.

Even from a distance, I saw the battle already in full swing. In lieu of an air-dome, Asteria had chosen to barricade her camp with high, heavy sand walls that the galla were now busily slamming themselves against. Parts of the defenses had already fallen where the horde was at its thickest.

The sight alone, of the black tide of darkness besieging Asteria's territory from the east, was enough to induce panic. The galla army seemed twice as large as the one we had fought the last time.

And Ereshkigal. The sight of that shadow-titaness filled me with dread, with that familiar panic that had been my only constant in those early days after Nuala and the other rangers' deaths, when I was fresh off injuries that were physical, and injuries that had remained invisible. I had passed my days then convinced that every shadow was out to get me.

And now, standing before the amalgamation of all my nightmares, all the work I'd put into healing myself felt like it could come undone in one moment, and I trembled.

This wasn't Inanna. This was her sister, *Ereshkigal*, hate manifested in a twisted, corporeal form.

"Ereshkigal," Odessa whispered, echoing my thoughts. "She won't ever stop, will she. She'll never rest until she finds Inanna again."

Or the next closest thing.

"We can't beat that," Lisette muttered.

"Yes, we can." The swarm might have grown in size, but so had our numbers. Whatever my feelings about Janella, I wasn't going to turn my back on my people. The bigger problem was losing our only two Firesmokers capable of wielding blue flames. I pushed my sorrow over Arjun away, to focus on everyone else who could still be saved. He would've been angry at me if I hadn't. "If you wish to sit this one out, Lisette, then step aside and let us take up the fight."

"The hell I will. I'll fight till my last breath." The girl gripped her Howler tighter. "We owe it to him."

"We will honor our promise to the people of Aranth," Tamera said crisply. "Salla and the others are inside Asteria's encampment, and they have our protection. But we will demand a reckoning for any others who conspired with Arrenley."

The Hellmakers' rigs pulled away, charging ahead to be the first to attack; with joyous shouts they targeted the first row of galla, firing indiscriminately into their midst. With a wince, I tugged out my sword as we skidded to a stop. As long as I could still hold a weapon, I could fight.

"Their right wall is failing," I growled. "They're too focused on where the bulk of the shadows are concentrated and they're not paying attention to the groups sidling around their shields. It will only take one to breach the camp."

"Haidee?" Odessa asked.

Her twin said nothing, only watching as we drew nearer to the fighting. Her pale eyes were hard.

"Haidee?"

Slowly, the Sun Goddess stood. She raised a hand, pointed a finger at the nearest cluster of shadows. Her eyes glowed amber.

Giant spikes of densely packed sand ripped out of the ground, impaling several of the creatures. Another wave followed, and the galla crumbled into nothingness as the sharp stakes tore through their bodies. When they attempted to scatter, Haidee changed course; large blocks of sand rose and fell onto the galla, like hammers striking an anvil.

"Haidee!" Odessa caught her sleeve. Haidee yanked her arm back just as I caught hold of Odessa's other arm, and felt myself tumbling into a riot of unexpected emotions. I felt guilt, anguish, fury—Haidee's. Guilt, terror, shame—Odessa's.

This had happened to me before. I'd been in physical contact with Asteria when I saw her visions foretelling Asteria's destruction. Odessa's touch allowed me to see the galla for the first time.

"Stay away from me!" Haidee shouted at Odessa.

"I know what you're planning to do! Arjun didn't give up his life so you can waste yours!"

Haidee stared at her sister, clearly enraged that Odessa had finally put into words what everyone else had been dreading to say. "Arjun is gone because neither of us were strong enough," she said through gritted teeth. "You're the reason—you're the last person to tell me how sacred life is!"

You're the reason he's dead. That was what she'd almost said.

Haidee's expression shifted to distress, regret. "No. I'm sorry, Odessa. I didn't mean it. You wield the galla's gifts. And I'm the one to be sacrificed. We could just—we could just perform the ritual the way they expect us to. Sacrifice me, like they intended all along—"

"No!" Odessa shouted, her features twisted in agony. "It will never stop, Haidee! We'll just be another pair in a never-ending cycle of death. I was always too weak, too frail, too sick. And when I accepted those gifts I became overconfident, cruel, willing to do anything to get what I wanted. And that's why I need you here, Haidee. I need you to keep my sanity."

A well-placed strike from her froze more fiends for several yards, clearing a path between us and a group of galla that stood apart from the rest of the horde. Blue gemstones glinted back at us.

Haidee staggered, and so did I, as a wave of nausea assailed me. My legs and arms felt like they had turned to lead. Odessa's attack had sapped at my strength, diminished her twin's—and mine. She'd done it deliberately.

Odessa climbed out of the jeep and walked toward the creatures. The crackle of energy around her was unbelievable. It felt like far more than I knew she could handle. She took in patterns until she was at her limit, then kept on going.

"You fool!" I forced myself up, ignoring the light-headedness, and stumbled after her. I caught her hand. "What are you doing?" I grated out.

She smiled at me, her eyes a prism of colors. "I've always been afraid of the damage I could do," she said candidly. "But every time I hold back I wind up hurting someone else." She took my face in her hands, smiled sweetly up at me. "Now I'm embracing it," she said, and brought my head down so she could kiss me. I felt strength flow from me to her, only augmenting her spells further.

And then she let go.

The patterns ripped through the galla. Fire incinerated them; Water froze them, shattered them into millions of pieces; Air shredded them into ribbons; Earth swallowed them up. Lightning bolts traveled from one fiend to the next, frying their bodies in an instant. By the time Odessa was done, we were standing in a circle of blackened ground, every galla within at least a two-hundred-yard radius of us destroyed.

The lapis lazuli–wearing demons had vanished, and only one remained: a small, shriveled thing.

"Odessa," I choked, still clinging to her, still too weak to use my abilities to keep her from expending more of herself. All I could do, all I could think of, was to funnel everything I had left into healing her, into keeping her alive. "Stop it."

"In a moment."

A wave of sand rose again, and crushed the tiny galla under-foot.

And then Odessa tottered, swooning against me. The rest of the galla turned toward us. My own strength gone, I cursed, holding Odessa's unconscious body against mine while I tried to level my sword at those attempting to draw closer. It felt as heavy as lead, and I could barely raise it.

More lightning sizzled across the sky and broke the ground apart, taking two dozen of the galla nearest us. "You will not harm my daughter," Asteria seethed. She was pale, her face streaked with soot, and more light sizzled against her palms. She flung them out in an arc, taking down more of the monsters.

Gracea appeared at her side. Her own lightning was weaker and smaller than the goddess's but it did the job, mowing down several more galla. A loud *whoop* sounded on my left, and I saw Slyp and Bergen attack, the latter lashing out and striking down any galla that drew too close while the old Stonebreaker manifested fists of stone, using them to punch through the rest.

Miel, Filia, and Halida had apparently resolved their Gareen problem while we were away, banding together to slice through as many galla as they could find. Tamera and her clan raced into position behind them, leveling their Howlers and firing. Sonfei's Mudforgers turned the sand underneath the galla into near-liquid, trapping them. Sonfei propelled himself through the air, launching a downward kick at the galla, wind cutting them into ribbons.

Noelle and Lisette had caught up to me, and we three stood side by side, grimly taking down all nearby galla. A hand fell on my shoulder and I spun with my sword raised, my other arm still cradling Odessa protectively. At the same time I felt glorious warmth running down my sides, my aches and pains falling away.

"Sumiko," I breathed. "I am so very glad to see you."

"The feeling is mutual, Lady Lan." Sumiko looked more exhausted than when I'd last seen her, but there was a smile on her face.

"And who is *this* pretty lady?" Lisette asked, though more out of habit than anything else, as she shot down another galla.

A loud scraping sound ricocheted around us. I tensed.

"The air-dome's coming down!" Charley called out, just as a spinning sandstorm erupted underneath the galla's feet, whipping them into the air.

I could make out someone standing at the highest point of the Golden City. Despite the miles that lay between her city and the camp she was efficient, and deadly. With every gesture she made, the sandstorm followed, pummeling more galla. There were soldiers stationed atop the gates, too, lobbing glow-fires and cannonshot at the horde.

Latona was aiding us.

Odessa had taken out a huge portion of the army. With all three groups fighting, it was only a matter of time before the tide turned in our favor, and we were able to eradicate the rest of the swarm. Tired, I slumped down and allowed Sumiko to work more of her healing magic on me.

Asteria strode forward, staring up at the lone figure above us. "We need to talk, Latona!" she shouted.

Silence. The figure turned away. There was a humming

noise as the air-dome flickered back into life over the city. Asteria remained standing there, her jaw clenched, long after her sister was gone from view.

"It's about time you returned," Mother Salla said with a sniff. Her eyes flitted from one face to another, and then back again, searching. "Where . . . ?" she began, and then stopped, horrified. "Where . . . ?" she started again, but couldn't finish.

It was Lisette who spoke, voice low and eyes glittering with emotion. "Salla. I'm sorry."

The Oryx clan mistress took a step back, like she'd been dealt a physical blow. "I see," she said, in a voice too high for comfort.

A scream rose from behind her. "That's not true!" Imogen cried. "Arjun can survive *anything*. He rode out to the Great Abyss and came back against all the odds. He fought a million Hellmakers and came back. He fought shadows and all sorts of horrors, and he *came back*."

"Immie," Haidee said helplessly, "I—"

"No! Don't you *Immie* me! He would have ridden through hell for you, and you couldn't even protect him! What kind of goddess are you, that you can't even save someone you said you love?"

"Imogen!" Salla exclaimed, but the younger girl spun on her heel and fled, crying, pushing past her siblings, who looked at each other, anguished, then back at Haidee. The goddess stared after her, trembling, before slowly walking away in the opposite direction.

"Let her be," I said softly. In the space of a couple of days

Imogen had lost two brothers.

Odessa stirred in my arms, blinking. "Are they gone?" she asked, almost timidly.

"I'm not happy with you, love."

She smiled weakly. "Sorry. I had to—I *needed* to prove to myself that I could help save everyone even without the radiances."

"There was a stone within the temple," clan mistress Tamera was saying, her face now a careful, contained mask. She'd wasted no time filling the other clans in, which I was grateful for, having no desire to do so myself. "It purportedly contained Inanna's immortality, a key to defeating Inanna's twin who, incidentally, is the massive piece-of-shit shadow we've been fighting all this time. Unfortunately, the Golden City army attacked us, and the stone was lost."

Salla nodded curtly, her face giving no indication of her grief. "Are you saying, then, that there is no hope left?"

"Not necessarily." This from a subdued Vanya. "If the texts are right, the only option left is for both of the goddesses to enter the Cruel Kingdom together and face the trials there, much like Inanna and Ereshkigal did once."

"But without Inanna's immortality . . . ," Lars began.

"The goddesses can enter the Cruel Kingdom without it," Vanya said. "It's getting out again that's less certain."

"We'll take that chance," Odessa said.

"Odessa—" I began, but she interrupted me.

"All that talk to Haidee about duty," she said, her face intent. "I meant it. I told my sister that she had to sacrifice the person she loves most in the world for *duty*. It would be hypocritical of me if I weren't willing to do the same."

"You're not sacrificing me. You're sacrificing yourself."

"I know. And that's why it was harder on her." She stroked my hand, taking great care not to put pressure on my wounds. "I started this journey because I didn't want to die. But what I am slowly realizing is that death will happen to all of us. Even goddesses. *Especially* goddesses, given our people's penchant for sacrificing us. I would much rather do it on my own terms."

"You know I can't allow that," I said harshly.

"You'd sacrifice the world just to keep me? You'll let everything else fall apart, allow the galla to overrun Aeon? They'll grow in number every day. They've gone two generations now without a sacrifice, with nothing for their hunger to gnaw on. They'll consume the world."

"You know I'd die first before I'd let anything near you."

"I know. And I'm afraid of that. If you die, Lan—if the only choice we have is to sacrifice you—then know that I won't survive you long."

"Odessa—"

"You know I'm right. I was so angry when Mother and Latona did the same thing. It's so easy to judge from the outside, believing that they ruined the world in their selfishness. Until the same thing happens to you. Latona lost her lover—my father. She resented Asteria for it."

"Haidee won't resent you."

"Maybe. But it was my recklessness that got Arjun killed all the same. And anger—anger festers, even in the best of us. We lost the stone. I don't know what's happened to it, but I know Arjun died making sure Janella would never get her hands on it. He saved us." She began to tear up. "Let's end the cycle, Lan. I will go into the Great Abyss, descend into the Cruel Kingdom as Inanna instructed, and put my trust in Haidee. Even if I can't come back."

"Then I'll go with you. Inanna had companions to defend the seven gates after she and her sister passed through, so they could return. For all your talk about duty, you still didn't accept the seventh galla. If we fail, if we have no other choice left, then you'll need me to finish the ritual."

"Lan—"

"If something happens to you, then I won't survive you long, either. I will follow you into hell and back, Odessa. That's *my* duty."

Finally she nodded, even smiled a little. "All right. Haidee intends the same thing, I think. I just don't know how to approach her yet."

"Talk to your mother first, Odessa."

She clearly didn't want to, but nodded again. "What will you do?"

I thought about Nuala, about my rangers. "Let me talk to Haidee." If there was anything I knew about, it was loss.

"I've already talked to the clan leaders," Haidee said stiffly as I approached. "I'm not interested in whatever else you have to say." She'd remained apart from the camp in the hours after the attack, preferring to sit alone atop one of the sand dunes. Arjun had been fond of doing that whenever he was on watch.

"I know. But I'm here anyway." I set a small bowl of fruit beside her. Sumiko had allowed me to leave my tent for this, after extracting my promise to return and remain abed until she deemed me well enough.

"What do you want?"

"I'm a Catseye."

"I would never have known." She was starting to sound like him, too.

"I thought you might want to know a little more about my past."

"What does that have to do with anything? Odessa's already at camp, and safe." A brief spurt of anger sparked behind her rigid monotone.

"I was in charge of a team of rangers back in Aranth, tasked with finding the safest way to the Great Abyss. It took us many months of travel, and despite the demons we encountered along the way, we did a fair job of overcoming the odds until we reached the mountain by Brighthenge." I kept my own voice neutral. "I was the only survivor."

She eyed me carefully, not without a trace of concern. She'd heard the general story before, was no doubt wondering why I was bringing it up now. "How did you survive?" she finally asked, when minutes of silence had passed.

"Luck, I think. I was no more equipped or better skilled than any members of my team. The galla came without warning, ripped up half of my companions before we'd even realized the danger." A soft gasp rose from her, but I was already lost in my own memories, forcing myself to finish. "In the end, there were only three of us left. Something rose from within the Abyss—Ereshkigal—and asked me to choose."

"To choose?"

"Which of my two teammates I was to sacrifice, to open the portal leading back into Aranth."

Haidee drew in a quick, sharp breath.

"I refused. It didn't matter. It killed them both, then tossed me into the gateway. One of them . . . was a lover. This was before I'd met Odessa."

"Oh, Good Mother . . ."

"Asteria found me just outside the city, out of my mind and raving." This was the part I'd never told anyone, save Sumiko. I'd never even gone into this much detail with Odessa. "I screamed for days after. They had to chain me up. I remember one of the Devoted suggesting to Asteria that I should be put out of my misery; they never thought I would make it back to sanity. I tried to . . ." And here I paused, idly stroking my neck. "Odessa doesn't know. I didn't want to remember what I'd almost done. I was ashamed."

Haidee's hand was against her mouth, her eyes large. "Good Mother. I'm sorry."

"I got better, as much *better* as anyone could be after what happened. But I still haven't told Odessa. That tells me I'm not completely where I want to be just yet." I hated that my voice

358

was trembling. "Physically, I made a full recovery. But I had nightmares. I had . . . panic attacks. I pursued Odessa a little more aggressively than I should have, like it could compensate for my shortcomings. I love her, but I was also desperate to feel alive again. I insisted that I was fine, that I needed nothing else. It took nearly getting Odessa killed for me to realize I needed treatment, and that I had to do it because no one else could help me if I wasn't willing."

"What was the treatment?" Haidee asked softly.

"Talking about it. Trying to process the trauma. That's the most important part. It sounds simple, which was why I'd scoffed at first. But it's working."

She said nothing for a while, and neither did I. She looked up at the sky, as if noticing something within the stars for the first time.

"I should have died then," I said.

She swung her head to look back at me, outraged on my behalf.

"No. It's not what you think I mean. Just that as hopeless as the choices they presented to me seemed, I realize that there was one more I could have made, though I didn't think of it then. One those creatures wouldn't have wanted me to make. If I'd chosen to die then, it would have taken them longer to lure Odessa to the Abyss. Or maybe they never would have been able to. Maybe it would have taken more generations after her. Maybe they would have spared either Merritt or Nuala, or both, in my place. They presented me with choices I could not have lived with. Maybe the right choice was to make one that *they* wouldn't have wanted. Everything always seems clearer in hindsight."

"I am sorry you had to go through all that. But it's not the same."

"I know. All I'm saying is that I know what it feels like, to carry that kind of burden. And that although you may feel like you are alone, I want you to remember that you're not, and that we don't want you to go through this alone."

"I don't know," she said. "I don't know if I want to . . . do anything." But she looked at me, and there was a softening in her gaze, a relaxing of the hard lines that had crept across her face in those hours after learning Arjun was gone.

"Thank you," she said, and that was a start.

A hooded figure waited for us by the boundaries of camp when we returned, and I stiffened, prepared for the worse. But when it reached up and tugged off its hood, it revealed a tumble of long, colorshifting hair. Haidee made a startled sound.

"I'm listening now," Latona said.

Chapter Twenty-Three

ODESSA AT THE CROSSROADS

— ☾ —

NIGHT HAD RETURNED TO THE desert.

As the light faded, a contingent led by Piotr of the Rockhopper clan, the one who had previously accused us of selfishness, approached Haidee. "We leave when the light returns," he said. "I care nothing about our leaders' promises. You will lead us to annihilation. You allow Latona, that accursed bitch, into our territory. She, who has hunted us for as long as we can remember. We cannot forgive this."

"You won't survive out there on your own," Lan said.

"Perhaps, but at least we can choose our own way to die. If the goddess cannot save even her own consort, then what chance have we?"

Haidee said nothing. She watched them leave before she, too, stood and walked away.

It took everything I had not to run after her. My sister's

anger had not yet run its course, and I knew she would not appreciate my presence just yet.

Unsurprisingly, Noelle took charge, supervising the Mudforgers' and Stonebreakers' efforts to erect more sand-tents. "The temperature will drop drastically, without warning," she informed Lars when the latter volunteered to do without that luxury. "Winds aren't uncommon out here, and at night they'll be freezing. None of you are used to the colder weather, and you'll be chilled before long. I'll distribute blankets for those who need them, and I want everyone slated for patrol to carry another while on duty."

"There are several back in the rigs," Lord Vanya said. "I'll give them to Mother Salla to dole out."

"Keep one for yourself," Noelle advised.

"I'll live."

"He survived, you know," said Lisette, who was watching him closely. "Latona confirmed it when she arrived. She said he was at the Citadel, recuperating. Doesn't mean he's not a coward who doesn't deserve your loyalty, but I thought you ought to know."

The boy's face crumpled. "I shot at him."

"And I'm very sorry you missed."

"I didn't. I hit him in the leg."

"If it doesn't kill him, you missed." She paused. "I'm glad he's still breathing, if only for your sake. But after everything he's done, you shouldn't feel like you owe him anything."

"He's my father. That's not something you can throw away so easily."

"He betrayed his own liege. Why is that someone you would ever defend?"

"Because he's still my father. Just because you discard people once they've outlived their usefulness doesn't mean I do the same."

Lisette blinked. "I've lost friends, too. This isn't a paradise. I'm just a realist about it."

"A realist? How much do you know of what's real, when you push everyone away?" Vanya paused and looked down. "No. You're right. That was uncalled for. My apologies. Noelle, tell me where to bring the blankets. I'll get them now."

"Have you ever had honey?" Noelle asked Lisette, who was still staring hard at Vanya as he walked away.

"What's that?"

"A rather sweet nectar; my mother gave me a taste of it once as a child, and I've never quite forgotten it. A rather funny animal called a 'bee' made it, and humans collected it for various condiments and medicines. There was a popular saying about it: 'to attract more bees, you must do so with honey. With sweetness.'"

The girl scowled. "And what would I possibly want with more bees?"

"To make even more honey, I'm told."

Lisette glared at Noelle, and stalked off.

"You have a way with words, Lady Noelle," I sighed.

"I've had to deal with squabbling children a time or two in the past." Noelle paused. "How is Lady Haidee?"

I looked down at my hands. I didn't know how to approach

my twin now, in the aftermath of Arjun's death. "She blames me. As she should." If I'd only had more control. If only I hadn't lost my composure when Lan had been hurt. . . .

"How long will it take for you to go to her, you think?" Noelle asked carefully. "A day? A week? Eighteen years, perhaps?"

I stared at her, and she shrugged. "It's the same with Latona and Asteria. It was the same with Inanna and *her* twin. As far as Aeon is concerned, it's a tale as old as time. I do not wish to see history repeating itself, Your Holiness. I think Aeon's seen enough goddesses sacrificed."

I didn't want that, either. But things, I felt, were already changing. Latona was here, and tensions in camp had risen, especially since word was already spreading about Piotr and his men leaving. But the older goddesses hadn't tried to kill each other yet, and I couldn't help but hope. "You are very wise, Noelle," I said gravely.

"A foolish steward doesn't last long in their job, Your Holiness. If you will excuse me."

Mother and Latona were still in talks with the clan leaders, the grudge between them temporarily set aside. They had no doubt been told of what Haidee and I intended for the morrow.

It was a simple enough plan: Open the portal leading down into the Cruel Kingdom, and face Ereshkigal once and for all. If four goddesses weren't enough to defeat the demoness, then our last resort was to complete the ritual.

It wasn't the best strategy. I didn't want to fail. I didn't want to complete the ritual. But as Lan had already pointed out, the chances of all of us returning from that fight were slim.

And if Lan wasn't coming back, then neither was I, because I was going to take every galla down with me.

It wasn't the best strategy, but it was the only valid one we had. The question was whether the nomads would oppose it because of the risks on their end, and whether our mothers would oppose it because of the danger Haidee and I would be putting ourselves in.

Haidee and me. Latona and Mother. Inanna and Ereshkigal. I knew that our mothers had once been close, but what of our two ancestresses? Did they love each other, share secrets, know each other's minds the way I did Haidee's and she did mine? Were Haidee and I doomed to follow in their footsteps, to be driven apart like our mothers had been? Haidee was still angry, still grieving. Her mind was now closed to me, and I didn't know how to overcome that barrier.

I was in no mood to confront Mother. I visited Lan instead, who was confined to her bed under Sumiko's orders. She was sitting up when I entered, an arm folded across her chest while the other was in a makeshift sling.

"Convince Sumiko that I'm good to leave," she pleaded. "It's barely an injury."

"As always, an understatement." I sat beside her, and stroked her brow. "But are you feeling better?"

"My arm itches, a good sign it's stitching together nicely, which I know because I know more about medicine than anyone else here."

"Except Sumiko."

"She's deliberately healing me in tiny doses instead of all at once. So I could rest longer, she said."

"She's right."

Lan grumbled, then softened immediately. "There's something else, isn't there? Are you worried about Haidee?"

I nodded, not trusting myself to speak.

"I talked to her. She's hurting and she's angry, but neither of those are directed at you."

"How can you be sure?"

"You were raised differently, but in many ways you are both still too much alike. She has your penchant for placing blame on herself most of all."

I bit my lip. "But she's not wrong, what she said back there. It's my fault Arjun's gone."

"Odessa, love." Lan shifted with a groan, then reached across to kiss me. "Your self-control is beyond anything else. Haidee's been inside your head enough times to know that. She wanted to lash out at someone she loved, one she knows will forgive her while she's still hurting, and that happened to be you. Talk to her. Don't let this stretch on between you two."

"I will. I'll do it tonight."

"How are you holding up?"

"I feel—out of sorts. But no more inclinations to murder anyone." Arjun's death had shocked me back into my senses. The voices in my head had been silent ever since.

"Odessa."

"I promise. If I feel those old urges coming back, I'll tell you immediately."

"Good." It was her turn to hesitate. "I haven't talked to Asteria yet."

"I'm going to. It's time Mother and I had it out once and for all."

"I should be with you."

"Absolutely not. Sumiko's orders."

She scowled, and I giggled. It felt good to laugh. "There are some things I need to discuss with her in private."

She nodded. "Come back when you're done. I miss you already."

I felt better after I emerged from Lan's tent, and decided to face Mother before I'd lost my newfound bravery. Much to my surprise, Haidee was there, idling by the clan leaders' tent. She caught sight of me, motioned me over. "Don't make a sound," she whispered.

It was obvious that she intended to eavesdrop. Latona's voice rose from within, clear as a bell. "I don't blame any of you for remaining distrustful of me."

A scoff that sounded like Tamera was the response. "We could pack up and leave this instant, let you deal with the galla on your own. We owe you no allegiance, after how you've treated us."

"Yes." Latona didn't even sound regretful. "There were only so many resources I could spare back then. It was either take you all in at the cost of the city's sustainability, or save a portion of my people and be assured of their survival. But afterward, once we'd stabilized the aquifers . . . I should have extended you all sanctuary then. But you had already grown to resent us.

You are free to leave. I will do what I can to ensure the galla do not follow."

A pause, and then Tamera again, grudging. "No. I promised your daughters I would keep them safe. Abandoning them now would make us no better than you."

"I can extend the city's air-dome to accommodate your clans, or we can offer you places to stay within the districts. No matter how strong the galla are, we can wait them out for years. For as long as—"

"No!" Haidee exclaimed. I groaned, but followed her into the tent. "Mother, you're talking about a siege!"

Latona turned, her mouth thinning. "Far better than your proposal to enter the Cruel Kingdom and fight that demoness yourselves! I won't allow you to throw away your lives!"

"The galla grow stronger with every attack! How long will it take before the city's resources are overtaxed and the air-dome falls? A week? A month? You're only delaying the inevitable!"

"A week's reprieve is far better than throwing yourself into an Abyss tomorrow!"

"It's been seventeen years' worth of reprieves at this point. You've been running away for too long!"

"I forbid you from sacrificing your life just because he's dead!"

Haidee stiffened. Across from me, Mother chose silence, and I followed her lead. Mother Salla cleared her throat. "I believe we've discussed all that we can for tonight," she said calmly, rising to her feet and gesturing for the other clan leaders to follow.

"We have much to do tomorrow, so let us prepare and catch up on our sleep. Good evening, Your Holinesses."

They left. I realized that it was the first time that the four of us had been alone together.

"I lost your father," Latona said steadily. "And I wanted to die, too. But I also knew that few would survive without me. So I built the city and protected it as best as I could. But all I wanted then was to travel back to the Great Abyss and throw myself into its depths, hoping that somehow, I would find him within it. The future of the Golden City lies with you, Haidee. You cannot be so careless, when so many are counting on you. Even more so now that the world is turning."

"And now that Aeon spins, Mother, tell me: Will it be Odessa or me your Devoted shall choose to sacrifice?"

Latona froze.

"Did you decide to stop the world from turning to halt the galla's advances?"

It was my mother, Asteria, who answered, shaking her head. "We still don't know how we did it. We were both grieving, and angry. All I remembered was wanting to lash out at everyone . . ."

". . . like we would tear the world in two in our grief," Latona finished softly.

"We must enter the Cruel Kingdom and find Ereshkigal," I said. "I know that it's a risk. The Devoted didn't want to gamble on losing two goddesses. Sacrificing one twin for a short bounty was better than risking both. I don't want that."

"Odessa," Mother said gently.

I turned to her. "You'll always be my mother, regardless of what anyone says. I know I haven't always been grateful for that, and I'm sorry. But we have to do this. And you know it, too."

She bowed her head. "I haven't always been the best parent for you. You were the only link I had to everyone I ever cared for—to my sister, to Aranth. I wept when I first learned of your sickness. It felt like you were being punished for my sins." She looked back at Latona. "I thought you were gone. I always thought that I would feel you somehow, no matter how far away you were. That was what convinced me that you were dead."

Latona sighed. "As did I. I thought Aeon was doomed, that it was my duty simply to delay the inevitable for as long as I could. I knew that anything else I tried to do would fail because . . ." She let out an unexpected sob. "Because you weren't with me."

"I am sorry about Aranth," Mother said, and I was stunned to see her eyes, too, fill with tears. "I never meant to, Latona. I thought you were safe. If they'd decided to kill me, I was prepared to let them, because I was convinced you were out of harm's way, and happy."

For many long minutes they were silent; both simply looking at one another, trying to navigate the distance between them widened by time, trying to overcome old hatreds that had once spanned a distance as vast as the icy seas that surrounded Aranth.

"Do you remember how we first met?" Latona asked softly. "It was a hot summer day, and I had balked at being cooped up in my room for geography lessons. I thought it would be good to put those lectures into practice, and snuck out to the nearby market—"

"—unaware I'd done the same thing," Mother finished with a faint chuckle. "We both reached for a pomegranate at the same time. The shock I felt then, seeing my own reflection gaping back at me in amazement. The panic we caused that day. The people were convinced we were demons."

"The tower they kept you in was at the other end of the city from the one where they kept me. I could see it from my window, and realized it was identical to mine. I'd always wondered what they kept there, never realizing the irony. Surely they should have expected us to cross paths, given that they'd housed us in the same city?"

"They'd had little trouble with the goddesses that came before us, I suppose."

Latona let out a teary laugh. "Aranth and I weren't happy, Asteria. Not even at Farthengrove. We'd shoved all the responsibility on you, and we felt guilty. Someone tried to kill me. We were no longer safe there. We feared that if they couldn't get me, that they would turn on you instead."

Mother closed her eyes. "We were both fools."

"All these years apart, and yet we have somehow raised our daughters right, for all our faults."

Mother smiled. "We did, didn't we?" She looked at us. "They've shown more understanding of the world than we ever did. I'm afraid for what might come tomorrow, but you're both old enough to know your own minds. We won't let you face the dangers alone, however. We're coming with you."

I leaped up and threw my arms around Mother. She hugged me back, and I felt her draw in a shaky breath.

"When Lan returned from the Great Abyss that first time, you fought to heal her," I whispered. "It wasn't just because you cared about her, was it?"

"Brighthenge broke me," she said softly. "I was in no better shape in its aftermath than Lan was after that first expedition. I recognized her suffering as my own. She was far stronger than I could ever be. She returned to the Great Abyss for your sake. I—I couldn't."

Until now, I thought, holding her tightly. It was not selfishness that had prevented her from returning to Brighthenge. And unlike Lan, her trauma had continued untreated for all this time.

"When you arrived here, Mother, did you . . . ?" I dreaded asking the question, but I had to know.

Mother sighed. "The waves turned violent when the world started turning. Not even the ice walls could stand before them. It decimated the city, and we had to evacuate. I remembered the gateway, then. There were a couple of young men who had been mortally injured, who had no hopes of surviving." She looked away. "They didn't suffer. I made sure of it."

"Why didn't you tell me earlier?"

"Because that wasn't the first time I tried to access the portal from Aranth."

"Tell me," I insisted.

"It was when I first learned you were sick, and nothing the Catseye did could heal you. I remembered the portal, knew I needed a sacrifice to gain access to Brighthenge. There was a criminal in the gaols who'd murdered his wife, waiting for me to pass sentence." She stared straight ahead. "Except the gateway never opened. I believe it was because Aeon had stopped turning, that it wouldn't work while the world was still." Her head dropped. "I killed a man for no reason. My shock when I learned Lan had reappeared through the portal, that Inanna— no, Ereshkigal—had opened it herself . . . I was terrified."

"It's not your fault."

"It's still my burden to bear." Mother met my gaze. "I was terrified when you first exhibited the same sickness I had— but in a strange way I'd been expecting it as well. We were in unfamiliar territory, in so many ways; I had no precedent to fall back on. The galla's gifts I'd acquired disappeared when the world stopped, leaving only the visions. I thought it must mean that the demons were gone from Aeon for good. That's why I was terrified when the shadow appeared over your heart. I thought it could be purged in the same way mine was. Yes, I gambled with Lan's life. I had only my own experiences to guide me by, the knowledge that I needn't accept the final gift to be cured. I had hoped the same for you."

"But Father died," I pointed out.

Mother smiled sadly. "Your father wasn't the sacrifice that was demanded of me."

Haidee had embraced Latona; the older goddess was weeping openly as well, but Haidee's eyes remained curiously blank, a part of her still tucked away and grieving.

"We need to figure out how to open the portal without killing anyone else," I mumbled several minutes later, once all our tears had run out.

Latona and Mother looked at each other. "I believe we know a way," Mother said finally. "But that can wait until tomorrow."

Sonfei was waiting when we emerged from the tent, looking more nervous than I'd ever seen him. Mother froze, her eyes wide and mouth parted, suddenly looking years younger. Latona glanced at him, and a slow smile spread across her face.

"A—Asteria." The usually confident Liangzhu man was stammering. "May I have a word with you in private?"

"Yes," Latona said, before Mother could answer. There was an impish glint in her eyes. "She's been waiting to talk to you for a long time."

Mother glared at her twin, but allowed herself to be led away.

"Sonfei was always smitten with Asteria," Latona said, watching them leave. "But Asteria only had eyes for . . ." She paused, her eyes falling shut. "I am sorry I never told you about your father, Haidee."

"You have the rest of our lives to tell me," Haidee said.

"I do, don't I?" Latona looked at me next. "I should have searched for you," she said, her voice harsh with self-recrimination. "I would have torn the world apart all over again, if I'd known."

"I had Mother," I said, smiling. "There is nothing to be sorry for. I only wish I'd met you and Haidee sooner."

Latona opened her arms, and I stepped into them. She smelled like Mother, too.

"I'll leave you two alone," she said. "I still need to talk to my commanders about how to proceed tomorrow. I have ordered Torven Arrenley detained in the gaols until further notice. I could forgive him perhaps, for seeking out the stone of immortality without my knowing, but I cannot forgive him for putting you two in danger to get it."

She left, leaving us looking up at the night. There were stars, I saw, and a full moon. It was a rare sight in Aranth, where the sky was constantly enveloped in dark clouds and unrelenting rain.

"We've been doing this all wrong," Haidee finally said. "Your galla's gifts. Some of the passages we've read about Inanna or Brighthenge talked about how we could use them to save Aeon."

"I'm not sure what you mean."

"You told me that every time you make something grow, you wind up poisoning the soil underneath and making it barren. I read a journal once, written by my—our—ancestor, Nyx. She talked about being able to resurrect a dead bird. The way she described it was similar to how you described resurrecting your . . ." She paused, looking worried.

"My Devoted," I finished for her.

"Yes. But at the shrine, when we combined our abilities—"

"—we could channel the Gates of Life and Death. If we do it together," I continued, growing excited. "You could nullify what repercussions there should have been—"

"Never tested it yet. But the passages about channeling these gates could have been the key all along. We were too focused on the prophecies and on Brighthenge and *The Ages of Aeon*, and we never thought we could—"

"There was a reason why Inanna couldn't fix the world without her twin. I still don't know how we were able to get Aeon to spin again, but when we did it together, somehow we—"

"I'm sorry."

I stopped, puzzled.

"I resented you. When Arjun died, I went down a list of things that went wrong, things I could have rectified if I'd been stronger, or faster, or thought it through better. And for a short time, I blamed you."

"You had good reason to."

"I don't, actually. That's what happened with Latona and Asteria. They were goaded into distrusting each other, into hating each other." Haidee still wasn't crying, like there was something inside her that was too broken now for tears. But her smile was soft and warm, more like the cheerful sister I knew. "I don't want us to be like that."

"Haidee." I was crying enough for the both of us. "I wish I'd known you when I was younger. I wish we'd grown up together. All I can think about is all the time we've wasted."

"So we shouldn't waste a second more." She was firm. "Mother Salla thinks it's a suicide mission, to enter the Cruel Kingdom without having any way of getting back. I feel like we don't have a choice. But I don't want you to do this without talking to Lan first. If you decide not to go with me, then I'll—"

"Don't be ridiculous," I interrupted. "Of course I'm going with you. Lan knows more about duty than I ever could. She knows what the risks are, and she agrees with me."

A cry sounded from camp, and we turned to spot a mass of frothing shadows in the distance, partly swallowed up by the night. "They're attacking with greater frequency now," Haidee observed quietly.

This time, though, we felt no fear. I heard the alarms sounding at the encampment, everyone scrambling to find weapons and a position to shore up against the approaching swarm.

The stars disappeared behind heavy clouds. I heard the steady thrum of the familiar, detested voices inside my head, whispering *join us*, but Haidee was here, her presence overpowering, and the miasma in my mind hissed and fled.

I wove the incanta needed to create the Gates of Death. At the same time, Haidee wove the incanta for the Gates of Life.

Lightning sizzled down. It caught a group of galla midcrawl, blasting them into nothing. We were relentless. More bolts rained down on the gathered horde, striking endlessly. I should have felt exhausted; we were using too many patterns, expending more energy than should be healthy. But I felt refreshed; without the constant murmur of voices plaguing my mind, I felt rejuvenated and happy and free. Haidee's mind was an interlocking piece, falling into place perfectly against mine, with a strange contentment in that joining that bordered almost on euphoric. It felt like I was a half who'd never known I could be whole.

We were ruthless. Even the shadows sensed that there was something new to our partnership, something they could not seek to comprehend nor overcome. I could see pockets of them attempting flight, the first time I'd seen any of them retreat from battle. And still we pursued, lightning coming swiftly down to savage the lot. At intervals we shaped the air into a mile-wide cleaver, and cut many of them in half in one fell swoop, the bodies falling away and evaporating like the desert rain. The clans were no longer gearing themselves up for battle; they watched the carnage with open mouths and wide eyes, and eventually, scattered cheers rose from our audience.

Darkness rippled through the Inanna—no, the Ereshkigal!—demon, like a disturbed reflection on a lake's surface. Something like hair flowed around her, curled like snakes waiting to strike.

But there was nothing vulnerable about us now. I knew ice and water best, and so I shaped my weapons into a glittering shard, the pointed tip sharper than even the best of swords. Haidee knew light and fire best, and so her flames wrapped around my blade, hot as hell yet never melting the ice or blunting its edges. With my strength merged with hers, her fires blazed blue and deadly.

We launched it right into the approximation of the creature's heart, heard the satisfying *thunk* it made as it tore through its chest, cleaving it almost in half. It bent backward, maw agape, and the rest of Haidee's fires were quick to consume it all, until there was nothing left, until there was nothing unnatural about the darkness around us.

Now that the threat was gone, we stumbled and clung to each other, shaken by our combined ferocity but also elated. "I've never used that many incanta at once before," Haidee said, awed. "All this time, killing one goddess and dooming the other to misery, when together, they all could have been this . . ."

"Your Holinesses!" Noelle was trotting out to us, and even her normally stoic expression had turned to reverence. Latona was there, matching her stride for stride. "I have water and a bite of food prepared," the steward said.

Haidee and I looked at each other, and we both began to laugh; mine loud and clear, Haidee's soft, like she was relearning how. Trust Noelle to be pragmatic.

Latona's eyes were a mystery, but when she spoke, the pride in her voice was evident. "My daughters," she said softly.

My sister nudged at me. "Go to Lan," she said softly, reading my mind. "Have no regrets this night."

I hesitated. "But . . ."

"I want to talk to Mother for a bit." The skies cleared again. Now there was only the pristine desert, white against the moonlight, and empty of danger. "And I want to look up at the full moon a little while longer." She turned her head and gazed upward. "He would have liked seeing this," she added softly. Her voice had regained some of its impassivity, but her fingers were still wrapped around mine.

"You know I love you, right?"

"Always. And I love you, too."

I hugged her then, but knew our moment of connection had passed. She was somewhere else now, back among thoughts of Arjun and happier days, and not even I could trespass there.

"What's a joust?" Lan asked when I returned. She was still in bed, but this time reading a book—a romance book, I realized. *The Lady's Pirate. My* romance book.

"You said you're not a romance reader."

"I had very little else to do. And now that I've started, I must confess it's a lot more interesting than I thought. What is a joust?" Trust Lan to be interested in the parts of the book about weaponry. "How do these lances work? It sounds a bit ungainly to handle, given the length the book describes. And atop a horse? What is that? Is it possible to bring beasts onto a ship—"

"How fully recovered are you?" I asked abruptly.

Lan blinked. "Well enough."

"Can you move without tearing anything?"

"Yes, thanks to Sumiko, I'm only slightly sore in places. What—"

I took the book and tossed it aside, pulled her close to me, kissed her. *No regrets*, Haidee had said. And I fully intended to take her advice. I mourned for her, and for Arjun, but I wanted to celebrate what little life I might have left with Lan.

"Quite the instruction manuals, these romance books," Lan murmured, mellower now than when we first started. I was snuggled beside her, sated, happy, and pliant, tracing small circles on her bare skin. "I think I have a better understanding of why you like them now."

I muffled a giggle. "I should have brought the raunchier ones for the trip."

"Is there no romance book you don't like?"

"A few. The ones where the heroine or their love interest dies. Or both."

She paused, stroking my back. "I suppose that's a realistic outcome? Surely they can't all have happy endings."

"Real life is harsh enough that I'd rather not be reminded of it." Wanting to lighten the mood a little more, I quipped, "Wouldn't you rather read naughty scenes instead? You did say they made good guides."

"I look forward to testing more of them out in the future." She gave my backside a quick squeeze. "How is Haidee?"

"I'm worried about her. She's still hurting badly. I know I have to give her time, but it's paining me to see her like this."

"That's the nature of losing someone you love," Lan said softly. "It never completely goes away."

"Was it like that with you and Nuala?"

"Leave it to you to talk about an ex when you're in bed with me, my *yexu*."

I laughed. My old jealousies felt ridiculous now, assured as I was of her love. "I was only curious. As much as you claim it was nothing serious, I know you better. You leave a little of yourself in everyone you care for. You can't help it."

"I left a lot of myself in you, if tonight was any indication."

There was a leer on her face, and I blushed. She sobered. "It's not always about the pain going away. It's about learning how to live with it."

I didn't think Haidee was going to learn how to live with it. If the worst happened tomorrow, in the Great Abyss, she intended to sacrifice herself. She still thought it was her destiny to. "If anything happens to me, I want you to mourn, and I want you to move on."

Lan could have protested, insisted that nothing would. But the stakes were too high, the future too unpredictable. She'd been a soldier for almost all her life, too long not to know the risks. "If anything happens to you," she said simply, "then that means something has already happened to me."

I could have made the same protests, but didn't. I placed my head on her shoulder instead, and breathed in her warmth, accepting this as truth.

Presently, she shifted. "You never told me," she said, her voice coy, "how salacious some of these romances of yours are. A few scenes made me wonder if they were even physically possible."

"You're still injured." I gasped as she moved over me, kissing up my neck.

"Not where it counts," Lan said, before setting about proving me wrong.

Chapter Twenty-Four

HAIDEE AT PEACE

I DIDN'T SLEEP. INSTEAD, I sat outside my tent and waited for the sunrise.

It was beautiful. More than that, it should be a sign of change. Today, we would journey into the Cruel Kingdom. Today, we would face Ereshkigal once and for all. In a few hours, it would be over. Either we would have destroyed Ereshkigal's hold on the world, or Aeon would be destroyed.

But at the moment, I couldn't bring myself to care either way.

The coming dawn painted the sky in orange and vermilion hues. I watched the stars wink out one by one, unwilling to compete with the growing light. There was a comfort, I thought, in knowing that they were still there looking down at me, though I could no longer see them.

The remaining clan leaders had been solicitous, a shade more respectful than I was used to. The soldiers stood to attention a little more forcefully, a little too self-aware in their discipline. Strangely enough, it was the cannibals who seemed most comfortable; their leader, Bull, met my eyes with a newfound gravity, as if he'd never tried to hunt me down as food several weeks earlier. He saluted me with a clenched fist, a sign of respect among them. I suppose it was easier for them to shake off the loss of one of their members; their whole lifestyle had been based on always expecting the worst.

But this wasn't just a comrade I'd lost. It was . . .

My twin sister never blamed me, even despite the accusations I'd flung her way. I knew the guilt weighed heavy on her still, no thanks to my thoughtlessness—even after our conversation, even after we routed the last swarm of galla together. Secretly I was grateful, that she'd never thought my grief was something to be pitied. Neither did Lan, nor Noelle. Given what the former had told me about her own past, she was probably the one who understood best.

The other Catseye, Sumiko, had offered her services to me. Lan had sung her praises, but I'd made excuses, pleaded for more time to process my feelings on my own. Talking didn't feel like it was going to help me. Not right now.

I stood and wandered the outskirts of camp for several minutes, and nearly stumbled upon Mother and Asteria, talking quietly. I crouched behind a dune, knowing I shouldn't be eavesdropping but unable to help myself. "Did Devika ever tell you about this stone of immortality?" Mother asked.

"I found one mention of it in a book before. I wondered about it being called that, because I knew we weren't immortal. Devika was quick to tell me it wasn't real. Only Jesmyn thought there might have been more to it, but even she told me it wasn't a viable alternative."

"What did she say?"

"That we were better off without it. That to use the stone that way would mean sacrificing the both of us, since it would require both aspects of Inanna's nature. I had no idea what she meant, and she realized pretty quickly she'd divulged information I wasn't supposed to know. She never said anything about it after that, no matter how many times I asked. I didn't know then that they were planning to . . . that by 'sacrifice' she meant . . ." Her voice trailed off.

There was silence for a while. "Where did we go wrong, Asteria?" Mother asked, sounding weary. "We knew they were keeping things from us. We promised we wouldn't let them tear us apart."

"And they did anyway."

"And all for Aranth?" Mother let out a teary laugh. "We actually allowed a boy to come between us?"

"You love him, Latona. Don't diminish what he meant to you."

"I am sorry that he loved me, Asteria. I'm sorry that . . ."

"Don't be. I'm glad he did. I cared for him too, but . . . I was jealous of him more than not."

"Of him?" Mother sounded amazed.

"You and I were always together, until he arrived. He took up all of your time, and I was left alone with the council, with the duties we should have been sharing. I rarely saw you after you took up with him. I missed you more than anything. But with the final galla, he . . ." She hesitated. "He would have been safe. I swear it."

"But you named your city . . ."

"Mainly out of spite. I was angry. You were right. I wanted to have some kind of control over him, but not in the way you thought. It faded after a few months, and for the longest time I just wanted to shut myself away and cry. I should have searched for you to be sure, but I was terrified of going back. I went so far as to try to access the portal, but it didn't work. If I'd been more honest with myself, I would have named my city after you instead."

"I wanted to die. I wanted to just lie down under the sun and close my eyes and stop thinking. It was Lord Arrenley who convinced me to keep going, to find a way to protect what remained of my people. This doesn't excuse his betrayal, but it's the only reason I haven't done more than imprison him. I owe him that much. But more than I lost Aranth, I lost you. I had Aranth's coat, but I had nothing to remember you by. When I learned you were still alive . . . I reacted badly."

"We are both good at reacting badly, I think," Asteria said softly. "I am so sorry. I wish we had more time."

"I wish that, too. I wish we could do everything differently again, Astie. But I'm glad we can make things better for our daughters now. I'm so glad we at least have today—" Mother's voice broke off. "Haidee," she began, her voice louder. "Is there something you would like to discuss with me?"

I started on my feet, stammering out apologies and hurrying away, though my heart felt lighter than it had a few minutes before. At least they were talking. At least they were trying to forgive each other. It was the best I could hope for.

I found another dune to perch on. He was fond of doing that, I remembered. He'd climb the highest one he could find and stand guard like he was solely responsible for the protection of the whole camp. He always liked to act tough, but it could never hide his kindness. He was . . .

Tears blurred my vision. I'd almost forgotten that I knew how to cry.

There was movement behind me, but I ignored her, continuing to stare up at the rising sun even as Mother settled herself beside me, carefully rearranging her robes.

"Aranth could never figure out if he preferred the sunrise or the sunset more," she said. "He was the scholar of us two, interested in all the complexities of how the world turned, and how its turning affected us. He built astrolabes to study the stars, and tracked the changing patterns in the weather, hoping to refine his ability to predict the rain and the snow. I never had his mind for mechanika, but he never made me feel like I was foolish for not knowing as much as he did. You are a lot like him in that, I think. You are a lot like him in many ways."

I said nothing. The pinks gave way to yellows, clouds slipping across the sky. From the corner of my eye I saw Mother's hair billowing in the wind, mimicking those colors.

"I kept his favorite jacket in my wardrobe. For years I would take it out and breathe in, trying to remember. But his scent would fade a little every time, and I had to decide if I would rather stop bringing it out so his scent could last longer, or keep it closer to me, even if I had to let him go quicker than I wanted. It took me two years before I could speak his name out loud. And even then it hurt so badly that I never said it again."

"His name is Arjun." She was right; the pain scraped at my throat, and the words came out raw and aching, stripped of anything that could protect me from the hurt. "And if I'd chosen to imprison myself for over seventeen years, never seeking to undo the mistake I'd made, he would hate me for my selfishness."

She bowed her head, accepting the barb. "From the little I've seen of him, I find that unlikely. You convinced him to travel with you to the center of the Breaking, with nothing more concrete than a mirage's word, a couple of letters, and your own convictions. He might have disapproved, but I doubt he would have hated you when it's clear he trusted you almost from the start. Despite everything I've done to harm his family." There was a light touch against my hand. "Haidee. I know I haven't been a very good mother to you. Ever since I was a young girl I've always had someone to rely on. First it was Namu and my Devoted, and then Asteria, and then Aranth. But after the Breaking, I was alone for the first time in my life, and I was afraid. I thought I'd lost everyone who'd ever been important to me, and so I sought to protect the little that I had left. And you—you were all I had."

I couldn't say anything. She squeezed my pinkie finger.

"I'd always believed Odessa gone. I would have fought Inanna herself, if I'd known she was still alive."

"And Asteria?"

"Asteria and I parted on the worst possible terms. She had always been better at everything. Better at incanta, better at leading, better at getting people to love her. I was willing to give her the Devoted, the people, rulership of Aeon. All I wanted was Aranth, and perhaps a quiet little corner of the world so we could live in peace, with you and Odessa. But even Aranth she wanted. I started to hate her after that, but that didn't mean I never stopped loving her, either. I just didn't want to be looked at as an inferior version of her. And in the end, I wept for her just as much as I had wept for Aranth."

I finally tore my gaze away from the sun. Mother looked forlorn and exhausted. She'd always appeared so perfect and aloof before, carrying on like she could never make a mistake.

"And now that you know she's alive? And that Odessa is alive?"

"I didn't want to step outside the city. I didn't try to bring Aeon back to the way it was, because I knew I couldn't have done it on my own. But now that you are both here with me again . . . I will help. I have been running away, for far too long." She turned to face me. "I think," Mother said, "that I would like nothing more than to fight alongside Asteria, alongside you

389

and Odessa. I am so sorry, my love."

I understood her a little more now. She had lost my father and hadn't known how to stop grieving. His jacket had stayed in her closet, his scent lingering longer, but so had her pain.

I didn't know if I could stop grieving, either.

"Maybe . . ." Mother's voice wavered. "Someday, maybe we can all be a family again. You and me and Haidee and Asteria."

I stepped into her outstretched arms and, finally, allowed myself to weep—huge, racking sobs that took bits and pieces of me with every tear, until I had nothing left inside me to break.

"I want to conduct an experiment."

Odessa was sitting on a sand dune, watching Lan confer with a few of the other clan members, and she glanced at me as I walked up. "What do you mean?" she asked.

I took her hands in mine. "Do you think you could . . . ?"

"Yes. But are you sure that you're—"

"I'm positive. We've done it before, we can do it again. Besides—"

"All right. I trust you."

We fell silent, our eyes closing at the same time. I could feel a strange glow emanating from within us both. As before, I saw her weave the incanta to grow her tree, watched as they sank into the sand beneath us. But for the first time I reached out to join my gate with hers, our patterns intertwining until they felt strong and intractable, bursting with the promise of change.

There was a strange cracking sound, and a green sprout rose

from the ground before us. The bud grew, flowered briefly, and then surged upward, twisting around itself to form braids of twigs and branches, continuing above us until, finally, a massive tree trunk stood in its place; branches growing, leaves forming.

Some of the clans who'd been watching us had never seen a tree before, and their gasps were loud as they watched this fresh miracle.

The tree was now roughly six feet tall, and still growing; from among its leaves more flowers sprouted, shed their petals, and formed small fruit that ripened before our eyes. Some grew round and orange, a sharp sweetness carrying in the air; others grew lengthwise and curved, or yellow and bottom-heavy, or red and puckered. I had never thought that one tree alone could produce different kinds of fruit. But there they were, begging to be plucked and consumed, promising sustenance. Shadows stretched over the sand, offering us shade.

With a cry of happy surprise, Noelle leaped up, pulling herself up through the branches to retrieve some of the lower-hanging fruit. Soon many others crowded around the tree, hands raised as Noelle tossed the ripest of the fruits down to them.

"See?" I whispered, opening my eyes.

"Yes," Odessa said. "I felt—I feel—" She lifted her hands to her face, looked surprised to find them shaking. "It feels . . . good."

"I think we need each other to do what we both can't alone. I couldn't have done it on my own. And that's why I don't want you ever talking like you're less than what you are. I've only just found you. I don't want to lose my sister all over again. We can do this. I know we will."

Odessa smiled, her eyes coming alive with tears. She hugged me. "You will never lose me," she whispered.

I hugged her back, looking up at our tree. *I wish Arjun could have seen this*, I thought. *He would be stuffing his face along with the rest of them.*

Odessa must have known what I was thinking, because her arms around me tightened.

A broken column was all that was left of the statue marking the portal's location. Had Asteria and her people not pointed the way, I would never even have known its significance. Opening it would have demanded another blood sacrifice, but I was adamant that there would be no more of that for this journey.

Except the alternative was to travel to the Great Abyss through the Sand Sea, a journey that would take weeks we couldn't spare. Especially if there would be galla dogging our steps the whole time.

Instead, Odessa and I were ready to perform yet another miracle.

"I'd like some further information regarding this gateway," Lan grunted, irritable. "Where is Vanya?"

The boy himself chose that moment to come trotting up, nervously smoothing down his rumpled clothes and studiously avoiding looking in Lisette's direction. I wanted to sigh, but didn't. Vanya could very well die today, as could so many others who'd chosen to follow us, and I couldn't fault him for making the most of his time here. "There's an inscription on the monument outside the Brighthenge temple, where the portals originated," he said immediately, once we'd posed our question. *"'A life for the west. A life for the east. Immortality, below.'* The first two sentences are self-explanatory, but sacrificing a life doesn't seem to gain us access to the *below*, which I assume is the way into the Cruel Kingdom."

"We know that already, Vanya," Latona said brusquely. "Out with it. Tell us what you think."

The boy gulped. "It's those paintings back in the underground temple, Your Holiness. They were very specific when it came to Inanna's legend, and quite detailed. The one in which both Inanna and her sister descend into the underworld does not depict them making use of a blood sacrifice to enter."

"Would a temple dedicated to Inanna portray her initiating something so cruel as a blood sacrifice?" Tamera scoffed.

"She was depicted as running away while her sister called out desperately to her for help. If it didn't shy away from that act of cowardice . . ."

"I think I know," I said. "We need a goddess with the Gates of Life, and the other with the Gates of Death."

"Yes," Asteria said thoughtfully. "I believe that's right. Latona and I've hardly ever used our powers together in that way before—"

"—and only on trivial things," Mother chimed in. "Pranks on some of the Devoted—"

"A few spells to impress some of the city folk, mostly to show off. We were so young and foolish then. We didn't know—"

"—that we could have done so much more for everyone, should have realized that was the reason the Devoted wanted to keep us separated. But it was too late."

"Good Mother," Lisette groaned. "They're doing it, too."

The Golden City mechanika had been busy. Jes and Rodge were overjoyed to see me again, neither willing to relinquish me from their hugs until I'd told them they still had a job to do, and not a lot of time to finish it. Yeong-ho was more reticent— no doubt he was still smarting over my decision to have him knocked unconscious—but he softened well enough when I apologized, and beamed when Mother made it a point to thank him for his ingenuity. "I understand that this was on such short notice," she said. "You more than exceeded my expectations. Thank you."

"It's always been my pleasure, Your Holiness." What Yeong-ho had done was fashion a smaller version of the air-dome, to be set up around the perimeter of the small monument and afford everyone within it some measure of protection. It would be stronger than the dome we'd managed to create back at the neutral grounds, and its compactness made it even more durable than the Golden City's.

Odessa spent most of the morning being mobbed by the other Aranthians. My twin's fears that she would be seen as a traitor by her people were instantly dispelled when many of them converged on her, laughing and clinging. It had not taken long for her to dissolve once more into tears, her guilt all the lesser than it had once been. Quite a few had latched on to Lan as well, her surprise turning to something bordering on bashfulness as other Catseye healers checked her wounds in between scolding her lightly for being reckless. Lan, I felt, had very little idea of how beloved she was among her own colleagues.

"You have done better than I have," one of them, Lenida, bemoaned. "To look after Her Holiness Odessa was not an enviable position. We frequently drew straws to determine which of us would be assigned to the Spire. Of course, I was quite vigilant, but—" She broke off at Odessa's sudden peal of laughter, and I had to smile at the sound.

"Lan," said another of Asteria's Devoted—a Starmaker called Gracea, I remember. The Catseye paused, and they eyed each other warily. "I am glad that you are safe," the former finally said, if a bit stiffly, and held out her hand.

After a moment, Lan took it. "So am I."

"I heard about Janella."

"I am not sorry for it."

The other woman finally smirked. "Well, now. So we *do* have something in common."

At least one person from Aranth didn't agree. Asteria remained apart from the rest, placing a Howler on one of the small stone cairns that bordered camp. "Janella's," she sighed, looking up when she saw me approach. "She told me she had received several of these from Lord Arrenley as a gesture of goodwill. She thought she could reach an agreement with Latona's people, persuade her not to fight. I didn't know about the stone of immortality."

"I'm sorry."

"Don't be. In many ways, Janella was my creation. Have I

ever mentioned that I saved Lan once, took her out of the streets? I once did the same with Janella, who I discovered in even more dire circumstances than my Catseye. For many years, she served as my weapon within the Devoted. But I never realized the toll that would take on her, just as I didn't realize the toll it would take on Lan." She turned away sadly. "She's another soul on my conscience. That she could never wield a fire-gate had always been a source of disappointment for her. I'm glad she had the chance to use it, however briefly."

It was a good day to reestablish connections. Two men waited for us by the monument, looking so much like Vanya that I didn't doubt who they were, and they knelt before we could bid them otherwise. "I am Captain Misha of the Tenth division of Silverguards," the taller of the two said. "This is my brother Ivan."

"There is no need for this, milords," Odessa protested.

"We must undo the damage our father has done to our family honor, Your Holiness," Ivan said grimly. "My brother personally arrested him and saw him to the gaols. His actions have besmirched both our names and Vanya's."

"We are not so cruel as to blame you for that, milords," I assured them. I turned to Vanya, who looked both surprised and hopeful. "I think there's someone who's been wanting to talk to you both, though."

Both brothers visibly relaxed. "Vanya," Ivan groaned. "Did you know how worried we were, you little twit? Our pardon, Your Holinesses."

"None taken. Go on," I told the boy. "You've got a lot of

catching up to do, it seems."

The lordling shot us a grateful look, before hurrying forward to meet his brothers, his relief and joy clear for all to see.

"You know, I see no problem with using blood sacrifices just this one time," Lisette said. She stared at the Hellmakers, making it no secret who she had planned on volunteering.

"No more killing, Lisette," Odessa said sharply.

"We've got four goddesses on hand," Mother Salla said. "A rare occurrence in the history of Aeon. That's at least two chances, and I suggest making good use of them."

"They will succeed," Sonfei said confidently, drawing nearer to us. "I have every belief."

What I wasn't expecting was for Asteria to promptly turn red. "Sonfei," she managed, looking everywhere but at him.

To our shock, Sonfei took her hand, pressed a kiss on her wrist. "The Liangzhu are standing by, and ready to move at your command, Your Holiness. Half of us will stay behind to protect both the camp and the city, and the rest shall accompany you to the Great Below." He bowed to the rest of us and left, Asteria still staring at the ground in apparent mortification.

"Oh," Noelle breathed. "*Oh.* Good on her."

"Noe!" Odessa gasped, looking scandalized. Lan, on the other hand, threw her head back and laughed.

Since it was Odessa who possessed the galla's gifts, she and I were to make the first attempt. As before, I channeled every conceivable pattern and felt Odessa do the same. Our incanta swirled together in a dazzling display of blues, red, whites, and greens before coalescing into something solid and sure, with all our hopes contained therein. We poured all of it into the small monument before us.

The air around the broken column sizzled, flickered, died down. We waited expectantly, but nothing else happened.

I turned around with a cry of dismay. "It didn't—"

The gateway burst into being, knocking us back a few feet. Before our eyes it grew in size until we found ourselves staring through the portal and into a shadowy, fog-ridden darkness. Gasps rose from the others.

"How long will the gate last?" Lars asked Asteria.

"Almost indefinitely—as long as nothing within makes an attempt to close it."

Lan shuddered. "When I was tossed back into the city of Aranth, the demons pulled it shut behind me."

"We'll need to keep this gateway open for as long as necessary," Mother Salla said crisply. "Should it close . . . it will take weeks before we can stage a rescue."

"Activate the dome, Yeong-ho," Mother commanded. With a whir, the air around us hardened and took on a thick, glassy sheen.

The strategy was simple enough. The monument's proximity to the Golden City meant that it would be easier to defend both at once, with the mechanika monitoring the monument and making sure the new, smaller dome was running smoothly. The bulk of Mother's army was to use cannons and other long-range weapons to attack the swarm. The clans and some of the strongest of the Silverguards and Redguards were to defend the monument should any galla break through. Noelle, who had been making estimates of the galla swarm's attacks, believed that the creatures arrived in roughly twenty- to twenty-four-hour intervals, allowing us to plan the journey before their expected assault. Latona ordered her men to keep watch all the same.

Yeong-ho's barrier also covered a path back to the city, in case our forces had to retreat. I didn't want to think about the circumstances that would lead to that. It would mean the team within the Great Abyss was—that *we* were—already lost.

The most difficult part of the mission lay with us. Guided by the paintings in the temple, we were bringing others with us, people who could defend each of the seven gates we would have to pass through before entering the Cruel Kingdom. I hadn't been shocked to see Noelle volunteer, as if venturing into the underworld was something she did often. Nor was I surprised when Sonfei offered. He looked softer somehow, happier than I'd ever seen him. Asteria, too, had lost some of her harder edges, and her gaze as she looked back at the Liangzhu man was warm. I was stunned to see Mother with a gentle smile on her lips as she snuck a few glances their way.

"I've never seen Mother smile like that before," Odessa admitted quietly, looking like she was itching to eavesdrop on their conversation.

"I've never seen *my* mother smile like this, either." It was hard not to hope that we would all come out of this alive, even knowing the odds.

Vanya had also insisted on coming with us. "My brothers

will be fighting with you at the Abyss," he said stubbornly. "They volunteered because—because they wanted to bring back the honor Father had lost with his betrayal."

"Your brothers are good men," I told him.

He lifted his chin, tone pleading. "I have to be there with them, too. I can be useful. Don't make me stay behind."

I hesitated. "It's one thing to permit Ivan and Misha to fight. They both have more experience in battle. But the extent of yours is the two expeditions you've gone on with us."

"Let him go," Lisette said.

The Addax clan mistress was the last person I would have expected to side with him. "I'm not sure—"

"Let him go. This is something he has to prove. My siblings and I didn't have a choice. He does, and he's choosing to help."

"Thank you, Lady Lisette," Vanya mumbled.

"Oh, so it's *Lady* Lisette, now?" But there was a tiny, happy smile on her face that I doubted she was even aware of.

Both Mother and Asteria were to accompany us, dismissing Tamera's protests that at least one should stay behind. "The real battle will be taking place underground," Asteria told her. "While we are away, I expect you, Lars, and Yeong-ho to remain in charge. I am counting on you three to keep my sister's city safe until we return."

"I will, Your Holiness." There were tears in Tamera's eyes. "We'll fight them off for as long as you need, I promise you that."

I gazed back at our armies standing at attention before us.

Their generals and clan leaders had informed them about the shrine paintings, told them what to expect. They'd chosen to come with us and fight all the same, and my heart swelled with gratitude, but was gripped by fear at the same time.

What if we were wrong?

I stared past the portal and into the swirling darkness beyond it. This was the Cruel Kingdom, I thought. We'd followed the paintings in the cave as best we could, obeyed the instructions within *The Ages of Aeon*. The only thing we hadn't been able to bring was the stone of immortality; the payment for our exit, the reason Inanna had invoked the Cruel Kingdom's wrath. What would it demand from us in exchange, if we didn't have that?

Odessa and I looked at each other. There was no going back now. But I felt a strange comfort in knowing that whatever we might face within, we at least were going to do it together.

"Ready?" she asked me. I saw the same nervousness on her face that I was feeling, but the same determination there, too.

"You don't have to do this," I said suddenly.

"What do you mean?"

I gestured at the gateway. "You don't have to go to the underworld with me. You can stay here and help defend the city instead."

"Haidee . . ."

"You know that I was the one who was going to be sacrificed, anyway. They don't sacrifice the goddess who accepts the galla's gifts. This is the world you're supposed to be ruling.

If anything happens to me, then at least it's something that was always supposed to happen." A few days ago, the thought had terrified me. Now, it was something I accepted as truth.

Odessa turned to me, smiling gently. Ever since successfully defending against the galla horde with me, pooling our abilities together, she was different. Whenever she'd channeled her incanta before it was almost always from a place of anger, or from impulsiveness, and I was afraid that she wouldn't be able to come back from that. But now that she'd realized that the galla's corruption no longer had a hold on her, she was more relaxed, more controlled—but at the same time, more determined. "I'm not going to abandon you, Haidee."

I stepped away from her, crossing my arms over my chest. "You have everything to live for." Odessa had Lan to think of. I had no one.

Odessa's jaw was set in a stubborn line, something I'd done frequently enough to recognize when it was done by someone who looked exactly like me. "Lan and I talked, and we both agreed. We know the risks. We know this is greater than any of us. Wherever the Cruel Kingdom is, I intend to walk into it with you."

I closed my eyes briefly. "Thank you." I wanted to sound grateful, but I wasn't in a place to accept gratitude just yet.

She understood. She drew me closer, hugged me. "I love you," she said firmly. "I know you know that. Whatever happens, I'm not letting you go."

Mother, to her credit, said nothing. Like me, she'd been the one who was supposed to be sacrificed, though she'd fought against that fate by defying the Devoted and finding love. She'd fought harder than I had, I realized; I'd been mistaken in thinking she'd always been passive.

Instead, she turned to Asteria. "I could say the same thing to you," she said quietly. "You were meant to rule Aeon, after all."

"I don't want to. I don't want to pretend the Brighthenge ritual has any validity. The Devoted kept us apart because they knew we would be stronger together. Generations of goddesses died because of them. We should have fought harder to break the cycle. And now our daughters are paying for our mistakes. I won't tell them they can't fight with us. But I'll face Inanna, or Ereshkigal, or whatever in that kingdom wears their faces, with you."

Mother let out a soft, tearful sob. And then she was hugging Asteria with all her might.

Bells sounded in the city. Lan cursed.

"I wasn't expecting another wave so soon," Noelle pointed out, sounding grim.

"Perhaps the Cruel Kingdom is aware they're about to have visitors," Tamera said grimly, "and they've prepared an early welcome party."

Mother and Asteria looked at each other. Their hands were clasped together. "Defend our people, Tamera," Mother said crisply, and both turned to step through the gateway, even as a fresh wave of galla appeared on the horizon, easily double the size of the last swarm. I heard the call to arms, the soldiers who were to defend us aboveground forming ranks, preparing themselves for one final stand. Those who were to join us underground were already forming up behind me, ready to follow us into the literal pits of hell. My mouth tasted like ashes, dread seizing me once again. Had we led these people this far, only to lead them to their deaths now?

But Odessa linked her fingers with mine, and the calm, determined look on her face gave me strength.

Shots rang out as the desert tribes, the Aranthians, and the Golden City army began raining fire down on the incoming demons.

Odessa and I tightened our grips. "Let's go," we said in unison, and stepped through the portal as well, our soldiers close behind.

Chapter Twenty-Five

ARJUN IN HELL

———————— ✹ ————————

I WAS AT LEAST 90 percent sure that I was dead. The last 10 percent was only holding out because I didn't think the dead would be this self-aware.

The first clue was that nothing hurt. Not the ankle I'd broken, not the wound on my chest where Janella had stabbed me, which was the kind of thing I'd always assumed would be fatal. When I ran my fingers across where the injury had been, just to be sure, I found nothing but unbroken skin. There wasn't even scarring.

I *was* dead, right? Even if my wound had somehow been miraculously healed, the fall would have killed me.

I glanced up, but saw only darkness. There was no indication of an opening above my head. The cavern, the treasures, Haidee—they were gone.

If I was dead, then why was there a familiar bad feeling

settling at the pit of my stomach, a suggestion that some part of me was still human, still able to be afraid?

And where was Haidee? If anything had happened to her—

The dead should be cold, right? So why did I feel so warm?

I glanced down at my hand, and realized I was holding a stone.

A stone that was shining so damn brightly, in a way it hadn't done while it was mounted at the altar. I could feel its energies traveling up my arm. I'd never felt stronger.

Right. Inanna's immortality stone.

"Am I immortal?"

My voice echoed across the empty space, unanswered. As far as questions went, it felt like a pretty stupid one.

"Hell and sandrock. The fuck."

No response to that one, either.

I willed myself to be calm. I wasn't dead. I couldn't be dead. Being dead felt too much like being alive to actually *be* dead. And if I wanted to stay being not-dead, then I needed to figure out how I was gonna get out of here.

Which begged the question: Where was *here*, exactly?

I was in a large tunnel; that much I could make out. I opened my fire-gate, relieved that I could still use incanta, and conjured small, tapered flames atop my fingers—I'd lost my Howler in the fall, dislodged from my arm during that long, terrifying plunge down—to survey my surroundings. The walls looked to be made of the same type of rock as the small temple, and I wondered if this place was located beneath it, even farther underground. I didn't want to think about whether or not I was trapped here.

I didn't have much choice. The way forward led into more darkness. Turning in the opposite direction, I found myself staring at a wall—a dead end. If I wanted to leave, I'd have to keep walking, and hope there was nothing else down here with me.

Minutes passed. How long had I been here? An hour? Two? A hundred? I felt like I'd been walking forever. How many more miles before the path ended? I glanced down at the stone in my hand again. If I was still alive, then this must be the reason for it.

I could see now why someone would have secreted it away, built traps around it and cast illusions to hide it from the rest of the world. I thought about Janella; she had plunged into the chasm with me. What had become of her? And where was Haidee? The thought of her potentially injured somewhere made my chest hurt, made me feel inadequate and useless. She needed the stone; I didn't.

Something snagged my ankle, and I stumbled. With a grunt, I looked down.

A hand had sprouted out of the ground. It had wound itself around my foot, and its grip was strong.

I blurted out every expletive I knew, kicking frantically at its wrist. It relinquished its hold, but more began to creep out of the floor, fingers curling, the paleness of their skin stark against the muddy earth. More ripped at my pants leg and climbed up my arms, tried to sling themselves around my neck. Some clearly had an objective in mind: hands clutched at my wrist, fingers attempting to pry the stone out from my grasp.

I set fire to the whole damned floor.

They fell away, and I didn't bother to see if that had killed them, only scrambled up off the ground and ran for my life. The darkness yawned before me, but I was more eager to chance what lay in its depths then remain with those ghastly hands.

The Corridor of Yearning, I thought without breaking my stride. Wasn't that some of the tripe in *The Ages of Aeon* that Vanya had yammered on about? An area of hell where souls greedy in life were doomed to spend an eternity. Maybe I wasn't dead. Maybe I was unconscious somewhere, and this was all a nightmare fueled by the lordling's damn tall tales that had embedded themselves in my subconsciousness. Or maybe my injuries had driven me mad somehow. This couldn't be real.

The ground gave way without warning, and I skidded to a stop, scrambled back. I stood before the edge of a cliff, looking down into a gaping black hole that showed no signs of a bottom. *The Gorge of Wrath, then,* I thought numbly, where those unable to control their rage in life were made to fall forever.

Arjun.

It was a whisper of a sound, soft and coaxing. It came from behind me.

Arjun.

I knew that voice. I hadn't heard it in nearly eight years.

I found myself trembling. The stone felt unbearably hot against my palm.

Arjun.

I didn't want to look behind me. But I knew that they would be willing to wait as long as they needed, until I did.

I turned.

Had Jerbie still been alive, he would have been about the same age as I was. But death had cursed him to be ten years old forever. The hole in his head obscured his features somewhat, but I would recognize him anywhere. I had buried Jerbie myself. My fire-gate had first manifested the day he'd died. I'd lost my hand because my rage had caused me to lose control.

Arjun, it said. *Arjun, you promised me I could have a turn with it.*

A small spinning top. Mother Salla had salvaged it from some old wreckage. She'd given it to me as a reward because I'd found the most fish that week. The day before his death, Jerbie had needled me endlessly about it, asking for a turn to play. He never had his chance.

It's my turn now, it insisted, inching closer. I backed away, and felt loose rocks crumble beneath my feet, the heel of my boot scraping along the edges of the cliff. Jerbie's eyes were nothing but hollow sockets now, but his ghost's gaze was trained on the stone in my hand. Its voice rose, the pitch rising.

You promised, Arjun! Let me have it!

He wasn't alone.

Multitudes of eyes shone out from the darkness behind him; hundreds of ghosts were crawling out to confront me. That they were victims of violence was evident in their maimed bodies, their malformed and bloody faces. The stone was a beacon to them; they shuffled forward, gazes hungry.

You said you'd let me have it, Arjun, Jerbie said. *I want it! You promised!*

I couldn't let them have it. I didn't know if I was alive or dead, but if I let Jerbie have it, then I would absolutely be 100 percent dead. What was going to happen if any of them got their hands on the stone? Countless scenarios flitted through my mind, all of them horrific and involving me actually dying, and in all the worst ways.

I had two choices.

I took the only one I could make.

I threw myself off the cliff.

The wait to hit bottom was endless; it felt like I had fallen for a day and a half, and I was convinced that falling forever would truly be my punishment, until I finally saw the ground rushing up to meet me. I closed my eyes, prepared for the impact, prepared to die for real and take all doubt about my mortality away.

I hit, bounced, hit again, rolled.

Nothing hurt. I had expected shattered bones, my brains splattered on the ground.

Instead, I sat up. Got to my feet. Looked up to see none of those ghosts had followed my lead. Looked down at the stone.

It sparkled, winked at me.

At this point, nothing would have induced me to give it up.

I wanted this to be a dream. I wanted to wake up. I wanted to open my eyes and find my head on Haidee's lap where it rightfully belonged, where she would tease me for snoring too loudly, that I'd slept too long but she couldn't bring herself to . . .

"The hell," I said, then sank back to my knees and threw up.

Once I'd gathered myself well enough to continue, I made my way down the solitary path leading into another narrow corridor. I would learn nothing, I decided, until I'd reached the end of this path, wherever it would lead. In the meantime, I took stock of what I did know. I'd fallen down the shrine and into this personal hell. I would have died if it hadn't been for this stone. That there was another passage underneath the shrine wasn't surprising to me, upon hindsight. If the cave walls and *The Ages of Aeon* were right, then the stone of immortality granted entry to the Cruel Kingdom, and it could be used to barter a return to Aeon.

Was this the Cruel Kingdom, then? Was it Inanna I was going to find at the end of this journey? Ereshkigal? And if I had the stone, what was Haidee doing right now?

I had to find my way out.

No; I had to find *her*. Haidee would go to the Cruel Kingdom regardless. If she thought I was lost—my heart twisted—then she'd be reckless enough to come here and face the demoness even without the stone.

I had to find her.

"I'm sorry, love," I whispered. If I hadn't let down my guard, Janella wouldn't have gotten me. Haidee wouldn't have had to try to save me. If I'd thought to throw the stone up to her, I would have gone to my death knowing she could save Aeon.

Apologize to her in person then, you ass.

The passage widened, opening up into another cavern.

"Arjun!" The cry was both unexpected and unexpectedly welcome; it sounded real, like it was just as terrified as I was, and like it was actually human.

"Faraji?"

The boy was shivering, his teeth chattering, and his face lit up with relief when he saw me. He was wearing the same clothes he'd had on during that fateful ride, but I couldn't see any evidence of his wounds. "I've been wandering around here for days!" he babbled. "Is this what it feels like to be cold? How did you get here? Where are we?"

I stared at him.

"Arjun? You all right?"

This was a trick. It had to be some trick. Because the grief bubbling up in my chest felt almost too painful to bear. Of everything this hell had thrown at me so far, this was the most agonizing.

"You're dead," I said, rather stupidly.

"Am I? Are *you*? Are we both dead?"

"Maybe." I gripped the stone tighter, comforted by its weight. Was that the reality of this place? Was I dead, and this rock the only thing keeping me from that final oblivion? But how did that explain Faraji?

He smiled nervously at me, just like the Faraji I remembered.

No. They couldn't fool me into thinking he was real. I couldn't take it.

Didn't stop me from reaching out for him with shaking hands. He was solid and breathing and had a heartbeat, and I couldn't help myself. Surely the dead couldn't be this warm.

I yanked him into an embrace, choking on my next words. "On the assumption that we're not . . . I'm glad to see you again, brother." My voice cracked. "Real glad to see you. But we have to get out of here."

"I don't know how!" Faraji burst out. "What do you think I've been trying to do all this time?"

"How did you get here?"

"I don't know. All I remember is the pain, and then I must have lost consciousness. When I woke up, I was here." He shuddered. "The things I've seen in this place . . . once we get back I'm finishing the whole bottle of whiskey Kad's been keeping under his bed. Then I'm crawling into my cot and not getting up for at least three days."

"I know you're scared, but we need to keep moving, see what's at the end."

"I tried. I keep getting turned around or something, like I've been going in circles. What's that you're carrying?"

"Just . . ." I stepped back, my hand closing over it so he couldn't see. "Just a stone."

"Can I have a look?"

I hesitated.

Faraji blinked, confused. "Just asking. Just show me how to get out of here. How did *you* even get here?"

"Time enough for that later." I wasn't about to tell him he'd

413

died. "Let's follow the path and hope it leads to an exit."

We walked as fast as we dared, Faraji keeping up a nervous commentary about his time here. "I've been chased by creatures I can't even put a name to. There were—things—on the ceiling, trying to grab at me as I ran. I had to jump off a cliff."

"You did?" I asked, impressed despite myself. Faraji hated heights.

"There were these shadows chasing after me, and they had teeth and fangs, you know? I figured jumping would be a better death than getting ripped to shreds by an army of those. Just like back in the desert, when I—" He cringed. "The fall knocked the wind out of me, but I didn't die. What about you?"

"Fell." I hefted the stone. As long as he couldn't take it from me, I should be good. He sounded like Faraji, but I wasn't sure if this was some new illusion. Good Mother, I hoped this really was Faraji. "We found this in some forgotten shrine of Inanna's. Haidee thinks it will put an end to the rituals, stop the galla without a goddess having to die."

Faraji looked away. "What about us?" he asked, obvious resentment in his voice. "The goddesses get to live, but we don't? What about everyone who's died over the years since the Breaking, huh? Why do the goddesses get all the second chances?"

"I know." He was right. Assholes like me and him didn't get the same opportunities as people above our stations. "Haidee and Odessa aren't just doing this to save themselves. They want to stop the people from suffering, too."

"Too late for us, though." Couldn't blame Faraji for sounding bitter. Maybe he was right. Maybe it was too late for us. Maybe we were just a couple of dead guys too moronic to know we were already dead.

My chest constricted. No. I was *not* dead.

"Maybe not. I think I see some light up ahead."

Eager now, we pushed on. But as we stumbled out of the passageway, I saw that our optimism had been premature.

There were fires everywhere. They burned all around us, the flames rising to as high as twenty, twenty-five feet. I could feel the intense heat; even as accustomed as I was to the hot sun and the desert, this was incomparable.

"We can't go through here!" Faraji gasped.

I turned, and swore. The entrance we had come through was gone, and I found myself staring at nothing but a smooth cave wall. It was like we had stepped out from solid rock. I ran my hands across the surface, but could find no opening, no illusion.

"What are we gonna do now, Arjun?"

"This is another test," I said tersely. "I'm sure of it. We need to get through to the other side without getting our skin burned off."

Slowly, we inched our way past the flames. There was no clear path before us, and the loud, crackling roar soon drowned out any conversation we attempted to make. Faraji fell silent, following my lead as I used my incanta to prevent the fires from drawing too close.

415

I didn't know how long we wandered through this forest of fire, but I was too busy forcing the heat back to notice the images in the flames at first. It was Faraji's whimper that alerted me, and I turned to find him frozen in place, staring into one of the fires. "I'm sorry," he sobbed, and raised his hand like he was trying to reach out to something within its center.

"No!" I grabbed his arm, jerked it away. "There's no telling what it's going to do to you if you touch it!"

"Don't you see them?" The boy sobbed. "They're in there. Mother Salla, Immie, Kad, Millie—all of them!"

Suddenly I did. I saw the shadows converging on our camp, overwhelming all within. I saw some of the clans valiantly standing ground, only to be overrun. I saw several of them being torn apart, the same way I had seen Faraji being torn apart, and I felt sick.

Was this still an illusion? A vision of the future? Or of the present?

"All the more reason for us to start moving faster, Faraji!"

But he wouldn't budge. "There's no point! If we make it out of here in one piece, then they're going to come after us anyway! They'll kill us all over again!"

Arjun!

I made the mistake of looking into the flames again, and saw Haidee.

She was on fire. Parts of her clothes had burned away, and the sudden smell of searing flesh filled my nostrils. She was dying. If I did nothing, she was going to die.

416

The Cave of Realities. Where the sinful were punished with neverending visions of their worst nightmares come to life.

Hell and sandrock. Please let this not be real.

"You need to save them, Arjun," Faraji begged.

The stone. I could save her with the stone. If I could somehow reach out and give it to her, then she would be immune to the fires.

The conflagration raged all around me, but the stone had gone cold in my hand.

I took a step back, away from Haidee.

"What are you doing?" Faraji cried.

"This is a lie." Vanya never said if those images in the fire were true. But I had to believe that the images were what people felt they deserved, as part of their punishment.

And this wasn't my punishment, because I didn't deserve to be here.

I backed away farther.

The expression on Haidee's burning face changed—from desperate and pleading to calculated and cruel. She reached out to me, but something shifted in the space between me and those flames, and what stepped out of the fire was not Haidee.

It was a gray shapeless thing, writhing and so hideously contoured that I recoiled from looking at it. It could have almost passed for human, had it not kept forgetting itself, sliding into asymmetrical, gelatinous shapes.

Arjun, it said, in Haidee's voice.

I grabbed Faraji by the arm and dragged him into a run,

even as the fires around us began to die down, as more of those vile apparitions took their place. Faraji stumbled as we raced through another, smaller passageway—the only exit I could see—but I never lost my grip, forcing him along until we had nothing but darkness to see by again, the hideous moaning in that beloved voice fading until not even its echoes were left.

"What was that," Faraji babbled. "What was—"

"Quiet, Faraji." I packed Fire into my palm, fearing the light might attract those strange wraiths, but knowing I had no choice.

"I saw them. Mother Salla and Immie and everyone else. They were all burning. Is that what's happening? Are they all—"

"They're not. Keep going."

He whimpered, but followed me without comment. I willed my blue flames brighter, higher, hotter, because if there was anything in this place that was gonna burn, it wasn't going to be us.

The Gorge of Wrath. Before that, the Cave of Yearning. And now the Cave of Realities. What was the last one Vanya had mentioned?

We emerged from a corridor and spotted an exit, the bright glint of sunlight telling me we'd reached the end of the cave. Eagerly, we hurried forward.

Then we stopped, and stared. Sand greeted us for miles.

It was almost as if I was back in the desert. Above us was something resembling a sky rather than a ceiling, though to call it a sky was a poor description; its swarthy colors were stretched out like a thick layer of dust, like a frayed rag thrown over an uneven surface.

Then there was the moaning.

There were people here—if you could call anything here *people*—up to their waists in sand, struggling and crying for help. They were wrapped in death shrouds that obscured their faces, and they twisted and turned, fighting to escape the trap of their eternal fates. They numbered as infinite as the grains of sand, as far as the eye could see.

The Sands of Punishment. Right. I could only imagine what went on here.

And past this lay the palace of the Cruel Kingdom. There was no castle to see, nothing that even remotely resembled the ugly pile of bedrock Haidee called the Citadel. But there was a hole in the ground several hundred meters away. The sands surrounding it were slowly trickling down into its depths without making a sound.

I started toward it.

There was very little space to maneuver my way around the wraiths but they ignored me, so I tried my best to blot out their screams. I strained not to accidentally glimpse what lay behind their shrouds. I feared that the sand would trap me like the rest of these people, but I lifted my foot with little difficulty, placed it in front of the other, and continued to move.

"Arjun. Don't do it."

"We have to get out of here. We have to save Haidee."

Return Ereshkigal's immortality, right? The passages never said that a goddess had to be the one presenting this stupid stone.

"Arjun."

The sand was smooth, almost like powder. My boots sank down an inch or so with every step; I looked back and saw it reclaiming the footsteps I had left behind, pouring into the imprints until there was no trace left.

"Arjun!"

But Faraji was struggling, sinking down. Tendrils of dust were winding around him, imprisoning him as they took root around his ankles and calves, keeping him immobile.

I swore and ran back toward him. "You need to go back to the passageway!" I tried to shove him back out of the sands, tried to direct blue fire at the sentient creepers pulling at his feet. "You have to—"

Faraji's hand closed around mine, and he attempted to pry the stone from me. The winding cords of sand around him retreated; at the same time, I felt something hook around my leg. The sand-vines had attached to me instead.

"I'm sorry," Faraji sobbed, trying to force my hand open. "They brought me here so I can take it. They want it. You understand, right? I have to bring this back, or they'll keep me forever."

"Faraji," I whispered, horrified. The sand climbed up my thighs. I felt it tighten around my torso. The shrouded dead turned toward us. I could hear their moans; those who were close enough grabbed for the stone as well, frantic and hungry.

"Please, Arjun!"

I ripped myself free from my friend's grasp, and he stumbled back with a screech as blue fire enveloped his arms. The dust-vines receded, and I ran.

"Don't leave me, Arjun!" I could hear him screaming after me. "Don't leave me don't leave me don't—" The words cut off in a gurgle.

That wasn't Faraji. It couldn't be Faraji. Nothing, *nothing* would ever convince me that that had been Faraji. That ass was in paradise right now, chilling with all the pretty girls. He would never have wound up in hell like this, crying and begging for—

Bony limbs snatched at my shirt and pants, and it was my turn to trip. The stone fell out of my hand and onto the ground a few feet away.

The vines returned, and I lunged desperately, only to miss the rock by a couple of inches. I tried to burn them away, but it felt like my strength was sapped, and I could muster no more than a flicker before I was overwhelmed. More hands dragged me back, and I fought not to scream, even as they closed in around me, obscuring my view. It couldn't end like this, I thought frantically. I had to return to Haidee. I had to give her back the stone. I couldn't die here, and be another nameless shroud. I *wouldn't*—

A hand plucked the stone from the sand.

And placed it back on my outstretched palm. At the same time, streams of blue fire enveloped the revenants, and they reared back.

The vines slithered away. The other dead continued to paw

at me, but I pulled away and fled. I tore through the rest of the faux desert, ducking and swerving and dodging until I'd reached the hole. Only then did I turn around.

My mother didn't wear the death shroud the other sufferers did; she wore something more familiar—a dark cloak, a star brooch pinned against her shoulder. The blue fires around her died away.

She said nothing to me despite saving my life, only bowed her head and turned, walking until she was lost among the writhing dead, until I could no longer see where she had gone.

There was nothing left for me here. Nothing but another leap of faith to take.

I gazed at the stone, reassuring myself that I still had it. Beyond the hole was the entrance to the Cruel Kingdom. I had no idea what I was going to find there.

But I'd find Haidee.

My sweet, stubborn, exasperating Haidee would have found a way. I knew she was here in this godforsaken kingdom somewhere.

And I was going to find her, so I could yell at her for being a bonehead.

I closed my eyes, sucked in as much air as I could, and leaped one last time.

Chapter Twenty-Six

'LAN AT THE GATES

───────────────── ☾ ─────────────────

WE STOOD IN ANOTHER CAVE, before a massive set of doors hewn from the same kind of rock as the walls. A thick stone arch loomed over our heads. The grotesque statue was the next to catch my eye as my vision adapted to the darkness. It was carved on the right side of the gateway—it looked not unlike a galla, though the carving gave it more definition than their shadowy forms had in reality. Unusually, this one sported a beard made of lighter gray stones.

Odessa drew in a sharp breath. "The galla of clarity," she said. "'A radiance at every door, the price for passage.' That's what was written on those shrine walls."

Soft curses and muttered exclamations filled the air as the others took stock of our surroundings and decided they didn't like what they saw. I pushed against the doors, but they refused to budge. "Now what?" I muttered.

"Now this." Odessa pressed her hands against the frame, looking up at the towering stone galla. "Accept this gift, and grant us entrance."

The stones around the galla's neck blazed a sudden blue. Odessa let out a soft, aching sound, like the wind had been knocked out of her. With a heavy grating noise, the doors slowly slid open, revealing another dark corridor beyond.

Odessa staggered, the color rushing out of her face.

I was already by her side, ready to physically carry her if that was necessary. Asteria was only half a step behind, her hand on her daughter's elbow.

"I'm fine," Odessa said weakly. "It doesn't hurt. I just went numb for a bit. But even that's gone now."

"That's the key," Vanya whispered, somehow managing to sound excited still. "This is the real purpose of those galla's gifts. To be able to access the Cruel Kingdom. It's why every goddess loses these radiances after her twin is sacrificed. It's always been a choice between facing Ereshkigal and giving up their sibling."

"Except the Devoted made the choices for them," I muttered.

There was a collective pause as it dawned on all of us just then that all the galla's gifts that Odessa possessed would be gone by the time we reached the last gate. We should have expected that; we were rejecting the Cruel Kingdom's terms, and therefore were forfeiting its benefits. We would be even more vulnerable at the end of this path.

And it was always possible that I might not live past the seventh gate.

I could see the thought on everyone's minds, in the hardening of Odessa's expression. "I never gave you up," she said. "And so they have even less of a claim on you now."

"And if they try anyway?" I asked, because we could not afford to dismiss any possibilities at this point.

It was Haidee who answered. "Then we'll fight our way through," she said, and the others rumbled their agreement. My chest tightened, gratitude and fear wrestling for space.

"One gate down, six more to go," Latona said grimly.

To follow Inanna's instructions, we had to leave a contingent behind to defend every gate. Each group was a balanced mix of experienced gunners, skilled infantry, and spell wielders; among the latter, a fair representation of fire-, water-, terra-, and air-gates. At least one healer was on hand in every contingent, and we'd chosen leaders who had enough authority and a good enough reputation among the factions that all would accept their command. The defense of the first gate was to be led by the Sidewinder and Dorca clans. "Don't keep us waiting for too long," Lars joked.

"I don't know how to thank you all," Haidee said, a soft catch to her voice. "You left the safety of your clan territories to aid us. I can never—"

"As far as I can see, Your Holiness, our territories will never be safe unless you goddesses emerge victorious here. I shall pray to the Good Mother to see us *all* out of here soon."

The ground rocked underneath us, and we scrambled for balance. The very earth seemed to shudder, heave up, and then shudder again, like a gigantic heartbeat. And then there were footsteps, I realized, of something very large headed our way.

It was a galla, as tall as those Odessa and I had first glimpsed from the Spire, shadowed and forbidding; its beard glittered blue.

Odessa cried out, shrinking back from the demon. "No! I refuse!"

There was a reason why Inanna had instructed us to leave warriors at every gate.

"That is your cue to leave," Lars said sharply. "Quickly!"

My heart in my throat, I could only clasp the man's shoulder in gratitude and duck through the gate, where we found ourselves before the next portal.

This and the third gate were dispensed with in the same manner; Odessa willingly gave up her gifts of courage and harvest, to a galla with a turban of jewels and another with beaded horns, respectively.

Odessa had managed to get through the first two gates on her own, but her legs gave out by the third gate and I'd insisted on carrying Odessa on my back through every archway we passed through after that. It was taking her longer and longer to catch her breath, which was coming in shallow gulps. "Keep moving," she whispered when I paused, wanting to stop and give her a few minutes' rest.

"But—"

"This is supposed to happen. I'll be all right. But we need to keep moving." I reached out with my aether-gate and could feel the shadow in her heart, nearly double the size it was when we'd entered the portal. Awareness of it burned a hole in my back where her chest was pressed against me. "I'll be fine, Lan. We can't stop now. Everyone's counting on us."

We dispatched the Ibex and Gila clans to defend the second gate, and the Pronghorn and Rockhopper tribes at the third doorway. "We will be very put out if you do not return," Minh said, as now-familiar footsteps told us that another galla had come to take umbrage at our trespassing. "I do not expect to spend the rest of my life battling galla."

"I appreciate your putting your trust in our daughters," Latona said, "when I have given you every reason not to over the years."

"They are more persuasive than I would have thought." Minh drew out their sword, eyes flashing green. "Hurry now!"

Gracea took up position by the fourth gate. Lights swiveled around her after Odessa had opened the doors, and the other fighters of Aranth opened their ice- and water-gates. "There is still much left unresolved between us, Tianlan," she said severely. "We have not had the opportunity to converse at length, here in this desert."

I nodded. "We should have more than enough time to do so once we return."

A ghost of a grin stole across her face. "I hope that this time you will honor your promises, for a change."

"I will." I turned to Sumiko. "Thank you for everything. More than you can ever know."

A roar sounded; a galla with a scepter of lapis lazuli lumbered into view.

The other Catseye beamed at me. "It was my pleasure, Lady Tianlan. Guard Their Holinesses for us."

"Go!" Light sizzled from Gracea's palm. Her aim was true; the galla howled, and we made our escape.

"I'll stay with them," Vanya said after the fifth gate was opened. Lords Misha and Ivan were to defend it with the rest of the Silverguards.

Lisette paused. "Vanya, you said that we would—"

"I know, but I have to do this." The boy's eyes were pleading. "I need to reclaim my father's honor. I need to reclaim *my* honor. I need to stay and fight with my people, too. Would you choose not to fight with the Addax clan?"

Lisette paused, her eyes very soft. "No," she said. She leaned over and gave him a quick, fleeting peck on the lips. "But I will be very cross with you if you die."

The boy blushed. He caught a Howler Misha tossed his way, saluted smartly at us, then turned to face the arriving demon as we went through the gate.

"Well," I said. "It's about time you made a move."

Lisette looked me steadily in the face, couldn't keep up the pretense, and blushed even harder than Vanya.

"I'm scared," Imogen said as we approached the penultimate gate.

428

"By all accounts you needn't be," Haidee assured her. "Vanya believes that the galla that attack here will not be as numerous as the ones above—"

"No, I mean I'm afraid for you. For all of you." Imogen was crying. "I'm so sorry. For what I said before. I didn't mean it. You love Arjun just as much as we do. It wasn't right for me to—"

"It's all right, Immie," the goddess said hoarsely. "I've never held that against you. You had every reason to be angry."

"I wasn't angry at you. Not truly. But what if you don't come back? What if we've planned for everything and still fail?"

"The best thing you can do for both Odessa and Haidee," I said gently, "is to defend this gate to the best of your ability. Trust them to do what needs to be done, and know that they trust every one of you guarding these gates. Aeon is worth fighting for, don't you think?"

"You are all worth fighting for," Asteria said quietly.

"I am sorry that Asteria and I did not resolve this sooner," Latona added soberly.

"What's done is done. I cannot condone the sins those before me have committed against you both, either. It is time that things must be set aright." Tears prickled at the corners of Mother Salla's eyes. Haidee's cheeks were already wet.

"I miss him so much," she whispered.

"I miss him, too. But Arjun wouldn't have you crying when you're this close, my girl. Do him proud."

"We need to go," I said softly, as another roar echoed through the cavern. I felt Odessa tense up behind me.

"Give Ereshkigal hell for him," Kadmos added fiercely, cocking his Howler.

My own trepidation grew as we approached the seventh gate. Despite all our planning, none of us knew how to get past the seventh gate without a sacrifice. *I could die here. I could die in the next few minutes.*

I also knew that I would sacrifice myself in a heartbeat if that was the only option we had left, before Odessa or anyone else could stop me.

My love's hands tightened around my shoulder. Air patterns wrapped around us, pressing us closer together.

"Do you know what Marianna did?" Odessa asked. "She bound herself to Dianae with a spell, so the bad guy couldn't kill her knight without killing her—something she knew the villain didn't want, as he planned to marry her."

"Odessa—"

"I won't let you go. I won't."

But the final gate was unlike the others. There were no doors here. There was no grotesque galla carved over the entrance, either, waiting for its tithe of a radiance. All we could see through the opening was even more darkness.

"I don't know what this means," Asteria said, sounding grim. "Odessa rejected the last galla. Will that prevent us from crossing through? Or has this gateway always been just so?"

"It doesn't matter," Latona said, examining the stone archway. "We can enter this gate without anything to stop us. If we are to sacrifice anything else, it will not be here."

I could feel Odessa sink down with relief by my side, though the Air patterns still swirled around us, keeping me by her side.

"If we are to sacrifice anything else," Haidee echoed, "it will be within Ereshkigal's lair."

It was a reprieve of sorts. But that could change soon enough once we entered. What if there was a trap waiting on the other side, and this was to lull us into a false sense of security? What had Inanna and Ereshkigal done to get past that seventh gate? She'd already lost the love of her life. Had she given up something else? Too many questions, with no way of knowing the answers at this point. "Lisette, remain here and defend this gate with your clan anyway," I instructed. "Sonfei, you and your people as well."

"No," Sonfei said. "I will be accompanying you until the end."

"Don't be ridiculous, Sonfei," Asteria said sharply.

"I am not ridiculous, though I am very much in love with you, which I admit is a different kind of foolishness. I will keep you within my sights from this point on. I told you as much last night. Or are you saying that you lied about what you said then?"

Asteria colored. "You were always so impertinent. You've changed so much over the years, but that has clearly stayed the same."

"What has also stayed constant is my fidelity," the man announced proudly, with no trace of shame, even as Asteria looked more and more horrified. "For over seventeen years I have not lain with anyone else, so strong was my admiration for you. Imagine my joy to learn you had done the same. Only last night did I—"

"That is enough, Sonfei!" Asteria had grown scarlet with embarrassment, and her eyes were blazing with some other emotion I didn't understand. "If you must come with us, then do so silently!" And with that, she stalked through the gate, like she would rather brave the dangers within than hear more. Latona followed her, bemused. "Stop that, Latona!" I heard Asteria say.

"I said nothing, dear sister."

"I could *hear* you thinking."

"I'm going in with you as well," I told Odessa.

"It would be safer for you to wait here with the others."

"That's not a guarantee."

"Lan—"

"You know why I have to be there. Don't fight me on this. If they're going to kill me, they'll do it just as easily here as they can past that gate. At least give me the chance to tell you goodbye."

Odessa had tears in her eyes, but she nodded, unable to say anything.

"Take care of Sonfei's men," I told Lisette.

She nodded. "And who will take care of you?"

"I will," Odessa said, and she sounded so sad.

"She will," I said, and accepted the inevitability, the possibility that she might not.

432

"Lan." The hardness hadn't quite completely left Haidee yet. She was keeping that part of herself in reserve until the worst was over and she could finally mourn Arjun in her own time. But not even she could hide her worry.

"I'm prepared to take the risk."

She looked like she was about to say something else, then changed her mind. She shook her head and sighed. "All right."

"She's made her decision," Odessa said softly. "And I'll honor it."

I looked at her. She smiled and tugged me close to kiss. "I love you," I whispered.

"And I love you. Tell me again once this is over." She let go of me, then reached out with her other hand and found her sister. "I'm ready."

"Let's do it."

Together, they walked through the stark, forbidding gate after their mothers, and I followed.

Chapter Twenty-Seven

THE TWINS IN THE KINGDOM

———————————— ☼ ————————————

WE STOOD BEFORE A THRONE crudely hewn from rock, slicked in black ichor.

The darkness hemmed us in from all sides, but strangely there was enough light to see by. It took several moments for me to realize the cause; the throne itself was glowing faintly, pulsing at intervals like it possessed its own heartbeat.

Other strange creatures slinked through the shadows. They were shapeless, constantly shifting, but there was something about them that suggested they had once been human too, were trying to remember how.

Something else loomed over the throne.

It was a woman.

It was not a woman.

It had arms and legs.

It had neither.

It had a face.

It had no face.

It was hideous.

It was beautiful.

I remembered the cave painting, the massive void etched across the wall. I recalled how uneasy it had made us, though it was nothing more than a blob. The unknown artist must have seen it themselves, in order to portray even a sliver of how it truly looked—it was everything and nothing all at once.

It was smiling.

It was *smiling*.

Gems clustered around it, on it, within it, and yet the overall impression remained of a black, shapeless being. We could see nothing beyond it, as if the world had shrunk down until there was nothing left but this grotesque, living hole.

There was an even darker chasm burrowed into its center; never fading, never healing. Like an incurable sickness hovering above its heart.

It raged. It wanted. It hated. It yearned.

It wanted us. It wanted our mothers. It wanted every goddess that had come before us, every goddess that had escaped its clutches by dying the way nature intended, instead of suffering under the endless torment it relished. It had claimed only half of those goddesses. Half was not a whole. It demanded both.

It demanded Inanna.

It demanded Inanna's progeny.

We heard shouts—from our mothers, we realized. From Latona, from Asteria.

Fight it. Fight it!

And we did. The world erupted back into light around us as we brought forth fires as blue as lapis lazuli, scorching the throne and whatever lay around it.

The void struggled. It was angry, and its hatred was contagious. It stole over us like a dark fog, and we could feel grief, agony, rage. While its sister had found peace in death, it had remained in this never-ending limbo, deathless and dying at the same time. It hated its twin for abandoning it. It hated Inanna for never returning, and it saw Inanna in us.

Its fury emboldened it. It hammered against us, our flames snuffed out as it gained the advantage. The darkness stole back in, entangling us, steeping us in its malice. We couldn't move. We couldn't breathe. Lethargy sunk into our minds, robbing us of thought, the will to push back. *Sleep*, a voice soothed. *Let go.*

No more struggling. No more pain. No more sadness. The Above was a constant struggle full of strife and suffering. In the Below, we could finally rest.

No! somebody screamed. And then warmth gathered at the back of our necks, Aether patterns spiraling through the darkness to settle everywhere, newfound strength blooming within us, shaking us free. We clung to it, and our fires burned hotter.

It screamed at our fresh assault. We guided our aim toward the shining blue jewels, and one by one, they exploded from the force of our will. At each shattering the void jerked back, again and again and again, until it had shriveled up into nothing. There weren't even embers.

And then the overwhelming presence was gone, and we

were back at the seventh gate, blinking at each other against the sudden brightness.

"Odessa? Haidee?" Lisette approached, her eyes wide and her voice awed. "Did you do it? Did we win?"

We glanced at each other, and at our mothers. They had relaxed, with the smiles of those who had expected little and found much. "I think we did," Latona said, her voice shaky. "I had no idea . . . I never . . ."

"It's done," Asteria said. "And that's all that matters. We're free. Haidee, Odessa—we're all finally free."

It was so simple. Inanna and Ereshkigal had entered the Cruel Kingdom without fully trusting each other. We had gone through so many trials together that the tests of the Cruel Kingdom were almost child's play. This was why the Devoted had feared us together. They could not control us, and they knew it.

And now, we had a second chance to rule Aeon the way we always should have.

In a daze, we traced our route back toward the portal that opened on the Skeleton Coast, collecting allies along the way. Mother Salla, Imogen, and the rest of the Oryx clan were giddy with relief, the other clans thrilled at the chance of starting anew. Sonfei was laughing, his arm carelessly looped over Asteria's, and she made no move to pull away.

The celebration was already in full swing by the time we stepped back onto the dunes. The galla army was nowhere in sight. For the first time since the Breaking, the dark clouds pulled away from the sky above the Great Abyss and the miasma of fog was lifting—revealing, for the first time, rocky ground underneath a bright sun, overlooking flatlands that, with time and effort, could be induced to flourish again.

Breathing hard, Lan surveyed the sands, blinking against the light. "I can't believe it's over," she said, her voice hushed. "I can't believe it."

There were no more galla. And in time, as the world continued to turn, Aeon would return to normal. Forests would grow, and seas would rise again.

It was more than we could ever hope for.

"Arjun," we whispered. We were still so closely linked, our minds intertwined, and the grief that rushed through us at the reminder was enough to incapacitate us both. We sank down to the ground, our arms around each other, our weeping lost amid the celebration.

It wasn't fair, that life could begin anew on Aeon without him.

He would have wanted this. He would have laughed, told us it was useless to dwell on the past, surrounded by the possibilities of the future.

"Is it over?" we whispered to each other, a part of us unwilling to let go. "Is it really over?"

It was. We had defeated Ereshkigal. Despite Odessa's and my short time together as sisters, our closeness and mutual trust had been stronger than anything Ereshkigal could throw at us. We mourned both Ereshkigal and Inanna as well, for what they could have been together. For what they could have given Aeon that we could now provide in their stead, and for all our ancestors who had suffered after them.

For the moment, any hostilities that still lingered among the different armies were forgotten. Many wept, and others shouted their joy. Clan members hugged Silverguards hugged the people of Aranth hugged the Liangzhu.

A hush fell over the crowd as we stepped through the portal, the last to do so. Immediately the people fell on their knees— even the clans that had long fought against Latona, even the faction from Aranth that had conspired against Mother. Even proud Lisette succumbed, as did Noelle and Vanya, all looking like they'd never truly seen us before.

"I have no intentions of ruling," Asteria began.

"Nor do I," Latona added. "Neither of us are fit to lead."

"I propose instead that we let our daughters rule Aeon jointly, and in whatever capacity they wish."

Lan came to us then, and threw her arms wide enough to draw us both into her embrace. She held us tightly as we wept, laughed, wept again.

But even as we celebrated, we could not shrug off the uneasy feeling that we had forgotten something important. What would happen next? Would Aeon return to how it had once been? Had we completely banished all the galla? Out here in the sun, everything seemed possible.

Was it truly over?

"No," Noelle said suddenly, in a voice not her own. "It's not."

And then, in the blink of an eye, the world changed once again.

The darkness returned. The air grew chilly, and the winds

picked up. We could feel the heat of the sun and the cold lash of rain all at once.

We were no longer at the Skeleton Coast. We were back at the edge of the Great Abyss as if we had never left, and the mist had returned with a vengeance, enveloping the gathered crowd until all but the barest outlines were obscured by fog, our people dressed like moving shadows until they resembled galla themselves.

Our mothers were gone. Lan and Noelle and Sonfei were gone. What remained was us and the yawning pit before our eyes.

We'd been wrong. There was always going to be a sacrifice, no matter how hard we fought against it. One of us was always going to have to die.

Choose, we heard a voice intone. The void we thought we had defeated loomed again, triumph in its gaze, pleased by the illusion it had fooled us with, and hungry.

It was the same test. They were always going to make us choose. The only decision we really had was deciding which of us was going to die.

Choose.

I stared helplessly back at my twin, only to find her mirroring my expression.

Was it a choice at all? We would be perpetuating the cycle all over again. Our mothers' attempts to free themselves had been futile, though they'd broken the world itself. Our journey to the Great Abyss to undo the mistakes our mothers had made—all had come naught. In the end, we faced the same decision. The same wrong choices.

Our father had died, and still they hungered. Arjun had died, and still they demanded more. It wasn't fair! He wasn't supposed to die, *Lan* was—

A part of us fractured, the old anger boiling back up to the surface. But the hate was brief, anguished, remorseful.

No. It wasn't fair for *anyone* to die.

Bitterness slid away. Sorrow, contrition, forgiveness—they took its place.

We heard Ereshkigal howl, displeased.

This was how it had all begun. This was how Ereshkigal was sacrificed. Some past animosity between the two that had festered, was emboldened by the malice here, led one sister to do the unthinkable.

This was how their Devoted justified their manipulation, their lies. How they had decided, in the generations to come, to make the choice for them. Both goddesses could have so easily been lost, Aeon destroyed.

After all, if a sister could bring herself to give up her own twin, then why couldn't they do the same thing on her behalf?

One of us had to die.

But even as the thought passed through our heads, a new kind of anger stirred inside us.

No.

This isn't who we are.

There is a choice.

There is always another choice.

Because if you weren't given a choice that you could live with, then you had to decide on the choice *they* would never allow you to make.

Vanya had said that the goddesses' lives were tied to Aeon; kill both goddesses without a spare, and the world died with them. Death required life. Even the galla knew this. Only Ereshkigal cared nothing for the rules, shrouded as she was in her fury.

They would never permit *both* of us to be destroyed. The Devoted had understood that well enough.

I looked back at my twin sister again, and this time I saw the same resolve, the same acceptance. No regrets.

Holding each other tightly, refusing to let go, we both stepped over the edge, and into the endless chasm below, *together—*

Chapter Twenty-Eight

THE TWINS AND ERESHKIGAL

☾

WE WERE BACK AT THE throne. The malevolent shape-less void was gone. My first instinct was to scramble for Lan, and I saw that she looked no more worse for wear, though she appeared as dazed as I felt. "What happened?" she asked weakly.

"An illusion," I whispered, heart still beating madly. It was getting harder to breathe; the realization that this wasn't over, that we had not yet beaten Ereshkigal's demon, was finally set-ting in, and I wasn't sure if my body could take any more of these shocks.

Haidee refused to let me go. She clung to me, wild-eyed. "That was the test Inanna failed," she gasped. "Did we pass it? If we did, then why does it feel like nothing's changed?"

Because Ereshkigal had upset the natural balance of the world, I realized. The Cruel Kingdom on its own would have accepted one goddess's sacrifice and allowed the other to live, so the cycle could repeat into perpetuity. But we had solved its riddle. We should have been allowed to leave. But the way back to the seventh gate was still shrouded in darkness, the exit still barred to us. Because not even the Cruel Kingdom could contain Ereshkigal's malice without being warped by it. And if she was to suffer, then the whole of Aeon was to suffer, even if that rage would wipe out every life.

No. Wait. If Haidee and I had sacrificed ourselves, that still left our mothers. They were both young enough to produce more offspring. Even if we'd both chosen to die, the Cruel Kingdom would have turned its attention to them—

Would have forced them into the same dilemma.

Panic set in. The last time they'd been put in this situation, they'd broken Aeon. The Cruel Kingdom had tried to divide us by placing Arjun's death between us—and for a few moments, we had fallen for it. If they had tried to use Father once again . . .

We spun, searching frantically for them, wondering if we would find only one of our mothers present, the other gone forever.

We needn't have worried.

Mother's head was in her hands, and Latona had thrown her arms around her sister, rocking her gently back and forth.

"I couldn't save him. I failed him—I failed you—again." The words came out through gritted teeth, because Mother never cried. "I'm sorry. I tried to reach for him. But the ground gave way. I knew it was coming. I knew what was going to happen. I should have reached out quicker, moved faster. Why didn't I? Why couldn't I—"

"It's not your fault," Latona said softly. "It took me seventeen years to understand all the ways you were not at fault."

"Why did you come back to Brighthenge, Latona?" It was very nearly a wail. "You could have stayed at Farthengrove with Aranth. You both would have been safe there." She turned, as if searching for something, and then finding it when Sonfei's large hands settled on her waist. She leaned back into him.

"That's not true, and you know it." Latona had never sounded so raw. "You had to accept the final galla's gift, didn't you? And you loved Aranth, too. You refused to sacrifice him. That meant the ritual would have failed anyway."

Asteria stared at the ground. "No," she whispered. "Aranth was not who I refused to sacrifice."

"I don't know what's supposed to happen now," Noelle said, sounding harried, and this time she sounded exactly like the Noelle I knew. My relief was immense. "But we need to get out of here."

A low moan met our ears.

Without the camouflage of the void, Ereshkigal's true form was a horrific sight. There was nothing left of her but a rotting skeleton, a dozen feet tall with arms that spanned nearly half the width of the cavern. Black hair hung from the skull in clumps, and the pale skin was stretched over ruined muscle, revealing bone in all the wrong places. Parts of a jaw swiveled loosely from where throat and chin met. Worst of all were its lidless eyes, pecked and maggoted in places, its gaze never leaving ours.

And then its features warped further. Skin formed, knitted against muscle; more hair grew from the top of its skull; sentience brought a glimmer of awareness back into its eyes. Its face shapeshifted into something more familiar.

Someone more familiar.

Asteria made a quick, shocked sound.

You left me. It was Janella, and it wasn't. Unseen things moved beneath her stretched flesh, her mouth opening and closing like a dying fish. Something dark and heavy settled against the hollows of her chest, and I could see more people swirling within. Some were unfamiliar to me, but in others I could see a trace of color-changing hair, a flash of pale eyes. Goddesses sacrificed to the Cruel Kingdom over the years; not even their privilege had saved them from Ereshkigal's torment.

"It's mocking us," Latona hissed. "It's trying to frighten us."

"It's working," Lan muttered.

A hole gathered above Janella's heart, empty and gaping and black. My hand clutched at my own chest, remembering the darkness I'd kept there, too.

Janella's shade made a loud, keening cry, its fingers reaching eagerly for both Haidee and me.

Asteria and Latona channeled blue flames that took out a part of its arm, but it cared nothing for the injury, reaching out for us again. Though it was still shrouded in shadow, Lan was angling toward the gateway we'd come from, shouting instructions at us to do the same.

"We passed the trials," I heard Haidee cry out, frustrated and fearful. "It should have let us go."

"She's been here too long," I whispered. "She's spent an eternity waiting, yearning, hating. The rules here be damned. She's not going to leave until she has her hands on Inanna. We have to find a way to put her at peace, too."

"That's not good to hear, considering Inanna has been dead for thousands of years at this point. The stone was our only hope of appeasing her, and it's gone!"

The black void was gone, but Ereshkigal remained. We had passed all the trials and earned the right to return to the surface with our lives intact. But the demoness was a different story. Her whims were separate from the laws of the underworld. The void had retreated because it had given us a reprieve, but Ereshkigal had not. And what Ereshkigal wanted was to see us all dead.

The air whirred, Latona setting up a barrier in between us and that horrific shadow. Grimly, I added all my strength to hers, could feel both Haidee and Mother following suit. It clawed against the barrier, screaming. But in time we would be exhausted, and it would find a way through.

"There's no way out," Lan said heavily. "Odessa, there's no other way."

I threw myself at her before she could move, refusing to let go. "If you even think about knocking me unconscious," I hissed, "I'll knock you out first."

"Odessa, we knew going in here that I might have to do this."

I knew, but I had bet everything that she wouldn't have to. Even here, with the threat of death hanging over all of us, I couldn't let her go.

"You know those romance books I said I hated, the ones that didn't have any happy endings? I still hate them, but I understand it now, why some people die for love that way. I will follow you whether you like it or not, Lan."

"We won't let you," Haidee swore, eyes blazing. The Air barrier thickened, became harder than even steel.

"What do we do, Asteria?" Latona panted. "What do we do?"

"I . . ." Mother faltered. "I—"

A sudden streak of blue fire blazed out of nowhere, striking the Ereshkigal-Janella hybrid dead in the chest. The monster reared back, as if stunned that anything could hurt her.

The attack had not come from any of us.

"Lady Odessa is right," a voice drawled out, painstakingly, achingly familiar. "Dying for love isn't all it's cut out to be. It's been a huge pain in my ass so far."

I lost the ability to think. As more flames tore into Ereshkigal I tore through the barrier and started running, not stopping until I threw myself into his arms.

"Hi, Haidee," Arjun said, grinning down at me. He looked like crap, but somehow still gorgeous. His clothes had been ripped and torn, and his eyes seemed a little haunted despite his glib tone, but he was in one piece. A part of me was terrified, wondering if he was another illusion sent to taunt me, because I knew I would shatter from that. But I was desperate to believe he was really here, that he'd somehow fought his way through everything to find me.

Then his mouth swooped down, planting a firm kiss against my lips. "I literally went through hell just to see you again," he rasped, and I knew then he was real, and I couldn't stop my tears. "Damn hands crawling out of the ground. Pitching myself off even more cliffs. I've got sand everywhere. Remind me to punch Vanya the next time I see him."

"How?"

He held up his hand, and I saw the stone, now gleaming with a strange, unearthly light. "Had the presence of mind to keep it with me when I fell. Saved me every step of the way."

Inanna's stone of immortality.

A piece of Inanna that we could offer to her sister.

Ereshkigal knew; already it was turning toward us, a keening sound splitting the air, its whole presence focused on the shining rock.

"Arjun! Keep shooting at it!"

"Right." His flames were more powerful than ours had been, and the shadow flinched back from them. Was it because of the stone?

I placed my hand over it, fearing what my touch might do— last time, it had given me painful visions of Inanna and the rites, and I didn't want to experience that again.

But nothing happened, save that the rock turned warm

underneath my palm. At the same time, I felt newfound strength pouring into me. It felt the way Lan's healing often did. I responded with blue fires of my own and this time, Ereshkigal staggered.

"She's frightened," Noelle said, stunned.

"Arjun . . . ," I began, but he'd already anticipated my question. He swallowed hard, steeled himself, then dropped the stone into my hand. I braced myself for visions likes the ones that had overwhelmed me at Inanna's small temple, but nothing happened.

"Oh, thank the goddess," Arjun rasped, visibly relieved. "I thought I was going to crumble into dust as soon as I let go of it."

There was no time to ask Arjun what he was talking about, because Odessa was already running, her hand finding mine just as the demoness shook itself off.

As soon as my twin's hand touched the stone it suddenly flared with the same bright light we had witnessed back in the shrine. Power coursed through us, more than any we had ever felt.

Ereshkigal roared and flung itself at us with shocking quickness. A swipe crumbled the wall behind us, cleaving easily through the thick stone. Odessa raised up a wall of Air just in time, but the demoness' attacks made deep grooves in the dense patterns, sinking farther past the barrier with every slice.

With a scream, Odessa went down. Her eyes were wide, her breathing stuttered, and she was clutching at her chest. Now that she had given up the radiances, her sickness returned with a vengeance. I cried out for Lan, but the Catseye was already scrambling for her, funneling her own energy into her weakened body.

"No!" Mother and Asteria linked hands; even this deep below Aeon they could somehow summon lightning, and the shadow-goddess arched up, hissing as the energy lanced across its form. Arjun ducked to the side and shot more fire at it. All their efforts only seemed to increase its fury. With an inhuman howl it lashed out madly at anything that moved, carving fresh grooves in the floor and shattering more stones.

"'Place immortality into Its heart,'" Noelle quoted, grunting as she fought to keep the shadows out of range with her spear. "'And bring her the freedom and peace I could not.' That's all we need to do, right?"

"Let's do it," Odessa breathed, pushing Lan away so she could stand. "We have to do it now."

"Distract her," Asteria instructed.

We all obeyed. The caves lit up with the brightest of blues, the Janella-Ereshkigal hybrid thrashing wildly as the flames pummeled her on all sides. As one, Odessa and I ran, leaping together to shove the stone of immortality into that dark hollow where the creature's heart should have been.

And then the creature flung its arms out at us, trying to deflect our attack. Its blow when it connected with my side was the worst pain I'd ever felt in my life .

It threw us several feet away. The impact sent the stone rolling across the floor, away from us.

The creature screamed, and sharp tendrils made of shadow

lashed out, striking madly at everything. I heard Noelle scream, saw Lan drag her away as red blood seeped through the steward's breeches, where she'd been stabbed in the leg, before the Catseye braved the sharp talons to return for Odessa. I held tightly to my twin, who was in a half faint, overcome by exhaustion. The demoness shrieked again, then focused its attention now on both Asteria and Mother, its blades tearing through their shields like the latter was made of paper. Triumphant as it shredded through the last of their defenses, it stabbed its way past the shield.

There was a harsh, agonized grunt. I heard Asteria scream.

And Sonfei was falling, his eyes dimming. With a horrific tearing sound, a blade of shadow jerked away from him, its edges stained in bright blood. Asteria caught him before he struck the ground, and it was her turn to lash out blindly in rage. The demoness was hurled back in a surge of lightning.

"*Yexu*," Asteria wept. Lan had dashed to her side, her hands pushing down around the wound on the Liangzhu's chest, trying frantically to put as much pressure on it as she could. But I knew that it was too late; the attack had pierced Sonfei through the heart, a fatal injury not even a Catseye could heal.

"I do love you, you fool," Asteria whispered.

Sonfei laughed, a faint, gurgling sound. Something he saw in Asteria's face made a warm smile break over his. "At last, I can protect you," he wheezed, then let out a long sigh, and never took in another breath.

Chapter Twenty-Nine

THE TWINS AT THE END

———————— ☼ ————————

WE KNEW WHAT WE WERE supposed to do now. We could continue the endless cycle, dooming more goddesses after us to sacrifice, or we could risk everything in the here and now and put Ereshkigal's spirit to rest once and for all, even if it meant we were to die.

Painfully, we picked ourselves off the floor. Lan looked back at us, her eyes full of grief. Poor Sonfei lay there, a gentle smile on his lips.

There was no time now to weep. There would be more to mourn later.

After its initial, rabid attack, Ereshkigal had weakened considerably, the shadows around it diminished somehow. Janella, poor Janella—her features had shrunk, the illusion of maintaining her appearance taking its toll.

We ran to where the stone lay, bent down and seized it. It

glowed again, instilled us with newfound energy.

My twin looked at me. There was no anger there, not even fear. It was like the years we had spent apart had only made us stronger, had given us the time we needed to be better, even if it had taken close to two decades.

"I'm not afraid," she said. "Isn't that odd? All those years, terrified and alone and wishing for more—and now I am not afraid."

"I feel the same way." I wished we had more time together. I wished we hadn't had only these last few days to discover who we really were, for her to know who I really was. But our short time together would be more than enough. It would sustain us for what was to come, for however long that eternity might be.

Her hand was warm against mine. "I am sorry," I said.

"I am sorry," she echoed, but it was *I love you* I heard, the same as she had.

"What are they doing?" I heard Noelle cry from behind us, but we were already moving, and nothing above or below Aeon could have stopped us.

The poor creature gave one last keening, shuddering cry as we pressed the stone of immortality against its chest. For so long we had regarded Ereshkigal's spirit as a vengeful monster, blinded by its hate. Now we saw it for what it was; the goddess Ereshkigal lashing out, hurt and lonely, yearning for a love she thought she had lost, for the sister who had betrayed her.

There was pain, but it was nothing we could not endure. The stone pulsed between our palms, our fingers intertwined.

There was pain, but behind that lay the promise of peace.

"The day of the Breaking—I couldn't bring myself to accept the final gift. But it wasn't Aranth's life they asked for. It was yours. I'd always loved you best. I loved Aranth, too, but not . . ."

"I know. And I love you."

For the briefest of instants, we saw Ereshkigal break apart. Her husk split open, revealing something dazzling underneath. For a moment, we swore that we could see something take human shape before fusing itself into that sparkling form.

I am sorry, sister.

We turned to look at our daughters one last time. They gaped at us, shock clear in their expressions. We smiled, at peace. Our time was done. Let them start new lives together, without the mistakes of our past.

Let them be happy.

Let them learn to love their sister better.

We stepped into the light.

Chapter Thirty

THE TWINS AND AEON

———————— ✺ ————————

THEY WERE GONE.

The cave was dark and empty. There were no more shadows crawling out to find us, no more galla seeking blood. Bereft of their presence the throne looked powerless, decrepit. Ereshkigal was gone.

And so were our mothers.

With a low cry I scrambled forward, convinced that this was yet another illusion. I saw Odessa doing the same, looking like she wanted to tear down the throne stone by stone, as if they were hiding behind it.

But we knew.

I cried. For Sonfei, for Mother and Asteria, for all the sacrifices we had made to arrive at this moment. Odessa clung to me, and our tears fell.

"This is why the Devoted's plan was always to separate the

sisters." I understood Noelle a little better now. Looking for rational explanations was her way of keeping herself calm, but her voice still shook. "Why they could not allow them to grow fond of each other."

I could sense Arjun before I could see him, let him fold me into his arms as I wept. To have him here after those painful days spent believing I had lost him, and then losing Mother— happiness and heartbreak were intertwined, and I could no longer distinguish the bitter from the sweet. Only Arjun could help chase away the pain of Mother's death. I knew he must have gone through his own torments to reach us, and my heart swelled knowing how he must have struggled. "I love you," I whispered, my voice muffled against his chest.

"You bonehead," came his fond reply.

But even as I cried, there was a decided shift in the air. The weight of Ereshkigal was gone; in its place was something lighter, more hopeful.

I saw them sprout through the cracks in the stone; tiny vines that stole out of the rock, giving way to small buds that sprouted and bloomed, until a fresh, fragrant scent filled the air. As we looked on, we saw plants stealing across the once-dark throne, more flowers wrapping around it.

Dazed, I got to my feet. "They planned this." They'd put up too little of a fuss when we insisted on coming here. And the talk between them I'd overheard earlier this morning: *But I'm glad we can make things better for our daughters now*, Mother had said. *I'm so glad we at least have today. . . .*

I was furious. I was heartbroken. "How could they?" I choked. "How could they?"

Mother had promised me more time together. She and Asteria had asked us to become a family again. They'd lied. As always, they'd lied—

Odessa blinked back at me, the palm of her hand pressed against her chest. She was weeping, but behind the tears was a stunned look of wonder. "It's gone," she said softly. "There's no pain."

Lan fell to her knees beside my twin, held her close. "You're right," she said, awed. "The shadows over your heart—they're gone."

I didn't know what to think or feel. I felt lighter. The demons that had curled at the edges of my mind, since the last time I performed the Banishing, since I first saw the galla rise out of the oceans of Aranth, were gone. The black hole within my chest had disappeared. I was finally, blessedly, undeniably alone.

But I wept. I wept for what Mother and Latona could have been, for everything that had been lost to bring us here.

I wept for poor Sonfei. Lan had shut his eyes and crossed his arms over his chest to hide that terrible wound, and I mourned what he could have been with Mother. Hoped that wherever he was he would at least be with her, with them, and happy. Noelle guarded him, her own face drawn, but she turned at some sound I didn't hear, and gasped when she saw the vines steadily climbing out of every nook and cranny the cave held, the scent of fragrant blossoms filling the air and overpowering the dampness of the cave.

I reached out to touch one of those flowers with my fingertips, and it was then that I saw it; it felt like Aeon's life force ran through my blood, because I could see the changes being wrought on its surface. I saw the plains flushing green, sprawling on for miles. I saw light rain showers blanketing them in soft dew. I saw the seas washing closer and closer toward empty shores, the black murky dregs changing into a clearer crystal blue. Gone was the dark mist that had always plagued the boundaries of the Great Abyss, dissipating as sunlight pierced through it for the first time. And this time, unlike the illusion Ereshkigal had woven for us, I could feel the sun's heat, felt it spark against my soul. And then, from the depths of the chasm came a grinding sound. The earth rocked hard against our feet, but this time it was for a better purpose. Yard by slow yard, the Abyss began to close, the opposite sides inching closer until it narrowed, met, and was gone, without even a scar to mark its place.

Aeon was healing. It had always been so with the sacrifice of every goddess, though man's corruption had ensured the reprieve could never last.

That cycle would end with us. I swore it.

It wasn't completely over. Ereshkigal's vessel had been destroyed, but so had the stone of immortality.

There must always be a steward within the Cruel Kingdom. Someone had to take Ereshkigal's place.

"What do we do now?" Lan asked me softly, her gold-and-ivory eyes worried. I smiled, overflowing with love for her. She had come intending to die. It was a miracle that she was still here with me. I intended to cherish her every day of my life. Just as I knew Haidee would do with Arjun.

Haidee and I looked at each other.

"'A half-life is better . . . ,'" I began, remembering that curious phrase that had been etched on those shrine walls.

"'. . . than no life at all,'" she finished.

We smiled then. We knew what we had to do.

EPILOGUE

"JUST AN HOUR MORE," I grunted, rolling over on my back and taking her with me, so that she was draped over my chest. Morning light filtered through the window; six months after moving in, I'd replaced the wooden frames with something more stable: a metal alloy blend that proved capable of weathering bad storms without rusting. It was a recent invention of Charley and Imogen's, one they hoped to mass-produce within the year. Bad weather was a rare occurrence on this side of the world, anyway, but I'd learned never to leave things to chance.

Over the months I'd tried to add little flourishes to our house; things I hoped Haidee would enjoy, like a glasshouse and a small atrium so she could enjoy the sunlight while she read, even finally splurging on a bathtub with connected plumbing. Haidee had protested; she was happy with how things were, she said, and didn't need anything else. But I didn't mind; I liked the permanence of it all, the idea that we could both put down roots after a lifetime of roaming.

It felt right to settle here, in this small village. It felt fitting, too, since this was the very same place we'd stopped to rest on our way to the Great Abyss all those years ago. This was the very same house, the same bed I'd once stretched a canvas over in lieu of a mattress, nervous about our sleeping arrangements and stammering over how I respected her too much to take advantage of the situation, until she'd surprised me and made the first move.

It had been Haidee's idea to make our home in this village. "We had some good memories here," she'd said then, placing her hand on the rickety wood, trying to figure out what parts were salvageable and what parts we had to build back up from scratch. "What's the first thing you'd like to improve?"

I'd given her a slow, shit-eating grin. "A bed," I said, knowing exactly why Haidee had such fond memories of this place, and watched her blush.

We never knew the original name of this village; any records of it had long been gone. We were overjoyed when Mother Salla and the rest of my siblings elected to make this their home too, together with most of the Liangzhu tribe. Mother Salla had been in her element, planning, organizing, and overseeing the construction of more houses, with an eye toward expanding.

Farthengrove was as good a name as we could think of christening it with.

The first thing we'd done after coming here had been to lay Sonfei to rest. "He would be very much liking it," Oda told us, "being as close to her as we are able to. The presence of the goddesses through the ages smiles down on this place now. It would ease his soul, knowing this."

They'd been gone for three years now, but Haidee told me one of the other reasons she liked it here was because she could still feel her mothers close by.

The Salt Sea had finally returned to the Skeleton Coast, and we'd received word from Yeong-ho that they'd finally been sighting fishes larger than salmon. Tamera and the Gila clan had elected to remain there. They had formulated a plan for sustainable fishing, among many other things, and it was keeping them busy. Lan and Odessa were scheduled to travel there in a month's time, to oversee that and other policies the council was hoping to implement before the year was out. They'd already extended an invitation to me, to travel with them.

I'd been tempted to turn down their offer, but Haidee had talked me out of it. "Lan told me all you did the last time was mope around the house," she said firmly. "I know you'll be lonely, but I want you to keep busy. Help Lan and Odessa run things. Lan's been invaluable to us while Odessa's been gone."

"Are you saying I'm useless?" I couldn't help it. Maybe it was easier for Lan to compartmentalize, but those six months were always rough on me.

She giggled. "Yes, when I'm not around. Go with them, boss people like I know you're itching to do. You have some sway over policy, too, and you can speak for me as my official *consort*."

She took special care to emphasize *consort* every time she mentioned it. I had been clueless as to why, until Lan had taken pity on me, took me aside, and told me they were not-so-subtle hints; Haidee was expecting me to formally ask her to become something more. Courtships and betrothals were things I had little experience with, and Haidee had previously been skittish when it came to talk of marriage, since her suitors in the past had offered their hands with politics in mind instead of love. Lan and Odessa had wasted no time getting married six months after spring first returned to Aeon, but I'd always thought Haidee didn't want or need it.

I'd ask her when she returned from this next trip. I'd drag Lan and Odessa into it, wheedle them into helping me make the preparations. I wanted Odessa to have as much input with the planning as she could, perhaps have the wedding exactly half a year from now when they could meet again, so she could take part—just like Lan and Odessa had delayed their own nuptials so that Haidee could attend. A short ceremony or a long, drawn-out one where the whole of Aeon celebrated—I didn't really care, as long as Haidee was willing to settle for me.

Haidee laughed, snuggled up against me. "You know I have to go," she said softly. "Lan misses Odessa too, you know."

I knew. Didn't stop me from making the same complaints every time *she* had to leave. This was becoming something of our own ritual now, in a way. Damn lot better than the ones we had to go through before.

Haidee was contented with the arrangement, and I knew it was selfish of me to ask for more than what she'd already given up. But I was going to miss her. It was going to be another long six months.

"One more hour," I insisted, rolling over so I could kiss her hair. She laughed.

"One more hour," she breathed, conceding, before tugging me down.

Haidee and Arjun were running late, but I didn't mind. I drew in a quick breath of air, taking in the wind, brisk and chilly despite the sun overhead. I had never known the combination could be possible, but the years had taught me how little I'd known about everything, and how grateful I was for the chance to learn more.

But for now, my body hummed with expectation. Good Mother, I missed her so.

Odessa had admitted that she didn't quite know how to describe her time in the underworld. She'd likened it to a dreamless sleep, where she was conscious of Aeon around her, like she was one with it, tied irrevocably to it in ways that went beyond words. Noelle had surmised that the goddesses would continue to flourish for as long as the world did, and that any more harm to it could result in them suffering, in returning to the very situation that facilitated Ereshkigal's corruption. Arjun and I had been very particular about reinforcing this notion, to great effect. Noelle now led Aeon's highest council, with both Haidee's and Odessa's approval. "From a tower steward to the most powerful position in the land," I had teased her, and she had sighed. "Not much difference," she'd said, "given the responsibilities required for both."

We were planning to travel back to the Golden City to meet with her, to discuss other locations earmarked for repopulation, as well as opening more schools for botany and agriculture. Charley, Jes, and Rodge were also attempting to start a school for mechanika, and Odessa had promised to visit on Haidee's behalf. Three years of hard work hadn't been enough to completely reverse the ravages of the Breaking, but it was a start, and everything I'd seen so far had given me hope.

Lisette had elected to stay at the Golden City, Arjun wryly noting that he would give her two months before her wanderlust got the better of her. He'd underestimated by ten. But Vanya had still been despondent when she'd informed him of her intentions to leave.

"Maybe I wasn't enough for her," he mourned, scarcely minutes after her departure, just as we'd arrived for our official visit.

Arjun had snorted his irritation. "Go with her, you fool."

"What?"

"Lisette would have up and left without telling anyone if she wanted to go alone. She told you for a reason. Yeong-ho can spare a rig. I bet you'll find her idling down the road, waiting and hoping you'll take the hint."

Vanya had gaped at him, then rushed away without another word. A couple of hours later, we found Lisette's jeep abandoned a few miles outside city boundaries. Apparently, the car the lordling had filched was better for off-road traveling. "Oblivious lovesick saps," Arjun had muttered, which was a bold thing to say, considering that Haidee had been trying to get him to propose for months and he'd been just as much of a blockhead.

We'd left the Golden City and traveled down the Sand Sea, to ascertain how Aeon's turning would affect it. Haidee had estimated the returning Salt Sea would claim most of its territory; the gradual decline of volatile patterns indicated the Sand Sea would eventually die out, its inhabitants either following suit or readapting to water. Sumiko had also reported that the waters near where Aranth had been were finally receding, that the acidfall was tapering off, and that the riverwinds were in decline. She, Slyp, and many others were currently conducting a detailed study of the Lunar Lakes.

Arjun later admitted to me that the main reason Haidee had insisted on traveling here was because she wanted to reconnect with some old friends, which turned out to be a pod of dolugong that accompanied us everywhere for several days.

"Hope you don't mind," Arjun muttered to me, apologetic, while Haidee giggled and romped around with some of the younger colts. "They're not exactly housebroken, and Madeline has been spoiling Shepard rotten since the last time we saw them. She's the head of their pack now."

"I don't mind at all. Clearly they're important enough for you to actually give them names," I said, and was surprised when he reddened.

But no matter where we visited, we always found ourselves returning to the small village near what had once been the Great Abyss. In many ways Farthengrove was our home away from home. It was where Odessa needn't be one of Aeon's twin goddesses, where she could be what she'd yearned to be when she had pretended, in Aranth so long ago, to be Ame. With Noelle in charge, we knew the Golden City was in good hands.

None of that meant I didn't miss her when she was gone.

Arjun and Haidee had finally arrived. The latter was smiling, the former looking a little surly. I couldn't blame him. It would be another six months before he would see her again.

Just like it had been six months since I'd seen Odessa.

"We're ready," Haidee said softly. Arjun grunted, nodded.

As much as I missed Odessa, I knew that this was even harder for the twins. I had six months out of every year to be with Odessa, to love her. But the sisters only had minutes to talk and share and express their devotion to each other, before one would have to take the other's place. They wrote each other often, leaving letters, drawings, and confidences behind for the other to peruse during her months above. It wasn't the same, but they were both determined that it would be enough.

Sacrifice came in different forms.

We stood before the Brighthenge monument. Over the years it had been transformed from a dreadful place of blood and carnage to one of pilgrimage and solitude. Gracea had been put in charge of maintaining the temple, and while I was never going to be friends with the Starmaker, I was astounded at how well she'd managed it so far. She agreed when I told her there was to be no audience present when the exchange between the twins happened. I didn't want to sully the moment for them, didn't want anything to intrude on the short, precious time they had with each other.

We didn't have to wait long. A glowing hole appeared in the air before the statue, growing in size until it was a doorway. From within a girl with long, flowing hair in a riot of colors emerged. Her pale eyes turned in my direction, and my *yezhiyao*, my *wife,* smiled, love clear in every feature. My heart swelled.

Haidee turned to kiss Arjun, murmuring her goodbyes. Then she stepped forward to meet her twin, Arjun letting out a small sigh of acceptance as he let her go.

Together, we watched as Odessa and Haidee made their way toward each other, grief and love and hope undeniable in every touch and word as the sun broke free of the horizon, promising better days to come.